Sleigh Bells in the Snow

Dear Reader,

Sleigh Bells in the Snow is the first in a series of three books set in the fictitious resort community of Snow Crystal, Vermont, with its beautiful lakes, mountains and forests. It's the perfect romantic setting for both summer and winter stories, and this series brings you both.

I love writing about families and I'm particularly fascinated by the way individuals respond differently to the same upbringing, which is why I chose to write about three brothers.

Jackson, Sean and Tyler O'Neil all left the family home to pursue their own ambitions. Older brother Jackson has built a successful winter-sports business in Europe, Sean is focusing on his career as an orthopedic surgeon and bad boy Tyler was recently forced to retire from the World Cup ski circuit after a nasty injury.

The sudden death of their father changes everything. The future of Snow Crystal is in their hands. Tough, responsible Jackson is determined to save the place that has been home to the O'Neil family for four generations, but he can't do it alone.

I loved developing these characters—three strong, sexy men, each with different temperaments and life goals, but sharing powerful brotherly bonds. I hope you enjoy reading about Jackson's path to love as much as I enjoyed writing it.

I love hearing from readers and you can email me via my website, or contact me via Twitter or Facebook:
www.twitter.com/SarahMorgan
www.facebook.com/AuthorSarahMorgan.

Thank you for choosing this book!

Love,

Sarah

xx

SARAH MORGAN

Sleigh Bells in the Snow

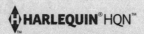

HARLEQUIN® HQN™

Recycling programs
for this product may
not exist in your area.

ISBN-13: 978-0-373-77855-3

SLEIGH BELLS IN THE SNOW

Copyright © 2013 by Sarah Morgan

Printed in U.S.A.

For my family, with love.

CHAPTER ONE

KAYLA GREEN CRANKED up the volume on her favorite playlist and blocked out the sound of festive music and laughter wafting under her closed office door.

Was she the only person who hated this time of year?

Surely there had to be *someone* out there who felt the way she did?

Someone who didn't expect Christmas to be merry or bright?

Someone who knew mistletoe was poisonous?

She watched gloomily as soft snowflakes drifted lazily past the floor-to-ceiling glass windows that made up two sides of her spacious corner office. She hadn't been dreaming of a white Christmas but it seemed she was getting one anyway.

Far below, the streets of Manhattan were jammed with tourists keen to enjoy the festive sights of New York in the holiday season. A giant spruce twinkled in front of the Rockefeller Centre, and the Hudson River glinted in the distance, a ribbon of silvery-gray shimmering in the winter light.

Turning her back on the snow, the tree and the glittering skyscrapers of Midtown, Kayla focused on her computer screen.

A moment later the door opened and Tony, her opposite number in Entertainment and Sports, appeared carrying two glasses of champagne.

She unhooked her headphones. "Who the hell is picking the music out there?"

"You don't like the music?" The top button of his shirt was undone and the glitter in his eyes suggested this wasn't his first glass of champagne. "Is that why you're hiding in your office?"

"I'm searching for inner peace but I'd settle for outer peace so if you could close the door on your way out, that would be perfect."

"Come on, Kayla. We're celebrating our best year ever. It's a British tradition to get drunk, sing terrible karaoke and flirt with your colleagues."

"Who told you that?"

"I watched *Bridget Jones's Diary*."

"Right." The music made her head throb. It was always the same at this time of year. The tight panicky feeling in her stomach. The ache in her chest that didn't ease until December 26th. "Tony, did you want something? Because I'd like to keep working."

"It's our office party. You cannot work late tonight."

As far as she was concerned it was the perfect night to work late.

"Have you seen *A Christmas Carol?* Or read the book?"

A glass of champagne appeared on the desk in front of her. "I'm guessing you're not Tiny Tim in this scenario, so that makes you either Scrooge or one of the ghosts."

"I'm Scrooge, but without the tasteless nightwear." Ignoring the champagne, Kayla glanced through the doorway. "Is Melinda out there?"

"Last seen charming the CEO of Adventure Travel who has been looking for you all evening so he can thank you personally for the incredible year their company has enjoyed. Bookings are up two hundred percent since you took over their account. Not only that, you got his picture on the cover of *Time* magazine." He raised his glass and his mouth twisted into a smile. "Until you arrived in New York, I was the golden boy. Brett used to give me tips on how to be the one on top. I was all set to be the youngest vice president this firm has ever appointed."

Alarm bells rang in her head. "Tony—"

"Now it's likely that accolade will go to you."

"You're still the golden boy. We work in separate divisions. Could we talk about this tomorrow?" Kayla delved into her bag for a report, wishing she could push herself inside and snap it shut until January. "I'm really busy."

"Too busy to nurse my ego a little bit?"

She eyed the champagne. "I've always believed people should be responsible for their own egos."

He gave a low laugh. "Coming from anyone else I'd assume there was innuendo in there, but you don't do innuendo, do you? You don't have time for it. Just like you don't have time for parties or dinner or drinks on the way home after work. You don't have time for anything *except* work. For Kayla Green, associate vice president of Tourism and Hospitality, it's all about the next piece of business. Do you realize there's a bet going in the office as to whether you sleep with your phone?"

"Of course I sleep with my phone. Don't you?"

"No. Sometimes I sleep with a human, Kayla. A hot, naked woman. Sometimes I forget about work and indulge in a night of really incredible sex." His eyes were on hers, his message unmistakable and Kayla wished she'd locked her office door.

"Tony—"

"I'm probably about to make a giant fool of myself, but—"

"*Please* don't." Deciding she might need both hands, Kayla gave up looking for the file. "Go back to the party."

"You are the sexiest woman I've ever met."

Oh, shit.

"Tony—"

"When you transferred here from London straight into the AVP role, I admit I was ready to hate you, but you charmed us all with your cute British ways and you charmed Brett with your killer business instinct." He leaned forward. "And you charmed *me.*"

Kayla eyed the glass in his hand. "How many of those have you had?"

"The other day I was watching you in the boardroom presenting to your client. You never stand still."

"I think better when I walk around."

"Yeah, you walk around in that tight little pencil skirt that shows off your ass and those skyscraper heels that show off miles of leg, and all the time you were walking I was thinking, 'Kayla Green has the sharpest mind in the business, but she also has a *great* pair of legs—'"

"Tony—"

"'—and not only does she have a great pair of legs, she also amazing green eyes that can kill a man from a thousand paces.'"

She stared hard at him and then shook her head. "Nope. Not working. You're still alive, so that's something else you're wrong about. Now go back to the party."

"Let's get out of here, Green. My place. Just you, me and my super big bed."

"Tony—" She tried to inject just the right tone into her voice. Firm, professional and absolutely not interested. "I understand how much courage it took for you to be honest about your feelings, and I'm going to be equally candid." *Well, not quite, but as close to candid as she ever came.* "Quite apart from the fact I would never get personal with a colleague because it would be unprofessional, I'm totally rubbish at relationships."

"You couldn't be rubbish at anything. I heard Brett telling a client this week that you're a superstar." An edge of bitterness crept into his voice and she sighed.

"Is that what this is about? Competition? Because honestly, when Brett was giving you tips on how to be on top, I don't think he meant you to take it quite so literally."

"Hot, dirty sex, Kayla, and just for tonight." He raised his glass. "Tomorrow doesn't exist."

As far as she was concerned tomorrow couldn't come soon enough. "Good night, Tony."

"I would make you forget your emails."

"No man has ever made me forget my emails." Contemplating that depressing fact did nothing to improve her mood. "You are drunk and you are going to regret this in the morning."

He sat down on her desk, flattening a stack of invoices awaiting her signature. "I thought I worked hard and then I met you. Kayla Green, public relations genius who never puts a foot wrong."

She tugged at the invoices. "My foot will be in your butt if you don't get off my invoices."

"Butt? I thought you British called it an arse."

"Butt, arse—call it whatever you like, just get it off

my desk. Now go home before you say something you shouldn't to someone important." About to stand up and eject him physically, she was relieved when her office door opened and Stacy, her PA, walked in.

Her gaze fixed on the empty glass in Tony's hand. "Ah, Tony—Brett is looking for you. New business opportunity. He says you're the man to handle it."

"Really? In that case—" Tony scooped up Kayla's untouched glass and strolled toward the door "—nothing stands in the way of business, does it? Certainly not pleasure."

Stacy watched him go, eyebrows raised. "What's got into him?"

"Two bottles of champagne got into him." Kayla dropped her head into her hands and stared blankly at the screen. "Was Brett really looking for him?"

"No, but you looked as if you were about to punch him, and I didn't want you to spend Christmas in custody. I've heard the food is terrible."

"You are one in a million and you're in line for a fat bonus."

"You already gave me a fat bonus. I treated myself to this top." Stacy twirled like a ballerina and black sequins gleamed under the lights. "What do you think?"

"Love it. Just don't stand too near Tentacle Tony."

"I think he's cute." Stacy blushed. "Sorry. Too much information."

"You think he's hot?" Kayla stared at the door where Tony had exited a few moments earlier and wondered what was wrong with her. "Seriously?"

"Everyone does. Everyone except you, obviously, but that's because you work too hard to notice. Why don't you come and join the party?"

"Everyone will be chatting about the holidays. I'm

fine talking about work but I'm useless with kids, pets and grandmas."

"Talking of work, we have a potential new business lead. The guy is coming in tomorrow to brief us. Brett wants you in on that meeting."

Relieved the topic had shifted, Kayla perked up. "What guy?"

"Jackson O'Neil."

"Jackson O'Neil." She filed through her brain. "CEO of Snowdrift Leisure. They own a handful of luxury hotels specializing in winter sports. Mostly European based. Zermatt, Klosters, Chamonix. Impressive track record. Very successful. What about him?"

Stacy gaped at her. "How do you *know* all this stuff?"

"It's what I do when other people have a social life." Kayla typed *Jackson O'Neil* into the search engine. "Do they want us to work with them? I can talk to someone in the London office."

"It isn't the European business. And it isn't Snowdrift Leisure. He took a backseat in the company eighteen months ago so he could move back to the U.S. and focus on the family business."

"Really? How did I miss that?" Kayla looked at the photographs that came up on her screen. Jackson O'Neil was at least two decades younger than she'd imagined him to be. Instead of the usual corporate head and shoulders shot, there was a photograph of him skiing down what looked like a vertical slope. Her head spun as she looked at the gradient. "Is that Photoshop?"

Stacy peered over her shoulder and made an appreciative sound. "That man is seriously hot. I bet he drinks vodka martinis, shaken not stirred. It's not Photoshop. All three O'Neil brothers are skiers. Tyler

O'Neil was on the U.S. ski team until he injured himself. They're always flinging themselves off some cliff or other."

"So I'd probably better not mention I feel dizzy at the top of the Empire State Building." Kayla clicked off the picture. "Snowdrift Leisure is a fast-growing, successful company. Why isn't he focusing on that?"

"Family. The O'Neil family owns the Snow Crystal Resort and Spa in Vermont."

Family. The most destructive force known to man. "Never heard of it."

"I guess that's why he's contacted us for help."

"If he'd wanted to run the family business, why didn't he do that straight off instead of setting up his own company?" She clicked through the Snow Crystal website, looking at images. A large Alpine-style hotel and log cabins nestling in a forest. A couple, smiling adoringly in the back of a horse-drawn sleigh. Laughing families skating on a frozen pond. She quickly returned to the images of the cabins. "Maybe he's a guy who prefers a challenge."

"No doubt he'll tell you why when you meet. He asked for you. He saw what you did for Adventure Travel."

Kayla stared at the log cabins, and thought how peaceful they looked. "Are they putting the business out to pitch?"

"Brett thinks if you can impress Jackson O'Neil tomorrow, the business is ours."

"Then we'd better make sure we impress him."

"I'm sure you will." Stacy hesitated. "Have you ever skied?"

"Not exactly. I mean, I've never actually worn a pair of skis *as such,* but I skidded on the snow outside

Bloomingdales last week. I felt as if my gut was going to come up through my mouth. Skiing must give you a similar feeling."

Stacy laughed. "My parents took me to Vermont when I was little. All I remember was ice. Even the trees were frozen."

"That's perfect because I love ice."

"You do?"

"Absolutely. Ideally I prefer it crushed in a margarita or carved into a swan as a centerpiece on a buffet table, but I can go with it under my feet if I have to. I'll be fine, Stacy. I'm helping them promote the company, not going on holiday there. When I worked on that African Safari account, did I have to hug a lion? No, I did not." Kayla felt the familiar buzz that always came when facing a new business opportunity. Her fears of the dreaded Christmas period were soothed by the knowledge she now had a legitimate reason to bury herself in work. She'd get through it, as she always did, and no one would be any the wiser. "Be an angel and dig up as much information as you can on Snow Crystal and the O'Neil family, particularly Jackson. I want to know why he took a backseat in his highly successful business to return home and run a place I can't even find on a map."

"I'll have it for you first thing tomorrow." Brisk and efficient, Stacy made a note in her book. "Maybe you should take a break, Kayla. You're forgetting it's Christmas!"

"I'm not forgetting."

She'd been trying to forget for a decade and a half. *There was no forgetting.*

Whenever she left her apartment or her office she walked with her head down, avoiding glimpses of glittering window displays and twinkly lights, but nothing helped.

Stacy tidied the stack of invoices. "Are you sure you won't change your mind and join our team trip to see Santa?"

It felt as if someone were sawing through her stomach.

Dragging open her drawer, Kayla pulled out indigestion tablets and swallowed two. She wondered whether taking the lot would put her out until after Christmas. "Can't, sorry, but I appreciate the invitation."

"There will be Christmas trees, elves—"

"Oh, God, poor you."

"Why poor me? I love Christmas." Stacy shot her a puzzled look. "Don't you?"

"I adore Christmas. I'm totally gutted I can't make it. I meant poor me, not poor you." The effort of smiling was making her jaw ache. "Think of me while you're mingling with elves."

"Maybe you should come anyway and talk to Santa. You can give him your Christmas list. Dear Santa, please give me the Snow Crystal account together with a massive budget, and, while you're at it, I'll have Jackson O'Neil naked. Hold the gift wrap."

The only thing she wanted for Christmas was for it to be over as fast as possible.

Memories hit her with a thump, and Kayla stood up abruptly and paced to the window. All around her were reminders of Christmas, so she paced back to her desk and sat down again, vowing to book a cruise to Antarctica next year. Whale watching. Whales didn't celebrate Christmas, did they?

The phone on her desk rang and she breathed a sigh of relief. *Thank goodness.*

Stacy snapped into professional mode and reached across the desk, but Kayla stopped her.

"I'll get it. I'm expecting a call from the CEO of Extreme Explore. I'd rather the man wasn't deafened by the sounds of sleigh bells, or jingle bells, or whatever bells are ringing out there, so it would be great if you went back to the party and closed the door behind you. Thanks, Stacy. If anyone asks, you haven't seen me." Waiting until she closed the door, Kayla whimpered and leaned forward, banging her head on the desk. "Christmas. Crappy, miserable, horrible Christmas. *Please* be over quickly this year otherwise I'm going to need every last shard of ice in Vermont to chill all the alcohol I intend to drink." Pulling in a deep breath she sat up, raked her hair away from her face and picked up the phone. "Oliver?" Afraid he might hear her desperation, she pinned the smile back on her face, thankful it wasn't a video conference. "It's Kayla. Great to speak to you. How's it going? I read through your business plans for next year. Exciting!"

This, she thought, *this she could do.*

No Christmas. No Santa. No memories.

Just her job.

If she kept her head down and focused on winning the O'Neil account, it would eventually all be over.

"WHAT THE HELL kind of nonsense is this?" Eighty years old, but with all the energy of a man half his age, Walter O'Neil thumped his fist on the kitchen table while his grandson Jackson lounged in his chair, biting his tongue and reining in his temper.

Every meeting was the same.

Every battle they fought came back to the same theme.

This was why he hadn't wanted to work with his family. It wasn't a job—it was personal. There was no space to operate. Any hint of a new idea was strangled at birth. He'd built his own successful company from the ground up and now he felt like a teenager helping out in the store on weekends.

"It's called public relations, Gramps."

"It's called a waste of money. I wouldn't have done it that way and neither would your father."

The blow landed deep in his gut. Jackson exchanged a swift glance with his brother, but before either of them could respond there was a crash. His grandmother stared in dismay at the shattered remains of the plate.

The puppy whimpered and retreated under the table for safety.

"Grams—" Jackson was on his feet, his own pain forgotten, but his mother was there before him.

"Don't worry, Alice, I always hated that plate anyway. Ugly thing. I'll clear it up."

"I'm not normally clumsy."

"You've been baking all morning. You must be exhausted." She sent a reproachful look at her father-in-law, who glared right back, unrepentant.

"What? Are you saying I can't talk about Michael? Are we all going to pretend this isn't happening? Do we brush his memory under the rug like crumbs?"

Jackson didn't know which was worse—the sight of his usually feisty grandmother so subdued or the shadow in his mother's eyes.

"I need help decorating the gingerbread Santas." She cajoled and soothed, keeping everyone happy while ignoring her glowering father-in-law, and within seconds she had Alice seated at the table in front of a rack of

freshly made gingerbread men, various bowls of col-
ored icing laid out in front of her.

Tyler sat at the far end of the table, restless and impatient. "I thought this was going to be a family meeting, not a family argument."

"Argument?" Alice turned troubled eyes to Elizabeth. "Is it an argument?"

"Of course it isn't. People are just having their say."

"Families are supposed to stick together."

"We're together, Alice. That's why it's noisy."

"Happy to reduce the numbers." Tyler half rose to
his feet and Jackson shot him a look.

"Sit down. We're not done here."

"I'm done." Always one to reject authority, Tyler's
gaze burned into his and then he looked at the set of his
brother's jaw and sat. "Remind me why I came home?"

"Because you have a daughter," Walter barked. "And
responsibilities. And there comes a point in a man's
life when he has to do more than tear up the slopes and
chase after women."

"You were the one who taught me to tear up the
slopes. You gave me the genes and the skis and you
showed me what to do with them."

Jackson wondered how the hell he was supposed to
run this place when his "staff" had more baggage than
an airport departure lounge.

"We need to stick to business." His tone got him the
attention he needed. "Tyler, you're going to help Brenna
run the winter activities program." And that was another problem brewing, he thought. He had a feeling
Brenna wasn't too pleased to see Tyler back at Snow
Crystal, and he was pretty sure he knew the reason.

He waited as his mother added a bowl of white icing
to the table and handed his grandmother a knife.

With Alice occupied, Elizabeth O'Neil turned her attention to the broken china on the floor.

Jackson felt as if he were walking over the fragments in bare feet.

"I intend to make this business work but to do that I need to make changes."

His grandfather glowered at him. "It worked just fine when I ran it and when your father ran it."

No, it didn't. It was on the tip of his tongue to tell the truth about the state of the business but then he saw his mother's fingers whiten on the broom. *Did she know what a mess his father had left behind?*

He should have told them straight-out, he thought, not tried to protect them. If he'd done that maybe they wouldn't be fighting him now.

Jackson looked at his grandfather. "I came home to run the business."

"No one asked you to."

Elizabeth O'Neil straightened her shoulders. "*I* asked him to."

"We don't need him here." Walter thumped his fist on the table. "He should have stayed where he was, running his fancy company and playing the big boss. I could have run this place."

"You're eighty years old, Walter. You should be slowing down, not taking on more. For once, swallow your pride and take the help that's offered." Elizabeth scooped up china fragments. "You should be grateful Jackson came home."

"I'm not grateful! A business is supposed to make money. All he does is spend it."

Jackson sat still, holding back the anger that simmered. "It's called investment."

"It's called wasting money."

"It's my damn money."

"No swearing in my kitchen, Jackson O'Neil."

"Why the fuck not?" Tyler was as restless as a caged beast. Jackson knew his brother hated being trapped indoors only marginally less than he hated authority. All he'd ever wanted to do was ski as fast as was humanly possible, and since the injury that had curtailed his racing career, his mood had been volatile.

"Don't wind your grandfather up, Tyler." His mother tipped broken china into a bag. "I'll make tea."

About to point out that what they needed wasn't tea but teamwork, Jackson remembered his mother always made tea and baked when she was stressed. And she'd been stressed for the past eighteen months. "Tea would be great, Mom."

"If you expect me to sit here I'm going to need something a hell of a lot stronger than tea." Tyler helped himself to another beer from the fridge and tossed one to his brother.

Jackson caught it one-handed. He knew that for all his outward impression of indifference, Tyler hated this situation as much as he did. Hated the fact they might lose this place. Hated the way his grandfather refused to let go of things.

He wondered if he'd been wrong to come home.

And then he saw his grandmother's lined, anxious face and his mother focusing extra hard on icing gingerbread Santas and knew there was no way he could have stayed away.

His grandfather might not want him here, but there was no doubt he was needed.

He watched as his mother bustled around taking comfort in the ritual of caring for people. She placed a plate of freshly baked cinnamon stars in the center of the scrubbed pine table and checked the bread she had baking in the oven.

The smell evoked memories of childhood. The large friendly kitchen had been part of his life forever. Now it was the closest he had to a boardroom and his infuriating, exasperating, interfering, lovable family were his management team. Two octogenarians, a grieving widow, his daredevil brother and an overexcited puppy with training issues.

Beam me up.

His mother placed a steaming mug of tea next to his beer and he felt a twinge of guilt for wishing he were back in his old office with his experienced team around him and only work to take up his attention. That time seemed so long ago. His life had changed. Right now, he wasn't sure it was for the better.

"The changes we've made will make a difference, but we need to tell people about those changes. I'm employing a public relations firm and I'll pay for it out of my own pocket." Given the state of the Snow Crystal finances, he didn't have much choice about that. "If I'm wasting money then it will be my money."

His grandfather gave a snort of disapproval. "If you're willing to throw away your own money you're even more foolish than I thought."

"I'm employing an expert."

"You mean an outsider." Walter sniffed. "And maybe you should be talking to your other brother before you make decisions about the family business."

"Sean isn't here."

"Because he has the good sense to leave the running of it to others. I'm just saying he should know what's going on, that's all."

"He'll be home for Christmas. I'll talk to him then."

Jackson leaned forward. "I need someone who can get Snow Crystal the attention it deserves. We need to increase occupancy. We need heads on beds."

"Is it about proving yourself? Because you've already done that with your big-shot ways, your fancy company and your fancy cars."

Change, Jackson thought. *They hated change.*

All his grandfather understood was blunt, so he gave him blunt.

"If we leave things the way they are, we'll lose the business."

His grandmother spilled a puddle of icing on the table, his mother turned a shade paler and his grandfather's eyes burned a fierce blue in his tanned, craggy face.

"This place has been in our family for four generations."

"And I'm trying to keep it in the family for the next four."

"By spending a fortune on a fancy New York company that can't even find Vermont on a map? What do they know about our business?"

"Plenty. They have a division that specializes in Travel and Hospitality, and the woman heading it up knows what she's doing. Have you heard of Adventure Travel?" Jackson leaned forward in his chair. "They were going under until Kayla Green took on the account. She had their business mentioned in every key media target."

"Jargon," Walter muttered. "So what is she? A magician?"

"She is a PR specialist. Right at the top of her game. She has media contacts that the rest of us can only dream about."

"She's not the only one with media contacts." Walter O'Neil sniffed to show exactly what he thought of Kayla Green's abilities. "I've been bowling with Max Rogers, editor of the *Snow Crystal Post,* for the past twenty years. If I want a piece in the paper, I ask."

The *Snow Crystal Post.*

Jackson didn't know whether to laugh or punch a hole through the table.

Wrenching the running of Snow Crystal away from his grandfather was like trying to pull fresh meat from the jaws of a starving lion.

"Local press is great, but what we really need is attention from the national media and international media—" He opened his mouth to add *social media* but decided not to get started on that one. "PR is more than talking to the press and we need to think bigger than the *Snow Crystal Post.*"

"Bigger isn't always better."

"No, but small can mean bust. We need to expand."

"You make us sound like a factory!"

"Not a factory, a business. A business, Gramps." Jackson rubbed his fingers over his forehead to ease the throb of his tension headache. He was used to walking in and getting the job done. Not anymore. Not with his own family because there were feelings to consider.

He decided that the only thing they'd respond to was hard facts. "It's important you know how things stand at the moment—"

His mother pushed a plate toward him. "Have a gingerbread Santa."

On the verge of revealing just how black the future looked, Jackson found himself staring at a plate of smiling Santas. They wouldn't look so damned cheerful if they knew how precarious their future was.

"Mom—"

"You'll sort it out, Jackson. You'll do what's right. By the way, Walter—" her tone was casual "—did you see the doctor about that pain in your chest? Because I can run you over there today."

Walter scowled. "I pulled a muscle chopping logs. It was nothing."

"He won't listen." Alice stuck a knife into the bowl of icing. "I keep telling him we should slow down during sex, but he ignores me."

"Christ, Grams!" Tyler shifted uncomfortably, and his grandmother looked up from the Santa she was holding, some of the old spark flaring in her eyes.

"Mind your language. And what's wrong with you? You think sex is just for the young? You have sex, Tyler O'Neil. Plenty of it if the rumors are to be believed."

"Yeah, but I don't talk about it with my grandmother—" Tyler levered himself to his feet. "I'm out of here. There's only so much family togetherness I can stand in one day. I'm going to tear up the slopes and chase women."

Knowing Tyler wasn't his problem, Jackson let him go without argument.

He met his mother's gaze and read the message there.

She was warning him to ease up on his grandfather.

The door slammed behind Tyler, and his grandmother flinched. "He was wild as a boy and he's wild as a man."

"He's not wild." Elizabeth poured milk into a pretty spotted jug. "He just hasn't found his place in the world since his injury. He'll adjust, especially now that he has Jess home."

It occurred to Jackson that his mother could have been talking about herself. She hadn't found her place in the world since losing his father. That wound was as raw as ever and she was stumbling around like a bird with a broken wing.

Smelling food, the puppy emerged from under the table. She looked up at Jackson hopefully, her entire body wagging along with her tail.

"Maple, sweetheart." Elizabeth scooped her up. "She hates all this shouting."

Walter grunted. "Give her something to eat. I like to see her eat. She was skin and bones when she arrived here."

Jackson closed his eyes. When he opened them again he was still in the kitchen. Still in the middle of this "meeting" where half the occupants of the room were made of gingerbread or had four legs.

"Mom—"

"When you get a minute could you bring down the boxes of decorations for the tree? Alice and I need to sort through them."

Jackson refrained from pointing out he hadn't had a minute since he'd arrived back at Snow Crystal. He'd been buried neck-deep in loans, business plans, staff who didn't do their jobs and finances that didn't add up. There were days when he ate standing up and nights when he lay on top of the bed, too tired to undress.

"We're off the subject. You need to learn to keep a meeting on track, Jackson." His grandfather reached for a biscuit. "So what does this woman from New York know about our business? I'll bet she's never even seen a sugar maple tree, let alone a whole damn forest of them."

"I'm not inviting her here to tap the trees, Gramps."

His grandfather gave a grunt. "She's probably never tasted good quality maple syrup. That's how I met your grandmother. She came to buy a bottle of our syrup." He snapped the head off a gingerbread Santa and winked at Alice. "She thought I was so sweet, she never left."

Watching his grandparents exchange loving glances, Jackson decided that not having tasted maple syrup was going to be the least of Kayla Green's problems. "If it will make you feel better I'll give her a bottle, but that's not our main business. It's a hobby."

"Hobby? The O'Neils are famous around here for the quality of our maple syrup—it's something we've been doing in this family for over a hundred years. Tourists come to see what we do here and you call it a *hobby?*"

"How many tourists?" Jackson ignored the food in front of him. "How many tourists do you think came last year? Because I can tell you it's not enough to keep this place going."

"Then maybe you shouldn't have spent so much developing those fancy cabins and refurbishing the lodge. Did we need a spa? Did we need a pool? Did you need to employ an expensive French chef in the restaurant? Extravagance, all of it." His grandfather was red in the face and Jackson rose to his feet, worry gnawing at his insides. He knew how much they were hurting. He also knew if they didn't face up to what was happening soon, Snow Crystal Resort would be going under.

He wasn't going to let that happen.

"I'm going to do what needs to be done. You're going to have to trust me."

"So now you're an autocrat." But his grandfather's voice shook a little, and Jackson saw something in the old man's eyes that nailed his feet to the floor.

This was the man who had taught him to whittle an arrow from a stick, to dam a stream and catch a fish with his bare hands. This man had picked him out of deep snow when he'd wiped out on his skis and taught him how to check the thickness of the ice on the pond so he didn't fall through.

And this was the man who had lost his son.

Jackson sat back down in the chair. "I'm not an autocrat but I have to make changes. We're operating in a stagnant economy. We have to stand out from the crowd. We have to offer something special."

"Snow Crystal Resort is special."

"It's Snow Crystal Resort and Spa now, and for once we agree on something. It's special."

His grandfather's eyes were suspiciously shiny. "So why change things?"

"Because people don't know about it, Gramps. But they're going to." The puppy nuzzled his ankle, and Jackson leaned down and stroked the dog's soft, springy fur. "I'm flying to New York tomorrow to meet with Kayla Green."

"I still don't get what a girl from Manhattan is going to know about running a resort like ours."

"She's not from Manhattan. She's British."

His mother brightened. "She'll fall in love with the place. I did. From Old England to New England."

Walter frowned. "You've lived here so long I don't think of you as British. Hell, I bet this Kayla woman has never even seen a moose!"

"Does she need to see a moose to get the job done?" But an idea was forming in his head. Not a compromise exactly, but a solution that might work. "If I can persuade Kayla Green to come and experience first-hand *exactly* what we offer here at Snow Crystal, will you listen to her?"

"That depends. She's not going to see much in a couple of hours, is she?"

Jackson stood up. "She can stay for a week. God knows, we've got enough empty cabins."

"No way is Miss New York or Miss London or wherever the hell she's from, going to want to stay in the wilds with us for a week in the middle of a Vermont winter."

Deep down, Jackson agreed with him but he wasn't about to admit defeat.

"I'll get her here and you'll listen."

"I'll listen if she says something worth listening to."

"Deal." He shrugged on his jacket while his mother looked on anxiously.

"Stay and eat. You've been working so hard I'll bet you haven't gone near the shops."

"He shouldn't have moved out." His grandfather clicked his fingers to attract the attention of the puppy. "He shouldn't have spent all that money converting that crumbling old barn into a fancy place of his own when we have all these empty rooms."

"I've trebled the value of that crumbling old barn." *And saved his sanity.* Jackson slipped his tablet computer into his bag and thought it might as well have been made of gingerbread for all the use it had been to him. "No food, thanks. I need to put together some figures for the people at Innovation. I'll do my own thing tonight."

"You always do," his grandfather muttered, and Jackson shook his head in exasperation and walked out of the warm, cozy kitchen into the freezing winter air.

His boots crunched through the thick snow and he stopped, breathing in the peace and quiet along with the smell of wood smoke.

Home.

Sometimes suffocating, sometimes comforting. He'd

avoided it, he realized. Stayed away longer than he should because at times there had been more suffocation than comfort.

He'd left the place behind at eighteen, fueled by a determination to prove himself. Why stay trapped in Snow Crystal when the whole world was out there beckoning him toward possibilities and opportunities? He'd been caught up in the excitement, the thrill of making something new, something that was *his*. He'd been riding the wave until that phone call. It had come in the night, like all the worst phone calls and had changed his life forever.

Where would he be now if his father hadn't died? Expanding his business in Europe? On a hot date with a woman?

Raising hell like his brother?

There was a whimper and he looked down to see the puppy by his ankles, snow clinging to her fur and mischief in her eyes.

"You're not supposed to be out here." Jackson stooped and lifted her, feeling the tremble of her body through her springy fur. She was small and delicate, a miniature toy poodle with the heart of a lion. He remembered the day he and Tyler had found her abandoned and half-dead in the forest, a scrap of fur, barely alive. They'd brought her home and coaxed her back to life. "I bet there are days when you wish you hadn't joined our family."

His mother appeared in the doorway, relief on her face as she saw the puppy. "She followed you." She took the puppy from him and gathered her close, stroking and kissing, pouring all her love onto the delighted puppy while Jackson watched, feeling the weight of responsibility pressing down on him.

"Mom—"

"He needs you, Jackson. Sooner or later he'll realize that. Your father made mistakes, but your grandfather can't cope with thinking about that right now. He doesn't need Michael's memory tarnished."

And neither did she. The shadows in her eyes told him that.

Knowing how much she'd loved his father, Jackson felt the tension increase across his shoulders. "I'm trying to get the job done without hurting him."

She hesitated. "You're probably wondering why you came back."

"I'm not wondering that."

Somehow, he had to find a way of making something that was his out of something that was theirs and making his grandfather feel as if the whole thing was his idea.

He had to save what they'd built.

Kayla Green might have worked with some of the toughest and most successful companies in her career, but nothing, *nothing,* was going to come close to the challenge of dealing with the O'Neil family.

He hoped she liked gingerbread Santas.

CHAPTER TWO

"ANGIE CALLED FROM the *Washington Post*. I told her you'd call her back. And I finished that media list." Stacy leaned across the desk and Kayla was nearly asphyxiated.

"Er—nice perfume." Her hand wrapped around the tall cappuccino she'd picked up on her way into the office. She unwrapped her cashmere scarf and dropped it over her chair, sending snowflakes floating across her desk. "It's freezing out there. If I'd known New York was this cold in winter I would have requested the L.A. office." Snatching a sip of coffee, she toed off the boots she'd worn to walk the short distance from her apartment and dragged her shoes from the drawer in her desk.

Through the glass wall that cut her off from the rest of the fortieth floor, she could see two of the junior account executives discreetly replenishing makeup. "What's going on? Brett will hit the roof if he walks past and sees lip gloss and girl bonding."

"Brett's with Jackson O'Neil. They're waiting for you in the boardroom."

"Jackson O'Neil is the reason for the perfume and the sudden run on cosmetics?"

"The man is *smoking*-hot, Kayla."

Only half listening, Kayla pulled her phone out of her pocket, checking new emails while she pushed her feet into her shoes. "Did you get any more information on him?"

"Yes. He is insanely sexy and—" Stacy blushed "—*single*."

"I meant on the company."

"I sent everything I found to your in-box this morning, but Kayla he's—"

"Somehow I've managed to amass fifty emails since I left my apartment. How is that possible? I cleared my in-box at 5:00 a.m." Kayla put down her coffee, slid her phone into her bag and scooped up the stack of notes she'd scribbled at three in the morning. "When I saw the snow, I assumed O'Neil would cancel."

"He took an earlier flight because the forecast was bad and he wanted this done. I collected him from the foyer. I managed to behave with dignity and not leap on him."

"That would have given a whole new meaning to the phrase 'full service agency.'" Grinning, Kayla smoothed her hair and took a deep breath. "Go and stick your head under the water cooler."

"Your in-box is the equivalent of a cold shower. By the way, this came for you. It's marked Personal so I didn't open it. I guess it's from someone who doesn't have your home address." Stacy handed her an envelope, and Kayla recognized her stepmother's handwriting.

Cold trickled down her spine. It was like landing naked in a snowdrift.

"Thanks." Stuffing it quickly into her bag, she strode out of her office and took the stairs down to the foyer, wishing she'd left the envelope on her desk instead of putting it in her bag. Now it was there, she couldn't stop thinking about it. It made the bag feel heavy even though it weighed no more than a few flakes of snow.

She stopped in the stairwell, pressed her palm to her ribs and took a few deep breaths.

The only things that should be on her mind right now were Jackson O'Neil and the Snow Crystal Resort and Spa. She shouldn't be thinking about her stepmother, not least because thinking of her stepmother always made her think of her father and then, inevitably, her mother.

She allowed herself a moment to stare through the window at the high-rises of Midtown, reminded herself how hard she'd worked to be standing here now, and then she continued down the stairs and pushed open the doors into the foyer.

The New York offices of Innovation were sleek and stylish, enveloped in floor-to-ceiling glass that offered breathtaking views over the skyscrapers of Manhattan. Usually Kayla found it the perfect working environment, but today chic minimalism had been displaced by festive touches. A huge Christmas tree dominated the foyer and someone had twisted a rope of tiny stars across the top of the boardroom door.

Everyone, from the receptionist right up to Brett himself, was in that smiling, energy-fueled phase that came between Thanksgiving and Christmas.

Maybe she *was* Scrooge, Kayla thought gloomily, her heels tapping on the polished oak floor as she walked past the receptionist and gave her a discreet wave. Maybe next year she'd book herself a log cabin with a view of a forest and a lake.

Maybe next year she'd arrange for someone to kidnap Santa.

She pushed open the door and Brett rose to his feet.

"Here she is! The star of the show. Kayla, meet Jackson O'Neil. Jackson, this is Kayla Green."

He was standing with his back to her, his eyes on the city spread out in front of him.

In those few seconds, Kayla decided Stacy had exaggerated his appeal. True, that jet-black hair looked promising, and he appeared to be taller and broader than the average businessman she encountered during her working day, but as far as she could see there was nothing else about him that warranted the volume of cosmetics and heavy breathing that was going on up on the fortieth floor.

And then he turned.

With hair that black she'd expected his eyes to be dark, but they were blue. A fierce, intense blue, and Kayla stopped breathing altogether because nothing about this man was average.

There was a hard strength to his features, a toughness that fitted everything she'd read about him in the cold chill of her early-morning work session. From the bold sweep of his eyebrows to the bump in his nose, he was wholly and unequivocally male.

That heavy-lidded gaze assessed her in a single sweep, and she felt as if someone had kicked her legs out from under her.

She thought about Stacy's suggestion that she ask Santa for Jackson O'Neil naked.

Dear Santa, it's been a long time since you've heard from me, but—

"Miss Green." His voice was deep and strong, and she was recovering from the shock of realizing that for once Stacy's taste in men made perfect sense, when he strode across the room and shook her hand.

The sudden jolt of chemistry unsettled her.

"Good to meet you, Mr. O'Neil."

For a fleeting moment it crossed her mind that this man might even have what it took to make her forget her emails. Then she remembered that the consequence of forgetting her emails was doing a bad job and there was no way she was ever going to let that happen.

"I hope your trip was good?" Kayla chose a seat as far away from those blue eyes as she could reasonably position herself. "I'm excited about this opportunity. Why don't you start by telling us a bit more about how you think we can help, Mr. O'Neil."

"Jackson."

"Jackson." It felt too personal. "I've followed the growth of Snowdrift Leisure."

"My focus right now is Snow Crystal, the family business. It was originally run by my father."

And his father had been killed in a car accident in New Zealand. She'd read about it in her research.

She was wondering how to tactfully ask the question that had been nagging her, when he raised an eyebrow.

"You have a question?" He was brutally direct. "It's important to me that this project is successful, so if there's something you need to know then ask."

"I don't want to be insensitive."

His eyes gleamed. "Do I look delicate?"

He looked like a man who could chop down a tree with a swing of his hand. "It would help to understand why you chose to take over the business now and not earlier in your career."

"Have you worked with family?"

"No." A knot tightened in her stomach. "No, I haven't."

"Good decision. A family business is driven by a great deal more than a concern for the bottom line. To describe it as complicated would be to simplify the situation." A wry smile tugged at his mouth, and Kayla found herself looking at the curve of his lips. She was sure Jackson O'Neil would be an exceptionally skilled kisser.

Irritated with herself, she opened her notepad.

Damn Stacy.

"I can imagine it isn't easy to agree on a business strategy when the people involved have an emotional investment. Perhaps you could outline their different responsibilities within the company?"

"I'd describe it as *flexible.*" He leaned back in his chair. "The company structure, if you can call it that, is informal. If anyone has an idea, they speak up, although that doesn't mean anyone is going to listen to them."

But they'd listen to *him,* she was sure of that. The air of power and authority was unmistakable.

"It sounds charming," Brett said smoothly, and Kayla kept her eyes on her notepad.

It sounded like chaos.

She looked up. "Tell me a bit about Snow Crystal itself."

"The O'Neils have owned the land around Snow Crystal for four generations. My great-grandfather bought it for the sugar maple trees and set up a business producing maple syrup. They did it the old-fashioned way, tapping the trees and collecting the sap in a bucket. My great-grandmother helped. They started selling the syrup and her syrup cookies out of their kitchen. Tourists enjoyed visiting the sugarhouse, so they started offering overnight stays. The business grew from that." He spoke with assurance, his voice deep and compelling as he outlined his family history.

It was a story of a family who had stuck together, a

family who had labored to build something. A family with a past and a future.

What did she know about that?

Nothing.

She reminded herself he was buying her expertise, not her pedigree. "I took a look at the log cabins online."

"Building those was the first thing I did when I came back eighteen months ago. They're built from reclaimed wood and have log fires, a hot tub and a view of the forest. If someone wants to escape, this is the place."

"Book me in." Smiling, Kayla scribbled *romantic getaway* on her pad. "And the rest of the accommodation?"

He talked, describing the resort and the changes he'd made.

She thought about the articles she'd read in the middle of the night when sleep had eluded her. A talented skier, he'd started a company for people like himself. The words used to describe him had included *focused, ruthless* and *visionary,* and his success with Snowdrift Leisure suggested they were accurate.

Kayla thought about the image of him plunging into a snow gully on skis.

Distracted by the image in her head, she rose to her feet and paced to the window. "I have a few more questions—what do you see as your main offering, Mr. O'Neil?" *Apart from killer blue eyes and a hot sexy body.*

"We offer the usual range of winter sports, together with skating on the lake and horse-drawn sleigh rides." He pushed a brochure across the table toward her. "Despite the addition of the spa and the cabins, we're losing money. Our occupancy rate is under forty percent.

The only part of the business currently in profit is our restaurant."

"Your strategy with Snowdrift was to target the high end of the market. Your clients were cash rich and time poor so you did everything for them apart from take the vacation yourself." She paused, thinking. "Who do you see as your main target audience? Families? Couples? Lone travelers? Adventure seekers?" *Christmas escapees?*

The corners of his mouth flickered. "At the moment it's anyone we can drag through the doors, but it's definitely a good place for families. We had fun growing up at Snow Crystal. Now we want to offer that same opportunity to our guests."

"How does your family feel about you bringing in an outside agency to work with you?"

"Unconvinced."

"You're confident you can persuade them to accept our recommendations?"

"It's your job to persuade them. Can you do it?"

"Of course she can. Kayla is the best there is," Brett drawled. "She'll have them eating out of her hand after five minutes. No worries."

"That's good, because eating is something of a family pastime." Jackson's gaze was fixed on Kayla. "I've come to you because you're reputed to be the best. It's essential that you can engage my family in whatever recommendations you make."

"Understood." Kayla sat back down and wrote herself a note on her pad. "It's always important to obtain buy-in from the whole management team."

"It's going to be a challenge."

Brett smiled. "*Challenge* is Kayla's favourite breakfast dish, along with a side of *difficult* marinated in the *impossible.* Isn't that right, Kayla?"

She wished Brett would shut up. "Who do you see as the most important person to influence?"

"My grandfather." He didn't hesitate. "He was born on Snow Crystal, lived and worked there all his life. He'd still like to be the one running the show. He resents the fact that he isn't."

And you resent the fact he won't let you get on with it, Kayla thought.

"So he doesn't leave you to run it yourself?"

"My grandfather lives and breathes the place. You know how it is with family."

Something twisted deep in her gut.

No, she didn't know how it was with family. She had no idea.

Kayla forced a smile. "So you'd like me to fly up there and meet them?"

"I want more than that. In order to persuade my grandfather to entertain the idea of taking on outside help, I've told them you'll spend some time with us. Show that you understand our business."

The fact that he'd done that without checking her schedule confirmed her suspicion that Jackson O'Neil was a man who hadn't often heard the word *no.*

She kept her smile firmly in place. "That sounds like an excellent suggestion."

"I want you to come for a week."

A week!

Even Brett was shaken out of his customary cool. "Jackson—"

A week?

"You'll spend quality time soaking up all that Snow Crystal has to offer."

It was a test of commitment.

Those blue eyes were deceptive, Kayla thought, and dangerous. On the surface Jackson O'Neil seemed civil and approachable, but he was a man who knew what he wanted and wasn't afraid to go for it. She had a feeling he used those eyes to lull his prey into a stupor before he pounced.

"A week could be difficult."

"But you feast on *difficult,* isn't that right?" He strangled her objections with the rope provided by Brett. "You'll find a way. Naturally I'll pay for your time."

Kayla could virtually see dollar signs tracking across Brett's eyeballs.

Her boss relaxed. "In that case, no worries."

She resisted the temptation to leap across the desk and squeeze Brett's throat until the words *no worries* never left his lips again.

She tried to work out how she was going to find a week in her packed schedule when even peeing required forward planning. A day would have put her in a cold sweat, but a *week?*

Trying to find a response that didn't include the words, *find me a time machine and I'll find you a week,* she opened her mouth to attempt to negotiate for an overnight stay in the new year, and then an idea formed in her brain.

"Did you say those luxury log cabins were secluded?"

"Yes."

"So secluded," she said casually, "that when a person is staying there, they could be the only human being on the planet?"

Blue eyes locked on hers. "The only thing a guest in the cabin will see as they're lying in the hot tub is local wildlife. White-tailed deer, raccoons, moose—the occasional black bear, although they're denning at this time of year so that's unlikely."

"Denning?"

"They're not true hibernators, but they den during the winter months."

Kayla decided that given the choice between an encounter with Santa or a black bear, she'd take the bear. And as for the rest of it—presumably the local wildlife wouldn't be banging on her door expecting her to celebrate Christmas. "You mentioned a log fire—"

"The cabins are luxurious."

She tilted her head to one side, mesmerized by the image in her head. Her mood lifted and this time her smile was genuine. "I agree it's important that I experience everything Snow Crystal has to offer. A week sounds reasonable. If there is a cabin free over the holidays, I'll come."

"The holidays?" Dark brows rose. "You mean Christmas?"

"If I'm going to feast on *difficult*—" she flashed a smile at Brett "—I like it served with cranberry sauce. Your grandfather needs evidence of my dedication... hopefully this will suffice. What better time for me to gain a feel for the charms of Snow Crystal? It will put me in a unique position to develop an integrated marketing plan that will make you stand out from the crowd." And it would also put her in a unique position to avoid the one time of year she hated more than any other.

Thank you, God.

A secluded log cabin and a business run by a family who would resent her presence at this time of year and undoubtedly leave her alone.

Perfect. Or it would be, if Jackson O'Neil would stop looking at her.

It was unsettling, and not just because he was spectacularly good-looking. Thick, dark lashes shielded eyes that saw far too much.

"Don't you have plans for the holidays?"

Yes. Her plan was to avoid the whole thing. To find a way of spending the holidays in a Santa-free zone. She was following the example of the black bear, which was clearly a highly evolved species.

"My plans, Mr. O'Neil, are to make sure that by this time next year you have a waiting list for cancellations and that *the* resort of choice for winter fun and relaxation is Snow Crystal. Together, we are going to drive your brand to the top. Perhaps you'd be kind enough to reserve me the most remote cabin you have available. It will be easier to focus if I'm far away from other guests." Oh, for goodness' sake, he was *still* looking at her. "Of course if you'd *rather* wait until the new year—"

"Tell me a bit about yourself."

"Me?" The question took her by surprise. "I read English at Oxford and then—"

"Not your academic background. Tell me something about you."

"Oh. I've worked for Innovation since—"

"Something personal."

It was Kayla's turn to stare. "Personal?"

"What do you do when you're not working?"

Kayla froze. No one had ever asked her that. Usually the questions were about forecasts, strategy, circulation figures—no one had ever asked her what she did when she wasn't working. "I—"

"It's a simple question, Miss Green."

No, it wasn't a bloody simple question. She decided to treat it like one of those interview questions where they asked your weaknesses and you gave them something they wouldn't see as a weakness, such as *I work too hard.*

"I work too hard." She gave an apologetic smile. "That doesn't leave much free time. Right now my focus is my career. I'd rather be working than doing anything else."

She'd especially rather be doing that than celebrating Christmas.

"Your family won't object if you work over the holidays?"

Why was the guy asking about her family? He wanted to buy her skills, not adopt her. No client had ever asked her a question about family. All they cared about was hearing what she could do for their business. No one had ever been remotely interested in the person behind the machine.

Her smile frozen to her face in a bizarre rictus, Kayla hunted for a response that was neither rude nor a lie. "They won't object. We're all busy people." Terrified that he might see through that neutral statement, she snapped her gaze from his and closed her notepad. "I will spend the week living and breathing Snow Crystal, write up my recommendations with input from the team back here and then we'll start work in the new year. Brett?" She glanced at him for support, knowing Brett was too hungry for the business to care if she drove a snowplow through her own vacation.

"Sounds good. I'll even provide the eggnog."

For once relieved that her boss was living up to his reputation for forgetting the people who worked for him had a personal life, Kayla relaxed. "Make it tequila and I'll put you back on my Christmas card list."

"Done. And you can put a pair of snow boots on expenses."

"You're all heart, boss."

"No worries."

Across the table, Jackson O'Neil was still watching her. Beneath the well-cut suit he exuded a raw sexuality that made it almost impossible for a woman to look away.

"Would you describe yourself as an outdoor girl, Kayla?"

Not in a million years. "I don't spend anywhere near as much time outdoors as I would like—" she adopted a regretful tone "—so I'm looking forward to rectifying that. And I love snow. Love it." Maybe she should have said that once. Maybe twice was overdoing it.

"That's good to hear." That hypnotic blue gaze didn't shift from hers. "So you ski?"

Remembering the picture of him plunging into a deep, snow-filled gully, Kayla decided it was safer not to lie about that. "Not exactly, but I've always wanted to, so this will be the perfect opportunity. I can't wait, although I think my preference will probably be for— er—flat slopes."

Dark brows rose. "Flat slopes?"

"Nothing too—" she tilted her hand to demonstrate a steep gradient "—terrifying."

"Right." He rubbed his hand over his jaw, and she had a feeling he was smiling. "Flat slopes. I admire your dedication." He rose to his feet, lithe and athletic. One glance at his powerful thighs told her that this man didn't expect his slopes to be flat.

She hoped he still admired her dedication when she was lying prostrate at his feet.

Belatedly, Kayla realized that spending a week at Snow Crystal meant spending a week in the close company of Jackson O'Neil, a man whose idea of fun was to jump off cliffs and land on a near-vertical slope.

Maybe she should have been more honest about her lack of experience.

Maybe she should book herself a hospital bed right now.

Gathering up her notes, she produced her most reassuring corporate smile and walked around to his side of the table. "Here at Innovation we're always willing to go that extra mile for a client." Preferably not downhill on skis, but if that was the only way then so be it. "Fast paced and focused. That's what we do." She stuck out her hand and then wished she hadn't, as strong, male fingers closed over hers.

She tried not to wince.

The guy was strong enough to kill a moose with his bare hands. And even though she was wearing her favorite confidence-inducing killer heels, he was taller. His hair was dark and gleamed under the harsh lighting of the boardroom. It should have been unforgiving, but it simply served to spotlight his spectacular good looks.

"Let me know when your flight gets in and I'll pick you up from the airport." He released her hand. "We'll do what we can to make the holidays special for you. It will give you a chance to try a variety of winter sports seeing as you—er—love snow so much." The glitter in his eyes told her he'd guessed that her only contact with snow up until now had been to stare at it through the office window and brush it off her coat.

She told herself it didn't matter.

"Secluded cabin, log fire, views of a frozen lake—"
No Santa, no store window displays or canned Christmas music and most of all, no memories. "It doesn't get any more perfect than that. Have a safe trip home."

THE WOMAN HAD obviously never been near real snow in her life.

Hiding a smile, Jackson snapped his bag shut and watched as she walked briskly away from him, those incredible legs accentuated by heels so high she almost needed to breathe additional oxygen. Her hair was smooth and silky and brushed her shoulders in a perfectly tamed curtain of pale gold. He was willing to bet Kayla Green had never had a bad hair day in her life. Everything about her was ruthlessly polished and controlled. He wondered idly what would happen to that hair after she'd spent a day in the mountains.

He wondered who she was under the gloss.

"I didn't expect her to be able to come over the holidays." He hadn't expected the chemistry, either, but he let that pass. He had enough complications in his life without adding more. "There can't be many people her age who would choose to spend Christmas in an isolated cabin, however luxurious."

"That's Kayla. If she's on a project then she's on it a hundred and fifty percent. She's brilliant and she has the best media contacts in the business. It's the reason I poached her from the London office. The girl is a tiger."

He was banking on it. He needed someone besides him who would take the business seriously. But still—

"She didn't have plans to return home for Christmas?"

Clearly that possibility hadn't occurred to Brett, who

shrugged. "If she did, she'll cancel. Snow Crystal is our top priority, and she's the woman to make it happen."

They walked together through to the foyer and Jackson paused, ignoring the long, speculative look the pretty receptionist sent in his direction.

"Does she never relax?"

"I'm not paying her to relax." Brett produced a smile in response to Jackson's raised eyebrow. "Sure, she relaxes. When she's asleep. That's the only time any of us relaxes. Drives my wife crazy. But Kayla's adaptable, and she'll do anything for her clients. If you need her to ski, she'll ski. Wrestle a bear—she'll wrestle a bear. No worries."

Jackson didn't reply. He was willing to bet if Kayla Green saw a bear they'd hear the screams back in New York.

For the past eighteen months, he'd thought of nothing but Snow Crystal, but suddenly all he could think of was joining Kayla in the secluded log cabin away from the outside world. His mind, starved of other outlets for creativity, used its creative talents to imagine her naked in the hot tub, cheeks pink, that smooth blond hair curling in the steam.

Damn.

Thanks to the influence of his family, he was taking *unprofessional* to a whole new level.

"YOU'RE WORKING OVER the holidays?" Stacy stared at her in dismay. "Kayla, that totally sucks."

It was a dream come true. "It's a bummer, but I'll live with it," Kayla said happily.

"But what about Christmas?"

"Christmas is canceled." She resisted the temptation to dance across her office.

"You're being so brave about it."

"I'm gutted, but there's no point in moaning."

"That is so unfair of Brett." Stacy was outraged. "You should be partying. Enjoying yourself. I don't mean to be personal, but when did you last go on a date?"

"Date?" Why did everyone keep asking so many difficult questions? "Er—there was that guy from the twentieth floor—I saw him a couple of times."

"If you're talking about the accountant, you saw him once."

"I'm not good at long relationships." Kayla piled everything she had on Snow Crystal into her bag. "Did you call everyone for a meeting?"

"Yes. And Kayla, one date is not a relationship."

"My point exactly."

"Are you sure you won't come with us tomorrow? We're meeting at 7:00 a.m. downstairs at the Rockefeller Centre for the first skate of the day. Full VIP package. Hot chocolate and skate concierge. We'd love for you to join us."

"What the hell is skate concierge?" Kayla reached for the bottle of water she kept on her desk.

"Some guy or girl pulls your skates on I guess." Stacy shrugged. "After that we're going to Santaland at Macy's. It's the whole Christmas experience."

Kill me now.

Kayla's jaw ached from smiling. She wondered whether she dared ring Jackson O'Neil and ask if she could have the cabin early. The way she felt, she was willing to camp in the forest. "Sorry to seem antisocial, but I just can't afford the time." She leaned back in her chair, stomach aching, head throbbing from too much time thinking about Christmas.

"Skating would be good practice for Vermont."

"I don't need practice. I'm going to be planning their campaign from the comfort of my log cabin."

"Won't your family be upset you're not coming home this year?"

"They're understanding." Now it wasn't just her stomach and her head, it was her heart and her throat. *Damn.* She'd thought she was tougher than this. "Thanks to Jackson O'Neil, I now have enough work to keep me going through the next five holiday seasons, so if you wouldn't mind—"

"Brett should have gone."

"Brett has a wife and four kids, although when he had time to *make* four kids I have no idea given that he's always in the office. Anyway, O'Neil asked for me—he's going to get me."

Stacy's eyebrows lifted and Kayla rolled her eyes.

"Not in *that* way. He's going to get the working, professional me." She tried not to think about those blue eyes or the width of his shoulders.

"Is there any other version? Kayla, you should not be spending the holidays alone."

"I won't be alone. There will be moose, raccoons and—and—" she racked her brains "—other lovely, cute Christmassy furry things."

"Have you actually ever *seen* a moose?"

"Not in the flesh, no." *Thank goodness.* "But I'm sure they're adorable. Why do you ask?"

"Because a moose is not a cute furry thing. I'm checking, so you know what you're getting into." Leaning across the desk, Stacy tapped Kayla's keyboard and a moment later a large image of a moose appeared, its elongated bony face filling her screen.

"Dear God—" Kayla recoiled. "That is the ugliest thing I've ever seen."

"I rest my case." Stacy straightened. "Still keen to spend Christmas there?"

"I won't be spending it with a moose, that's for sure. It will be fun. I've always thought log fires were romantic."

"Not by yourself."

"I won't be by myself. I'll take a pile of DVDs. My gift to myself is a boxed set called The Ultimate Horror."

"Kayla, that's terrible. Who spends Christmas Day watching horror movies?"

"I do." She picked up a stack of papers destined to be her bedtime reading.

"What about food?"

"According to Brett I feast on work, but I'll probably take popcorn."

"Christmas Day is about sharing good food with people you love, not microwaving popcorn."

"I love watching horror movies. It will be a treat. Now, kindly remove that moose from my desktop. I have work to do, and I can't do it with that thing watching me."

CHAPTER THREE

HE SAW HER before she saw him, striding purposefully through the airport, her shiny blond hair drawn into a ponytail that swung across her neck and drew glances from the men around her. She wore a long cashmere coat in a pale shade of caramel that brushed the tops of soft leather boots the color of dark chocolate. Over her shoulder was her laptop bag, and behind her she dragged a medium-sized suitcase.

Walking through the crush of tourists in their colorful ski jackets, she stood out like a gazelle in a shopping mall.

Eyeing the cashmere coat, Jackson hoped she'd packed something suitable in that suitcase.

Kayla Green might be an expert in integrated marketing, but she clearly knew sweet nothing about dressing for Vermont in December.

"Kayla!"

Seeing him, she lifted her hand in acknowledgment.

And then she smiled and the smile was sweet and genuine, as if she was really excited to be here.

It kicked at his ribs and lower. Heat shot through him. Every thought in his brain went up in smoke. Gripped by raw lust, he strode to meet her, reminding himself he had enough complications in his life without adding another one. "You were lucky. The flight after yours is grounded in Newark." Surprised his voice sounded even vaguely normal, he reached for her case but she gripped it tightly.

"I can manage, thanks."

"Right." Jackson decided the case would give her something to hang on to once those soft leather boots hit the snow outside and sent her spinning to the ground. "Then let's get going."

"I appreciate you meeting me." She was brisk and businesslike and he wondered how long she'd keep that up once she met his family. They had a way of sucking the professional from a person.

"You're welcome. As a matter of interest, did you pack any winter gear in those bags?"

She glanced down at herself. "Exhibit A. Warm coat. Boots. Scarf. What am I missing?"

He thought about pointing out she might be missing fingers and toes if she didn't find herself a few more layers, but decided she had brain enough to work it out for herself soon enough. She was dressed for Manhattan not Mount Mansfield.

"You look great." Truthfully she looked better than great. "You might need to add some thicker layers. The snow is pretty deep at the moment. We had a big storm a few days ago and another is forecast."

"Oh, I'm sorry. What a nuisance."

Her comment confirmed everything he already suspected about her relationship with snow. "We're a winter sports resort, Kayla. Snow is good. In fact it's essential."

"Of course it is." Her gaze didn't shift from his. "I knew that. I just meant, what a nuisance I didn't bring my other boots."

"You own a pair that doesn't have a four-inch heel?" He tried not to look at her legs and then decided *what the hell.* He hadn't seen anything that good in Vermont in a long time, and he was going to make the most of it.

"Actually, no. But it will be fine. I'm developing a public relations strategy for you, not skiing downhill."

He refrained from pointing out she was going to be skiing downhill the moment those heels touched the ice. "We'll find you something when we get to Snow Crystal."

He unlocked the car and stowed her bags.

Kayla sprang into the passenger seat and her coat parted, giving Jackson another glimpse of those incredible legs.

Lust slammed into him, and he was just recovering his balance when she turned and hit him with her smile.

Christ.

Felled by that smile, Jackson wondered how the hell he was supposed to focus on the words that came out of that mouth when all he wanted to do was kiss it.

He slid into the driver's seat and tried to erase those lips and legs from his brain. He couldn't remember the last time he'd felt this attracted to a woman. Lately he'd been working too hard to notice the sex of the person he was talking to.

But not this time.

Deciding that employing Kayla Green might just have made his situation more complicated, not less, he picked a neutral topic. "Have you seen much of the U.S. since you've been here?"

"I travel quite a bit meeting journalists and clients, but I mostly see the inside of an airplane and a hotel. You know how it is." She settled in her seat and her perfume wafted over him, swamping his senses.

Jackson kept his hands firmly on the wheel. It was that or grab her and haul her onto his lap. He was shocked by how badly he wanted to mess up that hair and ravage that soft mouth. Eighteen months at Snow Crystal and he'd obviously lost his grip on professional. "So you've never been to Vermont?"

"Never. But I've read extensively since our last meeting. You were born here?"

So she had the facts about the place, but not the feel. "Yes, but my mother is British. She came over to work in the hotel for a winter season and met my father. Married him and stayed."

"The last eighteen months must have been hard for all of you."

"She's struggling." He decided an understanding of his family was essential to understanding the unique needs of the business. "My grandparents live at Snow Crystal. My mother has been focusing all her energies on caring for them and making sure they're coping."

"And how are you coping?"

No one had asked him that question before. He hadn't even asked it of himself. Hadn't dared.

"I'm coping fine." He ignored the tension in his shoulders. "But it's been hard on my family."

"Is your mother involved in the business?"

"She helps out where she's needed." And that was part of the problem, of course. The lack of structure.

"What else do I need to know about your family? You mentioned a brother?"

"There are three of us. It's a wonder my mother is even remotely sane, given what we put her through growing up."

"Three brothers." Something in the way she said it made him turn his head toward her, and he immediately wished he hadn't because there was her mouth again.

"You don't have siblings?"

"Only child. You're the eldest?"

"Yes." The responsibility landed like a heavy weight on his shoulders. "Then Sean, then Tyler, who lives with his twelve-year-old daughter."

"He's the downhill skier—retired from racing after an accident. He's married?"

"Single parent. Jess's mother decided Tyler wasn't marriage material and married someone else instead." He was surprised by how much trauma could be condensed into one short sentence.

Kayla murmured words of sympathy, and Jackson thought back to that time, thought about the boy his brother had been and the man he was now.

He wasn't about to talk about the custody battle. Nor about the fact that Janet had never wanted Jess, just Tyler's money and a slice of the fame. "Burned him badly. He hasn't had a serious relationship since."

"Not surprising. But Jess lives with him now?"

"She's been back with us for a month." It had been a surprising turn of events, and he felt a rush of concern for his niece. "It's complicated."

"Relationships are always complicated."

"Are yours?"

"I keep mine simple."

"What's your secret?"

"Not to have any." Her tone was light and then she moved off the subject, talking about work again, grilling him on tourist numbers, hotels in the local area and transport links.

She'd whipped a tablet computer out of her bag and made endless notes as they talked.

The landscape was dotted with red barns and white-steepled country churches and the late-afternoon sun sent a wash of light over breathtakingly beautiful forests turned white by snow. The view caught him in the gut. He'd traveled the world, but in his opinion there was nowhere more beautiful. Expecting some comment from her, he glanced sideways and saw that her head was bent, her attention focused on the screen on her lap.

"You're missing the sunset."

"Mmm?" She glanced up and her expression changed. "Oh! That's stunning."

And Jackson realized her lack of response had nothing to do with indifference. She simply hadn't noticed. But she was noticing now, her eyes fixed on the snow-capped mountains that rose in the distance. "I can see why people choose to visit. It's beautiful. And relaxing."

For a person who knew how to relax, he thought, and that person was definitely *not* Kayla Green.

There was an almost-feverish energy about her, and already her head was back down, her fingers flying over the keyboard as she made more notes for herself.

She fascinated him.

"Where do you normally take your vacations?"

"I haven't taken a vacation in three years. I'm not good at vacations. But I'm good at knowing what other people enjoy—" she gave him a quick smile "—so don't start panicking about my ability to do the work."

He wondered what she'd say if she knew he hadn't thought about work since she'd climbed into his car.

They drove through villages, over covered bridges, past pretty clapboard homesteads and local stores. Doors were decorated with fresh evergreen wreaths and windows strung with sparkling lights and Christmas decorations.

Kayla alternated between looking at the screen and the gentle rise of the mountains, their snowy tops turning pink under the setting sun.

"That's part of the ski area?"

"Yes. See the mountains to the far right?" He gestured. "You're looking toward Stowe, home of the Front Four, some of the steepest and most difficult runs in the Northeast. And we have our share of steep in the mountains above Snow Crystal. The names are designed to make you think twice before getting off the lift—Devil's Gully and Scream being two of them."

"Scream? I think I could do that bit." She turned her head as they passed a sign by the side of the road. "Moose Crossing? How do the moose know they're supposed to cross there?"

Jackson laughed. "It's a warning to drivers that this is an area where moose are often spotted. You have to be particularly careful when driving at night. Moose have long legs. If you hit one, the likely scenario is that the moose comes through your windshield, and if that happens you might not live to tell the tale."

"That's one fact I don't recommend using in any marketing campaign."

"You might be surprised. Tourists love spotting moose."

"Really? I've only ever seen one in a picture. I think I might want to keep it that way."

As they drew closer to Snow Crystal, Jackson lifted his hand in greeting to the people they passed, and she raised her eyebrows.

"You know everyone?"

"Small community. Everyone knows everyone. I'm talking about the locals, obviously. The population swells by a few thousand tourists all year round." He turned the wheel and eased carefully into the long road that twisted and turned through the forest toward the lake. "Where did you grow up? I'm guessing not in the country."

"London." It was a typically brief answer and Jackson wondered whether it was because she didn't want to talk about herself or because she was careful to always focus on the client.

They passed the sign for Snow Crystal and she tilted her head. "Someone built a snowman."

"Favorite activity for kids around here."

She studied the carefully sculpted snow and the twig arms and mouth. "Was it yours?"

"Mine was stuffing snow down my brothers' necks and then running like hell before they could retaliate. We were more into destroying than creating."

"I suppose that's what happens when you have three boys. Tell me about your other brother."

"Sean? He's an orthopedic surgeon. I take credit for that choice...." He slowed as the surface became more uneven. "I broke my arm snowboarding when I was seven. Ran into a tree. Instead of running for help he stood there staring at the bone sticking out."

"Oh, please—"

"I was yelling at him to get help, and all Sean could do was wonder how it was going to go back under the skin. He insisted on coming with me to the hospital so he could find out. He went to Harvard and then spent time at the Shock Trauma Center in Baltimore indulging his fascination for difficult fractures, before switching to sports medicine. At the moment he's working in Boston and when he isn't wearing scrubs he dresses in smart suits, drinks fine wine and dates beautiful women."

He'd done the same, he remembered. There was a time not so long ago when he'd worn smart suits, enjoyed fine wines in good restaurants and dated beautiful women.

Now he rarely wore a suit, and apart from a couple of friendly evenings out with Brenna, who had grown up on the farm nearby and followed them around when they were kids, he hadn't dated anyone. For the past eighteen months his life had been about saving the business.

"So he's not back in the family fold?"

"No, but he'll be home for Christmas." Following an impulse, Jackson pulled over and parked. "This is one of my favorite views of Snow Crystal. From here you can see the lake, the mountain and the forest. If you come here early in the morning and late at night in the summer you can sometimes see black bear and moose."

"Thanks for the warning."

He smiled. "It wasn't a warning. The wildlife is important to the tourists. Have you ever seen a bear?"

"Never. And truthfully, I hope not to. I don't think it would be my thing, although I do meet quite a few sharks in my job." Her eyes gleamed. "Any other wildlife I should know about apart from bear and moose? Er—anything small and friendly and less likely to kill you? A cute rabbit perhaps?"

"The animals leave you alone if you leave them alone."

"I'll be leaving them alone. No doubt about that. So what else interests the tourists here?"

"The view." He considered himself good at reading people but he was finding it hard to read her.

"I've already written that down. *The view.* See?" She turned the screen toward him. "It's on the list, above 'moose.'"

"Instead of writing it down, why don't you try looking at it?"

"At a moose?"

"At the view. Get out of the car."

"Get out—you mean actually go outside and stand in the snow?" She said it slowly, as if he'd asked her to strip naked and run in circles. "You're the client, so if you think it's necessary then of course I'll—" Taking a deep breath she opened the car door and then gasped and slammed it shut again. "Crap, it's *freezing* out there."

The brief loss of control convinced him he preferred Kayla with her guard down. "If you wear the right gear, you won't feel the cold."

"I'm definitely wearing the wrong gear. I felt it right down to my bones." She shivered. "All right, I can do this. It's the whole Snow Crystal experience, frostbite and all." Opening the door gingerly she slid out of the car, one limb at a time, as if bracing herself to enter a cold swimming pool.

Jackson strolled around to her, his feet crunching on new snow. "Close your eyes."

He could see her weighing up the risk of trusting him against the potential downside of arguing with a client.

She closed her eyes. "If the next thing I feel is a bear's jaws closing on my arm, I resign the account. I really don't want the whole Snow Crystal experience to include being a bear's breakfast."

He closed his hands over her arms. "No bears. Turn around." Her hair brushed against his chin and the scent of it mingled with pine and freezing air. He decided that Kayla Green smelled as good as she looked. "Now open your eyes. Look through the trees."

"What am I looking at?"

"The lake."

She focused, her breath forming clouds in the air. "I— Oh. People are skating."

"In Vermont the weather is the ultimate wild card, but the one thing we always have in winter is ice.

"You can skate on the lake?" Her tone was wistful. "That's magical."

"You want to try it?"

"It's not *that* magical. I think I'm probably more of an indoor skater. But I can see others might find it charming," she added hastily. "I'll add it to the list underneath 'view' and 'moose.'"

"Skating is fun." He tried to imagine the business-like, composed Kayla Green falling on her butt and then decided not to waste time imagining something that was going to be reality soon enough. There was no way she'd keep her footing in those elegant and totally impractical chocolate leather boots.

Back in the car, he turned the heating up and steered the vehicle back onto the road. "If you look through the trees to the right you can see one of our log cabins."

She turned her head, the movement sending that blond ponytail swinging. "Is that mine?"

"No. You asked for secluded." Had he misjudged? Why would a single girl on her own over Christmas want to be in a secluded cabin? "You can change your mind and be closer to the main lodge if you prefer."

"A secluded cabin is my dream."

It seemed like an odd dream for a bright, twenty-something woman.

Then he thought about the life she led, the busy non-stop adrenaline rush that was her working day. Maybe she needed a rest. There were plenty of days when a secluded cabin sounded good to him, too.

"Your cabin is right on the boundary of our land and it backs onto a deer wintering area so you'll probably spot white-tailed deer. You might see snowshoe hare, fox, coyote, bobcats and the odd porcupine." He slowed as he negotiated the narrowing track. "I'll give you time to unpack and settle in before you meet the rest of the team."

Team? He almost laughed. *They weren't a team, they were a circus.*

"Do you live with your family?"

"No. I love them, but there are limits. I converted the barn." So that he could have his own personal brick wall to bang his head against when they drove him crazy.

He drove straight along the forest road that followed the edge of the lake and pulled up outside the little rustic gate that marked the track leading to the cabin.

"We have to walk from here."

It was perfect.

Kayla stepped onto the path and stood for a moment, breathing in the smell of the forest and the crisp winter air. Trees soared upward, branches drooping under the heavy burden of snow. The light was fading and the last rays of the sun glinted off the frozen surface of the lake, giving it a mystical, ethereal quality. Everything was still, the silence broken only by the occasional soft thud as snow tumbled from overloaded branches.

It felt a million miles from Manhattan. A million miles from her life.

A million miles from the all-consuming madness of Christmas.

She smiled.

She could have been the only person on the planet.

And then she heard the car door slam and remembered she wasn't the only person.

He was here.

The chemistry was a tight knot in her stomach and the frantic race of her heart.

She'd spent the journey with her head down, trying not to think about the man in the driver's seat next to her, trying not to think about his hands, strong and sure on the wheel or his thighs, hard and muscular, dangerously close to hers. But Jackson O'Neil wasn't easy to ignore. And he'd kept glancing at her, as if trying to work out who she really was behind the person she projected.

He made her edgy.

Striving for normality, she reached for her phone, but he shook his head as he put her bag down next to her.

"The signal is patchy here. It's better in the cabin. I'll leave you for a couple of hours to catch up on whatever you need to do, then I'll pick you up and take you to the main house. I'll do my best to keep the experience as painless as possible."

It seemed an odd thing to say. Or maybe he thought she was nervous with no team to back her up. "It's a meeting. I've taken plenty of meetings in my time."

"This one might be a little different."

"*Different* keeps things interesting. I'm looking forward to meeting your family and getting straight down to business." She emphasized the word *business* as much for her benefit as his.

She didn't want this to be about anything other than work.

As far as she was concerned, the chemistry was as unwelcome as Santa.

Telling herself that all she had to do was ignore it,

Kayla turned to pick up her bag only to find he was already holding it.

"This path can be icy. You might want to hold my hand."

What?

Certain that holding his hand would be a fast route to the dark side, she curled her fingers into her palm. "I'll be fine."

"We sweep the snow but there are always a few icy patches."

She'd rather hit an icy patch than lay a hand on any of his muscles. That was a line she definitely didn't want to cross. "I have natural balance." Trying to look professional, Kayla adjusted her scarf. "I do yoga and Pilates."

"Natural balance." He watched her with a lazy, hooded gaze. "That's good to hear." Turning away, he unlatched the gate, carrying her bag as if it weighed nothing. "The place should be warm. There should be plenty of logs for the fire but if you need more, let me know."

Kayla stared at those wide, powerful shoulders now encased in a warm, winter jacket.

It was obvious he'd chopped a lot of logs in his time.

Dressed in a suit, he'd unsettled her, but with a great deal of mental effort she'd managed to box him together with all the other men in suits she met on a daily basis.

Now he'd punched his way out of that box.

Given that he had his back to her she allowed herself one indulgent, entirely feminine glance of appreciation.

Stacy was right. He was insanely hot.

And because life had a way of doling out what you didn't want at the most inconvenient moment, he turned and caught her looking. "Something wrong?"

"Just enjoying the view." Hoping he didn't guess exactly which view she'd been enjoying, she kept her head down and walked quickly past him. Too quickly. Her feet made brief contact with ice. There was a horrible stomach-swooping moment where she fought gravity, arms flailing like the rotor blades on a helicopter, but it was a useless battle and she landed flat on her back in the deep snow at the side of the path.

Cold oozed through the soft wool of her coat, which she hadn't bothered fastening, and snow enveloped her. It tumbled on her face, on her chest and trickled down her boots. Snow crystals froze to the back of her neck and dampened her hair until she was chilled right through to her skull. Somehow, in the general indignity of the fall, her smart pencil skirt had managed to ride up high on her thighs, and she could feel ice numb her legs.

Kayla lay there, pinned to the ground by shock and snowflakes while Jackson strolled across to her, maddeningly secure on the slippery path.

She gritted her teeth. "If you so much as mutter 'I told you so,' I'm resigning the account."

"You should have held my hand."

"It would have felt weird holding hands with a client."

"More weird than lying flat on your back in front of a client with one leg in Vermont and the other in New Hampshire?" He was laughing now, and the sensual curve of his mouth made her insides curl.

"I always like to conduct at least one client meeting on my back. I find it breaks the ice, although in this case it may have been my head that's broken the ice."

"I warned you." His gaze moved from her face to her legs and the look in her eyes made her feel as if someone had touched her with the flame of a blowtorch.

"I preferred snow when it was my desktop image.

Wearing it doesn't feel so good." She was trying desperately not to laugh. Her dignity was already buried under snow; she didn't want to make it worse by having a fit of the giggles but she couldn't help it. A gurgle of laughter escaped. *So much for good impressions.* "Am I fired?"

"If I hadn't already given you the business, I'd give it to you now." He towered over her, six foot two of solid male muscle and raw power.

"Because you've seen my legs?"

"Because you laughed." His voice was dark velvet and any desire to laugh vanished.

"*I'm* allowed to laugh, but if *you* laugh I'm on the next flight back to New York and you will never find out what I would have done with this place."

"Noted." He held out his hand. "Do you want help getting up or are you planning on lying there for a while?"

She wasn't sure she trusted herself to touch him. She was used to feeling sure of herself. In control. Right now, she was neither of those things. "You wanted me to enjoy the whole Snow Crystal experience so I don't want to rush this. And then there's the fact that I don't think I *can* get up."

Dark brows met in a frown. "You're hurt?"

"My pride is mortally wounded and I have frostbite in unmentionable places, but really it's nothing to worry about. I'm looking on the bright side—at least I didn't fall into a bear's nest."

"Bears live in a den, Kayla, not a nest. And they're mostly asleep right now, although I suspect if you fell into their den they'd wake up soon enough."

Teeth chattering, she tried to reach his hand, but the snow was so deep she floundered.

Swearing under his breath, Jackson bent toward her. "Stop writhing or bears are going to be the least of your problems." There was an edge to his voice and the look in his eyes should have melted the snow around them. For a moment they stared at each other, and then he slid his hands under her arms and lifted her to her feet in an easy movement that confirmed her suspicion that the guy probably lifted tree trunks above his head for entertainment. She felt the strength in his grip as he steadied her on the icy surface. She stood toe to toe with him, her eyes level with the dark stubble that shadowed his jaw and pushed him over onto the wrong side of dangerous. If she leaned forward her lips would be against that jaw, and from there it was only a short distance to his mouth.

And she was willing to bet Jackson O'Neil knew exactly what to do with that mouth.

Unsettled by how much she wanted to test that theory, she gripped his arm and her fingers encountered tough, unyielding muscle.

She glanced up, and her gaze clashed with the brilliant blue of his.

They were surrounded by forest and space and yet they were standing close to each other, *so close,* and she could feel the power of his thighs pressing through the softness of her coat. Her stomach swooped and fell. She felt as if she'd slipped on the ice again, only this time she was engulfed by heat, not cold.

"Er—" Shaken by the flash of chemistry, Kayla extracted herself from the safety of his grip and willed her boots not to slip. She felt unbalanced, not just on the outside but on the inside. "I'm fine."

"You really want to do this again without help? As far as I can see there's no part of you that isn't soaked."

"I can do this. I'm a determined person."

"You're also a wet, freezing person, and your boots aren't designed for this."

If only it were just her boots. "I can manage."

"Right. That's why your ponytail looks like an ice sculpture." His tone was patient and he held out his hand. "Apart from my brother, you're the only person standing in my corner on this project, so it's in my interests to keep you alive. Hold on to me, or you'll be lying on your back making another snow angel."

"Snow angel?" Ignoring his hand, she scraped at her frozen ponytail, sending more snow sliding down her neck. She dreaded to think what she looked like but *groomed* wasn't going to feature anywhere in the description. "What's a snow angel?"

"It's when you lie on your back and move your arms and legs until you leave the shape of an angel in the snow." He looked curious. "Didn't you ever make a snow angel when you were a child?"

In normal circumstances her smile might have slipped. Fortunately for her it was frozen into place by the cold. "We didn't have much snow when I was a child. I grew up in England. Snow makes the national news."

"What about snowmen? You ever build one of those?"

"I prefer my men warm-blooded."

"Is that right?" The way he was looking at her made her suspect he could see straight into her head and read her mind.

Her teeth started to chatter, although whether it was from memories or her close encounter with a snowdrift she didn't know. "I think I need to get out of my clothes."

It was the wrong thing to say.

That disturbing blue gaze held hers for a moment and then dropped to her mouth and lingered there.

Chill turned to heat. "I meant my coat. I need to get out of my coat. There's an avalanche happening somewhere between my neck and my boots. I might need the mountain rescue team. Do you have one of those round here?"

"We do. My brother's a volunteer. Might get around to it myself if this place ever gives me some spare time." Jackson lifted his hand to her hair and brushed away another lump of snow. "Your hair is curling."

"Just one piece of good news after another." Kayla shivered. "Can we go indoors so that I can take a shower and have another stab at being businesslike?"

"While you're staying here stick to marked trails, and don't step into thick snow unless you know what's under it. This is a forest. There are ditches, streams, ponds, deep water—"

"I won't be stepping into thick snow."

But she already felt as if she were in deep water.

She wasn't used to feeling this way.

Didn't *want* to feel this way.

"I need to buy different footgear—you're right about that." She tried to ignore the dangerous simmer of heat low in her belly. She especially tried to ignore that part of her brain that told her coming here had been a very, *very* bad idea.

"Stand there while I fetch your bag." He was back in a few strides, her bag in one hand, the other outstretched toward her.

This time she took it.

She rarely held hands with a man. When she dated, which wasn't often, she followed a predictable routine.

Dinner then home. Sometimes it was theater, dinner, then home. Occasionally it was sex. But she always woke in her own bed. Alone.

She knew she wasn't good at intimacy, and holding hands was intimate.

Fortunately, the walk was short.

At the end of the path the forest opened into a clearing and there, nestled like something from a fairy tale, was the log cabin. A tasteful blend of wood and glass, it merged with the forest as if it had grown there.

"Oh." Enchanted, Kayla stopped. She forgot about being wet and feeling cold. She forgot that she was holding his hand. "It's like something from *Hansel and Gretel*."

"We can provide gingerbread, but finding a cannibalistic witch might be harder."

"It's idyllic."

"Glad you think so. Let's get you inside before frostbite sets in." He kept hold of her hand until they reached the front door. Then he released his grip on her and delved into his pocket for a set of keys. "Stand there and don't move."

Ignoring that instruction, Kayla stooped and unzipped her boots. "I don't want to bring all that snow indoors."

"There's more on you than on your shoes." He pushed open the door and handed her the keys.

Kayla stepped over the threshold and removed her coat, depositing half a ton of snow by the door. "I'm making a mess."

"The place is designed for people who enjoy the outdoors."

"What about people who are wearing the outdoors?" Kayla decided not to mention that she had snow in her bra. "Please tell me this place has a shower and unlimited hot water."

"All that and more. I'll show you around."

"Thanks." She would have preferred him to leave and give her nerves time to recover. "Where can I buy boots?"

"Brenna might have something that will fit you. If not, we have a small store in the resort that stocks a limited range."

"Who is Brenna?"

"She runs our ski program. She's lived around here all her life. She'll be a good person for you to talk to if you want to get a feel for the place."

"Right." Unsettled by those blue eyes, Kayla took a few steps into the room and looked around her properly for the first time. "I *love* this."

The main living area was double height with a cathedral ceiling and glass windows soaring up to the rafters. In the corner of the room a pretty iron staircase spiraled up to a sleeping "shelf" where a large bed was positioned to take maximum advantage of the views of the forest and lake.

"The master bedroom is downstairs, but you can lie up on the shelf and watch the lake and the wildlife. It can be used as a second bedroom, but we stipulate no kids under twelve because the only access is the spiral staircase. It's a perfect place to sleep."

Or a perfect place for insomniacs. At least here, when she was lying awake, she'd have a view.

Kayla wanted to climb up that staircase, lie down and not get up until January. All she'd see from that bed were glistening snowy treetops. No overdecorated shop windows, no festively fuelled Christmas shoppers and, most of all, no happy families.

"I don't understand why this place is vacant over the holidays. You should have been able to book it ten times over."

"I'm hoping once you've worked your magic we'll be doing that."

Kayla paced the length of the living room. "The way you've built it—the way it's designed—" she tilted back her head and looked through glass into the twilight and the forest "—it's as if the outside is inside. It's like being part of the forest and the mountains. You can virtually *feel* the snow, without any of the cold."

"That was the idea."

"It's magical." Forgetting she was wet and shivering, Kayla walked across the wooden floor, taking in all the tiny details from the basket of roughly chopped logs next to the flickering fire, to the twist of delicate lights that hung from rafters to floor turning the space into the equivalent of a fairy grotto.

Soft, deep-cushioned sofas in a deep shade of green faced each other across a rug. Tall bookshelves made from reclaimed wood lined one wall of the cabin.

It was a mixture of sumptuous luxury and cozy homeliness.

"Couples," Kayla muttered under her breath, pacing toward what she assumed was the master bedroom while Jackson stood in the center of the room, thumbs tucked into his jeans as he watched her. "It's romantic. This place has to be all about couples."

And that suspicion was confirmed when she opened the door to the bedroom and saw the large log bed dressed in colors of the forest. Deep greens blended with cream and hints of silver that shone like light reflecting off crystal. Glass doors opened onto the wide deck, and she smiled as she saw the hot tub.

"Definitely couples."

"That's how I planned it, but we don't seem to be attracting that segment of the market."

"Then it's because they don't know about it. But they will."

He leaned against the door frame. "You're confident."

"I know my job." Kayla strolled to the glass doors and looked out onto the deck. "If you were staying here you could lie in the hot tub, stare into the snowy forest and watch the wildlife on the lake." She could imagine that all too easily, imagine it with *him,* and imagining it brought the color rushing into her cheeks. "How private is it? Do people walk past here?"

"No. Hence the gate at the end of the path. I wanted each property to be secluded."

"So you could lie naked in the hot tub." She murmured the words to herself, thinking aloud and then realized what she'd said and felt the sudden shift in the atmosphere.

"Yes." He spoke slowly and there was a rough note to his voice that made her stomach flip and heat rush across her skin. "You could."

"Give me some time to think about it. I'll come back to you with some ideas as soon as I have something worth sharing." She could feel him watching her and knew that if she turned her head, the look they'd share would be more than a casual glance.

She kept her gaze fixed on the forest, feeling as if her body were on fire.

"I'll pick you up from here at six." His voice was husky. "That should give you time to unpack and settle in before you meet the rest of the family."

"I can walk. It will give me a feel for the place." And

time to refocus. And maybe roll naked in the snow to cool herself down. "I'll put my boots to dry. They'll be fine."

"Those are the same boots you were wearing when you slipped and almost knocked yourself unconscious?" They strolled back into the living area and Jackson reached for his jacket. "About tonight's meeting—" He shrugged on the jacket and zipped it. "It's not going to be easy."

"I do this for a living. It won't be a problem."

It was Jackson who worried her, not the prospect of meeting his family and talking business.

Why would it? She'd handled skeptical CEOs who thought PR was a waste of money. She could handle his grandfather with her eyes shut.

And once she'd done that, she'd be spending a whole week in a luxury log cabin with work, a stack of books and DVDs.

What more could a Santa-hating workaholic ask for?

CHAPTER FOUR

"So did Superwoman arrive?" Tyler strolled across his brother's kitchen and snagged a beer from the fridge. "I thought she might turn around and fly straight back to New York once she found out what she was dealing with."

"She doesn't know what she's dealing with, but she soon will. With luck all the flights will be grounded and the roads closed. Please help yourself to my beer. Don't hold back."

"I won't. Being in this family is enough to drive a man to drink, so the least you can do is supply the damn stuff." Tyler peered into the fridge. "This is the last one. You need to get to the store."

"That's one option. Another would be for you to stop drinking my beer and buy your own."

"I'll go with the first." Tyler elbowed the door shut. "I'm earning it this week. I'm giving private ski lessons to some spoiled teenage princess who cares more about her hair than linking her turns."

"Good to know you're earning your keep."

"I'm not going to dignify that with an answer. So does your woman ski?"

"I doubt she's even seen a ski close up, and she's not my woman." Jackson thought about how close he'd come to kissing her when he'd hauled her out of the deep snow. She'd been right there in his hands, soft and womanly and as aware of him as he was of her.

He'd seen her fighting it. He'd been fighting it, too, but she'd done a better job than him. She'd frozen him out. Smoothly and with finesse, but still the distance had been there. Which was probably a good thing. His life was complicated enough without adding to it.

Tyler raised his eyebrows. "It was a casual remark, but judging from your expression I hit a nerve. So is she hot?"

Jackson thought about her skirt riding high on her thighs.

Hot? *Hell, yes.*

"Our relationship is professional and it's staying professional. And that goes for your relationship with her, too."

"In other words you're struggling to keep your hands off her. Interesting."

"Why is it interesting?"

"Because for the past eighteen months you've been too involved with the business to notice a woman."

"Not true."

Tyler strolled to the central island in the kitchen and hooked a stool with his foot. "Tell me the name of the last woman you dated."

"Brenna."

"What? *Our* Brenna?" His brother's tone chilled fractionally. "Brenna we grew up with?"

"The same Brenna who stuffed snow down your pants when you were ten. The same Brenna who runs our ski program." Jackson watched as a snow bunting landed on a branch near the window. Through the trees the lake sparkled in the late-evening sunshine. If it had been a few degrees warmer he would have taken his beer onto the deck and watched the sun go down over the lake and mountains. He realized that the summer had passed and he'd had no time to sit and enjoy it.

Next year, he promised himself. Next year he'd slow down long enough to sit outside his own barn and breathe in the air.

"Well, hell—" Tyler sat down at the stone-topped island that formed the focus of the large kitchen, "did you and she—"

"What business is it of yours if we did?"

"So that means you did?"

Jackson turned with a frown. "Christ, Tyler—"

"I guess I just never saw you and Brenna together." His brother looked so shaken Jackson took pity on him.

"We're not together. There was no chemistry."

"So if there was no chemistry, why the hell did you date?"

"Let's just say our work conversations overran so we took it to the bar, and then we took it out to dinner a couple of times."

"But you didn't take it to bed?"

"You're asking who I take to bed?"

"Just looking out for her, that's all. She's like a sister to me."

Jackson wondered if his brother could really be so clueless about Brenna's feelings. "Ty—"

"And then there's the issue of working together. If you two are tiptoeing around each other, I need to know that."

"There's no tiptoeing." He decided it wasn't his business to say anything.

"For the record, I think Kayla Green would be perfect for you."

"You haven't met her."

"She's obviously clever and you think she's hot."

"She can't ski."

"So? No one can keep up with you on the ski slope anyway so you're not exactly looking for company. But if it bothers you, get her skiing. Take her to the top of a steep slope and she'll be so grateful when you rescue her, she'll think you're a hero and have sex with you. That one always works." Tyler lifted his beer and drank.

"Are you serious?" Jackson shook his head. "On second thought, don't answer that. As you pointed out, personal relationships with a colleague make things awkward. And it's unprofessional."

"To hell with professional, it's Christmas. People do crazy things at Christmas."

"Round here people don't wait until Christmas, they do crazy things all the time." Jackson leaned against the cabinet and nursed his beer while Tyler glanced around him.

"I like what you've done to this place." He scanned the custom-made cabinets, relaxed now the conversation had moved away from Brenna.

"Glad someone approves. Gramps thinks I've wasted money."

"Cheaper than the psychiatrist bills you would have been paying if you'd moved in with them. I'm thinking of doing something similar with the Lake House."

"Good idea, especially now you have Jess with you. How's that going?"

"I need a manual on how to handle women."

"From what I've heard, you wrote that manual."

"Not the teenage version."

The atmosphere shifted and Jackson put his beer down. "Something wrong?" Light slanted through the windows, reflecting off shiny pans hanging from wooden beams. It occurred to him that so far he hadn't cooked a single thing in those pans.

"Apart from the fact her mother had another baby and decided Jess was getting in the way of her new family and that this would be a good time to remember I exist?" Tyler's voice hardened. "What the hell did I ever see in Janet Carpenter?"

"You were young. Shallow. She had an impressive rack."

"There was that." Tyler stared at the bottle in his hand. "And I was flattered. Older woman and all. I thought it was birthday and Christmas rolled into one when she got me in that barn. All I ever got from that encounter was trouble."

Jackson watched as the snow bunting flew off over the lake. "You got Jess."

"Yeah—" Tyler's voice softened. "Yeah, I got her. And she's the best. You should see her on skis. Great balance, no fear. And that worries me. She'll ski down anything with a gradient."

"You were the same."

"Maybe I was, but that doesn't stop me wishing she'd show caution. She's lived most of her life in Chicago. She doesn't know mountains."

"If you're worried, take her out with you."

"And give Janet something to use against me? No way."

"Hell, Ty, she virtually sent the kid away. She's hardly in a position to challenge your parenting skills."

"Maybe, but I'm not taking the risk. I've finally got her back and I'm not going to screw this up."

Jackson knew his brother was still tormented by the fact he hadn't been given custody in the first place. It had been a hideous, ugly time, and he was one of the few who knew the truth of it.

Maybe it wasn't surprising Tyler hadn't noticed how Brenna felt. He hadn't just been hurt, he'd been scarred.

"Have you talked to Jess about it?"

"She won't talk to me." Tyler sounded tired. "I even tried asking her straight-out what's wrong. First time in my life I've asked a woman if she wanted to talk about what was bothering her. I even stayed around long enough for her to answer."

"And did she?"

"She gave me a look and told me I wouldn't under-stand." Tyler stared at the bottle in his hand. "Wasn't going to argue with that one. Truth? I don't think she wants to be here. She wants to be back with her mother."

"She's always loved being here."

"A visit is different to living somewhere perma-nently. Janet hated it here."

"Jess isn't her mother."

"But she's lived with Janet long enough, and we both know Janet hates me."

Jackson didn't argue. Knowing Janet Carpenter, he thought it unlikely she'd held back from expressing her views on Tyler. "Jess loves you, Ty."

"Does she?"

"I know she does. She's confused."

"She's not the only one."

"You're entering the realm of the teenage girl."

"Does that realm include multiple door slamming and hours spent alone in her room? If so, I'm already there." He shook his head. "I thought women were meant to be the communicators of the species."

"Maybe you should talk to Mom about it. At least having Jess back will give her something to focus on."

"You'd think so, but Jess is shutting her out, too. She's transformed overnight from sweet kid to reclusive teen."

"Give it time. She's only been back with you for a month."

"This was always her favorite time of year. She's spent every Christmas here since Janet took her away. What sort of mother doesn't want her kid around at Christmas? Not that I'm complaining about that part." There was an edge to Tyler's voice that only ever happened when he talked about his ex-wife. "But normally I can't get Jess out of their kitchen in the holidays. If she's not decorating Santa cookies, she's gluing snowflakes, cutting out reindeer, or singing 'Jingle Bells' all over the house at the top of her voice. When I asked her this morning if she wanted to go and bake with Grandma, she told me she's not a baby anymore."

"That's true. Twelve. Hell, how did that ever happen?"

"It happened, and all she wants to do now is ski vertical slopes. Do you think she's suicidal?" For once Tyler wasn't smiling or making light of life, and Jackson lowered his beer.

"No, I don't. What I think is that you need to chill."

"That's why I'm drinking your beer." Tyler glanced at his watch. "What time are we gathering to hear your woman?"

"If you're talking about Kayla, I'm picking her up from the lodge at six. You don't have to be there."

"A mad moose wouldn't keep me away. I have to watch how she handles Gramps. Think she'll cope with it, or is he going to walk all over her?"

Jackson couldn't imagine anyone walking over Kayla Green, but he was under no illusions. She was going to need all her skills to win over Walter Montgomery O'Neil.

"We'll see how she does." He picked up his jacket. "I plan on getting through the 'meeting' and then buying her dinner in the restaurant as compensation. I figure after an hour with our family, she's going to need a drink. Probably ten drinks."

Tyler lifted his eyebrows. "But this isn't a date, right?"

"It's work." Ignoring the look his brother gave him, Jackson scooped up his keys. "Buy some beer. That way there might be some in my fridge next time you open it."

IT WAS JUST a meeting.

She'd been to hundreds of meetings, and this one wasn't any different.

Energized after a hot shower, Kayla pulled another pencil skirt off a hanger and put it on the bed next to her black cashmere sweater. Smart *and* warm. Wearing it would show she could be practical when the need arose.

Grabbing her suitcase, she picked out her favorite pair of black heels. She'd walk over in her boots and then change into her shoes.

Wrapped in a towel, cheeks still pink from the heat of the hair dryer, Kayla mentally ran through the way she intended to play the meeting.

They'd be skeptical, so she'd show them what PR could do for them.

They'd assume she didn't know anything about their business, so she'd prove to them she'd memorized all the statistics and facts. That she *knew* Snow Crystal.

Finally, she'd show them what she'd achieved for other clients.

She'd show Jackson O'Neil that she might be useless at walking on ice, but when it came to understanding marketing there would be no slips. Her traction would be perfect.

She wondered why he was so concerned about the meeting.

Apart from my brother, you're the only person I have in my corner. It's in my interests to keep you alive.

The irony didn't escape her. She'd never met a man's family before. Never got to that point in a relationship, and here she was about to meet Grandma.

Kayla straightened her hair until there was no sign of her encounter with the snow, livened up the severe black sweater with a silver scarf covered in tiny stars and added a pair of silver hoops to her ears before checking her reflection quickly in the camera on her phone.

Go, Kayla.

By the time Jackson rapped on the door, she was confident she was ready for anything they threw at her.

He parked outside the main house. Tiny lights hung along the eaves and were twisted into the trees.

It could have been worse, she thought. At least there were no grinning Santas or illuminated reindeer with flashing antlers.

Jackson unclipped his seat belt. "Nervous?"

Yes, she was nervous, but she had a feeling that had more to do with the man sitting next to her than the prospect of the meeting. All he'd done was drive, but there was a tight knot in her belly and all she could think about was sex. Her gaze slid to the sensual curve of his mouth and then away again.

What the hell was *wrong* with her? Stacy was right. She needed to get out more. "I'm excited. You have a business issue to solve and that's what I do." What she didn't do was stare at her client and wonder how it would feel to be kissed by him.

"I hope you still feel the same way by the end of the meeting."

Anxious to get away from him, Kayla slid out of the car and stared at the path, weighing up her chances of making it to the door without falling over. "I might hold your arm this time."

"Good to know you learn from your mistakes." There was laughter in his voice and something else, something rougher and more dangerous that told her he was feeling exactly the way she was feeling.

Her gaze met the deep blue of his, and the sudden flash of chemistry punched the breath from her lungs.

It was like falling on an electric fence.

She grabbed his arm. "First thing tomorrow I'm buying proper footwear."

She held his arm for as little time as possible and then paused in the doorway to tug off her boots and slide on shoes that gave her at least another three inches in height.

Pushing her boots into her bag, she smoothed her hair. "I'm ready."

Jackson stared down at her feet. His gaze traveled slowly up her legs and finally ended up at her mouth. He hadn't touched her but suddenly her lips tingled and her throat felt dry.

"We should—"

"Yeah, we should—" His tone was thickened and then he frowned slightly and turned to push open the door.

Sleigh bells jangled, breaking the spell. Kayla stared at the pretty cluster of bells tied to the door handle below a glossy wreath made of juniper and spruce.

"What are those?"

"My father proposed to my mother in a horse-drawn sleigh. She kept the bells as a memento and hangs them on the door at Christmas."

Oh, great. That was all she needed. "Your mother loves Christmas?"

"Yes. She loves decorating for the holidays. Be warned—our tree is usually bigger than the one outside the Rockefeller Center."

Digesting that less-than-welcome news, Kayla stared gloomily at the bells.

They were just decorations, she reminded herself. And at least her cabin was a Christmas-free zone.

She walked into the house and stopped in surprise as she took in the details of the room and saw the number of people crowded around the large table.

"Oh, I— This is—" She turned to look at Jackson, confused. "This is the kitchen."

"That's right."

"The kitchen leads to your meeting room?"

The kitchen *is* our meeting room." He closed the door on the cold and Kayla felt a flash of panic as she turned back to face her audience.

They were holding this meeting in the kitchen?

She glanced around and saw shiny saucepans and stainless steel. Bunches of herbs hung drying above the range. Surfaces gleamed, but this was no show-room kitchen. It was lived-in and loved. There were boots of various sizes lined up by the door and shelves stacked with recipe books. It was easy to imagine the three O'Neil boys rushing in from the snow, hoping to grab some freshly baked treats.

A woman hefted a large blue casserole dish into the oven and gave them a welcoming smile.

"You must be Kayla. We've heard so much about you. I'm Elizabeth O'Neil, Jackson's mother. Alice and Walter, his grandparents—" she nodded her head in their direction "—and Tyler, Jackson's brother. Jess might join us later but I'm sure you won't mind that. Now come on in and let me take your coat." She closed the oven door and hurried over, the smile still on her face, her arms outstretched.

Kayla took a hasty step backward, and the sharp heel of her stiletto drove hard into Jackson's foot.

He swore under his breath and then his hands closed around her arms and he steadied her. "Do you have a license for that weapon?"

She didn't answer. Terrified she was about to be hugged, Kayla thrust her hand out, almost winding his mother in the process. "Pleased to meet you."

Jackson released her. "My mother is British, so you have that in common." He smoothed over the potentially awkward beginning. "Thirty-five years ago she arrived to cook for a winter season and never left."

"Why would I leave? I never saw anywhere more perfect than this place, and I'm sure Kayla agrees."

Kayla was ready to agree to anything in order to get out of this Christmas grotto as fast as possible. "Absolutely. It's stunning. Good to meet you, Mrs. O'Neil."

"Call me Elizabeth, dear. We're not formal." Warm and friendly, his mother took Kayla's coat, frowning as she hung it up. "It's wet. Is it snowing again?"

"No. I fell."

"You let her fall?" Elizabeth O'Neil turned reproachful eyes on her eldest son. "You didn't hold her arm? Shame on you, Jackson."

"It was my fault," Kayla said stiffly. "I'm not used to walking on ice, but it won't happen again."

Elizabeth nodded approval. "Because next time you'll hold his arm."

"No." Kayla had already promised herself she was going to keep physical contact to a minimum. "Next time I'll be wearing better boots. I'm going to sort that out first thing tomorrow."

Jackson's grandmother made a sympathetic noise. "I'm not surprised you fell. It's so icy. I'm afraid to go out in winter since I had my hip done and as for the cold—" Alice O'Neil peered at Kayla from across the table. "Are you wearing thermal underwear under that sweater? The wool looks thin. And your skirt is quite short. We don't want you catching cold while you're here. Jackson, you should take Kayla to buy underwear."

Kayla felt heat rush into her cheeks. "I—" *How was she supposed to respond to that?* She was used to small talk that involved observations on the weather or the traffic in Manhattan. Occasionally people touched on the economy. No one ever mentioned underwear. "I'm warm, but thank you for your concern." She shot Jackson a desperate look, feeling like a deer circled by a pack of hungry wolves. "Shall I begin my presentation?"

"Why do young girls wear so much black?" Walter O'Neil added his contribution from the far end of the table. "When I was young, black was for funerals."

"I love color. You'd look pretty in green, Kayla." Alice held out a ball of yarn to Kayla, who stared at it as if she were being offered a grenade.

Jackson's brother gave a slow, wicked smile. "We're *very* pleased to meet you Kayla. And I love the skirt. Don't change anything about it, especially not the length—unless you want to make it shorter."

"I didn't say it wasn't a nice skirt," Alice said stoutly. "I said it was short and with the weather like this—"

"She's warm, Grams. Don't worry." Jackson put his hand on Kayla's back and urged her into the room. "And she looks smart in black. If people would listen for a moment, you'd discover she's smart in other ways, too." He pulled out a chair and offered it to Kayla, who sat gratefully.

They'd done the small talk now, so hopefully they could move on to business.

"I'm really excited to be working with you." She thought she heard a snort from Walter O'Neil, but when she looked at him he was handing a fresh ball of yarn to Alice. "I've prepared a presentation that will give you a better picture of some of the ways in which we can help build your business." She pulled her computer out of her bag. Just touching the smooth surface helped her relax. It was like suddenly discovering there was a trusted friend in the room. "I'll start by going through a few of the campaigns we've run for other people."

Glancing up she noticed the photographs lining the walls of the kitchen.

There was Walter O'Neil looking handsome with an ax clasped in his hands in a photo taken at least forty years earlier. One of the family dogs. Another of the three O'Neil boys dusted in snow after a snowball fight. There was Tyler standing on the podium collecting a gold medal, and a man she didn't recognize—presumably the other brother—at his graduation. It was a visual record of the passage of time. The story of the O'Neil family.

Jackson followed her gaze. "My mother loves photographs. She also loves embarrassing us by displaying them for people to see." There was amusement in his tone and something else. Love. This man loved his family. That was why he was here and not thousands of miles away in Europe, running his own business.

Realizing she was supposed to smile, Kayla smiled obligingly.

"The kitchen is where I spend my time." Elizabeth turned on the heat under a pan. "Why wouldn't I hang them in here? It makes me happy seeing Michael on that sledge. And I love that one of you boys taken right after that snowball fight. Look at their faces, Kayla—you can see what a handful they were. They loved the snow. Show them a slope of any sort and those boys of mine would ski down it. Didn't matter what was at the bottom. They couldn't play together without fighting but nor could they bear to be apart. Turned me gray prematurely." But her face was all smiles, and she was clearly a woman whose life was fed and nurtured by family.

Feeling like an alien from another planet, Kayla hunted for something to say that wasn't "get me out of here." "They're lovely photographs." There was a thickness in her throat that hadn't been there a few moments before.

It was this damn place, she thought. This lovely, cozy kitchen all prepared for Christmas. There were bowls of pinecones and vases filled with long branches of forest greenery. Candles flickered on shelves next to handmade decorations and Christmas cards with scrawled messages of love.

She thought about her apartment in Manhattan. Sleek, stark and without a single homey touch. No messages of love.

"Kayla?" Jackson's prompt cut through her thoughts. "Are you all right?"

"Yes." But it was a lie. She wasn't all right.

Blocking out her surroundings, she tried to put her laptop on the table and discovered there was no room.

"Move your knitting, Alice." Elizabeth O'Neil swept a small pile of yarn out of the way. "Have you seen Kayla's computer? It's so small. Isn't technology fantastic?"

Kayla stared transfixed at the neat rows of gingerbread Santas waiting patiently in line to be iced.

A memory, long buried, awoke in her brain.

Despite the warmth of the kitchen, the chill spread through her. She felt horribly cold.

"Are you hungry, honey?" Alice carefully lifted a Santa onto a plate and pushed it toward her. "Aren't they beautiful? Try one. They taste as good as they look."

"No, thank you."

Alice clucked with disapproval. "You young girls are always dieting, but of course that's why you're so lovely and slim."

"I'm not dieting. I'm just not hungry right now." There was a sick feeling in the pit of her stomach.

Jackson's grandmother reached across and patted her hand. "You don't need to be nervous, honey. And we're just so grateful to you for giving up your holidays to help us."

The kindness almost finished her.

"Why are you doing that?" Walter narrowed his eyes suspiciously. "Why aren't you at home with your family?"

Elizabeth frowned. "Walter!"

"I'm just asking myself what sort of person chooses to work rather than spend Christmas with their family."

The sort of person whose family didn't want them.

Kayla gripped her laptop. "I've prepared a presentation for you. I hope it will help show some of the ways Innovation can help you with your business."

"This place is about families," Walter barked. "It's about togetherness and making memories. What do you know about that?"

Nothing. She knew nothing.

"That's enough, Walter." Elizabeth thumped a plate down in front of him.

"I just don't see what a Brit who works in Manhattan can possibly know about our business, that's all. She's an outsider."

The word slid into her like a blade.

She knew nothing about functioning families, but she knew all there was to know about being the outsider.

Just for a moment she was back in her stepmother's house, standing frozen behind the Christmas tree where no one could see her.

Why does she have to come to us, David? I want it to be just the four of us. Why can't she just go to her bloody mother?

It was as if Walter had found a loose thread in a sweater and pulled. Kayla felt herself unravel. Feelings she'd kept carefully locked away tumbled out.

Drowning, panicking, she turned to Jackson. "I need to plug my laptop into your projector, please." The feelings pressed in on her, dark and terrifying, and she pushed back, refusing to allow them to take hold.

"There is no projector."

"No projector?" She couldn't have been more shocked if he'd told her he'd built a hotel and forgotten to include bedrooms.

"It's not high on our priority list right now." That intense blue gaze was searching. "Just turn your laptop around and we'll look at your screen."

"No projector." Kayla snatched in a breath as she tried to navigate this latest obstacle. "No projector is just *fine*."

Alice placed a freshly iced Santa on the rack. "I always find icing something helps me relax. Give Kayla a knife, Elizabeth, then she can help."

"I can't cook. I've never iced anything." Fingers shaking, Kayla swiveled the laptop and fished her notepad out of her bag. "You're obviously busy so I'll be as quick as I can." For her own sake, if not theirs. She needed to get out of here.

"If she can't do something simple like ice a gingerbread Santa," Walter muttered, "how the hell is she going to work magic on this place?"

Jackson's jaw tensed. "If you ask her, she'll tell you. That's why she's here, but so far she hasn't been able to get a word in edgewise. And I don't need her to cook. I employed a chef."

"Even though we already had a perfectly good chef, but we're not going over that again now." Walter glared down the table at Kayla. "We're listening. Show us the magic."

An expectant silence spread across the room.

Feeling as if everything was happening in slow motion Kayla stared at Walter, then at Elizabeth and finally at Alice, who was carefully adding buttons to Santa's iced coat.

"Kayla?" Jackson's voice was controlled. "We're ready to hear what you have to say."

She didn't have anything to say. There was nothing in her head except the past.

Usually she was articulate, but panic had shorted her circuits.

Then she remembered it was all on her screen, but her screen was pointing toward them and she couldn't see it. "I prepared a presentation that demonstrates some of our experience in this area."

Alice squinted. "I might need my other glasses. Elizabeth, do you have my other glasses?"

"They're in your bag where they always are." Elizabeth handed them to her, and Alice slid them onto her nose and leaned forward.

Kayla adjusted the angle. "From the moment we get up in the morning to the moment we go to bed, we are deluged by messages." Oh, God, she sounded like a robot. She needed to liven it up and make it more personal. "We live in a fast-moving world where the news changes by the minute so the challenge is how to make yourself heard amongst the noise."

Alice looked confused. "There's not much noise around here, honey. Snow Crystal is a peaceful place, isn't it, Elizabeth?"

"Apart from Sunday mornings when you can hear the church bells. I swear there are times when I wish we hadn't given money for the restoration." Elizabeth stood up and removed a tray of baked potatoes from the oven. "One of these days I'm going to cut the ropes of those bells myself."

Kayla felt a flicker of panic. "I—was talking about media noise. It's an expression used to describe the amount of information we're subjected to daily from news channels, social media—"

"Social media?" Walter looked blank and Kayla gripped the edge of the table until her knuckles turned white.

"You're not interrupting." Elizabeth sounded confused. "We're having pot roast. Élise, our French chef, gave me the recipe. It's the perfect comfort food for a snowy day, and we have plenty of those around here. I'll give you the recipe, then you can make it when you're back in New York."

She wished she were in New York now, back in her soulless glass apartment sealed away from the world.

Coming here had been a bad idea. She was running away, but you couldn't run from something that was inside you.

"I'll leave you to your meal." Kayla stumbled toward the door and grabbed her coat. "Have a good evening." Her coat half on and half off, she yanked open the door.

A young girl stood there. Pale-skinned and thin, she wore a thick Fair Isle sweater and was holding a puppy in her arms.

"I found her outside." She put the puppy down, and it immediately ran over to Kayla and raced in circles around her, leaping up and leaving paw prints on her favorite black suede shoes.

"Oh, she's making a mess of your beautiful shoes, I'm so sorry—" Elizabeth brandished the serving spoon. "Go to your basket, Maple."

Maple paid no attention and Kayla heard Jackson sigh.

"Down!"

Responding to the voice of authority, Maple sank to her belly and turned wounded eyes to Kayla.

Kayla was willing to bet the look in her eyes was pretty similar.

I'm in much deeper shit than you are.

While the O'Neils were focused on the puppy, she seized the moment to escape.

"Social networking is playing an increasingly important role in travel planning right now. Many organizations are picking up on that and now run their own blogs, Twitter feeds and Facebook pages. It's a way of interacting with customers and personalizing your message. That's one of the things I suggest we look at when we're developing a plan for Snow Crystal."

The only sound in the room was the soft bubble of the casserole on the hob and the faint hiss of the kettle.

She'd silenced them, but it wasn't an interested silence. It was a bemused silence.

Icing dripped from Alice's knife onto the table, like snow falling from the branch of a tree.

The whole family stared at her, eyes glazed, and Kayla was reminded of the day she'd dropped a casserole dish while she was staying at her father's house. Her hands had been shaking, and she'd been trying so hard to make a good impression she'd caught her foot on the rug and tripped. She could still remember her stepmother's frozen expression as lumps of beef and red wine had spread across the expensive cream rug. She'd wanted to somehow melt away from the horrified stares. Wanted desperately for her father to hug her and tell her it didn't matter.

But it *had* mattered because they hadn't wanted her there in the first place.

She'd been the outsider then, and she was the outsider now.

The only person who wanted her here was Jackson, and he'd been relying on her to impress his family.

If she needed any confirmation that hadn't happened, Walter gave it. "That's it? If you ask me, we'd be better off leaving the money in the bank."

Kayla made a last desperate attempt to recover the

situation. "Why don't I take you through some of the integrated marketing campaigns we've run for other companies? It will give you a feel for what can be achieved. For example, our campaign for Adventure Travel generated in excess of three hundred million media impressions, including prime spots on daytime television."

"Media impression?" Alice looked blank. "What's a media impression?"

Walter glared at Jackson. "Why do we care what she's done for other companies? Is she saying we're not unique?"

He didn't even address her directly, Kayla thought. She might as well not be here.

"That's not what I'm saying."

This time he did address her directly. "So tell me what is special about Snow Crystal."

There was a hideous silence.

"I—I don't know yet." She had statistics, but that wasn't what was needed here. For once she wished she had the backup of her team. She even would have welcomed Brett saying "no worries" and committing them to all manner of unachievable goals. Anything that would give her a minute to refocus. "But I'll find out. That's why I'm here. I intend to find out what is special about Snow Crystal."

Jackson was staring at her with incredulity, and her cheeks burned because she knew she'd failed him. And herself. For the first time ever she'd failed at her job. There was no way, *no way,* he'd give her the business after her pathetic performance. And she didn't blame him. She wouldn't give herself the business, either.

Walter gave a grunt. "Then maybe we should be having this meeting when you've done that."

"That's enough." Jackson didn't move from his seat, but his voice was hard. "This family ma[…] things, but rude isn't one of them. Kayla is [...] at what she does."

Walter's expression was mutinous. "Maybe, [...] not an expert on Snow Crystal. She's just adm[...] and that's hardly surprising, is it? She's an ou[...] How can an outsider know more than us?"

"We need someone on the outside," Jackson [...] coldly, "because the people on the inside have d[...] things the same way for far too long."

"Because they worked. You want to change thing[...] for the sake of it."

"I have no idea who rattled your cage, Walter, but [...] you need to calm down or you'll be getting chest pains [...] again." Sending her father-in-law a reproving look, Elizabeth O'Neil placed the large casserole in the center of the table. "As for Kayla, she's probably starving hungry, and no one can think on an empty stomach. She had a long journey and traveling always makes a person hungry. Do you like pot roast, Kayla?"

They were looking for excuses for her fumbled, inadequate performance, and there were none. Or at least, none she could offer.

Kayla couldn't make her brain or her limbs work.

She glanced at the casserole as if a spaceship had landed in the middle of the table then stood up, graceless and flustered.

They didn't want her here.

Jackson reached out and caught her arm, his fingers like steel. "Where are you going?"

Why don't you eat in your room, Kayla?

"You're having a family meal. I'm interruptin[...] Shaking him off, she stuffed the notebook and com[...] into her bag without bothering to switch off the [...]

"Kayla—"

"I'm fine. Enjoy your meal." She took a last, wild look around the room and shot out of the door, slamming it shut behind her.

CHAPTER FIVE

WHAT THE HELL had just happened?

Jackson closed his eyes and spent thirty seconds mentally running through every swearword in his vocabulary while Maple leaped out of her basket and barked at the door as if she wanted to go after Kayla.

Everyone was talking at once.

"She seemed flustered." Alice put her knitting down. "Something was wrong."

Elizabeth took plates from the oven. "Of course something was wrong. She had Walter barking at her and on top of that she was hungry. No one can concentrate when they're hungry. You need to take her something to eat, Jackson. And, Walter, you need to show tolerance when we have a guest in our house."

"She wasn't a guest. She was here to make us change things that don't need changing. Things she doesn't understand." Walter pointed his fork at Jackson. "I told you it was a mistake to employ someone from New York."

"You didn't give her a chance." Jackson hauled in his temper. The fact that Kayla hadn't performed as expected intensified his feelings of frustration. She'd made his battle harder, not easier. "If you'd let her talk, you might have discovered she's good at her job." Except that she hadn't been. Not today. Not when it counted. She'd crumbled in front of his eyes and he had no idea why.

True, Walter had been difficult, but no more difficult than the senior company personnel Kayla Green spoke to on a daily basis in her role as associate vice president. And yet the ballsy, gutsy woman who had manipulated her tough boss like modeling paste had allowed his eighty-year-old grandfather to walk all over her as if she were yesterday's snow.

And Walter hadn't finished. "I don't care if she's from Alaska. If you put all your savings into her you're even more of a fool than you look. Might as well back a moose to win the Kentucky Derby."

"Better legs than any moose I've laid eyes on." Tyler's attempt to defuse the tension had the opposite effect on Jackson.

He was trying not to think about those legs, just as he was trying not to think about her mouth and her smooth blond hair. Most of all he was trying not to think about the panic in her eyes.

What the hell had happened to her?

He'd known it would be a difficult meeting, but not even at his most pessimistic had he expected her to actually walk out. If he hadn't witnessed it himself, he wouldn't have believed such a competent businesswoman could crumble so completely.

Had he underestimated the impact of taking her out of a minimalist corporate boardroom devoid of personality or character and transplanting her here, in the O'Neil kitchen?

He looked at his grandmother, knitting steadily, a ball of yarn at her feet and several more on the table, his mother stirring the casserole and his grandfather scowling from his favorite chair at the head of the table.

Jackson rose to his feet as his mother put a plate in front of him. "I'm not eating, thanks. I need to talk to her."

"Don't bother," Walter grunted. "She doesn't have anything to say worth listening to."

The comment snapped the leash on his temper. "That's enough." He saw his grandfather blink. "Once, just *once,* it would be helpful if we all acted as if we're on the same side. Do you think I'm doing this for fun? For my own entertainment? Because I could find other more exciting things to keep me awake at night than the state of the Snow Crystal finances."

Walter's mouth tightened, but his face turned a few shades paler. "Then you should do that. I ran this place before you were born. I can run it again with my eyes closed. It's what I want."

"I know you do. And your eyes *are* closed. As closed as your mind." Speaking through his teeth, Jackson strode to the door. "Unless you want to lose this place it's time you opened both of them. And the sooner you accept that I'm the one running it and I know what I'm doing, the sooner we'll be back in profit." Grabbing his coat, he strode out of the house, slamming the door behind him.

Walter's shoulders sagged.

The food in front of Elizabeth sat untouched. "I've never seen him so angry. And she's going to slip on the ice in those pretty shoes."

"She'll walk out," Walter muttered, "then at least he won't have sunk good money after bad."

"Was that your plan?" Alice glanced up from her knitting, her gaze steady and unflinching as she looked at her husband. "Jackson wants her here for a reason. Perhaps he'll surprise you, and perhaps she will, too."

"Maybe I have his best interests at heart."

"Maybe you don't always know best when you see it, Walter O'Neil."

"I married you, didn't I?"

Alice smiled. "Which proves you're capable of knowing what's best. Better do as Jackson suggests and open those eyes a little wider."

SHE'D BLOWN IT.

Stumbling through the snow on her high heels, Kayla knew she should stop and change into her boots, but she wanted to put as much distance between herself and the O'Neils as possible. Ruined shoes were the least of her problems.

For the first time in her life, she'd blown a meeting with a client.

How had that happened?

She was good at what she did. She *knew* she was good, and yet she hadn't controlled the meeting; she'd crumbled.

Cold crept over her legs and up her skirt. Her feet were freezing. Her hands were freezing.

Her laptop bag crashed against her hip and she hugged it against her, terrified of slipping and breaking it.

Her humiliation was total but worst of all were the other emotions. Emotions she hadn't experienced in a long time.

Over the years, she'd dealt with almost every situation except this one.

She'd come here to avoid Christmas and families and suddenly found herself slap bang in the middle of both. And the O'Neils weren't just any family. They were more closely knitted together than anything Grandma Alice produced with her needles and balls of yarn.

From the moment she'd stepped into the warm, cozy kitchen, she'd known she was in trouble. The kitchen in her New York apartment was ultramodern, and she rarely entered it except to reheat take-out food or make yet another cup of coffee. Yet the O'Neil's kitchen was clearly the heart of the home. With its cheery blue range cooker and huge scrubbed table with seating for their large extended family, the room had glowed like an advert for togetherness. The walls of her apartment were glass, her view the skyscrapers of Midtown. There were no photographs. No memorabilia. *Nothing personal.* The interior had a sterile, generic elegance that offered no clues as to the identity of the person who lived there.

Everything about the O'Neil home was personal. It was a place they'd created together. A place built on the foundations of a thousand precious memories unique to them, and those memories had been immortalized and proudly displayed for all to see. That cheerful catalog of family moments had ripped open her hidden vault of secrets and made it impossible to concentrate. Her focus had been constantly rocked until the lines between the business and the family had blurred to an indistinct mess.

And then there were the smells. *Oh, God, the smells.* Cinnamon and spice, freshly baked rolls and the sharp fragrance of pine. The association with Christmas had been so powerful it had taken all her willpower not to turn and run. If Jackson hadn't been standing behind her, she would have done just that.

Unable to feel her toes anymore, Kayla slipped but this time managed to stay upright.

"Kayla!" Jackson's voice thundered through the freezing air, and she gave a moan of denial.

She wasn't ready to face him. She'd snap, like one of the slender icicles dangling from the frozen fir trees.

He was going to fire her, and she was going to have to slink back to New York and face not only Brett and her colleagues, but also all the craziness of a New York Christmas.

"Kayla!" His voice was closer this time, but still she stumbled on, her feet soaked and freezing.

Panic lodged itself in her throat, as solid and real as a decoration from a Christmas tree.

Only when she heard the sound of an engine did she stop.

He pulled up next to her. The window was down, his breath making clouds in the freezing air. "Get in the car."

"I really don't—"

"Now."

She thought about arguing but one glance at the hard set of his jaw made her rethink. She wondered how she ever could have thought Jackson O'Neil friendly and approachable.

Right now he looked grim-faced and intimidating. It was obvious he was furious with her, and she didn't blame him. She was furious with herself.

Furious and humiliated. This was a million times worse than landing flat on her back in the snow. This was her *job*, and she hadn't been prepared for failure. She'd been flying high for so long she no longer even thought about flapping her wings. It just happened. But not tonight. Tonight, she'd fallen out of the sky and crashed to the ground, and now she had no idea what to do.

It hadn't occurred to her that she wouldn't be able to handle the Snow Crystal meeting. But it hadn't been Snow Crystal that had been her downfall; it had been the O'Neil family. Grandma, grandpa, mum, niece, pets, food, decorations, photographs—

"Kayla—" he spoke through his teeth "—get in the damn car."

Kayla slunk into the car, shivering like a puppy that had fallen into a snowdrift.

She expected him to drive but instead he sat there, his expression incredulous.

"What the *fuck* happened back there?"

She flinched. Yet another question she'd never before been asked by a client. At least no one could accuse Jackson O'Neil of not getting straight to the point. No *that didn't go quite as planned,* or *that could have been better.*

When she didn't answer, he spread his hands in silent question. "You're supposed to be the best. You handle CEOs who know nothing, but think they're experts. You've managed to build links with hardened, cynical journalists who won't even pick up the phone to most PR people. According to Brett you're the youngest associate vice president your company has ever appointed—you achieve all that and then you allow yourself to be bullied into silence by one eighty-year-old man? What is that about?"

It was about so much more than the man. "You have a right to be upset."

"I'm not upset. I'm confused. And, frankly, disappointed."

The word was like a blow in the gut. She'd never disappointed a client before. Never.

"Jackson—"

"I don't want excuses. I want the truth. I want to know what the hell went wrong! What happened? Was it the people? I told you it was a family business."

"Yes, but I didn't expect them to be so—so—" *So like a family.* She couldn't say that. It sounded ridiculous. "I expected to talk business. I didn't expect all the cooking and the photographs and all the small talk—the personal stuff."

"So? It's a little distracting, I admit. Annoying on occasion," he added under his breath, "but you're a professional. You told me there were no difficult questions you couldn't handle."

"I meant business questions." Her voice rose. "I didn't expect to be asked if I was wearing thermal underwear."

"Oh, for—" He broke off and leaned his head back against the seat, tension visible in his jaw. "Alice is eighty. Since my father died she worries about everything from hypothermia to avalanches. You should have just smiled and ignored her. You should have ignored all of them and said what you wanted to say."

"I couldn't ignore them."

"Why? It should have been obvious to you they don't understand public relations. They don't understand marketing. They've done things the same way for the past sixty years, and they're so terrified of change they'd rather sink like a stone than try something different. They're scared. Confused. They can't see the logic of spending money when we're losing it. It was up to you to convince them. That was *your job.*"

"Yes." And she'd failed. A lump wedged itself in her throat and she felt a rush of horror. Great. Now she was going to cry. Something she hadn't done since she was thirteen. "I'll contact Brett tonight and tell him to put someone else on the account. It's too late to get to the airport tonight so I'd appreciate if I could stay another night and then tomorrow I'll leave. I'll pay for the accommodation." She stared straight ahead. Straight into the snow and the dark, feeling completely alone. Even work, her closest and most trusted friend, had abandoned her.

"Leave? You're going to leave just because your pride is bruised? Hell, if I walked out each time my grandfather bruised my pride I'd never be home."

Kayla looked at him, confused. "I'm not leaving because of pride. I'm leaving because I assume that's what you want."

Fierce blue eyes locked on hers. "Why would I want that? If you've learned one thing tonight it's that I need all the help I can get. You're going to leave me to deal with them on my own?"

He didn't want her to leave?

Her heart started to pound. "I thought—I assumed—"

"You're not leaving. And I don't want anyone else on the account." His voice was roughened and deep. "I want Kayla Green. I mean the *real* Kayla Green, not the woman who turned up tonight."

She wondered what he'd say if he knew that the woman who had turned up tonight *was* the real Kayla Green. "I can't, Jackson. Even if I wanted to, there is no way I'll be able to persuade your family to take anything I say seriously after what just happened. I was unprofessional."

For the first time in her whole career, she'd walked out of a meeting.

"My grandmother knitted her way through the meeting, my mother was cooking and my brother was looking at your legs—" There was an edge to his voice. "So when it comes to unprofessional we are *way* ahead of you. I don't care about that. I care about getting the job done. We're just a family, Kayla. A family in crisis."

"I know nothing about dealing with a family in crisis." She heard desperation in her voice and knew he heard it, too, because those dark brows locked together in a frown.

"I'm asking you to focus on the work, that's all. You need to filter out the personal stuff. They don't understand the business and they help in the only way they know—by being there."

Being there. His words confirmed what she already knew. That the O'Neils were a family who stuck together no matter what life threw at them.

"They don't want my help."

"Welcome to my world. My grandfather resists all suggestions because he thinks he knows best. If he had his way he'd still be running Snow Crystal himself. I admit he can be difficult, but you feast on difficult, don't you?" The sardonic reminder of their conversation in New York made her wince. She made a mental note to strangle Brett when she saw him next.

"Your grandfather doesn't want me here."

Jackson's mouth tightened. "He doesn't want me here, either, but that doesn't mean I'm leaving."

"That's different. You're family."

"Which is why he dismisses me. He still sees me as the skinny kid he taught to ski. You're a professional, which is why you are going to make him listen to you."

"All I've done is convince him what a waste of money it would be to employ someone like me." The cold had penetrated her coat and she started to shiver. "You saw me in there! I am not the right person for this."

"Yes, I saw you in there, but I also saw you in your shiny corporate headquarters in New York. I have no idea what happened today, but I do know you're the right person. I've seen what you've done for other companies. I've seen what you've achieved. I've seen how passionate you are about your work. I want that passion working for Snow Crystal."

"But—"

"We're in trouble, Kayla." He sounded tired. "Serious trouble. I've ploughed as much into it as I can, but we're at the point where it has to start paying its way or we'll lose it."

"Lose it?" She absorbed that. "You mean lose the business?"

"Yes. Only it isn't just the business, it's their home. It's been their home for generations. If we're forced to sell, Alice and Walter will have to move out of the house they've lived in all their lives, and so will my mother." His fingers gripped the wheel, his knuckles white. "When my father died, I came back to support my family and help run the company. I didn't expect to have to save it. I had no idea how desperate things were. When I started to dig through the numbers, it was like a horror story."

She stared at him. "How much of a horror story?"

"Stephen King crossed with Hitchcock?" The corner of his mouth flickered, and she felt a rush of admiration that he could retain his sense of humor in the face of so much pressure.

She felt an inexplicable urge to reach out and offer comfort, and the urge shocked her because she wasn't a tactile person. She'd trained herself to keep her distance. She didn't form bonds.

To make sure she didn't do something impulsive like

touch him, she clutched her laptop bag. "You didn't suspect?"

"I had no reason to. Whenever I asked how things were, I was told they were fine. I didn't question it. Why would I? The business has been going forever."

"Do you know what went wrong?"

"My father made some bad decisions. And then there were the decisions he should have made but didn't. And the ramifications of that weakness on his part are huge."

Kayla thought of Alice knitting at the same table all her life. Of Elizabeth who had come here and never left.

An old wound ached deep inside her. "Do they know?"

"They know things are bad. They don't know how bad, or maybe they do know and just can't face the truth. They're scared. Afraid to make changes in case the whole thing comes tumbling down. My grandfather is looking for someone to blame, and right now he blames me for building the spa and the log cabins. Throwing away money when we needed every dollar."

"Those are the things that make Snow Crystal special."

"You know that. I know that. But *they* don't know that because right now we don't have heads on beds, so it looks as if I was wrong. I tell my grandfather they were a good investment, and he asks me to show him the bookings."

"If they're not booked it's because people don't know about them."

"So tell me how to make that happen." His tone was urgent. "Tell me what we need to do to get the sort of exposure you got for Adventure Travel. If this goes south, I lose everything my family built. And I'm not going to let that happen, so don't sit there and tell me you're leaving."

Pressure added to stress. Kayla felt as if she were swimming through thick mud. "I—I'm not experienced with family businesses."

"But you know how to get your message out there in a noisy media world, so do it." His gaze held hers. "I need you to do what you do best, Kayla."

Despite the mess she'd made, he still wanted her help.

Kayla clenched her hands in her lap. Her fingers were so cold she could no longer feel them.

It would mean staying.

It would mean getting to know his family. This job couldn't be done without getting close to them. Without understanding them. Without winning them over.

How the hell was she going to do that?

The thought of walking back into that kitchen and being confronted by the O'Neils made her want to run. "If I stay, I'd need to talk to them individually. It might be easier to win them round that way."

"That makes sense. One on one. And you need to know more about Snow Crystal. Spend time as a tourist."

"Fine." She closed her eyes. *This was madness.* She should be handing the account over to someone else. Someone who loved Christmas and families. She wasn't the right person for the job, but Jackson already had his phone in his hand and was texting someone.

"We'll start first thing tomorrow. I'll pick you up at nine."

"I'm awake at five." She spoke without thinking and saw his eyebrows lift. "I'm a morning person. I never sleep late. I don't like lying in bed."

His brief glance changed the atmosphere in the car.

Kayla turned her head away quickly, wondering how chemistry could exist in the middle of so much tension.

He was the sexiest man she'd ever met, and the fact that she kept noticing scared her. When it came to her heart, her instincts were as sophisticated as any virus software, detecting a possible threat and deleting it before it could threaten her or do damage.

Right now those instincts were flashing up red warning lights in her head.

"It's still dark at five." His voice was husky. "We'll make it eight, and I'll buy you breakfast in the forest. The Chocolate Shack serves the best hot chocolate and maple waffles in Vermont."

It sounded more like a date than a business meeting, and she felt a dangerous curl of heat low in her belly.

She sat still as Jackson eased the car forward and drove up the snow-covered track that led to the far end of the frozen lake and her cabin. Then he pulled in and switched off the engine.

"Thanks for the lift." Desperate to escape, she reached for the door handle, but his hand closed over her shoulder.

"Wait. You haven't eaten. Get rid of your laptop and I'll buy you dinner."

"No, thank you. I'd rather go back to the cabin. I have work to do."

The thought of eating dinner with this man terrified her.

And he knew.

She could see it in his eyes. Knew he could see right through the layers of protection she'd spun between herself and the world.

She was about to open the door and escape when he

lifted his hand and touched her cheek. "You still haven't told me what happened back there." His voice was soft, all trace of anger gone. "Why did you run? You could have slipped and broken something."

She could have told him she was already broken. She could have told him that Kayla Green had shattered into a million tiny pieces at the age of thirteen, and when she'd stuck herself back together she hadn't looked anything like the original version.

She could have told him that, but she didn't, because she knew that when a person bought something, they didn't want to know it was damaged. She looked good as new on the outside, and that was what mattered.

He wasn't interested in the real Kayla Green.

"I thought it best to leave. Thanks for the lift. I can walk from here. I'll see you in the morning." She slid out of the car, keen to put as much distance between herself and Jackson as possible. The moment her feet touched the snow she felt the cold ooze through her already-soaked shoes, but she knew the icy feeling inside her didn't come from the freezing temperatures or the thick layer of snow that blanketed the forest around her. The source was much deeper than that.

Pressed up against feelings she normally avoided, Kayla felt a flash of panic.

Who would have thought that a sleepy little resort in Vermont could have ripped at her like this?

Jackson appeared in front of her, his powerful shoulders blocking her escape. "Surely you're not planning to walk this path alone after what happened last time?"

"I'll be fine."

His muscular physique formed a sold barrier between her and her forest sanctuary. "You've suffered enough punishment for one day. I'll walk you to the door." He took her hand, and Kayla felt the warmth and strength of his fingers as they closed over hers.

"This is definitely breaking the client-agency code."

"There's a code? Damn. You probably should have mentioned that earlier." His tone was light and he tightened his grip. "On the other hand, I've never been big on rules and codes."

It was all too easy to believe that. He was a man who knew what he wanted, his toughness concealed under layers of velvety charm. She'd seen it in her offices that day in New York, and she'd seen it a moment ago when he'd refused to let her leave.

Desperate, she looked up at him. His jaw was strong and darkened by a day of stubble, his mouth a sensual curve in a face that made her want to revisit her own rules and codes. Never before had she been remotely tempted to kiss one of her clients, but neither had she ever walked out of a meeting. Apparently it was a day of firsts.

She rarely thought about sex, didn't have time to think about it, let alone do it, but she was thinking about it now. Hot sex, with no ties or promises, no past or future, just a moment of raw physical passion. And with Jackson O'Neil you just knew that moment would be good.

Heat rushed across her skin and desire uncurled inside her.

"I'm pretty big on rules and codes. And tomorrow I'm buying all the gear in the store. Any ice-walking-shoe-boot things that might help keep me upright." For the rest of her stay, she was going to be professional. No more falling on her back in snowdrifts. No more falling apart in meetings. That was a one-off lapse that wasn't going to happen again.

"We have some gear we can probably lend you. A decent coat and some ski pants. And some ice-walking-shoe-boot things." That mouth flickered at the corners and then he reached across and opened the gate.

The cabin glowed warm and welcoming in the darkness. The trees by the front door were studded with twinkling lights and the same tiny lights were twisted around the windows.

The cold numbed her face and seared her lungs. Her toes were freezing through her soaked shoes. She knew it was nothing that a hot shower wouldn't cure. The cold inside her? That was going to be harder to fix.

As they reached the door, she pulled out her keys. "I'll see you in the morning." She tried to tug her hand away from his but he tightened his grip, hauling her against him.

"Are you going to tell me what happened tonight? Because I sense it was personal."

The fact that he'd noticed her reaction made her feel as if she'd been caught sleepwalking naked.

"I'd like to forget about tonight and start again."

"Yeah, I get that. But starting again might be easier if you tell me what went wrong in the first place. You were in a panic."

There was a soft thud as snow slid from the roof behind her and landed on the deck. "I'm allergic to gingerbread." She kept her tone light. "It always has that effect on me."

He reached up and brushed flakes of snow from her hair. "Me, too. I can only eat a ton of the stuff before I want to resign."

Kayla relaxed slightly, relieved he'd backed down so easily. "Do you feel like resigning?"

"Every damn day." He smiled. A slow, sexy smile

that made her want to strip him naked and do bad things to him.

Oh, shit, she was in trouble.

"But you don't resign."

"The one thing a person can't resign from is their family."

Oh, yes they could. She knew that for a fact. And knowing it created the distance she'd been struggling desperately to find. They were on opposite sides of an enormous chasm. This man, wrapped in the big warm blanket of O'Neil love and affection, had no idea what it was like to be shivering in the cold by yourself.

The words snapped her back to her own lonely reality.

"Your family is lucky to have you. Thanks for walking me to the door. Good night." She unlocked the door but couldn't move, because he'd planted an arm on the door frame, trapping her. She stood there, locked in by muscle and hot man, staring into those knowing blue eyes.

"Tell me, Kayla. Tell me what happened in there." The gentleness in his voice matched the look in his eyes.

"Why? Why would you even care?"

"Maybe I can fix it."

She was willing to bet he did that a lot. Jackson O'Neil was a man who fixed things for other people. That was why he was here, fighting his family so that he could save their home.

And now he wanted to fix her.

A different type of woman might have been tempted. Maybe she was, too…a little.

But she knew some things couldn't be fixed.

"Thanks, but I've been fixing myself since I was thirteen years old so I've had plenty of practice. Good night, Jackson." She ducked under his arm and stomped over temptation into the warmth of the cabin.

I'VE BEEN FIXING myself since I was thirteen years old.

He wondered what she'd been fixing.

Whatever it was, something or someone had upset her tonight.

Jackson turned up his collar against the cold and took a long, last look at the closed door before crunching through the snow back to his car.

Maybe it was just being here.

Maybe it had finally hit her that in her eagerness for the business, she'd volunteered to give up her Christmas. Maybe seeing his family had made her think of hers. Maybe she was homesick.

It could have been any number of things, none of which were his business.

Ignoring the powerful urge to make it his business, Jackson reversed out of the parking spot and drove back down the track that led to the main lodge. He was guessing his brother would be there, and he was right.

Tyler was seated at the bar, entertaining a group of guests with stories of bear encounters and downhill daring. Spying Jackson, he threw a remark at the group that had them laughing, then made his excuses and joined his brother.

"You look as if you need a drink, and I guess I owe you one."

"One? You owe me at least a hundred."

Tyler reached across the bar and snagged a couple of beers. "So did you drive her back to the airport?"

"Why would I do that?"

"Because when she stumbled out of the kitchen she didn't look like she was planning on staying around."

Jackson closed his hand around the beer. "Does she seem like a quitter to you?"

"No. Anyone who can still be talking business while Mom is forcing food on them and Grams is trying to wrap them in lurid green is definitely not a quitter. But she seemed serious about her job and anyone like that isn't going to last five minutes in this place."

"Thanks."

"You don't count. You're tied here by blood and a guilty conscience." Tyler glanced over his shoulder as the door swung open letting in freezing air, a flurry of snow and another group of tourists. "So if she isn't on her way back to New York, where is she? The least you could have done was invite her for a drink. God knows, if she's working for this family she's going to need one."

Jackson wondered how his brother knew about the guilty conscience. It wasn't something he'd talked about. "I offered. She wanted to go back to the cabin and do some work. Talking of which…" He leaned across to the bar and called Pete over. "Can you send a pizza over to cabin ten please?"

"Toppings?"

Jackson glanced at Tyler for inspiration. "What do Brits like on their pizza?"

"How do I know? Stick to cheese. She might be vegetarian. She looked stressed enough to be one. Although, come to think of it she looked the way we all look after an evening with the O'Neils. My advice? Hold the pizza and send over whiskey."

"Cheese and tomato." Jackson dug out his wallet and handed over a note.

"Why are you paying when you own the place?"

"Because I want the books to balance."

"Fat chance of that. So she didn't want to eat dinner with you." Tyler shook his head sympathetically. "You're losing your touch, bro."

"Unless you like your eyes black and your jaw broken, I suggest you keep your thoughts on that subject to yourself." The door opened again, letting in more cold air and a young woman with a bright smile.

"Hi, Jackson!"

"Brenna—"

"Good to see you." Chocolate-brown hair peeped out from under a fur-lined hood. The pretty smile dimmed when she saw his drinking companion. "Tyler." She gave a brief nod and slipped her hood back. "Glad I caught you. I'm two instructors down. They're forecasting a foot of fresh snow and I've got a couple wanting to do Sunrise and Powder and no guide—you can take them."

Tyler choked on his beer. "Me?"

"It would make their day to be escorted by an ex-member of the U.S. ski team." She levered herself onto the bar stool and charmed Pete with a smile. "Coke, no ice, thanks. Are you a daddy yet? How's Lynn?"

"Big enough to be having twins. She can barely move, or that's the excuse she gives me when she asks me to make tea." Pete handed her a Coke. "Doctor thinks it will be here before Christmas." He looked dazed at the thought, and Brenna beamed as she unwrapped her scarf.

"Best gift of all. Text me the minute you have news. I cannot wait for our Snow Crystal baby to arrive." Sipping her Coke, Brenna turned back to Tyler, her gaze a fraction cooler. "About tomorrow—"

"Are they experienced? Last time I took a group into deep powder they were clueless. The woman thought powder was something she put on her face."

"These are experienced, but it's their first time skiing the East Coast." She tugged off her gloves and pushed them into the pocket of her jacket. "They don't want an instructor, just a guide, and you know this area better than anyone."

"Why can't you take them?"

"I'm teaching a 'bumps 'n' trees' class."

Tyler lifted his beer to his lips and drank, and Jackson wondered how two people who knew each other so well could turn every conversation into a combat zone.

They'd grown up together. Played together as children and skied together as teenagers. They'd been fiercely competitive and inseparable until the day Tyler had announced he'd gotten Janet Carpenter pregnant.

Soon after, Brenna had announced she was leaving New England to train as a ski instructor in Colorado. She could have done that here, of course, but she'd picked a place where there was less risk of bumping into Tyler. When she'd graduated, Jackson had offered her a job with his company running the kids program in Switzerland. She'd never once asked about his brother.

Jackson hoped it wasn't going to be a problem now that Tyler was back home.

The last thing he needed was to lose Brenna.

As if to prove that, she pulled out her phone and checked her calendar. "I'm running the teen course and taking 'bumps 'n' trees'. Then I'm filling in for Todd, who is taking his wife for a checkup. The only person without commitments is you. We can't afford to turn away the business. They're willing to pay good money for the privilege of leaving ski tracks in fresh snow. All they want is a cheerful guide. Think you can manage to hold the sarcasm for a few hours, O'Neil?"

"I'm not the only one with that name around here." Tyler glanced at Jackson, who shook his head.

"I have plans tomorrow."

"Fine, I'll do it. At least, I can do the guide part. Not so sure about *cheerful* if they want an early start. Smiles are extra at that hour of the morning."

"They're paying us extra, so you'll smile." Brenna slipped her phone into her pocket and picked up her drink. "By the way, Jess asked if I'd ski Devil's Gully with her someday this week. Says you banned her from doing that run."

"I banned her for a reason." Tyler's fingers tightened on the bottle and his eyes glittered dangerously. "And that reason is she's way too young and inexperienced."

Brenna lifted her brows. "You and I skied that run when we were half her age."

"And were grounded for a week as a result." Tyler gave a laugh and then remembered he was trying to be a responsible father and glared at her. "That's different. You and I skied more than we walked. Jess has been living in a city. Nearest she's been to mountains is a picture on her wall."

"She's your daughter," Brenna said softly. "She's inherited your natural aptitude."

"She's twelve."

"It isn't about age, it's about ability, and she's got it, Tyler. Talent. She feels the slope. She knows the mountain. Call it whatever you will, you need to let her do this."

"Kill herself?" Stubborn, Tyler shook his head. "Not on my watch."

Remembering their conversation earlier, Jackson felt a twinge of sympathy for his brother. It had taken long enough for him to have the opportunity to prove he could be a good father to Jess. He didn't want to blow it in the first month.

Tyler was frowning at Brenna. "How come you know so much about what she wants anyway? I can't get more than five words out of the girl."

"She often stops by my cabin." Brenna took a sip of her drink. "Yesterday we had lunch."

"Lunch? Why don't I know any of this?"

"Maybe she's afraid you'd say no. For a guy who never understood the meaning of the word, you sure as hell use it a lot now." Brenna slid off the stool. "I see our chief of police enjoying a quiet few minutes. Think I'll just interrupt that. I need to talk to him about our Emergency Response Plan."

"Wait, Brenna—" Jackson caught her arm before she could walk away, "don't you keep a supply of spare ski clothes in case someone needs them?"

"What size?"

"About your size. Maybe a little smaller. Not that I'm saying you're big," he added hastily, "but you're strong because of the skiing and—"

"You pick up many women with that line, Jackson?"

He cursed himself and then saw that her eyes were bright with laughter. "Brenna—"

"Shut up, before you fall into that hole you just dug for yourself. What do you need? Apart from a spade to dig your foot out of your mouth?"

"Whatever you've got."

"I assume this is for the woman from New York? Is she going to be able to help us?" Anxiety shadowed her eyes, and Jackson wondered how many of the Snow Crystal team were worrying about their jobs.

"She'll help us."

"In that case I'll drop off what I have at her cabin

on my way to the slopes tomorrow morning. If any of it fits, she's welcome to it." Ignoring Tyler, she flashed Jackson a smile and then turned and walked across the room, unzipping her coat as she went.

"How come she smiles at you and not me?" Tyler watched her. "If I'd made that remark about her being strong, she would have felled me, and not just to prove me right. And what is up with Jess? Why didn't she just ask me again if she could ski Devil's Gully?"

"Would you have changed your mind?"

"No."

"Probably why she didn't ask you."

"That makes no sense."

Jackson sighed. "When you were twelve, if there was something you wanted to do and Dad said no, what did you do?"

"I did it anyway. Most of the time I didn't bother asking."

"Right. And Jess is your daughter, so I'm guessing that, along with your ski talent, she also inherited a dose of the stubborn. Just saying." Jackson eased himself away from the bar. "At least she's crazy about skiing. In my book that's better than drugs or boys."

"Talking of boys, have you noticed Brenna's hair is longer than it used to be?" Tyler watched as Brenna slid into a booth next to Josh, the chief of police.

"I assume you know Brenna isn't a boy?"

"Can't help thinking of her that way. Back when we were growing up she hung out and did what we did. She was a fourth brother to us."

Jackson wondered whether decking his brother would bring him to his senses or just add to his problems. "I never saw her that way."

Tyler wasn't listening. "Think I should warn her about Josh? Guy's got a reputation."

"And you haven't?"

"I'm not the one looking at Brenna as if I'd like to strip her naked."

Jackson was fairly sure if he did then Brenna wouldn't object, but he decided that was something Tyler had to work out for himself. "Brenna can handle herself."

"So when the two of you went out—" Tyler's voice was casual "—it was like a guy's night, yes? You shared a few beers. Shot a few rounds of pool?"

Jackson decided this definitely wasn't the moment to mention that Brenna had worn a tight black dress and they'd shared a candlelit dinner. "She drank beer, yes."

"Maybe I'll see if she wants to spend a day skiing sometime, like we used to." Taylor scowled across the room. "She's smiling. What the hell is funny about an emergency response plan? Is she seeing Josh?"

Jackson glanced over his shoulder to where Brenna was laughing with the chief of police. "Looks like she's seeing him now."

"That wasn't what I meant."

"I know. But I don't insist on knowing the detail of the love life of my employees."

"Maybe you should. The last thing we need is the law hanging around Snow Crystal. Folks will think we've got trouble here."

"We went to school with Josh. He drinks here. Skis here. He's a member of the mountain rescue team."

"So he doesn't need to date the staff, too. Talking of business, I assume your plans for tomorrow involve a certain slick city girl with blond hair and great legs."

"She came here for the Snow Crystal experience. It starts tomorrow."

"It started this evening—" Tyler winked at a pretty blonde who walked into the bar with a group of friends "—when she was swallowed whole by the O'Neil family. I'd say that's a pretty standard Snow Crystal experience."

Jackson stared at the bottle in his hand, anger mingling with frustration. "Gramps didn't give her a chance."

"Yeah, well you know how he hates anyone messing with his toys."

"She looked shell-shocked."

"Probably the sight of Gram's knitting. That shade of green didn't do it for me, either. Please tell me that's not my Christmas present." Tyler shuddered and Jackson finished his drink.

"I have work to do."

"We all have work to do," Tyler frowned across at Brenna, who was still laughing with Josh. "What is she finding so funny? I don't think Josh has ever made me laugh. Certainly didn't when he gave me that speeding ticket last summer. Son of a bitch didn't even crack a smile."

Jackson was fairly sure the exaggerated laughter was for Tyler's benefit. He grabbed his jacket and stood up. "I need to get going."

"Me, too. I need to get back and try to have another conversation with Jess, which is going to be harder work than anything you're doing. It isn't easy saying no to a kid when her response is 'you did it at my age.'"

"You *did* do it at her age. All of it."

"So?" Tyler scowled. "That means I know what I'm talking about."

"Tyler?"

"What?"

"You don't know shit." Shaking his head, Jackson strolled toward the door.

INSOMNIA WAS A BITCH.

Kayla lay on the shelf, staring out over the forest. The moon sent a beam of light over the trees, turning the surface of the snow to shimmering silver. She'd started in the master bedroom but had been too restless to sleep, so she'd pulled on a warm robe, made herself a mug of tea and climbed the spiral staircase to this small patch of heaven.

She cradled the warm mug in her hands. It should have offered comfort, but inside she was cold, so cold she felt as if she'd never be warm again.

She'd discovered long before that loneliness could be a dull background ache or it could be sharp and painful. It could bite into the soft parts of a person leaving bruises, or it could just nip gently at the edges of your subconscious.

She'd learned to live with it, but tonight the O'Neils had ripped away all the protection she'd so carefully wrapped around herself, leaving her vulnerable and exposed.

It wasn't just the hostility, although there was no doubt Walter had been openly hostile. Alice and Elizabeth had been almost smothering in their affection and level of welcome, and that was almost as bad.

She kept her interaction with people superficial. She didn't bond. She didn't make attachments. She didn't *want* attachments.

But if she wanted this business, she was going to have to find a way of working with the O'Neils.

Snuggling against the pile of soft pillows, she sipped her tea and thought about what lay ahead.

The family setup might be unusual, but the business problems weren't.

Tonight had been a disaster, but not because she didn't know her job. Because of the people. Because she had no idea how to relate to them.

She told herself she didn't have to bond with them to help them.

No one was asking her to become part of the family.

All she had to do was win their trust, find out what mattered to them and what they needed and then produce a tailored marketing plan that would solve their problems.

It really wasn't that hard.

She had to ignore the other stuff.

She especially had to ignore the chemistry with Jackson.

CHAPTER SIX

SHE WAS AWAKE at five, after a night in which sleep occupied less than a few hours. That, at least, was familiar.

She stuck to her usual routine. Brisk shower followed by strong coffee and an hour spent on her laptop, first clearing emails and then working on ideas. This was always her most creative time of day, before the sun came up and her phone starting ringing. Ideas flowed, and she spread papers over the work surface in the kitchen, scribbled notes, wrote down what she'd learned, afraid to lose even a single thought, terrified that if she slowed down or stopped to think about the night before her brain would freeze again.

She paced the length and breadth of the vaulted living room, watching darkness turn to dawn and snowy treetops emerge from a blanket of early-morning mist.

The beauty of it soothed her.

Here, deep in the forest, there were no reminders of Christmas. No glittering decorations, no maniacally grinning Santas, no canned Christmas music playing on a loop. Just nature at its most peaceful.

Her emotions, violently disturbed by the events of the night before, gradually settled.

By the time she took a break, her list of questions were longer than her list of answers, and her coffee had sat untouched on the table for an hour.

Kayla drank it cold while reading the notes she'd

made. Her hair hung loose over the soft white robe that had been left for her use in the luxurious bathroom and her feet were bare on the wooden floor. It was the way she always started her day. The same routine she followed each day of her life and it felt familiar and yet unfamiliar.

Lifting her head, she realized the unfamiliar was the silence.

She was used to noise. Traffic noise. Street noise. The noise of a million people jostling for space in the same small slice of a city. First London, then New York. Here, there was no traffic, no people and no noise. The trees muffled sound and the snow fell in gentle silence.

Halfway through her third cup of coffee she heard a tap on the door and looked up in dismay, assuming she'd lost track of the time.

It wasn't Jackson who stood there, but a girl. Dark hair peeped from underneath a fur-lined hood, and she carried a large box in her arms.

Under the padded ski jacket and trousers she was slim and fit and, judging from the way she balanced the box and tapped on the door, she had no trouble walking on ice.

Resenting the disturbance, Kayla put down her mug and walked to the door. She was greeted by a punch of cold air and a friendly smile.

"Hi, you must be Kayla!" Her breath forming clouds in the freezing air, the girl walked in without waiting for an invitation and deposited the box at Kayla's feet. "I'm Brenna. Jackson asked me to find some gear. I hope something in this box fits." She narrowed her eyes. "Looking at you I'm guessing it might, although we might not be lucky with the boots. Your feet are smaller than mine."

Taken aback by the familiarity and unaccustomed to early-morning visitors, Kayla tightened the knot on her robe. "I— Thanks. I'm not dressed because I'm working—" She left the door to the cabin wide-open but the other girl didn't take the hint.

"Yeah, I saw you pacing and frowning to yourself. You should close that door. You're letting the heat out." Brenna pushed the door shut with her foot. "So if you're pacing, does that mean we should all be worried?"

Kayla glanced from the door to her uninvited visitor and wondered whether anyone at Snow Crystal had heard of personal space. "Why would you be worried?" Clearly the other girl wasn't worried about interrupting someone who didn't want to be interrupted.

"Jackson told us all you're a genius at getting folks through the door and making a business busy." Brenna unzipped her jacket. "Math has never been my best subject but even I can work out that empty rooms don't equal profit. I haven't asked him outright, because he looks as if he has enough on his mind, but it's obvious to me things are grim. It might be Christmas, but we've got plenty of room at the inn right now. We're pinning our hopes on you."

Kayla thought about the night before and how badly she'd performed.

"We'll fill those rooms." What she had to do was think of this as a business challenge, like any other. What she didn't need to do was think of the O'Neil family all together in that kitchen. "I was working on that when you arrived." If she thought the other girl might take a hint, she was disappointed.

Brenna nodded. "So do you want to try this stuff on? I'm assuming Jackson asked me to bring it over because he's planning on showing you the charms of Snow Crystal."

"You've spoken to Jackson?"

"Caught up with him in the bar last night. Told me you didn't have the right gear."

And that, Kayla thought, was an understatement.

Had he told Brenna about her undignified fall? Or, worse, about the meeting?

"Thanks for the clothes." Pulling her professionalism around her like a cloak she moved toward the door, but instead of following her Brenna walked farther into the room.

"Do I smell coffee?"

"Well, yes, but—"

"Great. You don't mind if I help myself? Looks like you have plenty and I could do with some help waking up." Brenna strolled to the kitchen and reached for a mug. "Need a top-up?"

"No, thanks." She was already on her third cup, the caffeine pushing through her veins and kick-starting her sleep-deprived brain. What she needed was silence. What she didn't need was to share her space with anyone.

The mornings were her time, before the madness of the day started in earnest.

But it didn't seem to occur to Brenna that she might be intruding on anything. She walked around the cabin as if she owned it. Unlike Kayla, it didn't take her five minutes of opening cupboards to find the mugs. She knew exactly where they were kept.

"I love this cabin, don't you?" Brenna tugged off her gloves and filled the mug to the brim. "It's my favorite. I could live here. I just love the shelf. The view is so perfect it seems like a total waste to fall asleep."

"You've stayed here?"

"Once or twice. I live in town, but if the weather is bad I sometimes sleep over at the lodge and if Jackson is feeling generous he lets me use one of the cabins. Any excuse to sample Elizabeth's cooking. Cooking isn't really my thing. Apart from bacon. I'm good with bacon." Brenna picked up the mug and nursed it, leaning her hips against the counter. "How was your welcome meal?"

"Welcome meal?" The mention of the night before was enough to make her feel as if she was rolling in snow naked.

"The pot roast. Elizabeth thought it would be the perfect meal to welcome you. She's been planning it for days."

"I didn't stay to eat." The revelation that the dinner had been especially to welcome her sharpened her guilt. "I had work to do. And I really should get on and do some more."

"If you worked all last night you deserve a break. And talking of eating—" Brenna glanced around the kitchen. "Do you have any food?"

Kayla stared at her in desperation. "Food?"

"Breakfast?" Brenna lifted her eyebrows. "First meal of the day?"

"Oh—I— No, I don't eat breakfast. I suppose there might be something in the cupboards, but really I should be getting on and—"

"You don't eat breakfast?" Brenna sipped her coffee. "That will change when you've been here awhile. Breakfast is an important meal in the O'Neil household."

When she'd been here awhile?

"I'm just here for a few days. Then I'm going back to New York."

Brenna shuddered. "In that case, all the more reason to make the most of breakfast while you can. You haven't lived until you've tasted Elizabeth's pancakes with maple syrup. Did you know they make their own maple syrup here? Come back in February and you can see them tapping the trees. They have a working sugarhouse." She chatted away, open and friendly, apparently oblivious to Kayla's discomfort.

"I won't be coming back in February. I'm just here until Christmas."

"You'll be back. Everyone who visits Snow Crystal wants to come back. You'll book a vacation."

Kayla didn't point out that if that were the case, Jackson wouldn't need her help. "I don't take vacations." She cast a desperate glance at her laptop. "I should probably get dressed and I expect you'll have finished your coffee by the time I'm done, so I'll say goodbye and—"

"I'll wait while you try it on. If nothing fits, we can sort something else out."

Realizing that the sooner she did this the sooner she'd be allowed to get back to work, Kayla grabbed the box of clothes and retreated to the bedroom.

Guilt pulled at her.

Elizabeth O'Neil had spent all day in the kitchen preparing a meal to welcome her, and she'd rejected their hospitality and walked out.

How on earth was she was going to recover this situation?

Jackson had told her he was having trouble getting them to support his ideas. They were already suspicious of her as an outsider. Even more so since she'd acted like one.

Her head started to pound, and she rummaged through the box and found a pair of black ski pants. They fitted perfectly, as did the fleece zip sweater and ski jacket. Socks in her hand, she walked back into the living room.

"This is all great, thanks."

"Wow." Brenna whistled. "Ski pants make most people look fat. Not you. I might have to hate you."

Join the rest of the O'Neils.

"Don't bother. People will know I'm a fraud the moment I step onto the snow. Horizontal and soaking wet isn't a good look."

Brenna studied her over the rim of her coffee mug. "You don't ski?"

"No. In fact I suspect I don't do anything that is going to endear me to the O'Neil family."

"They're a sporty family but they're not employing you for your ability to ski a double-diamond-black trail."

Kayla felt a rush of despair. "I don't even know what that is."

"It's a difficult one that makes you want to throw up your breakfast. Hey—cheer up." Brenna grinned. "We're all expert at different things. I don't know anything about public relations or whatever it is you do."

Right at that moment Kayla didn't feel as if she knew much about anything. Her confidence was at rock bottom. She sank down onto the sofa. "But you know Snow Crystal."

"Grew up here. Went to school with the O'Neil boys, although they were a few years ahead of me. I skied with them. Followed them wherever they went."

"Even down those—what did you call them?— diamond-black trails?"

"Those, too. Gave my mother panic attacks. Whatever they did, I had to do it, too, and they never once slowed down for me." She grinned. "Bastards."

Kayla remembered what she'd read about the O'Neil brothers. "And you run the ski program?"

"Yes. Although now Tyler's back I guess that could change." Brenna finished her coffee, strolled to the kitchen and rinsed her mug.

"What do you mean, now he's back? Has he only just come back?"

"Tyler's never been one to hang around Snow Crystal for long. Too wild." Brenna bent to straighten her socks. "Came back for the funeral and then flew off again. He and Walter drive each other crazy. The more Walter tries to control him, the more Tyler rebels. It was the same when he was a kid. If Walter says white, Tyler says black. In many ways they're alike but neither of them can see it."

"So what made him come back?"

"Jess—that's his daughter—announced she was coming to live with him."

"Oh." She remembered the brief glimpse she'd had of the girl before the puppy had trampled her shoes.

"She has spent Christmas here for the past twelve years, but now she's here for good. Her Mom just had a baby." Brenna's voice changed. Hardened. "I don't know the truth, but I'm guessing she and that guy she picked instead of Tyler don't want poor Jess around. I can't even imagine how bad she feels."

Kayla sat still, staring straight ahead.

She didn't have to imagine it.

She knew.

"It's a mess," Brenna said, "but she won't really talk about it. And Tyler isn't really helping. For some reason he's being really strict with her, and it's driving her crazy."

"But he's here." Somehow Kayla formed the words. "He didn't send her away."

"I guess not." Brenna looked thoughtful. Then she smiled. "I brought you some snow boots. They should be fine for walking around the resort. When you're ready to ski, we'll kit you out. I'd offer to give you a lesson, but I'm guessing Jackson wants to be the one to do that. You'll be okay with him. Unlike Tyler, he slows down for beginners."

Kayla was relieved by the change of subject. "Tell me a bit about Jackson. He handed over the running of his business to someone else and came home. That must have been hard."

"Jackson has always been the responsible one. More controlled. Tyler is impulsive, but Jackson—" Brenna frowned. "He's different. He weighs up all the options and then picks the best way, and once he's picked it, he won't deviate. He has total faith in himself. I saw it when he was younger. When we were skiing backcountry, Jackson would pause at the top of a slope and take a minute to pick his route. It was as if his brain was computing all the dangers. Tyler would just hurl himself off and trust his ability to get himself out of trouble."

"And did that work?"

"Most of the time. He's very gifted. Has strong instincts." Brenna stooped to pick up her boots, her dark hair swinging forward and obscuring her features. "Trouble has always followed Tyler, and he's never been one to run from it. Now Jackson—" straightening, she pushed her feet into fleece and warmth "—he treats trouble like a puzzle to be solved. When they were young, he was the one who refereed the fights between Sean and Tyler."

Kayla thought about the way he'd handled the different personalities in the meeting. "He's good with people."

Brenna pulled a hat down over her ears. "He must be or I wouldn't have come back here. I was perfectly happy in Switzerland, and at least there I didn't have to—" She broke off and gave a distracted smile. "I should get going. I'm teaching a class in twenty minutes. Perhaps we can grab a drink sometime. Thanks for the coffee."

"You're welcome." Kayla wondered what it was Brenna hadn't had to do in Switzerland. "Thanks for the clothing."

"Glad it fits. Hope you can fill this place with people."

"Brenna?" She stood up and followed her to the door. "What do you love about Snow Crystal?"

"What do I love?" Brenna tilted her head back and stared at the tops of the trees and the mountains beyond them as if she was surprised Kayla couldn't see it for herself. "All of it. I love the crunching sound of snow under my boots and the way the cold air feels on my cheeks. I love the summer here and the fall foliage of course, but winter is special. You'll understand that as soon as we put you on skis. There is no better feeling than being alone on the mountain skiing the last run of the day when the only sound is the soft rush of your skis over fresh snow."

"If I find myself alone on a mountain it will be because I'm lost."

Laughing, Brenna opened the door, letting in a stream of cold air. "The snow patrol are last off the mountain. You're going to be fine. Here's Jackson now. I'll see you later." She walked across the deck and down the steps, sure-footed and confident.

Kayla stood watching her for a moment, feeling better.

The feeling lasted right up until the moment Brenna reached up and gave Jackson a kiss.

Jackson glanced toward the cabin. "You found something to fit?"

"Of course." Brenna zipped her jacket. "But I don't think she was pleased to see me. It's frostier in the cabin than out. That girl is stiffer than a fir tree after an ice storm. If that's what working in Manhattan does for you, I'm glad to be at Snow Crystal. You need to get her to relax, Jackson."

"I'm working on that." He could see her through the windows of the cabin, head bent over her laptop. Black ski pants showed off her long slim legs and that sleek curtain of blond hair was twisted neatly into a clip at the back of her head. She looked businesslike, but there was a vulnerability about her that hadn't been visible in New York. Or maybe he hadn't been looking.

"I have a feeling that getting that girl to relax will be one of your more challenging projects so I'll leave you to it." Brenna flashed him a smile, and Jackson caught her arm as she turned away.

"About Tyler—"

Her smile didn't slip as she extracted herself gently. "What about Tyler?"

"Is it all right, working with him?"

"Fine. As long as he doesn't decide to take my kindergarten class down a diamond black, we'll be good. See you later, Jackson."

He knew she wasn't telling the truth, but he decided

that as long as she wasn't resigning, that was all he needed to know for now. He'd handle the problems one at a time, and the next problem on his list was currently pacing the cabin in front of him.

She met him at the door.

Their eyes held for a fraction of a second and then she was smiling, brisk and efficient.

He remembered what Brenna had said about her being frozen and wondered why his friend couldn't see what he could. If there was ice, then it was on the surface. Underneath, Kayla Green was a simmering cauldron of suppressed emotions.

"Good morning." She was formal and distant, and he wondered how the hell he was going to break down those barriers and get her to relax enough to enjoy Snow Crystal. Somehow he had to teach a woman who lived her life indoors, to enjoy the outdoors. Have some fun. And the first thing he needed to do was make sure she was suitably dressed because nothing killed "fun" faster than cold.

"Brenna found you some gear. Did she wake you?"

"I'm an early riser."

"Yeah, I remember now. The five o'clock start. And late to bed." He knew, because he'd seen the light from her cabin glowing long after the clock by his bed had told him it was the next day.

He wondered what it was that kept her awake when others slept. An overactive mind? Or something else…

She stood aside to let him in, but Jackson shook his head and handed her a bag.

"Let's make a start. I want to show you Snow Crystal. We'll grab breakfast while we're out." He put the boots he was carrying down in front of her. "You need to wear these. I'm taking you on a tour."

"On skis?"

"Not yet. I'm still searching for that 'flat slope' you requested. When I find it, I'll let you know. In the meantime we'll try something else."

"Something else?" Her expression was comical. "When is your brother coming back for Christmas? I have a feeling I might need the services of an orthopedic surgeon. And I already have boots courtesy of Brenna."

"What she gave you will be fine for walking around the resort, but you need these for what we're doing today." He watched as she slid her feet into them. Felt a flash of satisfaction that he'd guessed the right size. "Cinderella, I presume."

"Her footwear was a little more delicate, and you are definitely *not* Prince Charming."

"You don't think I'm Prince Charming? You sure about that?" He straightened and found himself closer to her than he'd intended. She made him think of summer. Her hair smelled of flowers and her eyes were the same washed green as the trees emerging from a cobweb of early-morning mist.

Chemistry punched him hard in the gut, and the shock in her eyes told him she'd felt it, too.

"I stopped believing in Prince Charming around the time I stopped believing in Santa and the tooth fairy." Dressed in ski gear she looked younger than she did in her businesslike skirt and stilettos. Softer.

Jackson felt an urge to power her back into the cabin and put some color into those pale cheeks. Instead he forced himself to step back and give her space.

"Santa's not real? No one ever told me that. You just ruined my day." He kept it light and saw her relax slightly.

"If you dump me in the snow, you'll ruin mine." She zipped the jacket to the neck and pulled on the gloves he handed her. "I hardly dare ask why I'm dressed like this. I'm not sure I'm going to like the answer. Does it involve bear or moose?" She turned to lock the cabin door.

"It might do. And you don't need to worry about locking up. My mother hasn't locked her door since she arrived here thirty-five years ago."

"I live in a city. Force of habit." Dropping the keys into her pocket, she stepped gingerly onto the deck, testing the surface. "These feel more stable than my other boots."

"Anything would feel more stable than your other boots. Those should be fine on most surfaces, except for sheet ice. Here—" He handed her a helmet and she looked at it in alarm.

"I need a helmet?"

"For protection."

"Protection from what?" Their feet crunched on snow as they walked down the path and she turned the helmet in her hands, looking at it from all angles. "I should have worn one of these last night when I met Walter. And maybe a bulletproof vest."

He was impressed that she could treat it with humor despite feeling bruised. "Put the helmet on. We're going to explore some of the Snow Crystal trails and back-country."

"How? I saw that picture of you jumping off a cliff, and frankly I don't think I could— Oh—" She stopped at the gate and saw what was parked there. "What's that?"

"That, Cinderella, is your carriage."

She eyed the snowmobile. "We've been reading different fairy tales."

"Cinderella would have loved a snowmobile. You've never been on one?"

"Er—no. There's not a lot of call for them in London or New York."

"They're the most flexible mode of transport around here. They can cope with the forest tracks and the frozen lake. Guests love them. We have forty miles of groomed trails through the forest and the mountains."

"The guests use these?"

"Tyler and a couple of the other instructors take small groups on snowmobile rides through the forest. We're careful to stick to a defined route so we're less likely to disturb wildlife, but it's something most people enjoy around here. You need to put that helmet on and to do that you need to remove this…" He removed the clip from the back of her head and her hair slithered down in a sheet of tempting honey-gold. One strand curled across her cheek and brushed the corner of her full mouth.

Lust slammed into him.

Deciding he was in more trouble than he'd thought, Jackson took the helmet from her and pushed it onto her head. He secured it, noticing that she was avoiding eye contact. He might have thought nothing of it had it not been for the streak of color across her cheekbones and the fact she was barely breathing.

He knew the feeling.

"Are you ready?"

"Ready?" Her voice was a startled croak.

"For our trip." Damn, he wasn't doing any better than she was. All he wanted to do was pull off that helmet and kiss that mouth. "Through the forest."

"You want me to drive that thing?"

"Not this time. This time I'll drive 'that thing.'" And the sooner the better, for both their sakes. "You're the passenger."

"Mmm—" Her eyes were fixed on the snowmobile now. "I'm not a good passenger. I prefer to be the one in the driving seat."

He had no trouble believing that. From what he'd seen so far, Kayla Green was big on control, most especially when it came to her own emotions. "But you've never driven one before, so if we both want to live it would probably be better if I drove this time." He pushed his own helmet onto his head. "I'll teach you. But not today."

She opened her mouth to argue and then closed it again. "Does it go fast?"

"Only if I make it go fast."

"Tell me you're not a speed fiend like your brother."

Back in control, Jackson smiled and pulled on his gloves. "I could tell you that—" he flipped down the shield on her helmet and swung his leg over the saddle "—but I was raised not to tell a lie. Move when I move and lean when I lean."

"Jackson—"

"Hop on, Cinderella, or that clock will be striking midnight before you've even arrived at the damn ball."

Gingerly, she slid her leg over the back of the snowmobile. "I'm really not sure about this—"

"You have to be sure of something before you do it? That must be limiting. Hold on to me."

"I can sit without help." Her voice was muffled by the helmet, and he realized that if it did nothing else, the helmet would stop him kissing her.

"Just like you could walk on ice without help. We

both remember how that turned out." Smiling to himself, Jackson gave it some choke and cranked the engine—and felt Kayla's arms shoot around his waist. He shook with laughter. "You okay back there? Only I thought you said you could sit without help."

"If you're laughing at me you're going to be sorry."

But he wasn't sorry. He wasn't sorry about any of it. Not about bringing her here and certainly not about taking her on this trip. He spent his days trying to make numbers add up into a different pattern, defusing tension, soothing anxieties while all the time trying to do things the way he knew they had to be done if this whole place was going to thrive again. He was weighed down by duty and responsibility, and he didn't often get to throw off that weight. But Kayla Green made him feel lighter. She also made him feel a hell of a lot of other things he was trying to ignore.

He took it steady to begin with, allowing her time to get used to the rhythm of the snowmobile and the feel of moving across the snow and ice. At one point he heard her gasp and felt her tighten her grip on him, but then they left the resort behind and soon they were speeding along winding trails, through dense, heavily wooded forest.

It was a perfect blue-sky winter day. The overnight fall of snow had added a layer of soft powder to the groomed trail and the surface sparkled under the bright sun.

He thought he heard her laugh and he increased the speed, gently touching the throttle to keep the machine moving.

Jackson thought about the times he and his brothers had raced along this trail, risking life and limb, leaving their mother racked with worry. Sheer guts and enthusiasm had bred skill, and now he knew where to steer, how much throttle to use to get the best performance from the machine and he pushed it to the limits.

When they reached the Chocolate Shack, he slowed and pulled off the trail.

A curl of smoke rose from the chimney and a few skiers wrapped in warm layers were seated at tables outside, a slash of color against a background of white.

"That was *amazing!* I want to spend the rest of my life doing that." Breathless and laughing, she slid off the back of the snowmobile, flipped up the shield on her helmet and glanced around her, enchanted. "This place is gorgeous. How does anyone ever find it?"

"There are trail maps. And its reputation means people make the effort. They're famous for their whipped hot chocolate."

"Whipped hot chocolate? That sounds delicious." She pulled off the helmet and her hair flowed over her shoulders like sunlight, knocking all coherent thoughts out of his brain.

It wasn't just the color, although he wasn't about to object to natural blond—it was the way it swung, silky and soft, just inviting a man to reach out and slide his hands into it. Tangled and slightly messed by the helmet, her hair sparked thoughts of how she would look waking in the early morning after a night of hot screaming sex. Everything about her made him think of sex, and he realized how long it was since he'd had some serious rest and relaxation. Just for once it would have been nice to take a break from rescuing his family. He had several ideas of how he'd choose to spend the time, and none of them included rest. They did, however, include Kayla Green. Naked. Smiling at him the way she was smiling now.

He wondered how she'd react if he did what he was longing to do and kissed that mouth. Then he realized that mouth was moving. "Sorry—did you say something?"

"I said it sounds delicious."

"What sounds delicious?"

"The hot chocolate." She looked puzzled. "What else?"

What else? He was on the verge of revealing exactly what else but he stopped himself.

He had responsibilities, and none of them involved having hot screaming sex with Kayla Green. "Waffles," he said thickly. "The waffles are good."

"Sounds delicious." The cold air had put color in her cheeks. Or maybe something else was responsible for the sudden flush. The same something that was burning inside him. "The snowmobile was fantastic. I can't remember when I last had a high like that when I wasn't working."

It told him a lot about her that her highs came from work.

Unable to help himself, Jackson pushed her hair back from her face, and her smile froze as if she suddenly remembered that she didn't do this.

"Jackson—"

"Whipped hot chocolate." He heard the roughness of his own voice and pulled his hand away. "Let's go and have some of that." *Before he gave in to temptation and had something else.*

THE CHEMISTRY SWIRLED between them, brushing over her skin and darting through her body, sharp and terrifying. It drew her in, drew her to *him*. And she knew the source of the attraction was more than a pair of blue eyes and strong shoulders. His strength wasn't restricted to the physical. It went deeper.

Even after a comparatively short time in his company, it was easy to see why he was the one his family turned to in a crisis. Another man might have chosen to focus on his own business. Jackson O'Neil had chosen to come home and do what needed to be done. And from what she'd seen so far, it was a thankless task.

He glanced at her. "Inside or out?"

"Outside." She was breathless, and she didn't know whether it came from the sheer exhilaration of speeding through deep snow along a forest trail or being near him.

"You're not cold?"

"I like looking at the trees." She picked a table near to the cabin and breathed in the smell of wood smoke and forest. Sunlight filtered through the trees. The sky was a Caribbean blue, the temperatures Arctic. The contrast fascinated her. "I had no idea winter could be this pretty."

"It's the best time, providing you're dressed for it." Jackson put his helmet down on the table next to her and trudged through the snow to the door of the cabin.

She shouldn't have watched him, but she couldn't help it. He was in his element here, outdoors in the mountains, confident and comfortable in the harsh surroundings of snow and ice. And she wasn't alone in her appreciation of his qualities. Two women at the adjacent table were looking at him, too, gazes lingering.

Kayla looked away and focused on the snow-laden trees.

She couldn't remember ever being anywhere so peaceful. The only sound was the occasional dull thud as deeply piled snow tumbled from a branch onto the snowy forest floor.

It was a million miles from Manhattan.

A million miles from her life.

"Here." A large mug of hot chocolate appeared in front of her. Jackson pulled out the chair across from her and straddled it. "People ski for miles to sample Brigitte's Belgian hot chocolate. It's legendary around these parts." He'd pulled down the zip of his jacket and the neck of his jumper brushed his darkened jaw.

She rarely noticed men because she was too busy thinking about other things, too busy rushing through her life to ever take a second look, but Jackson was a man who deserved a second look. And a third. In fact the women at the table next to her hadn't stopped looking.

It bothered her that she didn't want to stop looking, either.

Instead, she focused on the swirls of cream that topped her hot chocolate. "So this is a special recipe? What's in it?"

"Calories," he said drily. "Brigitte guards the exact combination with her life, but I think it involves milk, chocolate, vanilla, fresh whipped cream and cinnamon. You might want to call your cardiologist before you take a sip."

"Is it worth the extra hours in the gym?"

"You're going to work off those calories fast enough. I'm taking you skiing this afternoon."

"I haven't already humiliated myself enough in the snow? You want more?" Kayla paused with the mug halfway to her lips. "Can't we just explore on the snowmobile?" She was surprised by how much she'd enjoyed being outdoors—the crisp fresh air and the sting of cold on her cheeks. Then there was the feeling of being pressed close to Jackson, but she wasn't going to think about that....

"You're getting the whole Snow Crystal experience, Kayla Green. No wimping out."

He had a way of persuading people to do exactly what he wanted them to do, she thought. He knew when to push hard, when to back off. When to employ a steely look and when to smile. He had his mother's warmth and interest in people. He was a man who took the trouble to look beneath the surface.

It unsettled her.

She didn't want him looking beneath the surface. She wasn't looking for depth. She didn't want depth.

"Just as long as the whole Snow Crystal experience doesn't include bear and moose." She sipped her chocolate and closed her eyes. It was the best thing she'd tasted, the hot velvety sweetness made even more perfect by the freezing temperatures biting through her clothing. "I've died and gone to heaven."

"Good, isn't it?"

She opened her eyes and saw that he was smiling. "Worth two solid weeks on the treadmill."

"You haven't truly lived until you've tasted Brigitte's hot chocolate."

"It's wicked." She tasted cream, chocolate and the burst of cinnamon and savored it all—flavor, scent and texture. As she licked cream from her top lip, she saw that he was watching her.

"I get the sense you don't usually indulge."

Kayla curled her fingers around the mug, warming her hands, staring down at the chocolate flakes sprinkled onto swirls of whipped cream. "That depends on what you mean by *indulge*."

"Doing something just for the sheer pleasure of it." Somehow the atmosphere had shifted. There was tension where tension shouldn't exist. Heat where there should have been cold.

"Work is my indulgence."

"Work can't be an indulgence. Not even if you enjoy it."

"Of course it can. There's nothing like the high you get from winning a big account, or getting a client profiled in their target media."

"Nothing?" He leaned across and brushed his thumb over her mouth, and she stilled, feeling that touch right through her.

"What are you doing?"

"Removing chocolate from your lips."

"I could have done that."

"I guess you could." He lowered his hand slowly. "But I did it."

Heart pounding, she touched her fingers to her mouth where his had been only moments earlier. "Do all the O'Neils touch a lot? Last night your mother wanted to hug me, and she'd only just met me."

"My mother has always known how to give a warm welcome. Does it bother you?"

Yes, it bothered her. "I suppose I'm not used to it."

"You don't come from a family of huggers?"

"Why are you so interested in my family?"

"Just a friendly question, Kayla. But if it makes you uncomfortable, you don't have to answer."

It made her uncomfortable. *He* made her uncomfortable.

She tried not to look at the width of those shoulders or the warmth of his gaze. "My family wasn't tactile."

"Wasn't?"

"I mean isn't." Unused to talking about her family, she handled it clumsily, but he let it go.

"How did you end up in public relations?"

The shift in conversation was a relief. "When I graduated, I went for an interview with an advertising agency in London. They had a sister PR agency and during my interview they decided I was exactly what they were looking for. It took about six months to discover I had an aptitude for finding media angles and selling them to the press. After that I was promoted pretty quickly."

"It must have been hard, moving to the U.S."

"Not really. I didn't have anything keeping me in London."

"Your family isn't there?"

And, just like that, they were right back to that question. "My mother lives in New Zealand. My father, in Canada."

"So you were on your own in the U.K.?"

She'd been on her own for as long as she could remember. "It's fairly common for families to be scattered these days." *Scattered* was a good word. *Lost* might have been a better one.

She thought about the envelope waiting for her back in the cabin. Last year, the envelope had stayed untouched until February when she'd finally cleared out the bottom of her in-tray.

She was terrified Jackson was going to press her for more details, but he levered himself to his feet. "Are you done? I want to show you the ice waterfall before I take you skiing."

Deciding that skiing had to be preferable to talking about her family, Kayla finished her drink and followed him to the snowmobile.

He stood steady in the deep snow, legs spread as he pulled on his gloves. "Do you want to drive?"

Remembering the twisty, turning trails and the skill he'd shown maneuvering the snowmobile, she shook her head. "Not this time. I'd rather let you do the work. When it comes to physical effort I'm inherently lazy."

"So you're a lie-back-and-let-it-happen sort of woman? That surprises me." The gleam in those blue eyes made her feel as if she'd stepped off a cliff.

"Are you flirting with me?" She breathed and felt cold air rush into her lungs. Unfortunately it did nothing to cool the heat of her skin. "Because if you are, I'd have to warn you that you're wasting your time."

"It's my time." His gaze steady on hers, he picked up his helmet. "Up to me how I choose to waste it."

"Just as long as you know I'm not good at personal relationships."

"Who told you that?"

"No one. I have impressive self-insight. I know what I'm good at. I know what I'm bad at. I'm bad at relationships. Not just bad, terrible. The truth is I find work more interesting than any man." There. She'd said it. And he was still standing there. Still watching her with eyes that saw far, far too much.

"Surely that would depend on the man."

"I'd rather check my emails than go on a date. And if I do go on a date, I still check them."

"Is that right?" He reached out and tilted her chin, and she froze, but all he did was zip her jacket to her throat and smile at her. "The internet connection is pretty unpredictable up here. You might have to find another way to occupy yourself on a date, Kayla."

"I don't intend to go on a date. I'm here to work."

"So your plan for dealing with chemistry is to pretend it doesn't exist?"

"Chemistry?" The word came out like a croak, and his eyes creased at the corners.

"Yeah, *that* chemistry. Seems to me we have two choices here. We can try to ignore it or we can go with it and see where we end up."

"Option one works for me."

"That could give me a problem."

Her mouth was dry. "Why?"

"Because I'm leaning toward option two." For a crazy, heart-stopping moment she thought he was going to kiss her. Then his smile widened and he stepped away. "The snow is likely to be deep up ahead. Hold on tight."

That was it? He was going to throw out a statement like that and then just leave it there? Leave her all jumbled up and thrown off balance?

Feeling as if she'd stuck her hand into a naked flame, Kayla climbed on behind him.

She hesitated and then curved her arms around his waist. The hardness of his thighs pressed against hers, and she was torn between pulling back and falling off or drawing closer. In the end she drew closer and found herself pressed against masculine power and strength. Her heart was banging against her ribs, and her hands were shaking so much she was sure he was going to feel it.

And no doubt he'd say something, because he wasn't a man who backed down from anything. Instead of ignoring the chemistry, he'd addressed it. Instead of being frozen out by her lack of response, he'd seemed amused.

As they traveled along the snowy trail she ceased to think about the forest or work, and thought about him.

She was so lost in the moment she didn't even realize they'd stopped moving.

"This is it. We walk the rest of the way."

"Walk?" She slid off the machine, conscious that
it was just the two of them. They were alone, and out
here in the wilds of the forest alone *meant* alone. "Just
how far away is this ice waterfall?"

"Through the trees. This is as close as we can get
on the snowmobile. We have to walk a little way down
the trail. It's groomed so you shouldn't have trouble."

She didn't.

Her feet crunched on the surface of packed snow
and soon they were enveloped by the silence of the forest. Jackson was slightly ahead and she was gazing at
the width of his shoulders when he stopped suddenly.
She crashed right into those shoulders and would have
fallen again had he not grabbed her hand and hauled
her against him.

"Look." It came as naturally to him to touch as it did
to her to keep herself at a distance, but she didn't have
long to dwell on that because they'd reached a break in
the trees and there, towering above them was a cascade
of ice, a frozen sculpture formed by nature and cutting
between the rocks.

"That's a waterfall?" She tried to imagine how such
a force of nature could ever freeze.

"During the summer the water tumbles down here,
but in exceptionally cold winters it freezes over."

"It's astonishing." And it was. Not just the spec-
tacle of an entire waterfall frozen in front of her eyes
but the detail, the colours and textures, from opaque to
translucent, silver threaded through bright white with
shimmers of green and blue as the sun hit the surface.

"Sometimes we climb here."

"You climb up the ice?"

"It's fun. And challenging because the conditions change constantly as the outer surface of the ice melts." His gaze shifted from her face to something behind her and his expression changed. "Kayla—"

"What?" Turning her head, she saw a large moose watching them through the trees. "Oh, crappity crap. That is *big*."

His fingers tightened on hers, his hand warm and strong. "Don't panic. He isn't going to be interested in you."

"That isn't flattering." Heart pumping, she stared at the moose. "The design is wrong. The legs are too long for the body, the body is too short for the face, and the antlers are the wrong size and shape for anything, but I'm willing to bet they'd hurt if he chose to drive them into someone." She hoped that someone wasn't her.

"The long legs enable him to walk through deep snow. Moose are fine as long as you don't get too close."

"Do I look like I intend to get close? I'm trying to run, but you're holding me. Let's go."

"No. This is all part of the Snow Crystal experience." His voice warm with laughter, he slid his arm around her waist, locking her against him. "Lots of tourists come here hoping to see what you're seeing now."

What she was seeing was a strong jaw shadowed by dark stubble and a firm mouth that was too close for comfort.

Suddenly the moose didn't feel as threatening as the chemistry. "With the benefit of many years of experience I can tell you that the moose is not going to be what gets you on the cover of *Time* magazine. Let's go—"

"The important thing to remember is that there is no safe way to approach a moose." He tightened his grip, holding her easily. She was pressed against the hard muscle of his thighs and it wasn't the moose she was thinking about, but him.

"I can assure you I won't be approaching it. In fact this might be a good time to show me your love of speed."

"They're not usually aggressive unless they're frightened. It's one of the reasons we tell people to keep their dogs on leads around here. During the mating season, in the fall, the bulls can become aggressive."

"Note to self—never visit in October." She tugged at her hand. "Now can we—"

"Kayla—" he tugged her back to him "—he's *not* going to hurt you."

The chemistry was suffocating. The knot in her tummy wound tighter and tighter.

"You don't know what his intentions are toward me. He might sense I'm a city dweller and decide to send me back to New York with one kick." She tried to joke. Tried to do anything she could to cut through the tension that was like a steel wire pulling her toward him. "I presume they kick?"

"Yes. Despite their size, moose are flexible. They can kick in all directions, including sideways."

"Sounds like my yoga instructor. Can we go now?"

He smiled that slow, dangerous smile, his mouth just a breath away from hers. "Don't you trust me to protect you?" He was all hard muscle and masculinity, and she no longer knew where the threat lay, but she had a feeling it wasn't behind her.

"I've always preferred to be in charge of my own protection." She felt weird, and she had no idea whether it was the proximity of the moose or the proximity of Jackson O'Neil. "I guard myself."

"Yeah, I got that." His voice was husky, his eyes on her mouth. "And what happens when you let your guard down, Kayla?"

"I don't let my guard down. I don't let people close."

But he was close.

Too close.

And then his mouth wasn't just close to hers it was *on* hers, sure and demanding, and his kiss felt as good as she'd known it would. Hunger ripped through her, the sexual chemistry so intense the heat threatened to burn right through them. It was the most erotic, sexually explicit kiss she'd ever experienced, and she wrapped her arms around his neck, lost in it.

"Christ, Kayla—" He groaned the words against her mouth, his voice thickened and rough. He had one hand locked in her hair and the other on her back, holding her hard against him. Pressed thigh to thigh, she was aware of hardness and heat, of the sensual stroke of his tongue against hers, and she grasped the front of his jacket, hauling him closer, wanting more, *needing* more. The sheer force of the chemistry shocked her because it was as sharp as it was unfamiliar.

She didn't do this….

But she was doing it now, her mouth as hungry for his as his was for hers. Her gut tightened. Nothing mattered except his kiss, and the skill of that kiss turned her brain to slush and her limbs to water. Her surroundings faded, and her entire world became this man, his mouth, his hands and the desperate heat burning through her body.

They were creating enough heat to melt the frozen waterfall, and yet still she wanted more. She wanted to climb all over him, rip off his clothes, get to see those muscles without the clothes, she wanted to—

He powered her back against the nearest tree and she would have lost her balance had he not steadied both of them. She felt the roughness of the bark pressing through the thickness of her jacket. He rested one arm above her head, caging her, and still he kissed her, as if he couldn't stop, couldn't help himself, and she moaned his name because she couldn't help herself, either. She fumbled with his jacket, pushed her hands inside and felt the hard swell of male muscle against her seeking fingers. The smell of pine mingled with the tantalizing scent of him. A shower of snow thudded onto her head from the branches above, but she barely registered the sudden cold because his fingers were on her zip, too, and when he cupped her breast she felt herself shiver. She moaned, twisted as the heat pooled low in her pelvis. She felt the skilled drag of his fingers over her nipple, the erotic slide of his tongue in her mouth and the only sounds were the pumping of blood in her head and the shallow rasp of their breathing.

All around them was silence, a mysterious magical silence as the snowbound forest cloaked their illicit moment of passion in wintery whiteness.

And then he lifted his head. Slowly, reluctantly, as if he were locked in a battle between willpower and desire, and Kayla opened her eyes, too, dazed and disorientated.

Maybe it was because they were standing in the shadow of a tree but his eyes seemed dark, an almost midnight-blue, and for once there wasn't a hint of a smile on his hard, handsome face.

And then he gently eased himself away from her and slid up her zip, protecting her from the cold. "So now we have the answer."

"The answer?" Her lips, still tingling from the pressure of his, could barely form the question. "What answer?" She didn't have the answer to anything, least of all why she'd done what she'd just done. He'd started it, but she'd been right there with him. The only difference between them was that she wouldn't have stopped.

"The answer to what happens when you let your guard down. If you feel the need to check your emails, go ahead." A slight roughening of his voice was the only hint that he was affected by what had happened.

"Emails?" She stared at him dizzily, wondering how a man's kiss could blitz her brain so completely.

"Yeah. Those things you check when you're bored by the man you're with." He paused long enough to let the words sink in. Then he stepped back and glanced over her shoulder. "I'm sure you'll be relieved to know the moose has gone."

Moose?

She hadn't given a single thought to the moose since he'd started kissing her.

In fact she was fairly sure that while Jackson's mouth had been on hers a whole family of moose could have stampeded right over her and she wouldn't have noticed. She was surprised to see the snow still thick on the trees and deep underfoot. She'd half expected to find herself standing in a pool of meltwater.

As reality slowly reasserted itself, so did the panic.

She never did this. Never *felt* this.

But maybe this happened to Jackson O'Neil all the time.

Judging from the way Brenna had hugged him that morning, she obviously wasn't the only one affected by Jackson O'Neil. The thought cooled her more effectively than the shower of snow.

"Does Brenna mind you kissing random women?"

Those blue eyes narrowed. "I've never asked, but I'm fairly sure she'd tell me to go ahead and kiss who I want to kiss."

Confused, Kayla stepped back, but he locked his hand in the front of her jacket and dragged her back to him. "I'm not with Brenna."

"I'm not interested in your love life, O'Neil—"

"Yes, you are. You saw her hug me and you wondered, but you don't need to wonder. You could have asked me straight-out, of course. For the record, that's the way I'd prefer it, because then there are no misunderstandings. But seeing as you insist on pretending none of this is happening, I'll answer the question you haven't asked. Brenna and I are friends. We've been friends a long time. If it was going to be more, it would have happened long ago." His hand was still on her jacket as he held her toe-to-toe with him and the power of the chemistry almost blinded her.

"Fine." Except it wasn't fine. *None of this was fine.* "I just have no idea why you kissed me, that's all."

"No?" A slow smile spread across his face. "You're a clever woman. I'm sure you'll figure it out. Failing that, why don't you ask yourself why you kissed me? That ought to give you some clues." With that, he released her and walked back to the snowmobile, the view of his powerful shoulders leading her to decide that Jackson O'Neil looked as good from the back as he did from the front.

CHAPTER SEVEN

JACKSON ENDED THEIR snowmobile tour at his favorite mountain restaurant.

"We'll have lunch here."

Kayla pulled off her helmet. Her gaze was fixed on the view, which could have been because it was spectacular, but he had a feeling it was because she'd rather look at just about anything but him. "I'm grateful for the offer of lunch, but what I'd really like is to go back to the resort and do some work."

She was running from him.

The kiss had shaken her, and he had some sympathy with that because it had shaken him, too.

For a brief moment in the forest, she'd thawed. Under his hands and mouth, Kayla Green had transformed from ice machine to warm, soft woman, but now she was frozen again, the layer of ice between her and the world thicker than ever.

He wondered what it would take to melt it permanently.

"This is work. You're getting to know Snow Crystal." Jackson chose the table with the best view. "Sit down. The specialty of this place is the hot spiced apple cider."

If they hadn't been on top of a mountain, she would have argued. He saw it in the way she held herself, tense and poised for flight. But there was no flight because her only way out of here was on the back of his snow-mobile, and he wasn't going anywhere.

So she sat. "If it's a local specialty I'd like to try it of course, thanks." It was a signal that she wanted to get this over with as fast as possible. "I'm interested in—" She broke off, her expression frozen, as a pretty girl wearing a red ski jacket and a Santa hat skipped across the deck to them.

"Jackson! I wasn't expecting to see you here today." The girl flung her arms around him and Jackson almost drowned in blond hair and perfume. As he gently extracted himself, he saw that Kayla was already on her feet.

"This looks like a good moment for me to use the bathroom." She smiled her most corporate smile, and Jackson sighed because she was back in hedgehog mode, complete with a full set of prickles. And they were aimed right at him.

"Kayla, this is Dana. Dana is my cousin." He emphasized the word gently and saw Kayla frown slightly.

"Oh. I assumed—" She stuck out her hand, as if she was making sure she couldn't be on the receiving end of the same effusive greeting. "Pleased to meet you."

"Hi, Kayla." Dana gave a friendly smile, shook hands and then turned back to Jackson. "Guess who I have in my kindergarten class this week. The Foster twins, can you believe that? I babysat them. Now they're on skis."

"That thought is close to terrifying. How are they doing?"

"They're awesome. Overexcited about Christmas, but who isn't? Hey, Cliff—" Dana leaned back and waved her hand to the owner of the restaurant "—starving to death and dying of thirst here. Any chance of some service?"

Cliff strolled over, eyebrows raised. "You just told me you weren't eating because you couldn't afford my shocking prices."

"I can't, but that was before Jackson showed up. He's paying." She peeped at him and Jackson gave a half smile.

"My debts are so huge one burger isn't going to make a difference."

"In that case I'll have the mountain burger with fries, thanks. Unless I'm interrupting—" Her eyes slid to Kayla, who was still wearing her corporate smile.

"What could you possibly be interrupting? It's great to have a chance to chat with someone who lives around here. It gives breaking for lunch a purpose."

She had a smile for different situations, he decided. And he preferred the one she'd given him when he kissed her.

She looked a whole lot healthier than she had when he'd picked her up that morning. The fresh air had whipped pink into her cheeks and added sparkle to her eyes.

Or maybe it was the kiss that had done that.

He pulled off his gloves and put them on the table. "Do you ever do anything just because it's fun?"

"I find work fun."

Jackson spoke to Cliff and ordered the artisan cheese board and the charcuterie plate, along with a basket of fresh rolls and Dana's burger.

Kayla stared at the food. "I'm really not hungry."

"You'll be hungry when it arrives. The food is sourced from local suppliers. The quality of food around here is exceptional. It's a definite draw for the tourists."

At the word *tourist* she relaxed. "So what would you say is the special appeal of Snow Crystal, Dana?"

"If I had to pick a favorite, I'd have to say dogsledding, but I'm biased because my parents run Snow and Sled from the farm right next to Snow Crystal. We have a huge network of trails, and when I'm not teaching classes, I help out in the kennels. We have eighteen huskies. Twenty-two if you count the four that are retired." Dana sat back as Pete delivered their drinks. "I can guarantee it is the most fun you will ever have in your life. If you like, I could take you out. We run daily most weeks and at this time of year we run at night, too."

Kayla sipped her cider. "You go out on the sled in the dark?"

"If there is enough moonlight we use that. If not, headlamps. Going out at night is special."

"It sounds romantic." Kayla's gaze connected briefly with Jackson's. Just for a moment they were both back in the forest, mouths hot as they'd feasted on each other. Then she looked away. "Romantic destinations are an important draw for the traveling public. We try to target a wide range of media so we're always looking for a story that's a little different. A new angle. Something that sets you apart. That way we get top-tier placements." She paused as Cliff delivered the food to their table.

"One artisan plate, one charcuterie and a burger. Enjoy. And don't forget to tell your friends how good we are."

"I always do. In fact this burger should be free, given the number of people I send up here." Dana bit into her burger while Jackson looked on in amusement.

"Technically that burger *is* free since I'm the one paying."

"You're still repaying the debt for all those snowballs you stuffed down my neck when we were growing up. So, are you flying back to the U.K. for Christmas, Kayla?"

"No, I'm staying here." Kayla reached across the table and helped herself to a thin slice of cheese. "I'm living the Snow Crystal experience."

"You couldn't find a better place to spend Christmas. It's magical." Dana slapped Jackson's fingers as he reached across to steal her fries. "If you wanted fries you should have ordered some."

"I ordered these and paid for them."

They played verbal tennis, the banter bouncing backward and forward between them as it always did and, as lunch progressed, other people drifted over and joined them until the table was crowded with a dozen people, most of whom Jackson had known since childhood.

Kayla was polite, factual and impressive as they encouraged her to talk about her work. She didn't seem overwhelmed as she had with his family, and he decided it was because the conversation wasn't personal.

He was surprised to discover how much he wanted it to be personal.

"We should go." He rose to his feet, exchanged a few words with one of the instructors about snow conditions and the forecast for Christmas itself, and checked his watch.

Dana was on her feet, too, pulling on her gloves and still chatting to Kayla. "If you want a sled ride, let me know. It's something everyone should try once in a lifetime."

"That would be interesting, thank you."

"Not interesting. Magical. And romantic." Dana gave Jackson a meaningful look, and he shook his head. He would have laughed but he knew better than to encourage her.

"Go! And keep those Foster twins out of trouble."

"Not possible. Bye. Love you." She stood on tiptoe, kissed him and then winked at Kayla. "I do that because it increases my cool rating among people who don't know we're related."

"Goodbye, Dana," Jackson said mildly. "Leave, now, before I charge you for the burger."

"I could give Kayla a ski lesson."

He reached for his gloves. "Or you could go do your job and leave me to give her a ski lesson."

Kayla didn't smile. "Maybe we should leave skiing for another day. I could use some time alone with my laptop, and I was hoping to talk to your mother this afternoon."

The words made sense. Her expression didn't. He saw panic in her eyes. The same panic that had been there when he'd kissed her. The same panic that had been there the night before.

It all added up to one thing.

She didn't want to be alone with him.

KAYLA PACED THE length of the cabin, trying to regain her balance.

She'd come here to escape Christmas, expecting to find calm and peace to work until the whole thing was over. She hadn't expected to find a hot guy with no respect for boundaries. It unsettled her. *He* unsettled her.

It wasn't just because of that kiss—although admittedly it had been enough to make a girl forget how to stay upright on her own two legs—it was the way he behaved around her. He wasn't prepared to be frozen out, and he seemed to have no issues with blurring the boundaries between business and pleasure.

Kayla opened her laptop. She wanted to work, but now her head was a mess, her concentration shot and all coherent thought tangled up with images of Jackson.

Trying to focus, she phoned the office and spoke to Stacy.

"I took a look at those activity reports—thanks for that. Any news from the Wexford Hotel Group?" She listened while Stacy updated her, calmed by the familiarity of the routine. "I need to call Howard—I'll do that from here—and ask Melinda to send me through the timeline, proposal and business deck for the airline pitch. I'll look at it in a quiet moment."

"Over the holidays?"

"I'm working."

"Not right the way through, surely. What about Christmas Day? Do yourself a favor and at least get up close and personal with that gorgeous guy. Find mistletoe if you have to."

They hadn't needed mistletoe.

They hadn't needed anything except each other.

She felt color rush into her cheeks and was relieved she and Stacy weren't in visual contact. "I would never get involved with someone I work with."

"Kayla, you work all the time. The only guys you are ever going to meet are people you work with, so unless you plan on leading a celibate life, you're going to have to cross your own line at some point. Brett wants you to bring back maple syrup. His wife and youngest daughter like it."

Kayla rolled her eyes. "He can buy it at the store."

"It's not the same as homemade in Vermont."

Homemade in Vermont. She thought about the gingerbread Santas and the smell of baking.

"That's it. I'm going to use that for our campaign. Homemade in Vermont. It's all about traditional family values. A place you can share idyllic moments with those you love. Don't most people want that?"

"Er—*you* don't want that."

"I'm not talking about me." Kayla felt the familiar rush of excitement that came with ideas, swiftly followed by relief that at least part of her was operating normally. "People lead busy lives. They don't have enough time for family and they feel guilty about that, and then the holidays come round and they want something that reaffirms their values. Snow Crystal does that. It's a perfect place for families. We'll put together some packages. And maybe we should profile the O'Neil family. They've built this place, stuck by each other—it's the sort of story people love." Her brain working, she strode back across the cabin and scribbled notes on her pad.

"That's great. Are you having any fun there?"

"Fun?" She thought about the snowmobile ride. *She thought about the kiss.* "Everything is fine. I need to go. I want to talk to Elizabeth O'Neil about cookery."

"You don't know anything about cookery."

"That's why I need to talk to someone with knowledge."

THE AROMA OF cinnamon and spice hit her as she walked up the snowy path to the front door. From the artful twist of fairy lights in the trees to the elaborate wreath on the door, the place sparkled with Christmas cheer.

Through the door she could hear Elizabeth singing along to Christmas songs. It made her want to run a mile and then she decided she didn't want to be a woman who could be unsettled by a few twinkly lights and someone's cheerful rendition of "Jingle Bells."

Nor did she want to be a woman who was unsettled by one man's kiss, even if that kiss had been insanely good.

Trying to push that out of her head, Kayla knocked briskly on the door and was greeted by ecstatic barking. Moments later, Elizabeth opened the door and Kayla saw the puppy springing up and down like a child on a trampoline.

"That's a warm welcome." Kayla was relieved at least one person in the family wasn't bearing a grudge. "I wondered if you had time for a chat? But if this is a bad time—"

"It's a perfect time! Tyler was supposed to be bringing Jess over, but there's no sign of either of them. Maybe they've gone shopping. You know how it is at Christmas."

Yes, she knew.

That was why she'd agreed to a week here. It was just a shame it wasn't quite turning out how she'd planned.

She stepped into the hallway, saw boxes of decorations laid ready and tinsel heaped high and backed away like a wild animal sensing danger. "I'm disturbing you."

"You're certainly not disturbing me. It's lovely to have company. I have biscuits in the oven and then we'll trim the tree together."

Kayla felt a rush of horror. She'd rather hug a moose than trim the tree. "No! I mean—I'm no good at it. I have no eye for what makes a pretty tree."

"It will be fun. You're so much taller than me, you can reach the top. Come through to the kitchen for a minute." Elizabeth removed several trays of freshly baked cookies, which she quickly and efficiently transferred to a cooling rack.

Kayla tried to work out how she could escape from decorating a Christmas tree without causing offence. "Are you feeding the whole of Vermont?"

"Sometimes it feels that way. We sell them in the café, and we put them in the rooms when we have new guests arriving. I think those little touches make it feel less like a hotel and more like a home. Let's go through to the living room. I'm waiting for Jackson to bring one more box of decorations from Alice's attic."

Kayla followed Elizabeth into the living room, careful not to tread on Maple, who was running happy circles around her feet.

Through the windows she could see past the trees to the lake and, beyond that, the snow-covered mountains. A log fire blazed and a large Christmas tree stood in the corner, waiting to be decorated. Kayla stared at it with an ache in her chest.

"Big tree."

"Isn't it a beauty? Tyler and Jackson dragged it from the forest on the sledge."

Kayla picked out a chair angled away from the tree. Unfortunately that put her in direct line of sight of the mantelpiece with its garland of twisted ivy and delicate fairy lights. Keeping her head down, she pulled her notepad out of her bag. "Do you have time to talk about Snow Crystal?"

"I always have time to talk about Snow Crystal. Walter has taken Alice down to the village to buy more yarn, so Maple and I are on our own here." Elizabeth carried the boxes in from the hallway and opened one of them. "I pack these away each year and then can't remember what's in them. Does that happen to you?"

"I— No. I rent a small apartment near Central Park. There's barely room for me. I don't decorate."

"Not even a small tree? That's terrible." Elizabeth opened the first box. "Still, I suppose you have all those glittering New York shop windows to enjoy. Michael took me once. We saw them lighting the Christmas tree at the Rockefeller Center. I'll never forget it, although I still maintain there is nowhere I'd rather be than Snow Crystal at Christmas. You'll never want to leave."

She didn't just want to leave, she wanted to leave *right now.*

Coming here had been a bad idea.

She'd thought she'd be able to escape, but there was no escape when the thing you were trying to escape was buried inside you.

Kayla's head was starting to pound. What had possessed her to offer to come here at this time of year? Thanks to that lapse in judgment she now had her back to a giant Christmas tree, while facing a box full of baubles and enough fairy lights to power Sleeping Beauty's castle.

"Is something wrong, dear?" Elizabeth's voice was quiet. "Did Walter upset you?"

"Nothing's wrong. Tell me about Snow Crystal," Kayla said desperately. "Tell me what makes it special."

Elizabeth watched her for a moment and then stood up. "Why don't I make us some tea? I could talk for hours about Snow Crystal."

Hours?

Kayla wasn't sure she'd make it through minutes let alone hours. "I don't want to take up too much of your time."

"I love the company." Elizabeth disappeared into the kitchen and was back a few minutes later carrying a tray loaded with a teapot, two bone china mugs and a plate of homemade cinnamon stars. "In the morning I drink English breakfast tea and in the afternoon Earl Grey with lemon. They all tease me, but it's my little British treat. That and HP Sauce and the occasional bar of Cadbury's chocolate."

"Do you miss England?"

"I did at first, but not anymore. As soon as I met Michael and had the children, Snow Crystal became home. And I had no family left in England, so I suppose that was another reason why it was easy to leave it behind. But I brought a few traditions with me, and tea is one of those." The puppy barked hopefully and Elizabeth glanced at Kayla. "Is she bothering you? I can put her somewhere else."

"No. Don't do that." Keen to make a good impression this time, Kayla reached down and gave Maple a hesitant pat. The puppy's fur was soft and springy under her fingers. "She's pretty. And so friendly."

"Did you have a dog when you were growing up?"

"No." Kayla felt the pressure build in her chest. "No pets. Did you breed her?"

"Jackson found her in the forest when he was out on one of the trails this summer." Elizabeth set the tray down on the low coffee table. "Someone had left her tied to a tree. Can you believe that?" Her mouth thinned. "She was skin and bones."

"That's terrible." Shocked, Kayla stroked Maple gently. "So you kept her?"

"There was no way we'd let her go to the pound, so we gave her a home. But it hasn't been easy. She's a miniature poodle and we have two Siberian huskies, Ash and Luna, and they play rough. Maple gets in the middle of that."

"I haven't met your other dogs."

"They're living with Tyler at the moment. It's good for Jess to have them around." Elizabeth picked up the teapot and glanced up. "Maple was a bit overexcited last night. I'm worried she ruined your shoes."

Kayla thought about the combined destructive power of paws and snow. "It was my fault for wearing unsuitable shoes."

"They were the prettiest shoes any of us had seen around here for a while." Elizabeth poured tea into the two china cups. "Now what do you want to know about Snow Crystal?" She was kind, warm and accepting, and Kayla felt a rush of guilt.

"I want to apologize for last night."

"If anyone needs to apologize, it's Walter."

"No. I talked about things that didn't interest you and didn't seem relevant and—well, I was rude." And it bothered her. Both the loss of control and the fact she'd offended them.

"You weren't rude." Elizabeth spooned sugar into her cup. "You were overwhelmed, and who can blame you. I remember the first time I met the O'Neils. It was like being buried by an avalanche. There were twelve of them sitting in the kitchen the night Michael brought me home. Twelve, not counting animals, all talking at once and not one of them stopping to listen to another, although somehow they seemed to manage to hear what was said anyway. I just wasn't used to it. I'm guessing you're not used to it, either. You're used to order and shiny meeting rooms and suited executives. We're nothing like your usual clients—I'm sure of that."

Kayla thought of Jackson. Thought of those strong hands controlling the snowmobile through the deep snow. She thought about his powerful shoulders and the warmth of his mouth as he'd kissed her.

No, he was nothing like her usual clients.

Her heart thumped against her ribs, and she glanced around the living room, trying to distract herself.

The afternoon sun slanted through the large windows, bouncing light off photo frames. Deep sofas piled with cushions in earth tones faced each other across a large cream rug. It was a room that had seen a family grow. A room with a thousand stories to tell. The slight scuff on the leg of a chair where an active boy had smashed into it, the rug slightly worn by eager feet. It was a family room, comfortable and comforting. Except that it didn't comfort her.

Kayla felt the ache build inside her. "You came here to cook?"

"It was meant to be just for the winter season." Elizabeth sipped her tea. "I'd finished a course in Paris. Learned to make so many fancy dishes. Michael always said the day he tasted my braised lamb shanks, he was lost." Smiling, she put the cup down. "He ate his way through the menu so he could have an excuse to talk to me. By the time he reached the last dessert we were in love. We were engaged after two weeks and I did all the cooking for our wedding."

"Two weeks?" Kayla blinked. "That's fast."

"I've never understood people who have long engagements. If you know, why wait? And I knew. Michael and I connected straightaway. Losing him was a shocking blow." Her eyes misted, and Kayla sat there feeling awkward and inadequate.

She knew nothing about the type of love Elizabeth had felt for her husband, but she knew how it felt to have your life irrevocably altered.

"It must be difficult for you, learning to live without him."

"I miss him every minute of every day. I don't talk about it much because I know Jackson worries about me, and he has enough to worry about." She picked up her cup again, as poised and elegant as if she was indulging in tea at the Ritz in London. "But I'm glad to be living here. I feel close to Michael and it's the same for Walter and Alice, of course. I have no idea how it would feel to have to leave this place—" Her eyes shone a little too brightly and Kayla sat still, staring hard into her tea because she knew.

She knew how it felt to lose a home.

She knew how it felt to be forced to move from somewhere safe and familiar. To have your roots wrenched from the ground so violently that only the scars remained.

And suddenly she understood why Jackson had come home. A man like him, with strong family values, would do that no matter what the cost to his own dreams and ambitions. It was about so much more than saving an ailing family business. It was about saving the memories for his mother and grandparents. Saving the jobs of people he'd known all his life. Saving the home he grew up in and the place he loved.

"I can help." She was surprised by how badly she wanted to. Surprised to discover the desire to help had nothing to do with personal ambition. "You need more people through your doors, sleeping in your beds and eating in the restaurant. More people need to know about Snow Crystal. That's what I do. I can put together a campaign that raises the profile of the resort."

"That's why Jackson brought you here, and I've never questioned his judgment."

"Why did he leave? Why not just stay and run Snow Crystal right from the start?" She told herself that information on Jackson O'Neil was necessary for her job. It wasn't because she had a personal interest and it definitely wasn't because of the kiss.

"Michael would have liked him to stay, but Walter didn't want him here. They clashed over it. Jackson found himself in the middle of that for a while, and then he went off to college and found his own path." Elizabeth set a pretty china plate in front of Kayla. "It was the right thing to do. If he'd stayed here he never would have found out how high he could fly. And he flew high, as I always knew he would."

Kayla heard the pride in her voice and wondered how it felt to be on the receiving end of that sort of love.

She'd given up telling either of her parents about her promotions and successes. Given up hoping they might be interested in anything she did.

"His father wanted him to stay?"

"Yes, but I think that was probably for selfish reasons," Elizabeth admitted quietly. "Michael didn't enjoy running this place. And Jackson was right to go. If he'd stayed, his wings would have been clipped by his father and his grandfather and those wings would have torn in the struggling."

The vivid imagery made Kayla wince. "Ouch."

"Eventually he might have resented them for holding him back, for standing in the way of him proving himself. He didn't want something that someone else had created. He wanted to create something himself. He needed that." Elizabeth passed Kayla a cookie. "They're my cinnamon stars. At Christmas we package them up in pretty packages tied with bows. Try one."

Kayla obliged, wondering if cooking was how Elizabeth filled the loneliness.

"Walter doesn't agree with the changes Jackson has made?"

"Walter doesn't understand why we would spend money when we're losing it." Elizabeth picked up a box of decorations. "I suppose I don't understand that, either. But I trust Jackson. I need to sort through these decorations. Some of them need tender loving care. Some just won't survive another year. Could you look through this one?" She pushed a box toward Kayla, who took it with all the enthusiasm of someone being passed a box of tarantulas.

It was just a few Christmas decorations. She could sort a few Christmas decorations without having a breakdown, surely?

Elizabeth smiled. "Why don't you start hanging those."

Kayla's mouth felt dry. "You want me to hang them?"

"Of course. If you're here with us over the holidays, the least we can do is let you share in our Christmas. I expect you have your own Christmas rituals. All families do."

Kayla gripped the box. "We had a few."

Put your stocking by the fire, Kayla. Let's see what surprise Santa brings you.

There was a hollow, empty feeling in her stomach. She recognized the feeling because she'd lived with it for such a long time.

Loneliness could be felt at any time, of course, but there was something exquisitely painful about the loneliness that came along with Christmas.

She lifted a decoration from the box and stared at it.

A moment later it was gently removed from her hand.

"You don't like this time of year, do you, dear?"

It embarrassed and frustrated her that she still felt this way. That she hadn't been able to put the past behind her and find the same joy in the holiday season that so many others did. "I find it difficult."

The box was removed from her hand.

"Leave it. I'll trim the tree later."

"I'd like to do it." She'd spent Christmas alone for the past decade. This time she was alone in the middle of a family. It couldn't be worse, surely? "It's been a while."

"You don't see your family at Christmas?"

Kayla hesitated and then the door opened, allowing a flurry of cold air into the living room along with Jackson. His collar was turned up against the winter cold, and he carried a large box in his arms.

Elizabeth gave Kayla's arm a brief squeeze and walked toward him. "Is that the box we've been looking for?" Her voice gave no indication that he'd disturbed a conversation of significance, and Kayla was grateful for that. At the same time she wondered how much she would have said if they hadn't been interrupted.

Jackson handed the box to his mother. "It was in the old barn tucked behind a stack of rusty machinery. I'm guessing Walter put it there after last Christmas." Spying her rescuer, the puppy gave a yelp of ecstasy and shot across the living room, leaping on the spot to greet him.

Jackson scooped her up and made a fuss of her. "Sorry I took so long. After I found the box I only managed to walk three steps without being grabbed. Misbehaving boiler in cabin four, a leak in one of the lodge bedrooms and a child with a painful knee after a fall skiing." He sprawled on the sofa and stretched out his legs. Maple snuggled onto his lap.

"I've been telling Kayla my life story." Elizabeth picked up another box of decorations. "And she's a good listener, unlike most of the folks around here. So where did you go this morning? I hope you took her somewhere nice." She moved the conversation on and Kayla felt a flash of gratitude.

Jackson stroked Maple gently. "We went to the Chocolate Shack and the frozen waterfall."

"Oh, that's beautiful! Clever of you to show her that first. It's my favorite place in the whole of Snow Crystal. Michael proposed to me there. Took me on a horse-drawn sleigh. The bells were tinkling, snow was falling…it was the most romantic thing you could imagine and even more so because he wasn't a particularly romantic man. He surprised me." Elizabeth lifted her hand to her throat. "He was romantic that night. Not just the proposal, but the way he did it. He'd thought it through, you see. Created something I'd remember. There was a fur rug and a bottle of champagne—" She broke off and Kayla saw concern in Jackson's eyes.

"That sounds like a perfect proposal." She took over the conversation to give Elizabeth a chance to compose herself. "Are sleigh rides popular among the guests?"

"Yes." He told her about the horses they kept, about the route they took along the lake, and Elizabeth seemed to recover.

"Talking of guests, we had a request from the family renting cabin one for a Christmas tree. I asked Tyler, but he had to take that group skiing and Walter shouldn't be chopping down trees and dragging them through the forest at his age."

"I'll do it." Jackson massaged Maple's tummy but his eyes were on Kayla.

She'd been trying not to look at him, but the pull of his presence in the room proved too much.

For a fleeting moment their eyes connected, and she knew he was thinking about the kiss. And so was she. The atmosphere was so thick she could hardly breathe. She was sure his mother should have been able to feel it, too, but Elizabeth's attention was focused on the box of decorations in her lap.

Kayla stood up abruptly. "I'll help you." She snatched up the box Elizabeth had removed from her hand and hung a silver ball randomly on a branch, her hands shaking.

"You don't have to do that, dear."

"I want to." It was just a tree. She ought to be able to decorate a tree. "I've been thinking we should definitely offer romance-themed packages."

Elizabeth gave a sigh of approval. "I like that. Most people are too busy for romance today. No one slows down long enough to take time for each other."

Jackson lifted Maple off his lap. "You think it's better to go that route than showing Snow Crystal as a family destination?"

"We're going to do both, although the method isn't clear in my head yet." It would be a lot clearer if she didn't have her face stuck in Christmas. Kayla hung the decorations as quickly as possible, trying to get the job done. Why did the tree have to be so *big?* Branches stabbed her in the arm and in the face. Then she turned too quickly and they caught in her hair. "Ouch!"

"Family destination *and* romantic destination? Can a place be both?" Jackson rose to his feet and gently disentangled her, the backs of his fingers brushing her cheek. "Won't we be diluting our message?"

Just for a moment she was back in the forest, surrounded by the smell of pine and the strength and power that was Jackson O'Neil. He smelled so good she closed her eyes, but that proved to be a mistake, because even though the baubles vanished her head was full of Jackson.

"Kayla?"

She opened her eyes, dizzy. "Mmm?"

"You're no longer a decoration on the Christmas tree." His voice sounded lazy and amused. "I was asking if you thought we'd be diluting our message?"

"No. We'll be widening our audience." Pulling away from him, she reached for the box and extracted another silver ball. "You can't afford to restrict yourself to families only. And you have plenty to offer couples in search of romance. Sleigh rides, romantic dinner with champagne, breakfast…"

"For someone who claims not to be romantic, you seem to have a pretty good idea of how to create the right surroundings." Jackson took the decoration from her and hung it from a high branch.

Kayla watched, distracted by the flex of male muscle. "I'm good at seeing what will work for other people. You just have to look at the facts."

"Facts?" Elizabeth tilted her head to one side as she looked at the tree. "It isn't about facts, dear. It's about a feeling. A feeling in here." She pressed her fist to her chest. "It sweeps you away and robs you of breath, and you know that no matter what happens in the future, this is a moment you're going to remember forever. It's always going to be there, living inside you, and no one can take it away."

Kayla stood there, drowning under Christmas decorations and emotions she didn't recognize.

She'd felt that way at the frozen waterfall when Jackson had kissed her.

She'd known right away it was a moment she wouldn't forget.

Shaken, she forced a smile. "Then that's the feeling we need to try to create. For other people, obviously." She met Jackson's searching gaze and saw Elizabeth glance between them thoughtfully.

"So what are your plans for the rest of the week? Are you taking Kayla skiing, Jackson?"

"Just as soon as I've found the 'flat slope' she's requested."

Elizabeth chuckled. "My boys tend to prefer the other sort of slope, Kayla. Steep ravines, gullies—the steeper the better. They loved the outdoors and they loved the adventure. They were wild."

There it was again, Kayla thought. Pride. She sensed Elizabeth was a woman who would never feel anything but pride for her children.

"Not wild." Jackson stooped and switched on the Christmas tree lights. "I knew what I wanted and I went after it." He turned his head to look at Kayla, his gaze loaded with meaning.

Oblivious, Elizabeth stacked the plates and cups on the tray. "You were all wild. And once Tyler started racing—I couldn't ever watch. I watched the recording, once I knew he was safe."

Kayla tried to respond, but her mouth was dry, her brain empty and her gaze captured by Jackson. And then he smiled and that smile caught her somewhere behind her ribs.

She'd thought she'd experienced chemistry before, but nothing in her life had ever felt like this.

"Come over for breakfast tomorrow," Elizabeth said.

"You can sample our maple syrup with my homemade pancakes."

Jackson's gaze dropped to her lips and lingered there.

"Pancakes." Somehow she managed to form the word, and she saw Jackson's smile widen. Then he dragged his phone out of his pocket.

"I need to take this."

She hadn't even heard it ring.

This was *not* good.

"Afterward, we'll make a batch of cinnamon stars together," Elizabeth was saying. "Then you'll be able to make them when you get back home."

Kayla didn't say that she was more likely to choose to poke herself in the eye with a pen than bake at home. She wasn't capable of saying anything.

Jackson strolled back into the room. "I have to go over to the lodge. Chef trouble. Darren is threatening to walk out."

"As long as it's not Élise. She's a fabulous cook," Elizabeth murmured to Kayla, "but hot-tempered. French. Cooks like an angel and swears like she's in the military. Darren drives her crazy because he likes to do things the way they've always been done. I expect she told him his food is boring, only not as politely as that. Go and soothe her, Jackson. Don't let her leave. I just love her duck confit. You should try it, Kayla."

Kayla decided she'd better sign up to Weight Watchers before she left Snow Crystal. "Maybe I will." Without looking at the tree or Jackson, she picked up her bag. "Thanks for the tea and the chat, Elizabeth. You've given me some ideas to work with."

Jackson slid his phone into his pocket. "I'll drive you."

Which meant being trapped in an enclosed space

with him. She didn't trust herself not to spontaneously combust. "I'll walk. You go and sort out your chefs before they chop each other into tiny pieces."

"In that case I'll pick you up at seven for dinner."

He was asking her on a date? *In front of his mother?* "Dinner?" She looked at him stupidly, and he gave her that slow, sexy smile that told her he knew exactly why she wasn't getting in the car with him.

"Dinner, Kayla."

She licked her lips. "I—er—"

"I'm keen to spend more time discussing your initial ideas for Snow Crystal. I presume you have no objection to dinner meetings?"

A dinner meeting.

No candles.

No seduction.

Work.

Aware of how close she'd come to making a total fool of herself, Kayla gave a relieved smile. "Dinner meetings work for me. Great use of time." She breathed again. "I'll see you at seven."

She left the house and closed her eyes for a moment, letting the freezing air cool her heated skin.

Snow Crystal might be in a whole heap of trouble, but it was nothing compared to the heap of trouble she was in.

CHAPTER EIGHT

JESS SAT CURLED up on the window seat in her bedroom, her arms around Luna as she stared at the snow falling in the darkness. Ash lay on the floor next to them, his head on his paws, watching her with those pale, beautiful eyes. The two Siberian huskies were her best friends, and Snow Crystal was her favorite place in the world.

Better than her home in Chicago, where there wasn't a mountain in sight. When she was younger she'd had no interest in dolls or anything pink and glittery, and a few years on she had no interest in boys or shopping malls.

Other girls had posters of Justin Bieber on their walls. She'd had a poster of her dad skiing the Hahnenkamm in Austria, one of the most terrifying and dangerous downhill runs in the world. A run so steep that only the best made it down to the bottom in one piece. The top of that slope was a terrifying seventy-three degrees. *Seventy-three degrees.* Shit. That wasn't skiing, it was flying. Or falling.

She angled her hand and tried to imagine it. Imagined the adrenaline and the death-defying speeds you'd reach shooting out of the start gate onto a slope so steep you couldn't see where you were landing.

One day she wanted to ski that course, but it was an ambition she'd shared with no one.

She felt out of step with her friends and even her family. Most of the time she felt like a stranger, living a stranger's life.

Only here did she feel as if she fit. Only here did life make sense.

This was the only place she'd lived that felt like home.

One hand buried in Luna's fur, Jess rubbed the windowpane with the other and peered into the darkness.

Her mother hated Snow Crystal. She hadn't been back since the day she'd walked out, taking Jess with her. She hated everything about the place. She hated the snow, the mountains and, most of all, she hated Tyler O'Neil.

She wouldn't have his name mentioned in the house so Jess made scrapbooks and kept them hidden under her mattress. Ever since she'd been old enough to know what to do with a stick of glue, she'd kept pictures of her dad. Her grandmother and great-grandmother had cut out pictures for her, and at Christmas when she'd come to stay, they'd stick them in a new book together. She had photos of him skiing the most famous and prestigious downhill runs on the World Cup circuit. She knew their names and all the details. As well as the Hahnenkamm there was the Lauberhorn in Switzerland, the longest downhill of them all and a real test of stamina—the list went on, and the one thing those runs had in common was that her dad had skied them all. And if that hadn't made her want to burst with pride, there were the two gold medals he'd won at the Olympics and the World Cup title.

She'd boasted about him in school once, but most of the kids hadn't believed Tyler O'Neil was her father.

She knew her mom wished he wasn't.

Her mom could have married him, but instead she'd chosen Steve Connor, because Steve had wanted to be a lawyer and could give them a better life than a guy whose only ambition in life was to get from the top of a mountain to the bottom faster than any person alive.

Once or twice, Jess had tried explaining how much skill that took, but her mother hadn't wanted to hear it. Skiing wasn't a "proper" job and Tyler O'Neil wasn't a suitable father figure.

The past year had been hell, not that she'd shared that detail with anyone.

She might have told her grandmother, but she knew she was still hurting, and Jess figured if her dad could break a leg and then get up and ski to the bottom of the run on the one leg that still worked, she could cope with the shit her family had thrown at her without falling apart.

The truth was, she was never going to be the daughter her mother wanted her to be.

Janet Carpenter had done everything she could to knock the O'Neil out of Jess. She'd dragged her to piano lessons, extra French, debating, dancing—

All Jess wanted to do was ski as fast as humanly possible.

The final straw had been when she'd skateboarded down the stairs in the house and almost broken her stepfather's leg.

"You're just like your father," her mother had screamed, and Jess had hugged the words tightly because they were the best words her mother had ever spoken to her.

She *wanted* to be just like her father.

She was her father's daughter and always had been, and that drove her mother mad.

And now the baby had arrived, her half sister, a squalling tiny being with a wrinkled face and a shock of hair, and her mother was too absorbed by this second chance at parenthood to waste time molding a child who was all the wrong shape and always had been.

Jess had heard her on the phone that night, yelling at Tyler.

"She's your daughter, so you can have her. I can't cope with her anymore."

And so Jess had been shipped off to Snow Crystal for Christmas, just as she always was, the only difference being that this time she wouldn't be flying home at the end of the holidays.

She was here for good.

It had come to her in a cold moment of realization that no one wanted her. Not her mother, not her stepfather, not even Tyler. She'd been forced on him.

In her dreamier, more optimistic moments, she'd imagined them spending time together, but so far all they'd done was ski on groomed, safe slopes. Jess was bored out of her mind, and he had to be bored, too.

He obviously didn't think she was good enough to ski anything else, and she couldn't prove him wrong because he'd virtually grounded her.

He didn't want her here.

Shivering, she hugged Luna closer, warming herself on soft fur and unlimited doggy affection.

She was a burden, cramping his style, ruining his carefree life.

Maybe if she could prove to him she could ski the way he did, he'd be pleased to have her around. Maybe then, he'd think she was cool.

Maybe then, everything would stop hurting.

Kissing Luna on the head, she slid off the window

seat. She dug her scrapbooks out from under the mattress, pushed the photograph of her baby sister inside her favorite, then picked up her pen and wrote *Jess O'Neil* on the cover in curly writing.

KAYLA HAD EXPECTED something in keeping with the rustic setting. A place a family could gather after a day of skiing and fun in the snow to exchange stories of daring exploits and slopes conquered. She hadn't expected elegance, but the Inn at Snow Crystal was definitely elegant. Candles and fresh flowers adorned the center of tables dressed with pristine white tablecloths. A large fire flickered in one corner of the restaurant adding a cozy, intimate feel.

She'd chosen to wear her favorite black dress. It had frequently taken her from a day in the office straight out to a dinner meeting with clients.

And that was what this was, she reminded herself. Dinner with a client. It didn't matter that their table faced the illuminated ski slopes and was perfect for a romantic, intimate dinner.

"Thanks, Tally." Jackson took the menu from the waitress. "How are things in the kitchen now?"

"All fine, sir." Tally's gaze slid from his, but not before Kayla had seen anxiety.

Jackson saw it, too. "Tally?" His voice was gentle, and Tally cast a desperate look over her shoulder just as a crash came from behind closed doors.

Calm and controlled, Jackson rose to his feet. "It seems I need to visit the kitchen before we eat."

Before he could take a step across the restaurant the kitchen door opened and a burly man dressed in chef's whites blundered out.

"That's it." He ripped off his chef's hat and thrust it

at Jackson. "I'm done being told what to do by a woman half my age and height. Either she goes or I go, O'Neil. Your decision."

Tally stood there, frozen with dismay, and Jackson smiled at her. "Thanks, Tally. We're going to need some time with the menu. We'll call you when we're ready."

The waitress shot him a grateful look and shot off, relieved to be out of the line of fire, while Jackson squared up to the furious chef.

"This is not the time or the place for this conversation." He spoke in a low voice that couldn't be overheard by the other diners. "Be in my office at nine tomorrow. We'll talk then. And now I'd like you to return to the kitchen. We're full tonight and I can't be a chef down."

"You should have thought of that before you hired that French bitch."

Jackson's expression didn't flicker. "You'll call her Élise, or Chef. And if you want to be on the team at Snow Crystal, you'll work with her."

"I won't work with her. One of us has to leave."

"If that's your decision, then of course you must go. I won't stop you."

Darren's face worked in fury. "Wait a minute—you want *me* to leave?"

"I have no use for people who won't work as a team."

The chef blustered for a moment and then stabbed a finger into Jackson's chest. "Your grandfather hired me. He never had any complaints."

"I'm not my grandfather." Those blue eyes were ice-cold, that same mouth that could deliver a smile both sexy and wicked, hard-set and grim. "Go. Now." His tone made Kayla wish she'd escaped along with Tally, and apparently Darren felt the same way because the bluster left him in a rush. He deflated like a balloon popped at a child's party.

"I'll reconsider if you'll talk to her."

"You threatened to walk out in the middle of service. I accept your resignation." The softness of his voice was a contrast to the flint in his eyes, and Darren's expression was wild.

"No one can reasonably expect me to work with that woman! Do you know what she said to me? She told me to get out of her kitchen because male chauvinist pig wasn't on the menu."

Kayla kept her head down and focused on her phone. She mustn't smile. There was nothing to smile about.

Jackson's chef was about to walk out and the restaurant was fully booked.

Darren was still blustering. "If you fire her, I'll reconsider."

"Élise has a job and a home here for as long as she wants." Something in the way he said it caught Kayla's attention, leaving her with the feeling that there was more behind his words, but Jackson was already walking the man to the door and she could no longer hear the conversation.

When he returned, she could sense anger simmering beneath the calm. "You're going to have to excuse me for a moment while I go and talk to my remaining chef."

At that moment a young woman with short dark hair emerged from the kitchen. She walked with the energy and grace of a dancer, head held high, eyes gleaming.

Assuming this to be Élise, Kayla braced herself for another explosion, but instead, the woman approached a young couple dining at one of the tables by the window. "You wanted to see me, *non?* You enjoyed my langoustines." She spoke with only a trace of a French accent, her movements fine and delicate as she used her hands to illustrate her speech. "You will come back again and I will cook you my pot-au-feu. It is perfect for this cold weather. When you 'ave tasted it you will never want to eat anything else." She beamed at the dazzled couple and then virtually danced across the restaurant to where Jackson and Kayla were sitting.

"Jack—" She softened the *j,* turning it into the French *Jacques,* and he rose to his feet, controlled and professional.

"Élise. Darren won't be coming back."

"Vraiment?" Something that looked suspiciously like happiness brightened her eyes. "He has decided he can no longer work with 'that French bitch'?"

Jackson had clearly decided to be economical with the truth. "I'm going to try to get you some help in the kitchen for tonight."

"There is no need. The French bitch can manage perfectly, thank you. You just sit down and enjoy your meal with your beautiful friend." She beamed at Kayla, but Jackson wasn't smiling.

"You can't manage on your own, Élise. We're full tonight."

"And each person will enjoy the best meal they 'ave ever eaten. I can 'andle it. I will promote Jeff for the night. He is excellent *chef de partie.* He will be excellent *sous-chef.* I 'ave—*have*—" her cheeks dimpled as she corrected herself "—taught him to swear in French so the customers aren't offended."

Kayla gave a choked laugh, and Élise looked at her with that bright, direct gaze. "You have ordered your food?"

Jackson picked up a menu, but Élise leaned across and removed it from his hand.

"I will decide. If you want to help me, you could find me one more kitchen assistant. Someone willing, with a good work ethic and strong, because a chef spends long hours on their feet." She eyed his shoulders and her eyes sparkled. "You are strong. If you are bored being the boss, I can find a use for you." Without giving them time to respond, she walked back through to the kitchen with that same lithe, catlike stride that made Kayla wonder if she'd had ballet training.

"I like the 'French bitch.'" She reached for the water that had been discreetly placed on their table while Élise was talking. "Where did you find her?"

"In Paris. She was cooking in a tiny restaurant on the Left Bank." He hesitated, as if about to add something, but then smiled. "Luckily for me it didn't work out for her so I gave her a job. She cooked for me in one of my hotels in Switzerland and then joined me here six months ago. She's a genius in the kitchen and very professional. You might not guess it, but she was upset tonight. You can always tell how upset Élise is by how French she sounds. In the right mood, her accent is virtually undetectable." He reached for his glass. "Bringing her in was the right thing to do, but it's shaken up a few people."

"I don't see you as a man who would have a problem shaking people up if there was a purpose to it."

His gaze held hers. "Then you'd be right."

Even in this moment of tension, the chemistry was still there.

She felt it, pulsing between them, and she knew he did, too.

"Darren didn't look too pleased."

"His ego is bigger than his talent. And he and Élise don't share the same vision for the restaurant. His objective is to feed people. Hers is to serve a meal you will always remember. That's what I want for this place." He sounded sure. "I want people going back to New York, or Boston or wherever it is they've come from and I want them talking about the Inn at Snow Crystal. I want them planning their next visit and sending their friends."

Kayla watched him across the table, thinking that he was as comfortable in these elegant surroundings as he was in the wild outdoors.

He'd chosen to wear a jacket and tie but those outward trappings of sophistication did nothing to disguise the strength and power of those shoulders. Did nothing to detract from that raw masculinity that was part of him.

"Will your grandfather be upset about losing Darren?"

"Probably. He wants me to go back to Switzerland and stop meddling." He seemed relaxed, but she knew he had to be feeling the pressure. The future of this place, the future of his family, rested on his shoulders.

She wondered how he coped with it. Just one meeting with Walter had been enough to send her running. The fact that the reasons for that had been personal didn't change the fact that Walter had been difficult, abrasive and combative.

It didn't make sense to her. "Without you, Snow Crystal would definitely go under. Surely he's pleased you're back to help."

"He's not pleased."

"Why? It isn't as if you're inexperienced. You have an impressive track record. I would have thought he would have been relieved to hand it all over to you."

He stared into his glass and then gave a humorless

laugh. "I guess to understand that, you have to understand what this place means to my grandfather. His
father, my great-grandfather, built Snow Crystal. Met
my great-grandmother on a ski slope, and they decided
that was what they wanted to do. And it was a tough
life. They built it from nothing. Walter was born right
here, in the house. Lived here all his life."

"Which should mean he wants to protect it."

"I guess it's hard to hand something over that means
as much as this place means to him. He wants it to stay
as it was. He resents the changes I make."

"But you're here anyway."

"They need me."

And that, she thought, said everything about him. He
was a man who believed in family, and stuck by them
even when things were difficult.

Something tightened in the pit of her stomach.
"There's no way he can argue that what you've done
here isn't a good thing." Glancing to her right, she saw
elegance, polished silver and a room full of happy diners.

"I expect he credits Darren." Jackson picked up his
wineglass. "If you hear an explosion tomorrow, it won't
be avalanche blasting. And I am going to have to find
more staff for the kitchen because, no matter what Élise
says, she can't manage the holiday season on her own."

Kayla thought about Elizabeth, trying to fill the gap
in her life with cooking. "Could your mother help? She
obviously loves feeding people."

Jackson lowered his glass. "That," he said slowly,
"is a great idea."

"Maybe she wouldn't like working with Élise."

"She loves Élise. They talk recipes all the time. Élise
is always popping over there to sample whatever my

mother has in the oven. And you're right—feeding people keeps her happy. Cooking relaxes her, which is why
your idea is such a good one. She needs something new
to focus on. I'll talk to them both tomorrow." He sat
back as lobster ravioli was placed in front of them, and
Kayla noticed how much attention Tally paid Jackson.

"Some people are pleased you're here." She waited
until the girl had walked away to make the observa-
tion, and Jackson smiled.

"That will be the people who are terrified of Walter. And maybe the people who can do basic math and
understand that this place needs paying guests." He
played it down but Kayla had already seen enough to
know the staff worshipped Jackson. She suspected it
wasn't just because he was the one standing between
them and unemployment.

She picked up her fork and looked at her plate. "This
looks amazing."

"Élise insists on using as many fresh, local ingredients as possible, and she changes the menu on the fly
depending on what's available." He waited while she
took a mouthful. "Is it good?"

"It's sublime—" She closed her eyes as flavor ex-
ploded on her tongue, and when she opened them again
he was watching her, lids half-lowered in a way that
took her right back to that moment in the forest.

"Jackson—"

"You must eat out all the time in New York." His
voice was level and steady, as if they hadn't just generated enough heat to light the candle in the center of
the table without the use of a naked flame.

Kayla relaxed slightly. If he could ignore it then she
could ignore it, too.

"I'm usually paying attention to the client, not the

food." She took another mouthful, wondering why this felt more like a date than a dinner meeting. "So Élise is your star?"

"Not my only star. We're building up a good team here. Brenna is awesome. Not just a talented skier, but a gifted teacher. She's a PSIA level 3 coach."

"PSIA?"

"Professional Ski Instructors of America. Level 3 is the most advanced qualification. Brenna grew up here, but she spent four years working with me in Switzerland and another two in Jackson Hole, so she's an experienced and gifted teacher. She can teach anything from a three-year-old who can't stand on skis to a teenager who wants to ski deep powder. Now Tyler is back, he is going to help her. Were your earrings a gift from a lover?"

The shift from professional to personal gave her whiplash. "I bought them for myself when I got my last promotion."

"A woman who buys diamonds for herself." He reached for his wine. "I wonder what that says about her."

"It says she knows what she wants and doesn't wait around for someone else to buy it for her."

"You got something against a man buying you gifts, Kayla?"

"Not in principle." She stabbed her fork into another delicious mouthful. "But in practice a man buying a woman gifts usually means they're in some sort of relationship, and I don't do relationships."

"*Relationship* is a broad term. Covers a lot of possibilities."

"Mmm—" she chewed "—and I'm equally bad at all of them. How is your langoustine?"

"Delicious. What makes you think you're bad?"

"Evidence and experience. Why are we talking about this and not Snow Crystal?"

"Because for five minutes of my life I'd like to think about something other than Snow Crystal."

She realized how utterly all-consuming it must be, trying to haul this place back from the edge, especially with Walter standing in his way.

"You have a difficult task. Which makes what you've accomplished all the more admirable." She glanced sideways. "Not a single empty table."

"Élise will be having a nervous breakdown."

Kayla thought of the fire she'd sensed in the other girl. "One person's nervous breakdown is another's opportunity. It's exciting. I think she'll fly." By the time she'd cleared her plate, she was sure of it. "That was incredible. What you've created here—" She tapped her fingers on the table, thinking. "You need a different strategy for the restaurant than you do for the rest of Snow Crystal." When he raised his eyebrows, she continued. "The Inn should have its own identity."

He leaned back, listening. "Go on."

She outlined her thoughts, relieved to focus on work because the alternative was focusing on him. When she paused to gauge his reaction he was watching her with those dangerous blue eyes that drew her in.

Her mind blanked.

The people around her faded.

She forgot the restaurant and the other diners. Forgot everyone except him. And still he looked at her until her heart kicked her chest like the hooves of a wild horse trying to escape captivity.

The silence was agonizing. The tension, torture.

And she knew he felt it, too, because when he spoke his voice was thickened and rough.

"When you're passionate about something, your whole face lights up. I love that. I love your energy and drive."

Her hands were shaking, so she put down her wine-glass. "I'm passionate about making this work for you."

"Why?"

It shouldn't have been a difficult question to answer. He was a client. But those weren't the words on her lips. "Because I can see how much it matters. I can see what you have riding on it." Forcing herself to focus, she outlined more suggestions, checked her hands weren't still shaking and reached for her phone so that she could make some notes. "What do you think?"

"What I think," he said slowly, "is that no matter what the situation or the conversation, you always bring it back to work."

"Work is the reason I'm here. I think we need to make dining here as personal an experience as possible. Maybe Élise could give away some kitchen secrets, offer recipes that diners can re-create at home. We can post photos of the food and maybe the occasional one of the chefs at work." She was talking too fast and too much.

She knew it.

He knew it.

He leaned forward, still watching her. "What happens if you don't talk about work?"

"You're paying me to talk about work."

"Your light was on at 2:00 a.m. and you were up again at five. Why don't you sleep, Kayla?"

The knowledge that he could see her cabin from his

barn gave her a jolt. "If you saw that, you must have been awake, too."

"I was working on budgets and forecasts. Not my favorite occupation for two in the morning. And now I want to forget about work."

She didn't want to forget about work. It was vitally important to her that she didn't forget about work or she'd start thinking about him and the chemistry. And that kiss. *Oh, God, that kiss.*

He was a client and she wasn't used to blurring the lines.

"Tell me about growing up at Snow Crystal."

"I'd rather talk about you."

"I'm boring."

"Most people who work hard, play hard." He sat back as Tally removed their plates. "You don't seem to be one of those."

"I have fun doing what I do. My clients are beneficiaries of that."

"I can think of at least ten minutes earlier today when you weren't thinking about work."

That moment had been simmering between them all day.

"What happened earlier was a mistake, Jackson."

"You think so?" His gaze flicked to hers. "Generally I know when I'm making a mistake. Coming back here sometimes feels like one. Working at 2:00 a.m. always feels like one. Kissing you, didn't."

Desperate, she latched on to the one part of the conversation that wasn't personal. "Why does it feel like a mistake to have come back?"

"I'm not going to let you do that. I'm not going to let you shift this conversation." His gaze was locked on hers. He didn't look away. Not even when Tally delivered the main course to the table—rack of lamb served with baby vegetables and crushed herbed potatoes. "Tell me why you were willing to work over Christmas."

"You heard Brett—I feast on difficult. Except right now I'd rather be feasting on this. Élise is a fabulous chef." Kayla focused on the food on her plate, wondering why being close to him made her nervous. "I'm not going to be able to move tomorrow."

"Tomorrow I'm giving you a ski lesson. You will have sweated off the calories by lunchtime. So you don't see your folks during the holidays?"

He wasn't going to let it drop.

Kayla put her fork down, leaving her food untouched. "What was it you said today in the forest? Something about preferring it straight? I'm going to give it to you straight, Jackson. This may come as a shock given that your home seems to be a sanctuary for decorations and a breeding colony for gingerbread Santas, but not everyone is addicted to Christmas. Some of us don't like the holidays too much. In fact—" she hesitated and then decided it was time to be honest "—I hate it. It's my least favorite time of year. I was willing to work over Christmas because it seemed like the perfect escape. Does that answer your question?"

CHAPTER NINE

IT DIDN'T BEGIN to answer his question, but that was probably because he had a bunch of them.

"You came here to escape Christmas?"

"I thought it might be easier." She picked up her knife and fork and sliced through the lamb. "I thought I had more chance of avoiding festivities here than I did there. You promised me a secluded log cabin. It sounded appealing."

"And then you found out my family makes a big fuss of Christmas."

"Mmm." She chewed. "That came as a bit of a shock, but I'm over it now."

"Why do you hate this time of year?"

"It's frustrating trying to get anything done. Publications run on a skeleton staff, opportunities for coverage go down, people in the office walk round wearing ridiculous bits of tinsel in their hair—"

"That tells me why Christmas is inconvenient. It doesn't tell me why you hate it."

A few seconds passed.

"It just isn't a happy time of year for me." She said it quietly and he felt something tug inside him.

In the flickering candlelight he could see the thickness of her lashes and the smooth curve of her cheek. In her black dress, she looked younger. More vulnerable. Less like the killer PR expert and more like a woman.

And he knew, deep in his gut, that there was some much deeper, darker reason for her dislike of Christmas than the inconvenience of the holiday season.

He remembered how pale she'd looked decorating the Christmas tree. She'd seemed as fragile as the frosted silver decoration she'd held in her hand.

"I'll try to make sure you're not subjected to too much Christmas during your stay."

"Oh—" she smiled, back to being her detached, professional self "—it's really not that much of a big deal."

It was obviously a huge deal. He heard it in her voice and saw it in the way she held herself.

"So let me give you some tips about skiing tomorrow—" He steered the conversation in a different direction, entertained her with stories about skiing exploits when he and his brothers were growing up and saw the tension gradually ease out of her shoulders.

By the time they reached dessert—a delicate trio of French patisseries that would have shattered anyone's resolution to forgo dessert—she was even laughing.

And she was still laughing as he drove her back to her cabin, regaling her with stories about Tyler.

"Seriously? He did that? It's a wonder he wasn't killed." Smiling, she pushed open the gate. She'd pulled on her snow boots in his car, and she walked confidently now, but he noticed that when he took her hand she didn't pull away.

The moon sent a ripple of silvery light over the snow-covered trees and she stood for a moment and breathed.

"It *is* beautiful here. Like being in our own world. The land of Snow Crystal."

"Occupied by aliens," he said drily, and she laughed.

"Occupied by brave fighters who refuse to be defeated by the big bad economy."

The smile stayed on her face all the way to the cabin. It stayed in place until she glanced into her glass-fronted living room and saw the enormous Christmas tree twinkling with lights and silver stars.

"Oh." Her tone was flat. "Who put that there?"

Jackson held his breath to prevent himself venting every swearword in his vocabulary.

"I'm guessing it was Alice."

"Your eighty-year-old grandmother dragged a six-foot tree through the forest? That's impressive."

"I heard her talking this afternoon when she came back from her shopping trip. She thought you were upset because you weren't home for Christmas." And his mother had tried to talk her out of it, he remembered. Somehow, his mother had known Kayla wouldn't want one. "She must have had Tyler help her or something. Hell, Kayla, I can—"

"No." She turned, her smile as fake as the spray snow they used on the windows of the village store. "She was being thoughtful and I don't want to offend her. I've done more than enough of that. It's fine. It's just a tree."

But he could see it was so much more than a tree. It was a reminder of a time of year she hated, and it had killed their brief moment of camaraderie.

The laughter, the humor, the connection—it had all gone. She'd pulled herself back, like a turtle retreating inside the protection of its shell.

"Kayla, if you don't like Christmas then you don't want to be walking around that damn thing each time you go to the kitchen. I can—"

"I'll just tune it out." She was already walking up the steps, pulling away from him physically and mentally. "I won't even notice it's there when I'm working."

Jackson wanted to ask how the hell she planned on tuning out something that was almost the size of the Empire State Building, but she had the door open and was giving him that fixed, formal smile she'd perfected. "Thank you for a lovely evening. I'll get to work on that proposal."

"JESS?" TYLER THUMPED his fist on the door and wondered whether this whole parenting thing would have been easier if he'd had Jess living with him all her life. At least he would have had more practice. "Open this goddamn door right now or I swear to God I'll break it down and I'll be patching up the wood with those skis of yours."

That threat received the same lack of response as the others he'd thrown at her.

Ash and Luna whined as they watched him from the top of the stairs.

"What?" He glared at the dogs. "If you know something, for fuck's sake tell me."

He'd started patient. Then patience had given way to manipulation. Turned out he wasn't above bribery— hell, he'd tried everything from promises of hot chocolate to new skis, but he still couldn't get the girl to open the door.

She'd been locked in there all afternoon, since he'd arrived back from guiding that group of powder hounds. He'd nipped out for an hour to cut down and deliver the tree to Jackson's woman from New York on his grandmother's instructions, and when he'd arrived back Jess had still been in her room.

Tyler planted his hand on the door frame and cursed. "Jess? If something is wrong, just give it to me straight. I can read the weather, I can read the snow, but I sure as hell haven't ever been able to read a woman's mind, so cut me some slack, will you?"

Still no answer.

Irritation mingled in with unease.

There was no sound from inside the room. Nothing.

In his experience a quiet woman was a dangerous woman.

Turning the air blue and trying not to think how much extra work this move was going to cost him, Tyler raised his leg and kicked the door hard with his boot.

It flew open and Ash barked loudly, bounding forward to investigate the source of the drama.

The room was empty except for a pile of scrapbooks on the bed.

Wasn't she too old for scrapbooks?

He flipped one open and saw a picture of himself standing on the podium receiving a medal.

"Shit." He sank onto the bed and carried on turning the pages until he realized that what he was looking at was basically a chronicle of his life.

Jess had kept a record of his entire skiing career. And there, in the front of the book, were two words written in a childish scrawl.

My dad.

His throat felt scratchy and raw.

He'd thought she didn't want to be here. He'd thought Janet had poisoned her against him, but the contents of those scrapbooks said otherwise.

He was about to close it when he saw the photograph of the baby.

And he saw something else.

Jess O'Neil.

Not Carpenter. O'Neil.

Unease turned to panic. "Jess? Where are you, sweetheart?" Closing the scrapbooks, he glanced around him, searching for clues. He yanked open doors, wondering if she were hiding. "If this is some sort of game, I'm not close to laughing so just—" He shivered as cold air brushed his skin and saw what he hadn't immediately seen when he'd walked into the room.

The window was open.

And Jess was gone.

KAYLA LAY CURLED up on the shelf, staring into the forest, watching the snow glisten in the light of the moon. She decided if there was anything lonelier than being on your own at Christmas, it was being on your own while surrounded by a big happy family.

For the O'Neils, it was clearly the highlight of the year. A time to get together and celebrate being a family.

Unable to sleep, she dragged on the luxurious robe that had been left for her use and went downstairs.

There, staring at her, was the enormous fir tree.

"If I thought I could lift you, I'd throw you back where you came from," she muttered, turning her back on it and opening her laptop.

At least her plan for Snow Crystal was coming together nicely. She'd even managed to speak to Brett and outline her ideas.

And she'd closed the door on Jackson, instead of inviting him in. It had taken willpower she didn't know she possessed, but somehow she'd maintained distance.

And she'd carry on maintaining that distance. She'd—

A hammering on the door made her jump and she turned to find Jackson standing by the door, gesturing for her to open up.

Her heart accelerated.

She knew he wasn't a guy who was used to hearing no, but she hadn't expected him to show up here hours after she'd already wished him good-night.

Wishing she were dressed, she walked to the door, but one look at his face told her this wasn't a social call.

"Jess is missing." His expression was grim and serious. "Climbed out of her bedroom window. Didn't leave a note. No clues. Her phone is still on her bed. Tyler is losing his mind. It's fifteen-below out there and she's just a kid. We're gathering together a group to look for her."

"Give me five minutes to get dressed."

She did it in two and was back by the door stamping her feet into her boots while Jackson finished up a conversation with someone called Josh.

"Yeah, right—" Still on the phone, he passed Kayla gloves and a hat and walked to the door. "We'll do that. And if we see anything, we'll call you. I don't want my mother involved yet. Or Walter. His heart isn't good. And don't let anyone contact Janet Carpenter, either. No way does she get to do more damage to my brother." He hung up and Kayla followed him through the door.

"Who was that?"

"Josh. He's chief of police and a member of the mountain rescue team. He's going to put the team on alert, but I'm hoping we won't need them."

"Could she have gone home?"

"To Chicago? Not at this time of night." He drove fast down the snow-covered track and pulled up outside a house that overlooked the lake.

The kitchen was full of people, most of whom she didn't recognize, and Brenna and Tyler were in mid-argument.

"So because I'm trying to be a responsible parent

this is somehow all my fault?" White-faced, Tyler paced the kitchen while Brenna spread her hands in exasperation.

"All I'm saying is that you don't listen to what she wants. You just say no, Tyler. You're making it too easy for her to rebel against you."

"I'm doing my fucking best!" Tyler rounded on her. "She wanted to throw herself off the top of a vertical cliff. You think I should have said yes to that?"

"*You* did it."

"I skied anything with a gradient, including old Mitch Sommerville's garage roof. I loved skiing. Speed. It had nothing to do with teenage rebellion."

"This isn't helping." Jackson strode between the two of them. "We need to work out what might have been going on in Jess's head."

"Good luck with that. I've been trying to work that out for the past twelve years, and I've gotten nowhere." Beside himself with worry, Tyler tugged on his jacket. "I'm done with standing around talking. I prefer action."

Jackson caught his shoulder. "Not without a plan."

"My plan," Tyler said grimly, "is to find my daughter. Finally she's back living with me, and I intend to keep it that way. The rest of you can stand around talking about teenage rebellion if that's how you want to spend the time."

It must have been so hard for him, Kayla thought, trying to bond with a young girl he only saw sporadically. But there was no doubting how much he cared.

As far as she was concerned, that was the most important quality in a parent.

"Maybe it isn't rebellion." She hadn't intended to speak. Her heart was pounding so hard she could feel it against her rib cage. "Maybe she's pushing you. Testing you."

Tyler looked at her, noticing her for the first time. "What are you talking about? You don't even know Jess. You met her for about ten seconds the other night."

He was right, of course. She didn't know Jess. Kayla wished she'd kept her mouth shut, but it was too late because Jackson was frowning at her.

"Testing what? What do you mean?"

"Nothing." Kayla backed off. "You're right. I don't know Jess."

"Why do you think she could have been testing him, Kayla?"

Everyone was staring at her. Even Tyler, his gaze so fierce it was as if he suspected she'd taken Jess and buried her body.

Kayla licked her lips. "I'm just thinking that maybe this thing with her mother has shaken her up. Maybe she's looking for proof that you love her."

Silence spread across the room.

Tyler swore fluently. "You think I don't love her? Have you any idea how hard I fought to have my daughter living with me?"

Kayla tensed. "I wasn't suggesting—"

"It sure sounded as if—"

"That's enough." Jackson's tone was hard. "There's logic in what Kayla says. Think about it, Tyler. Janet calls up and tells you she can't handle Jess anymore, and suddenly the kid is coming to live with you. No warning. Nothing. Your life is turned upside down."

"There's nothing wrong with my life!"

"Put yourself in Jess's shoes and think how that must have made her feel."

Kayla stood, frozen in silence. She had a pretty good idea how it had made Jess feel.

She'd felt it all herself.

Tension rippled across Tyler's wide, powerful shoulders. "I want her here. I'm not saying it's easy. I'm not even pretending I'm any good at it—we're both still finding our way, but that doesn't mean I'm not glad she's here."

"Have you told her that?" Kayla's mouth was so dry she could hardly form the words. "Because maybe she needs to hear it."

"That's good advice," Brenna murmured. "Maybe Jess is worried you don't want her here. That she's cramping your style. I hadn't thought of that."

"So what does that mean? You think she's run away?" Tyler's face was white with worry. "I've never once said I don't want her here. If that's what's in her head then it was put there by someone else."

Kayla wondered if that "someone else" was Jess's mother. She wondered whether Jess had overheard something. It wouldn't be the first time that had happened to a child torn between two parents.

Why does she have to stay with us at Christmas? Can't she go to her father?

She tried to push back the memories, reminding herself this wasn't about her. It was about Jess.

"We can deal with that part later." Taking control, Jackson strode to the door. "Let's start by searching the resort. Ask people if they've seen her. Brenna— you and Tyler take the trail by the cabins. Kayla and I will go to the far side of the lake."

Brenna reached for her keys. "Have you checked whether her skis have gone?"

Tyler threw her a look. "It's dark, Einstein."

"Not everywhere. The bowl is illuminated." Jackson stopped dead. "So is Devil's Gully."

Tyler's face lost the last of its color and Kayla glanced between them.

"What's the significance of Devil's Gully?" She'd heard Jackson mention it, but wanted to know why they all looked so worried.

"It's a double diamond black. A thousand feet of vertical drop, sections of it have a forty-degree pitch. About the same angle as the ramp of an Olympic ski jump." Brenna zipped her jacket to the neck. "Runs right under the chairlift. You want to make a fool of yourself with an audience, you're going to pick that one."

Tyler ran his hand over the back of his neck. "Or if you want to ski something challenging once it's dark. She asked me if we could do it together."

Brenna looked at him. "And?"

Tyler was white-faced. "I said no."

JESS STOOD ON the top of Devil's Gully staring at the re-flection of lights on the snow.

It was steep. And it looked worse with the dark all around and no people. There were still people skiing on the easier runs that led to the village, but this run was hard-core. Punishingly difficult. She remembered Gramps and her father talking about it.

Fall on that one and you'll fall all the way to the bottom.

For a stomach-lurching moment she wondered if she'd made a mistake. It had seemed like the perfect way to prove herself, but it seemed different with the dark pressing in on her and the eerie silence. And what was the point of proving herself when there was no one here to see it?

Her teeth chattered, and she wished she were back in her bedroom, looking at her scrapbooks.

"No different in the dark than in daylight." Tyler's voice came from behind her. "Either way it's still a hell of a drop."

He'd come looking for her.

Jess felt her heart lift and then plummet.

All that proved was that she was a responsibility he didn't need.

She felt something burn in her throat. Great. Here she was, proving how tough she was, and she was about to cry like a baby. "It's easy."

"It's not easy. It's for experts." Tyler stabbed his poles into the snow and reached across to fasten her helmet. "Good job you're one of those."

It took a moment for the words to sink in, and when they did, the stinging in her throat turned to a lump.

"You're not going to make me go down on the lift?"

"You can go down on the lift if you like. No shame in that. Tell people I forced you if it makes it easier." Tyler adjusted his boots. "Or we can ski this bastard and see how that turns out."

"Ski it?" Jess stared at him. Tyler O'Neil, skiing legend. The man they called The Bullet because he reached such incredible speeds in the downhill. *Her dad.* "You mean—together?"

"Sure I mean together. You wouldn't leave me to ski this on my own, would you?" Tyler stooped and checked the bindings on her skis. "You want to go first or follow?"

Jess tried to work out which would make him love her more and decided she didn't want to die just when she'd finally got her dream to live with him.

"I guess you could go first."

"Right. So count to five and then follow me. I'll meet you at the bottom. Then we'll get Grams to make us hot chocolate. How does that sound?"

It sounded good. Better than good.

"I want to ski like you." She blurted the words out, unable to stop herself. "That's all I've ever wanted to do. I want to make you proud of me. I don't want to hold you back."

Tyler's eyes glittered as he looked at the steep gradient that lay beneath their feet. "Does it look like you're holding me back?"

"I might slow you down."

"Are we still talking about the skiing here?" His voice rough, he reached out and zipped her jacket to the neck. "Because if we're talking about other things, I'd rather you said it straight-out. I'm not good at digging for meaning behind what people are saying. If a man's got something to say, I prefer he just says it. That goes for women, too, by the way. Not that I've ever met one that does it, except maybe Brenna, and she doesn't count."

"Having me here must be difficult for you."

One minute she was standing there drowning in her own insecurities, the next she was being hugged by her dad, and he held her so tightly it was the best feeling in the world.

"Having you here is easy. Having you here is the best thing that's happened for a long time." His voice was thickened. "*Not* having you here was difficult for me. Maybe we should talk about that sometime when we're not both about to get frostbite."

The burn in her throat was back, but this time it was mingled with relief and a happiness she hadn't known existed.

Not having you here was difficult for me.

"I won't be a nuisance—" The words were muffled by his jacket. "I won't stop you doing anything or hold you back. You can just live your life and ignore the fact I'm here. I'm okay with that. Whatever rules you make I'll stick to them, I promise. Just don't send me to boarding school."

"Boarding school? Who the hell ever mentioned boarding school?"

"Mom. She said that's where I'd go when you'd had enough of living with me." She felt his arms tighten around her.

"That's not going to happen, Jess. I'll live my life, that's true enough, but that life's got you in it now. You'll go to school in the village like the three of us did, and as for rules, I've only got the one—" Tyler gave her a squeeze and then released her and glided smoothly to the top of the slope. "Next time you're planning on locking your bedroom door and sneaking out the window, tell me where you're going so I can come, too. Now let's nail this. And if you fall, don't take me with you."

CHAPTER TEN

KAYLA LAY ON her face, inhaling snow for what felt like the fortieth time that morning, and heard a whooshing sound as Jackson arrived by her side.

"That was better."

Better?

She lifted her head. Spat out snow. "Which bit was better? The bit where I turned into a windmill or the bit where I hit the ground with my face?"

He hauled her to her feet in an easy movement. "Your weight was wrong. You leaned back. It's a natural response to a slope but you have to have the weight forward in your boot. Want to try again?"

"Why not? I think there might be a centimeter of my body that isn't bruised, and if I'm going to be black-and-blue I'd prefer to be black-and-blue all over. I like a uniform look. Matching black eyes is bang on trend, haven't you heard?"

He wasn't even bothering to hide the smile. "You need to trust your skis."

"I only met them a few hours ago. I never trust anyone on such a short acquaintance."

"Your ski is designed to turn." He skied down ahead of her and then paused and called up to her. "Try it again."

She tried not to think about the fact he made it look

easy. "Fine, but make sure you send Brett the bill for medical expenses."

"If you break anything, my brother Sean will fix you for free."

Baring her teeth at him in a mock smile, Kayla let her skis run across the slope and then transferred her weight as he'd taught her.

"Put pressure on the big toe edge." The instruction came from in front of her, and she realized that Jackson was skiing backward.

"Has anyone ever told you you're a flash bastard, Jackson O'Neil?"

The cold nipped at her cheeks. Her skis ran smoothly over the snow. In that fleeting moment, Kayla realized she was enjoying herself.

"Okay, this is fun—" The moment she said it her ski hit a bump and she lost her balance and would have crashed down again, but this time Jackson caught her. He locked his arm around her waist and steadied them both as she slammed into him.

Breathless, Kayla clung to the front of his jacket, wondering why it was that so many activities ended up with her cemented to his body. "Don't drop me."

"I won't drop you, but if you could stop digging your nails into my arm that would be good." He spoke through his teeth. "If it's not your stilettos, it's your nails."

She looked at him and saw his eyes darken.

"No," he said thickly. "Not here. I need to concentrate or we'll end up at the bottom of the mountain."

"I thought that was the objective."

"Yeah, but in your case it's best if it takes longer than twenty seconds." He eased away from her, but still held her steady.

"How old were you when you first skied down this run. Tell me honestly."

"Three."

"You're kidding."

"I was a late starter. Tyler was two. I still remember my father yelling at him 'Turn, turn' and Tyler whizzing straight down like an arrow from a bow, yelling back, 'Why?' He just didn't see the point of turning when he could go straight down."

Kayla laughed. "Is that true?"

"Yeah, it's true. Along with a million other stories that would make your hair stand on end."

"No wonder Jess thinks he's a hero. It must be cool having him as a dad." But coolest of all was having a dad who loved his daughter as deeply as Tyler clearly loved Jess.

She thought back to the way Tyler had handled the situation the night before.

Once they'd received confirmation from the lift attendant—a lift attendant who had been too overawed to challenge the daughter of a medal-winning downhill skier—Tyler had sent everyone home except Brenna, who had stayed at the base of the lift in case Jess had started the run before Tyler could reach her.

Jackson lifted his hand and brushed snow off her shoulder. "It was good of you to help us."

"I didn't do anything."

"You made us all see it from Jess's point of view." His voice was rough. "You were right that she was worried he wouldn't want her here. It didn't take him long to put her right on that score."

Kayla felt something squeeze her chest.

This time, it had just been a misunderstanding. A lack of communication.

"Looks like it's going to be a happy Christmas in the O'Neil household."

"Seems that way." He didn't release her. "So how come you know so much about the feelings of teenagers, Kayla? How old were you when your parents divorced?"

"Thirteen."

"That must have been tough."

She'd never talked about it with anyone. "It was hard at the time, but I guess it made me stronger. More independent. Life events shape us, don't they?" Except in her case she'd ended up misshapen.

She stood still, feeling the cold biting into her cheeks and the solid power of his body between her and the fall of the mountain. "Should I give up? I'm not sure I have an aptitude for skiing."

"The thing about skiing is that, even if you don't progress much past beginner status, you're still out in the fresh air, looking at those mountains and getting some exercise with it."

"So you're not big on the gym then?"

"I'll use the gym when I have to, usually for weights. I spot Tyler a couple of times a week. He does the same for me. But as for cardio—" he shrugged "—I've never been one for running without a purpose. Why would I when I have this on my doorstep? There are plenty of other ways to get the heart pumping." The glitter in his eyes made her heart pound, and she turned her head and focused on the mountains.

"I admit it's beautiful. I even admit that for thirty whole seconds back there when I was upright, skiing felt like fun. But the rest of the time I'm face-planting in the snow and that doesn't feel so good."

"Keep practicing and you'll face-plant less. Are you always this impatient when you're learning something new?"

"Yes. If I'm not good at something immediately, I'd rather do something else."

His eyes were on her mouth. "You got any ideas about what that something else might be? Because I might have some suggestions."

She felt the chemistry flare, live and dangerous, and this time it wouldn't be controlled. "Jackson—"

"Yeah, I know." His voice was husky and hot. "Public and all that. Getting naked on the slopes is still frowned on. Not to mention giving a person hypothermia." His phone beeped, and he dug the edges of his skis into the snow and reached into his pocket and checked his messages. "Another Christmas tree order. A family would like one by this evening in order to continue a family tradition of putting presents around it."

"Can't they buy it from a supermarket?"

"They could, but a tree freshly cut from the forest is the fairy tale—that's as long as they're not the ones cutting it." There was wry humor in his eyes. "Come with me after lunch and you can be part of that fairy tale."

"I've never been a believer in fairy tales."

"That's good to hear, because chopping down the tree and hauling it back through the forest when the weather is minus double digits certainly doesn't count as one. But it's all part of the fantasy. All part of a Snow Crystal Christmas."

"In that case, I should be there."

She told herself if there were one thing guaranteed to kill her libido stone-dead, it would be choosing a Christmas tree for another family.

HE TOOK HER deep into the forest.

The trail was hard-packed and well maintained, and he stopped the snowmobile at the end of a narrow track. Then he helped her fit snowshoes to her boots and they walked the rest of the way, making tracks through fresh snow. Trees reached high above them like tall, white-cloaked sentries.

The frozen air bit through clothing and sank its teeth into skin.

She shivered. "It's cold."

"Wicked cold. Typical Vermont winter. There are folks who spend most of it indoors. There are days when I don't blame them. Are you warm enough?" He put his arm around her and pulled her close. For once she didn't resist.

"Just toasty." Her teeth were chattering. "Never been warmer."

"Did you buy any of that thermal underwear Alice mentioned?"

"Are you asking me about my underwear?" The look she sent him sent lust slamming into him.

"Just looking out for your welfare. Don't want to send you back to Brett frozen like the ice pack."

"As long as I'm still able to work, Brett wouldn't care."

"Doesn't that bother you?"

"Why would it bother me? He employs me to do a job for him. It's perfectly reasonable of him to expect me to do that job."

Jackson decided not to point out that it was also reasonable to care about the welfare of your employees. "You like him?"

"I respect him." She peered at some tracks that disappeared into the trees.

"Squirrel." He answered her question before she asked it. "There are lots of them here. Sometimes you see snowshoe hare, although not so much in this part of the forest. Tell me more about Brett."

"What do you want to know? Innovation is one of the fastest-growing PR firms in the U.S. and a lot of that is down to him. He's driven. Focused. Can be visionary and inspirational at times. Drives you mad at others."

"So you're planning on staying with them for a while?"

"Yes. I only came over this summer and I'm enjoying the work. I'll do a couple of years. Then I suppose I'll move on."

"Move on to what?"

She shrugged. "Different company. It's what I do."

"Ever wanted to do anything else?"

"Like what?"

"If you're going to work that hard, you could start your own company."

"I've thought about it. I suppose most people do at some point or another. You did."

"That's right. I did."

"It must have felt good—creating something from the ground up. What made you decide to do that and not just work here?"

"Mixture of things." He hauled her out of range as a branch deposited its mantle of snow on the ground. "Ambition. Curiosity. Ideas. I had so many ideas I didn't know what to do with them all. There was no space for them here." *Still wasn't.* "Frustration."

"And rebellion? A desire to show Walter and your father that anything they could do you could do better?"

"Yeah, there was that, too." He acknowledged it and felt the guilt kick. "I should have come back sooner.

Should have asked more questions. My father hated it, you know."

"Snow Crystal?"

"Not the place. The business. He felt the business stopped him from enjoying the place. He resented the time it took to run it when he could have just been ripping up the slopes."

"So why didn't he do something else?"

Jackson had asked himself the same question repeatedly. "Only son. I suppose people just assumed he'd go into the family business. But he spent almost all his time skiing." Pain punched him beneath the ribs. "He was in New Zealand when he crashed the car. You could ask what he was doing in New Zealand when this place was in so much trouble, but that was my dad. He went where the snow was. I got the call in the middle of the night and flew back as soon as I could. Arrived back in time to collect his body from the airport." He felt her hand curl into his and squeeze.

"I'm sorry."

"It was tough. Still is, particularly on my mother. But the cooking was an inspired idea. Just the prospect of it has lifted her mood."

"I'm pleased." She tilted her head and looked at the trees. "It's so beautiful here." She was wearing the hat he'd given her, but beneath it her hair was loose. He noticed she'd stopped pinning it up. Sleek and smooth had given way to soft waves.

"You're only a couple of miles from The Long Trail, the oldest hiking trail in the U.S. It follows the main ridge of the Green Mountains from the Massachusetts-Vermont line all the way to Canada."

"I've always lived in cities. The nearest I got to hiking was walking through Hyde Park in London and

Central Park in New York. This is—" She breathed deeply and gasped as the cold air tickled her lungs. "This feels like a snowy wilderness."

"Not exactly wilderness. Backcountry." Jackson stopped. "I know you're not a lover of Christmas trees, but does that one look all right to you?"

She followed his gaze. "Looks fine to me."

He cut it down, secured it to the sledge and then dragged it home, taking each turn carefully as they followed the trail back to the resort.

A large SUV was parked outside the cabin and several sleds and boots lay abandoned by the entrance.

Jackson untied the tree and dragged it to the door. Then he picked up the chain saw, shaped the trunk and pushed it into a stand.

"Is that ours?" A young girl stood on the doorstep, watching as Jackson and Kayla hefted the tree up the steps.

"Yes. Do you like it?" He rested the tree and glanced at Kayla. Snow and pine needles clung to her hair and her cheeks were rosy from the cold. In his opinion she looked a million times better than she had in her office in New York.

"I love it." The little girl stared at it in wonder just as the door opened and a young woman appeared, a toddler in her arms.

"Sophie, what— Oh—" She paused, enchanted. "It's like a fairy tale tree."

Jackson caught Kayla's eye. Saw her turn her head away to hide the smile, because it was exactly as he'd predicted. That smile made him want to get the job over and done with as fast as possible.

Dinner, he thought. Only this time not at the Inn, but in his barn. In his large, custom-built kitchen with its views of the lake, and cooked not by Élise, but by himself. It was time to finally use those shiny pans.

And this time they wouldn't be talking about work.

He took the weight of the tree. "I'll bring it in for you."

"Thanks—" Smiling, the woman held the cabin door wide and called over her shoulder. "Todd? Come and see this tree. Better still, come and help carry it."

Jackson tried not to squash Kayla between the tree and the door but in the process ended up with his thigh jammed against hers.

"We'll have it in the living room. Sophie—move the Lego so Mr. O'Neil doesn't tread on it." Baby on her hip, the woman commanded operations, and Jackson dumped the tree and extracted himself from clinging branches.

"You need to keep it watered."

Sophie stared at the tree, eyes wide. "We have decorations."

"Sounds good." Jackson checked the tree was secure. "Well, I'll just be—"

"Stay for a drink." The woman smiled at him. "Todd just opened champagne. It's one of our traditions the night we get the tree."

"I'll take Charlie." The girl held out her arms for her brother. "See that, Charlie? Your present is going underneath it. And mine. Only four more sleeps until Santa comes."

Jackson was about to ask what she wanted Santa to bring when he caught sight of Kayla's face.

The healthy pink in her cheeks had faded and her skin was as white as the snow that clung to the branches.

Too late, he remembered she hated Christmas—and this whole damn place shrieked Christmas.

Damn.

He'd been ticking another job off his list. He hadn't thought about the implications for Kayla.

As Todd came through the door bearing champagne, she moved to the door. "I have to get back to work. Enjoy your tree and have a happy Christmas."

Jackson stepped toward her. "Kayla—"

But she was gone, out through the door, as light-footed as one of the white-tailed deer that sometimes ventured close to Snow Crystal.

He wanted to follow her, but a glass of champagne was thrust into his hand and Todd raised his glass.

"To the charms of Snow Crystal. The best-kept secret on earth."

Hoping that it wouldn't be a secret for much longer, Jackson drank. By the time he extracted himself from the festive glow radiating from the Waterman family, there was no sign of Kayla.

"ARE YOU SURE about this?" Alice watched as Elizabeth picked up Maple's bowl and rug. "What are you going to tell her?"

"The truth. That I need to go and help Élise in the kitchen and can't leave Maple alone for that long."

"I could watch her."

"You have your book group."

"I haven't even read the book. The print was too small and the first page was depressing. I only go for the cake." Alice studied her daughter-in-law over the top of her glasses. "You could give Maple to Jackson."

"I'm giving her to Kayla."

"She doesn't seem like a dog person to me." Alice unraveled a ball of yarn. "Doesn't know what to do with the puppy. Steps over the animal like a pair of shoes left on the floor. Did you see the way she stroked her? Vertical pats."

"She's not used to dogs. She'll work it out and working it out will be good for her. It's only for a few hours."

"You're interfering."

"Yes. Have you seen Maple's toy?" Elizabeth crawled under the table and retrieved the toy bone while Maple wagged her tail happily. "There. You are just what Kayla needs."

"Jackson may not agree when the animal does her business on his hardwood floors."

"She's not going to do that." Elizabeth scooped Maple up and kissed her. "Tonight you need to be extra cute. I've never seen anyone as lonely as that poor girl, and you're the family member designated to sort it out."

Alice looked at her. "Jackson could do that."

"He's next on my list."

CHAPTER ELEVEN

KAYLA SAT ON the sofa in her robe, an untouched bowl of popcorn on the floor and Maple curled by her feet.

When Elizabeth had arrived at the door and asked her to keep the puppy for a few hours, she'd been horrified, but Jackson's mother had been so excited at the prospect of helping Élise in the kitchen that Kayla hadn't been able to find a way of saying no.

"I don't know anything about dogs."

"All she wants is company. Wish me luck! Élise can be terrifying when she's cooking." Buzzing with excitement, Elizabeth had thrust a few things into her arms and hurried back down the path with a wave, leaving Kayla with Maple and no idea what to do.

She and the puppy had stared at one another and then Maple had settled down on the rug in front of the fire and Kayla had got on with her evening while keeping a cautious eye on the dog.

She'd taken a long, indulgent shower, rinsed away pine needles and bits of the forest that clung to her. Other things hadn't proved so easy to shift, like her mood. She'd stepped out of the shower lost in thought and almost slipped when she'd felt Maple licking her wet toes.

And now she was on the sofa staring gloomily at the puppy.

"I don't know why you're looking so pleased. I'm

lousy company. You couldn't have picked a worse place to spend a few hours."

Maple rolled onto her back hopefully, and Kayla shook her head.

"I'm not a tactile person. I'm sure someone better qualified will rub your tummy later."

Huge brown eyes stared at her mournfully.

"Oh, for—" She bent down and rubbed the puppy's tummy gingerly, her fingers tangling with fur the color of coffee and whipped cream. "Don't tell anyone how pathetic I am, will you? I'd be fired on the spot." Tears jammed her throat and she felt a flash of horror and then remembered the only witness was the dog. For once, she didn't have to hold it back.

"Honestly, it's just one day of the year. And it always makes me feel this way. It seems as though you're the only person in the world on your own." She'd never felt lonelier in her life.

A tear fell and landed on the puppy.

Maple whimpered, rolled onto her front and stood up.

"Sit." She managed to say the word through her clogged throat. "Sit. Oh, for—" The puppy sprang onto her lap and Kayla pressed herself into the sofa. "Down. *Down!*"

Maple ignored her and wagged her tail.

The dog felt warm. Solid.

"Honestly, I'm fine—" Kayla kept her hands in the air. "I've never been that big on hugs and— Oh—" The puppy snuggled down. "Right. I suppose you can stay there as long as you don't pee on me. And if you tell them I cried, our relationship is over." Slowly, gingerly, she lowered her hands to the puppy. The fur under her fingers was soft and springy, the eyes looking at her a warm caramel-brown.

Tears fell, slowly and steadily like the snow outside the window. "I never cry. This is your fault. You shouldn't be so cute."

She wished her phone would ring, but for once it was silent, and she knew it was because the people back in the office would be caught up in pre-Christmas madness.

So—" She continued to stroke the puppy. "I can't work with you sitting there so I suppose this is the perfect time to watch a movie. I hope you like horror because that's all I brought with me."

She pressed the remote control and started watching the movie she'd set up earlier while Maple dozed in her lap.

The cabin was in darkness. The only light came from the moon reflecting off the snow and the flicker of the television as she listlessly watched the story unfold.

She was lost in the dark and the horror when she heard a noise.

Her screams mingled with those of the woman on the screen, and Maple sprang from her lap barking. Kayla leaped after her, spilling popcorn.

"Shit—sorry, cover your ears, Maple—"

The door to the cabin opened abruptly. "Kayla?" It was Jackson, concern in his voice as he strode across to her, his feet scrunching on popcorn. Maple was leaping and barking. "Why are you screaming? What the hell has happened? Maple, sit. Sit!"

Maple ignored him.

"*You* happened—for God's sake, Jackson—" she put her palm to her chest, feeling her heart pounding

"—you scared me half to death and you scared the puppy. I thought you were a-a—"

"A what? All I did was knock on the door—" His gaze slid to the TV and his eyebrows rose. "Seems to me you were scaring yourself to death. *The Shining?* That makes perfect sense. An acknowledged feel-good Christmas movie. I guess you're going to follow that with *The Texas Chain Saw Massacre.* Every fir tree's nightmare."

Hand pressed to her chest, she forced herself to breathe. "I was just in the mood for it, that's all." Stooping, she scooped a shivering Maple into her arms and snuggled her close. "Shh. It's all right. It's just Jackson, arriving with his chain saw. Nothing to be scared about."

"I might have to disagree with that." He picked up the DVD box. "You were in the mood for Ultimate Horror? That must be one hell of a mood you've got going on there."

"It was my Christmas gift to myself. At this time of year the only thing that's showing on TV is movies with the word *miracle* in the title." Her legs still wobbly, she sank back onto the sofa. "Sorry. I didn't realize you wanted a meeting."

His gaze drifted to her robe. "Not a meeting. I came to pick up Maple. Thought I'd bring you something to eat at the same time."

Her heart rate finally slowed. For the first time she noticed the large box by the door. "Pizza?"

"Fully loaded, cooked fresh by Élise, who usually considers pizza beneath her, so you are now among the favored few. I was going to invite you to my barn for the evening but after you vanished I decided I'd bring dinner to you."

"It was kind of her—of you—" she hugged Maple closer "—but I'm not dressed."

"You have to be dressed to eat pizza? That's a new one on me."

"All right then, I'm not hungry." Her voice rose. "If you don't mind, I'd really appreciate an evening by myself. But—you can leave Maple." She was shocked by how much she didn't want him to take the puppy.

In usual Jackson style, he didn't budge. "Why do you want an evening by yourself? So you can cry on your own?"

"Don't be ridiculous." Panic flickered at the edges of her composure. "I've had a shower and washed off my makeup. The light in here is just—"

"You've been crying, Kayla. What I'd like to know is why. Is it because of that damn family and their Christmas tree? Or something else?"

"I'll drop Maple round to your mother in the morning." Putting Maple down on the rug, she walked toward the door, assuming Jackson would follow.

He didn't.

Jackson O'Neil was about as easy to manipulate as a solid lump of rock.

He strolled across the room and sat down on the sofa. Stretched out those long, muscular legs as if he was settling in for a long evening of entertainment. If he felt at all awkward that he might be intruding, it didn't show.

Kayla felt a rush of frustration. "Jackson—"

"I'm not leaving."

"But—"

"I'm partial to the occasional horror movie myself, although I generally prefer psychological thrillers to all that blood and guts and chopping that goes on in some films. So—" he tickled Maple with his toes "—are you going to tell me why you were crying or am I going to have to torture you to get your confession?"

Irritation mingled with something much, much more dangerous. "I found out Santa doesn't exist."

"He exists. I know it for sure because his reindeer left a hell of a mess on one of the trails last year. He also knocked a piece out of one of the chimneys. I blame my mother for leaving out too many cinnamon stars. By the time the guy had eaten them he was too fat to get back on his sleigh. Come and sit down and bring the pizza with you. We'll finish the movie together."

"I'm not in the mood for company."

"Too bad, because I am. I'm nervous." He was all power and strength. The least nervous-looking individual she'd ever encountered. "And given that you're responsible, the least you can do is make that right."

"I make you nervous?" She was willing to bet this man had never been nervous of anything in his life.

"You scared me with all that screaming—I need time to get my courage back before I walk home. I can't be alone right now."

"Yeah, right—" she eyed the muscles of his shoulders "—because you're so fragile, obviously."

"I'm scared of the dark, terrified of loose popcorn and frightened out of my wits by screaming women. Either you put some lights on right now or you're going to have to hold my hand." He rose to his feet and she took a step backward wishing, not for the first time, that Jackson O'Neil wasn't so damn sure of himself.

But he didn't approach her. Instead he scooped up Maple and the blanket and carried the puppy through to the bedroom, leaving the door slightly ajar while Kayla watched in bemusement.

"What are you doing?"

"She's too young to witness what we're about to do."

"We're not about to do anything." Her heart was pounding harder than when he'd emerged from the darkness. "This is *not* a good idea."

"I think it's the best idea either one of us has had in a long time."

"You should go home, Jackson."

"What I should do and what I often choose to do aren't the same thing. Ask any one of the teachers I had growing up." He was standing right in front of her now—lean, athletic and powerful.

She stared at the blue-black stubble that shadowed his jaw. And that proved to be a mistake because she just wanted to reach out and run her fingers over it. And she wanted to stand on tiptoe and press her face to his, feel that male roughness scrape the sensitive flesh of her cheek.

"You should go before we both do something stupid." Her voice came out like a croak, and the corners of his mouth flickered into a smile.

"Go ahead. Do something stupid."

Everything he said flustered her, and she wasn't used to feeling flustered.

"I'd be using you," she blurted out, "to fill this one night because I'm lonely. Do you really want to be used?"

"Hell, yes." His laugh was deep and sexy. "How soon can you start?"

"You're a client."

"I don't hear either of us talking about work right now." His hand slid behind her head and into her hair, and his eyes were suddenly gentle. "So you're lonely, Kayla Green?"

There was a long, pulsing silence.

"Yes." It was a simple truth, but a truth she never admitted.

"Because it's Christmas?"

"No. But it's worse at Christmas. There's nothing quite like being surrounded by family groups to remind a person they have no one. Not even someone to argue with or be irritated with."

"I know people who will be happy to irritate the hell out of you. Anytime you want to spend time with them, just say the word." His fingers were in her hair. His mouth close to hers. The gentleness had gone. His tone was rough and his eyes dark, the sexual chemistry so intense she couldn't breathe. It pulled at her, melted low in her belly and fired her nerve endings.

"This would be a mistake." She locked her hand in the front of his sweater, and his arm came around her waist.

"Mistakes are what make us human." He spoke the words against her lips and then he was kissing her, his mouth hard and hungry, and she kissed him right back because he was all she wanted and needed. There was nothing in her head except this moment, and she slid her hands under his sweater, moaned as she felt the warmth of his skin and the ripple of male muscle under her palms.

"You feel good—" Frustrated by the barrier created by his clothing, she tugged, pulled, and he broke the kiss long enough to yank the sweater over his head along with the T-shirt he was wearing under it. They both staggered but he locked her against him again, and she slid her hands over his shoulders, feeling the hard swell and dip of muscle. "You've lifted a lot of logs in your time."

"All part of the job." With rough, impatient hands

he parted her robe and inhaled. "If I'd known that was what you were wearing underneath there's no way our conversation would have lasted as long as it did."

She licked at his lips. "I'm not wearing anything."

"That's what I mean. Hell, Kayla—" With a groan, he backed her against the wall, trapping her between the smooth wood of the cabin and the hard heat of his body. And now, finally, she could see him properly. See the contours of those powerful shoulders, the dark curling hair that shadowed his chest, the swell of his biceps and the strength of his forearms as he pinned her there.

For a few indulgent seconds they just looked at each other.

She was breathing rapidly and so was he, his eyes so dark they no longer seemed blue.

"What happened to your underwear?" His voice was thickened and rough, loaded with the same tension that held her breathless.

"It got wet in the forest when that tree shook itself on me."

The corner of his mouth flickered and he lifted his hand to her cheek. "You make me smile, Kayla Green."

Her heart was pounding. "You make me smile, too."

He lowered his head fractionally, just enough to drive her crazy with anticipation, and the feeling terrified her because she couldn't ever remember feeling this way before.

Out of control.

He stroked her cheek with his thumb. "Have I told you you're beautiful?"

"No." Her fingers bit into the warmth of his shoulder. "Are you going to kiss me again or am I going to have to force you?"

His smile was slow and sure. "Just taking my time."

"How much time?" She could hardly breathe. "I need to know whether to take control or not."

"You're in a hurry?" His voice was rough and deliciously male. "Is there someplace you need to be?"

"No—" Her breathing hitched as she felt his hand on the base of her spine. "I'm just a person who likes to get things done."

"I never would have guessed that about you. You always seem so laid-back and calm." His hand was inside her robe and she felt the warmth of his palm on her bare skin, felt his hand linger on the dip of her waist and then lower to the curve of her hip. And his touch drove her crazy because she wanted this so badly—wanted to feel his hands on her, his mouth on her—and he was making her wait until she thought the waiting might drive her out of her mind.

She ached as she'd never ached before, and when his fingers closed on her thigh, she slid her leg around him, locking them together. She could feel him, thick and hard, his erection contained by the fabric of his jeans.

"You're wearing too much—" Her fingers searched for the snap of his jeans and she heard him suck in breath. Seconds later he was as naked as she was. Her hand closed around the pulsing thickness of his shaft and she heard the rhythm of his breathing change.

"Jesus Christ—"

The tension was incredible. All the more so because it had been slowly building since their first meeting.

She rose on her toes, her mouth a breath away from his. "You want to wait? Because if you do that's fine by—"

Their mouths clashed, sensation shot through her and after that there was no holding back. There was no slow. No steady. No careful. One word came into her head.

Wild.

He took her mouth with raw hunger, and she was the same—demanding, desperate as she felt the possessive bite of his fingers in her hair.

Without lifting his mouth from hers, he pushed the robe from her shoulders, leaving her naked. Cool air swept across her skin, but she was pressed against the heat of him. Flesh against flesh. Female against male. Fire against flame. It licked at her, driving her higher until she felt nothing like herself, nothing like she'd ever felt before. He held her locked there, trapped against the powerful ridge of his erection while they kissed, taking his time with her until the heat was so intense she thought she'd explode. She arched against him, pressing into that hardness, and finally he lifted his mouth, but only to explore another part of her—her cheek, her jaw, the base of her throat. She felt the scrape of stubble against the sensitive flesh of her breast and then gasped as he sucked her nipple into the warmth of his mouth.

"Jackson—" A gasp became a moan as he toyed with her, building arousal with every skilled, leisurely flick of his tongue. Heat pooled in her pelvis. She squirmed against him, feeling male hardness press against the most sensitive part of her, and just when she thought she couldn't stand it any longer, he scooped her up and the next minute she was lying on the soft rug in front of the log fire, pinned down by the weight of his powerful body.

He grabbed the remote and switched off the TV. The only light in the cabin came from the fire and the silvery glow of moonlight reflecting off snow.

Looking into those blue eyes, her tummy flipped and tumbled. She saw heat. Intent. And something else she didn't recognize. Nerves fluttered low in her belly along with other sensations more intense than anything she'd felt before. They danced across her skin and melted into her, pouring through her veins and weakening her limbs until she was relieved to be lying down.

Should she warn him again that she was no good at this?

What exactly were his expectations?

But he made his expectations perfectly clear as he eased away from her and kissed his way down her body, his tongue tracing a sensual line that made her shiver in delicious anticipation. He slid his hand under one of her thighs, bending her knee and giving himself access. Her naked body was warmed by firelight and lit by moonlight, but she had no time to think about being self-conscious because already he was parting her, his mouth on her slick heat, his tongue tracing sensitive flesh with knowing skill.

Kayla moaned and tried to move, but he held her fast, one strong hand locked on her hip to prevent the restless shift of her body, the other filling her with delicious pressure as he took what he wanted. And what he wanted was her and he used his warm clever mouth until she felt the first flickers of response. So did he because he withdrew immediately, eyes glittering as he eased away from her.

"Jackson—"

"I want to be inside you. When you come, I want to feel it. All of it. All of *you*."

The intensity of it, the desperation, was alien to her. Dimly, through the haze of almost-painful arousal, she felt a flicker of panic.

"This is just sex, Jackson." She struggled to form a coherent sentence. "Tell me you know it's just sex."

"Stop talking—" He cupped her face in his hands

and took her mouth in a hot, hungry kiss, the skilled slide of his tongue an erotic prelude of things to come. And she kissed him back, felt her thoughts fade to the edges of her mind but held herself together long enough to plant her hand firmly on his chest. He paused, eased his mouth away from hers with obvious difficulty.

"Are you— Is that no?"

"No." Her voice was as husky as his. "I mean—it's not no." She could see he was fighting for control. The muscles in his shoulders were pumped up and hard, his jaw tense as they struggled to have a lucid conversation when all both of them wanted to do was finish what they'd started.

"Kayla—"

"I may not believe in Santa, but I believe in safe sex."

Silence pressed between them.

His gaze held hers for a moment and then he cursed softly under his breath. "Yeah— I—" Shaking his head to clear it, he pulled away from her and reached for the clothes he'd discarded.

The sense of loss shocked her.

She felt a sick thud of disappointment, followed by a desperate desire to drag him back to her. And then she realized he wasn't getting dressed. Instead he was digging something out of the pocket of his jeans.

Seeing the condom in his hand, Kayla gave a laugh that was a mixture of nerves and relief. "Did that come with the pizza?"

"It came with me."

"You—why?"

"I thought if you got fed up eating pizza and talking about work, we could cement Anglo-U.S. relations." His mouth was back on her neck, his tongue on her skin, tasting. "How do you think we're doing?"

She didn't know whether to be shocked or laugh with relief. "I think this is going to be a hell of an alliance."

"I agree." He came down on top of her, all sleek male muscle and coiled strength. She dug her fingers in his shoulders, felt the hard thrust of him against her and wrapped her legs around him, drawing him closer. She should have been cold, naked in the middle of this wintery scene, but she was hot, hotter than she'd ever been in her life as she lay in front of the warmth of the fire pressed against the heat of his skin. The need simmered inside her, strong, powerful and right, and she raised her hips as he surged into her, matching his low growl with a soft cry of pleasure as each hard, velvet thrust took him deeper. Her body tightened around him and for a moment it felt like too much—the pressure, *the intimacy*—and she wondered if he guessed because he lowered his mouth to hers, kissing her, slowly and deeply, until she felt nothing except the need for this, for *him*.

Perhaps he'd intended it to be slow, but it didn't end up that way. They were both too desperate, the hunger too ferocious. His hand was locked in her hair, his mouth on hers as they moved together in a rhythm that was both wild and primitive. She felt flushed, feverish, bathed in a heat that had nothing to do with the flickering flames of the log fire, and with each thrust of his body she climbed higher and higher until everything inside her tightened and she balanced on that dangerous edge, held there by his skill and her own desperate need not to lose control. But she did, of course, because he drove her right over that edge, and she fell, tumbling, the contractions of her body gripping the length of his shaft, taking him with her. He groaned deep in his throat, a thickened sound, and then he was kissing her again, and he kept kissing her right through it so that they didn't just feel it, they breathed it and tasted it.

And as the storm faded, reality seeped back into her brain.

Her surroundings, which had faded from her consciousness, came back into view, and for the first time she registered that they were both naked and surrounded by floor-to-ceiling glass.

But outside there was nothing but the white silence of the watching forest, the trees the only witness to their uncontrolled passion. It was like lying in a glade on the forest floor, bathed in wintery silvery light with just the red glow of the flickering fire to warm them.

It was the most perfect moment of her life and she remembered Elizabeth's words.

It sweeps you away and robs you of breath, and you know that no matter what happens in the future, this is a moment you're going to remember forever. It's always going to be there, living inside you, and no one can take it away.

She knew this was one of those moments. But she also knew, better than anyone, that perfect moments didn't last. And the more perfect the moment, the harder it was to deal with the emptiness that came after.

Remembering that, she tried to ease away from him, but he rolled onto his back and covered them both with the soft throw from the sofa, his arm locked around her in a possessive grip.

"Are you warm enough?"

"Yes—" But inside she was cold, because she wasn't used to feeling this.

They lay in silence, watching flakes of snow float lazily past the windows, coating the trees in a luminous cloak of dazzling white.

"Have you always hated Christmas?"

She could have lied. She could have just kept their relationship physical, but she knew they were already past that, and it terrified her because if there was ever a man who was completely wrong for her it was Jackson. Jackson with his big, loving family and his unshakable strength and values. He was a man who deserved the truth. She couldn't give him anything else, but she could give him that.

"No. Once, I loved Christmas. It was my favorite time of year." She spoke softly, as if her voice might somehow disturb the wonderful peace of the forest. "My dad traveled a lot with his job, but he always made sure he was home for the holidays. I looked forward to it. Like most families, we had our rituals."

His arms tightened. "Such as?"

"We went to the forest to choose a tree, then we decorated it together...." She remembered the family earlier. Remembering their delight and excitement brought back memories both sharp and sad. "My dad would hold the box of decorations and I would hang them and he would do the branches at the top that I couldn't reach."

She lay tense, unable to relax. "On Christmas Eve I hung out my stocking. I was always too excited to sleep. Not because of the presents, although I always loved those, too, but because we were together. No work calls. No business travel. Family time. That was our Christmas every year until I was thirteen." Pulling away from him, she sat up and looped her arms around her knees, staring at the fire.

"What happened?"

"It seemed like a typical Christmas. There was no suggestion it would be anything different. I came downstairs that morning and found my parents at the breakfast table drinking coffee. Nothing odd about that. They told me to open my stocking. Bright voices, no clues. *Open your stocking, Kayla. See what Santa has brought you.* Not that I believed in Santa, of course, but it was another of our rituals. We used to leave a carrot for his reindeer. My dad even put teeth marks in it. When I was four I believed it, and as I grew older it became one of our family jokes." Her breathing was shallow, and she heard him curse softly and then felt the warmth of the throw on her bare skin as he wrapped it around her shoulders and pulled her back down into his arms. He held her like that, tight and close, until her heart rate slowed and his warmth became hers. It was a whole new kind of intimacy.

Outside, it had started to snow heavily, the flakes falling thickly, drifting past the glass as if the sky was crying in sympathy. The memories gnawed at her insides and chafed against her skin.

"They waited until the last present was opened. Until I was surrounded by wrapping paper and Christmas happiness and then—" she paused, breathed "—then Dad told me we weren't going to live together anymore. That we weren't going to be a family. And he stood up and left. He had another woman and he wanted to spend Christmas Day with her."

There was silence.

Jackson didn't speak, didn't ask questions, but his hold on her tightened.

"My mother knew about it. In the mess that followed she spilled the fact that they'd married because she was pregnant, and both sets of parents had insisted on it. They'd struggled through until he met someone else and couldn't play the game anymore." Her head was on his chest, her cheek pressed against warm flesh and hard male muscle. "I've heard people talk about how it was when their parents divorced. How there were rows and broken china. One girl I worked with actually said she breathed a sigh of relief when her parents separated, because it was like living in a war zone. For me it was nothing like that. My parents never argued. I thought it was because we were happy, but in reality it was because they were seeing other people. They'd made a deal to stay together because of me. One moment things seemed perfect and the next it was all gone. No rows. No broken china. The only thing broken was me."

He stirred and moved his hand down her back, gentle and protective. "You're not broken, sweetheart. You're strong and whole."

"You're thinking that this stuff happens all the time. That it is another sad tale of a marriage that didn't last. But he didn't just have another woman." She spoke softly. "He had a family. Twin daughters. His 'travels' weren't travels. He was living with her for most of the week. He went to them that day, as soon as I'd opened my stocking. It was surreal. There was the tree and the stack of presents. From the outside it looked like a normal Christmas. But my dad was gone."

"He had another family?" His tone hardened. "What sort of a coward does that?"

"I ran away that night. Pathetic, I know, but I felt as if they didn't care so what did it matter. I suppose I was hoping they'd come after me, realize how upset I was and get back together. I was thirteen and desperate. That was when I realized happy endings didn't happen."

"Where did you go?"

"I sat in Trafalgar Square. I'd forgotten my coat and had no money. Luckily a policeman saw me and took me to the station. Gave me hot chocolate and a blanket and held me while I cried. Then phoned my parents. My dad had already gone, of course, so it was my mum who came to pick me up. She was furious with me." She slid her fingers over his chest. "After that, I went off the rails a bit. She couldn't handle me so they sent me off to boarding school. To begin with I went home for the holidays, but Dad's new wife didn't want a teenager around. The way she saw it, she'd shared my dad for too long already. Dad felt guilty when he looked at me and my mother was dating again and doing all the things she'd apparently missed out on when she gave up her life to have me. Christmas became a time of guilt and duty on their part and agonizing discomfort on mine. My stepmother had waited years to have Dad all to herself. She wanted a dreamy Christmas with her new family and the legacy of my father's mistake didn't fit into that. I was the outsider."

Still holding her, Jackson swore softly. "Walter used that word the other evening. That's why you were upset."

"It was part of it. That word presses a button for me. And he was right—I am the outsider. It's my specialty."

"Kayla—"

"I actually prefer it that way. I run my own life. I'm happy. I'm proud of who I am and I like what I have. The only time I find it hard is at Christmas. At Christmas it's like standing outside a party you're not invited to, knowing that everyone else is inside having fun." She eased away from him and lay on her back, staring up at the soaring ceiling. "There's something about this time of year that makes your emotions sharper. You feel as if everyone else has someone, even though you know that isn't true."

"You never see your mother?"

"She moved to New Zealand."

"You don't visit?"

"I went once, a few years ago. Hard to say which one of us found the experience most painful. I'm just a reminder of a part of her life she'd rather forget. And my father just sees me and feels guilt." She turned her head to look at him and gave a crooked smile. "I know how to kill a romantic atmosphere, don't I?"

"We're naked in front of a fire and it's snowing outside." His voice rough, he hauled her back against him, holding her tightly. "You can't kill that."

She was silent for a moment, knowing what she'd told him had changed things.

There was the intimacy of sharing their bodies and then there was the intimacy of sharing inner secrets. That one was new to her, and she wasn't sure how she felt about it.

"Should we check on Maple?"

"She's asleep. She uses so much energy during the day she crashes out at night. She won't wake until morning."

"But she's in the bedroom."

His fingers were in her hair. "There's another bed."

He was planning on staying the night?

She never spent the whole night with a man, but he was already on his feet and tugging her upright.

Kayla felt a flutter of panic. "What are you doing?"

He cupped her face and kissed her. "It's time someone gave you some new Christmas memories."

CHAPTER TWELVE

HE WOKE IN the cold darkness of the early morning to find the bed empty.

It didn't feel right.

What would have felt right after a night filled with the best sex of his life would have been to wake up next to the woman he'd shared it with. Preferably with both of them still naked.

Unfortunately the woman in question obviously felt differently.

He wasn't surprised.

What surprised him was how much he minded.

Cursing softly, Jackson reached for his watch and checked the time.

Seven a.m. Where the hell could she have gone at 7:00 a.m?

"Kayla?" He called her name but he already knew the cabin was empty. And the fact that there was no answering bark told him she'd taken Maple. Which meant she'd gone over to the house.

His mother probably wasn't even awake yet.

Rubbing his hand over his face to clear the fog of less than four hours sleep, Jackson leaned back against the pillows.

She could have woken him so that he could walk with her. The fact she hadn't told him all he needed to know about the way she viewed their relationship.

She'd already pushed it into the history books.

He wondered how she'd react when she discovered he had no intention of stopping at one night.

Jackson smiled.

He wondered if she realized she hadn't once checked her emails.

CAREFULLY SUPPORTING THE bundle tucked inside her coat, Kayla tapped on the front door of the house.

Just one night, she told herself. *Nothing to panic about.* Other people did it all the time and then got on with their lives. It didn't mean anything. It wasn't a threat to who she was or what she wanted.

So why the knot in her stomach?

The door opened and Elizabeth stood there, her smile welcoming. "I got your text. You didn't need to bring her back. I could have come and collected her later, dear."

The endearment made her chest feel tight. She wasn't used to hearing it.

Yet another reason to stay away from Jackson. It wasn't just the man who was a threat, it was his whole family.

"I felt like the walk." Actually she'd felt like running. As fast as she could from the man lying in her bed. This woman's son. "Did I wake you?"

"I wake early."

Someone else who couldn't sleep, Kayla thought. "I'll bring her blanket over later and I couldn't find her toy. It might be under the sofa."

"I didn't realize she'd spent the whole night with you. I thought Jackson was picking her up."

"She seemed settled with me." Kayla gently extracted Maple, who squirmed with excitement and licked her face.

"I hope she wasn't too much trouble."

Kayla handed over the puppy, surprised by how much she wanted to keep her and relieved Maple couldn't talk because she was the only witness to what had happened the night before.

"She slept."

"When she's out, nothing will wake her." Elizabeth stood to one side. "Come on in out of the cold. We're all in the kitchen."

"All?"

"Brenna and Élise are here. Élise is making pancakes, although she calls them crepes or something French. All I know is that they taste good, but that girl can't make anything that doesn't taste good."

Kayla hesitated. She should have said no, but the alternative was going back to the cabin where Jackson was still asleep.

"I should work—"

"Brenna's just made a fresh pot of coffee."

The word *coffee* decided it. Kayla stepped inside and was once again enveloped by the welcoming warmth of the house. The delicious smell of coffee mingled with cinnamon and freshly baked rolls. Warm winter smells.

Brenna and Élise were both busy in the kitchen, chatting together as they prepared breakfast.

Kayla greeted them, feeling awkward, while Elizabeth filled a mug with hot coffee.

"So did you even see Jackson last night? I thought he was going to take Maple."

"I—" Thrown by that unexpected question, Kayla fumbled for an answer. "Yes, he—popped round."

Brenna sent her a quick look as she removed a box

of eggs from the fridge and clutched them against her chest.

Élise extracted them from her grip. "*Merde!* You're not supposed to squeeze the box! They are eggs, not boulders. They will break."

"Sorry. You know I'm not much of a cook. Except for bacon. No one fries bacon like I do."

Élise rolled her eyes and muttered something unintelligible in French. Then she smiled at Kayla. "So— how was my pizza?"

"It was delicious." She didn't tell them that she and Jackson had devoured it cold in the early hours of the morning, sitting naked in front of the warm glow of the fire while the snow fell outside.

"There is nothing better than pizza when you have done lots of exercise and are totally starving." Her tone innocent, Élise smacked the eggs on the edge of a bowl. "Don't you agree, Brenna?"

"I do." Brenna gave up on cooking and picked up her coffee. "And the best thing about pizza? It can be shared. So if other people have been raising a sweat along with you, you can both eat."

Oh, God, they knew.

She didn't know how, but they definitely knew.

Kayla bent and made a fuss of Maple, hiding her scarlet face.

"You ate pizza together?" Elizabeth's face brightened. "That's good. Jackson's been working too hard lately. He needs to relax. He carries so much responsibility on his shoulders. What time did he leave you? It isn't like him not to answer his phone. Walter is in a state about Darren. He wants to talk to Jackson. I really don't want him getting so worked up—" Worrying out loud, Elizabeth returned to mixing the ingredients for her cinnamon stars while Kayla kept her head down and tried to think up an answer that wouldn't reveal the exact whereabouts of her son.

"I—er—didn't look at my watch—"

"I just had a text from him," Brenna said smoothly. "He has a few things to do and then he wants to talk to me about the ski program. I'll tell him to look in on Walter."

"I had a text from him, too." Élise walked across the kitchen with a large bag of flour. "We are meeting to discuss the restaurant later. Brenna, you are supposed to be helping me."

"You keep complaining, so I've resigned as your *sous-chef* or whatever I'm supposed to be."

"A *sous-chef* has to be able to cook more than bacon. If you were my *sous-chef* I would have fired you long ago. You would last less than a minute in my kitchen. Fortunately I now have Elizabeth." She beamed at Jackson's mother. "You are the new shining star of my kitchen. So calm. I hear Darren already has a job at a café in the village. It will suit him better I think. Stop stroking the puppy and wash your hands, Kayla. I need your help."

"I don't know how to cook." She noticed that the French girl was pronouncing the *h* in her words this morning and remembered what Jackson had said about her sounding more French when she was stressed.

"Fortunately I *do* know how to cook and so does Elizabeth, which is a good thing or we would all starve around here." Measuring flour, Élise beamed at Kayla. "I will give you directions."

"And she gives clear directions. I enjoyed myself so much last night. If I'd known what fun it was work-ing in a restaurant I would have done it years ago. And

Jackson told me it was your idea, Kayla." Elizabeth removed a slab of cookie dough from the fridge while Kayla washed her hands, relieved that the subject had apparently moved away from Jackson's whereabouts.

"It seemed like a logical solution to a problem. What do you want me to do?"

"Sift my flour into a bowl for me. Easy. Here—" Élise handed her the equipment and picked up a whisk and started to beat eggs. "When I was a teenager I used to work in a mountain restaurant in the Alps. It was more of a hut than a restaurant—we sold crepes and *vin chaud* to skiers as they passed. Perfect skiing food."

"I had hot spiced apple cider for the first time." Kayla shook the sieve. "It was delicious."

Elizabeth shaped the dough. "Alice used to make it with apples from our orchard."

Élise glanced up. "You're getting flour on the table, Kayla. *Merde,* all I ask you to do is sift flour and you are making a mess. You are almost as bad as Brenna."

The insult warmed her. Ridiculous, but it made her feel included. *One of them.* "I warned you I couldn't cook." But she was smiling and so was Élise.

"This isn't cooking—" The French girl reached out and grabbed Kayla's wrist, moving the sieve over the bowl. "Don't shake so hard. You are covering everything, including Maple." She blew kisses at the puppy, who wagged her tail happily. *"Je t'adore mon petit chouchou. Tu es trop mignon."*

"So you ski, too?"

"Ben bien sûr, of course. Brenna, if I ask you to fetch me maple syrup, could you do it without breaking the bottle? At this rate I could just make the pancakes on the floor. Most of the flour is there."

"Ignore her," Brenna advised. "Élise, next time you

wipe out on the mountain I'm skiing right over your head."

"I never wipe out. I am elegant on skis." Élise added milk to her egg mixture, whisking all the time, the motion of her wrist barely visible. "I skied from the age of four."

"Four?" Brenna gave a disdainful sniff. "Late starter."

"I lived for a while in the Alps. I could see Mont Blanc from my bedroom window. And the climate is much better than here."

Brenna placed a bottle of maple syrup on the table with exaggerated care. "Are you criticizing our Vermont climate?"

"Only the winter—" Élise paused to test the consistency of the mixture "—in the winter it is freezing." She rolled her *r*s. "In France it can be cold, yes, but not like this where your eyelashes can freeze to your face."

"Hey, you could take us to Paris. You still have an apartment there, don't you?" Brenna grinned. "Girls' weekend."

Girls' weekend.

Kayla finished sifting the flour. *Maybe she would do that,* she thought. *Maybe she'd actually take a holiday.*

Paris in springtime.

She'd never done anything like that. What surprised her was how appealing it sounded.

Asking herself what a night with Jackson had done to her, she pushed the bowl toward Élise and suddenly realized the other girl was quiet. She wondered if all the talk of Paris had made her homesick. "All done."

Distracted, Élise stared at the mess around her and opened her mouth, but Elizabeth got there before her.

"Wonderful," she said quickly, swiftly wiping flour

from the surrounding surfaces and the floor. "Maple needed a bath anyway."

Élise shook her head in despair. "Did you never cook with your mother, Kayla?"

"My mother hated cooking." Kayla wiped her hands. "In fact she hated being a mother." She didn't know who was more surprised by that confession—her or them.

Elizabeth's eyes were troubled. "I'm sure she didn't, dear."

"No, she really did." Kayla sat down with her coffee. "She had me when she was seventeen. Instead of going to college, she was a mum at home with a screaming baby. She hated every minute of parenthood. Once, on one of the rare nights when we had a conversation, she told me that those years were like doing time with no opportunity for parole."

There was silence in the kitchen.

Brenna paused with her mug halfway to her mouth. Élise stopped whisking.

And Kayla sat, wondering why the hell she'd just told them that. It had been bad enough spilling her secrets to Jackson, but to just blurt out really intimate details to these people who she barely knew—she felt naked. Exposed. She wanted to drag the words back and return to hiding under the warm layers of protection she'd wrapped around herself.

Then Elizabeth's arm came around her shoulder and she was being hugged.

"But you came through it a strong, warm, clever woman who has achieved so much. I'm sure she is proud of you now."

"We don't speak. I'm a reminder of the worst years of her life. She moved to New Zealand to 'start fresh.'"

"And your father?"

Kayla thought of the envelope waiting back in the cabin. "He sends money every Christmas. He's always been generous financially. He was the one who paid for me to go to boarding school after they split up."

Another silence followed that statement, and this time it was Élise who broke it.

"Okay, that is truly shit. Are you sure you're not just telling me this story so that I feel sympathy and let you off cooking? Because it won't work. If your mother didn't teach you to boil an egg, then I will. No excuses."

It was the perfect way to handle it.

Kayla smiled, grateful for the sensitivity that came without sentimentality. "I can boil an egg."

"I bet you can't boil it without cracking it." Back to her old self, Élise measured out more flour. "I need to add some more flour to this or the quantities will be wrong. I didn't allow for you dropping most of it on the dog. I am going to run cooking classes for you and Brenna. Everyone should be able to cook. If nothing else, it is a useful seduction technique."

Brenna rolled her eyes. "If I need a seduction technique, I'm not going to pick up a frying pan."

"This is a good thing because if *you* cooked, the man would be dead before any sex took place." Élise finished off the mixture with a flourish.

"I can cook for a man if I have to. I just happen to believe a man should be able to cook for a woman."

"I agree. Particularly in your case, if you want the relationship to last."

Elizabeth laughed. "It's such a treat having you three girls chatting in my kitchen." She squeezed Kayla's shoulder and stood up. "I need to go and wrap a few presents before the day starts. You go ahead and eat. Don't wait for me. I'll be back in time to eat leftover pancakes and take the biscuits out of the oven. Thanks again for taking Maple, Kayla."

"Anytime you need puppy sitting, I'm a willing volunteer." She couldn't believe she'd said that. Puppy sitting? It was something she wouldn't have thought of a few days earlier.

She felt a stab of guilt. She wondered if Elizabeth would have been so warm and supportive had she known how Kayla had spent the night.

"So—" As the door closed behind Elizabeth, Brenna planted a fresh mug of coffee·in front of Kayla and folded her arms. "Tell us everything. Is he alive, or have you left him naked and unconscious?"

Kayla stared at her.

"Of course he is alive." Élise snorted. "Any woman with eyes can see Jackson is a man of strength and stamina. It is why she has black circles under her eyes. I am guessing that right now he is lying there, wondering why she ran out on him. Why *did* you run out on him? Me, I prefer to wake up slowly. But I like morning sex very much."

Kayla felt her face heat. "I really don't—"

Brenna planted herself in the chair across from her. "Élise and I covered for you. The least you can do is give us the details."

"I don't want details. I am not a voyeur." Élise put the bowl to one side to rest. "Or maybe I do want details. Jackson has so much sex appeal. He would be an exceptional lover, I think. Mmm. Give us details."

Kayla clutched her mug, feeling more vulnerable than she had when she was talking about her mother.

She didn't do details. She didn't do *this*. Have sex with a man, all night, and wake next to him in the morning. She hadn't had time to think it through or rationalize it. She certainly wasn't ready to talk about it with anyone.

"I don't know what makes you think—"

"Two things…" Élise lifted a heavy based pan from the cupboard. "First, the look of panic in your eyes when Elizabeth asked you what time Jackson left, and second, the slight redness on your neck, caused by the scrape of stubble over sensitive flesh."

"Jackson came round to pick up Maple—"

"But he stayed for you. And judging by the fact you slunk up to the door with Maple this morning, I am guessing you crept out before he woke."

"I didn't slink." Kayla caught the look they gave her and rolled her eyes. "Okay, yes, I left! I— It was just one night. I didn't know what I was going to say when he woke up. I still don't know."

Élise looked confused. "Why is that so difficult to find something to say? You say 'Great sex, Jackson.' Unless it wasn't great sex, in which case you say 'Boring sex, Jackson, next time just leave the pizza and I'll eat it by myself.'" She oiled the pan. "But I'm sure it was great sex. If it weren't for the fact we work together, I might have been tempted myself. Except for the complication of Sean."

"Sean?" Brenna stared at her. "What does Sean have to do with anything? He hasn't been home in months."

"No." Élise tilted the pan. "I hope that isn't because of what we did."

"Because of—" Brenna was gaping. "What did you do?"

"Last time he was home we had a crazy night of satisfying sex—" Élise increased the heat under the pan "—which is another reason why Jackson is off-limits."

Brenna put her mug down slowly. "You had sex with Sean? Jackson's brother?"

"Why are you using that tone? It was not a big deal. Just one night. In the meadow next to the lake. Normally I think outdoor sex is overrated— Brenna, watch that pan for a moment." Élise sped across the kitchen and pulled a tub of berries out of the fridge. "But with Sean it was not the case. He is very sexy and he has good hands. I suppose because he's a surgeon. And he is sophisticated. He enjoys food and knows as much about wine as any Frenchman. I also like that he can talk intelligently about European politics, but of course Jackson can do that, too."

Brenna lifted her eyebrows. "You talk about politics during sex?"

"Of course not, but I expect conversation afterward." She gave Kayla a pointed look. "I do not run off." She pushed the fridge shut with an elegant movement of her shoulder and Brenna shook her head.

"Are you and Sean in touch?"

"No. It was just a onetime thing for both of us and it was a very good one time. He has expert knowledge of anatomy."

Kayla exchanged glances with Brenna. "But when he comes home for Christmas—won't that be awkward?"

"Why?" Apparently bemused by the question, Élise emptied the berries into a bowl. "I don't really understand why it would feel awkward if you both chose to do it."

"In my case because I slept with a client! Oh, God—" Kayla groaned and dropped her head onto her hands "—how could I have been so unprofessional?"

"He already was your client so what is the problem?" Élise gave a Gallic shrug. "Maybe it would be different if you had sex with him to persuade him to give you the business. Although maybe not. Jackson is so hot I think any woman could be forgiven—" She thought about it for a moment and Brenna laughed.

"You're an alley cat, Élise."

"Sex is a normal part of life. Not something to be embarrassed about. Unless the sex is bad, of course. From the dark rings around your eyes I'm assuming the sex wasn't bad."

Bad? It had been exceptional. The first time, the second time, the third time…

Kayla dug her hands in her hair. "It was just the one night. Like you and Sean. That's it. I'm—I'm just going to carry on as if nothing happened." And she knew the real reason for her panic had nothing to do with being unprofessional and everything to do with the way she felt about Jackson.

Brenna sipped her coffee. "You think he's going to go along with that?"

She had no idea. She didn't want to think about it, and she certainly didn't want to talk about it. She wasn't used to confiding in other women. She wasn't used to waking up in a man's bed.

She wasn't used to feeling this way.

Élise poured a small amount of pancake mixture onto the center of the pan and spread it until it formed a thin, even layer. "Jackson will do what suits him. He is a man who knows what he wants and isn't afraid to go after it. He is very strong. I like that about him."

She liked that about him, too. Along with many other things.

A crepe appeared on the plate in front of her.

"Voila!" Élise dusted it with sugar and folded it with

a flourish. "*Crepe au sucre.* Eat. After a night of sex, you need food."

She ate, and of course it was delicious because she was fast learning that Élise was incapable of producing anything that wasn't delicious. To make sure the subject didn't return to Jackson, she revealed to them her initial ideas for Snow Crystal.

"There are lots of angles I'm going to try with the media, but the biggest one is you—" She looked at Élise. "Female French chef transforming the restaurant experience in this little corner of Vermont—the press will love you."

"*Vraiment?*" Élise's face brightened. "This is promotion from 'the French Bitch,' I think. From bitch to babe. I will be a celebrity, perhaps. I will be rich."

"You can open your own restaurant in Paris."

"I wouldn't want to do that." Élise turned her back to them and something in her voice and the set of her shoulders made Kayla wonder if there was more to that declaration than a simple statement of future plans.

She remembered how quiet Élise had been when Brenna had suggested a girls' weekend in Paris.

She remembered what Jackson had said to Darren.

Elise has a home and a job here for as long as she wants.

"I'm glad you're not going back to Paris," Brenna muttered, her mouth full, her fork already loaded. "You're a pain in the butt, but you can cook like no one I've ever met. This is delicious, although it kind of cancels out the hour I put in on the treadmill this morning. How can you cook like this and stay so slim?"

"Because I do not eat everything I cook, *imbecile.*"

Kayla decided that Élise's secrets, whatever they were, belonged to Élise. "I think Walter would also interest the press. A man who was born here, raised here and still runs the place." She sampled the maple syrup. "I'm a little worried about what he'd say to them. It could backfire in a spectacular fashion. Then there's Tyler, of course—ex-downhill champion now working here. I need to think how I can use that. It's got to be a draw for experienced skiers. I think we should put together packages that would appeal to the expert. Ski master class. We could offer a 'powder date with Tyler O'Neil.'"

"Except that this is Vermont, so the powder is about as predictable as Tyler, which isn't saying much." Brenna nursed her coffee and Élise looked thoughtful.

"Tyler is hurt, I think. I don't mean his leg, I mean his whole self. He loved ski racing. It was his everything. Like my cooking. If I could no longer cook, I would want to boil myself in oil."

"I want to boil you in oil most of the time." Brenna picked up her fork. "And Tyler can still ski."

"But he can't race and he is so competitive. It would be like me no longer cooking for appreciative guests, just people like you."

"Thanks. He was the same when we were kids. Had to be first down the mountain." Brenna took a mouthful of pancake. "Trouble was, Jackson and I wanted to be first down the mountain, too."

Kayla cleared her plate. "What about Sean?"

"He's a good skier, but not like Tyler. Sean treats the mountain the way he treats everything else in life—as an intellectual challenge. He waited for us to fall and then picked up the pieces. The family drives him crazy. He doesn't have Jackson's patience. And talking of the family, have you talked to Walter about your idea?"

"Not since the meeting on the night I arrived here,

which was an unmitigated disaster." Remembering made her insides quail. But she also knew she needed his support. Kayla stood up. "I'm going to go and do it right now. I've been putting it off."

"Walter can seem fearsome, but underneath he is a pussycat. I love him very much. I will give you pancakes for him. That will put him in an instant good mood." Élise pulled open a drawer and found a container. "Wait for him to eat exactly two mouthfuls and then hit him with whatever you want to say."

"Thanks. This was—" Kayla pulled on her coat "—it was fun."

Brenna waved her fork. "When you're ready to give us part two, send a text."

"Part two is me going back to New York. I bought some gear yesterday by the way, so I'll drop yours back to you soon, Brenna."

"No hurry."

It was still early and most of the occupants of Snow Crystal were asleep or occupied with breakfast. Her feet sank into new snow and she thought how peaceful it was, how restful. The cold froze her cheeks. Her breath clouded the air. The sky was a perfect winter blue. The only sounds were the occasional snap of a twig and the whispery rush of snow falling from branches onto the forest floor.

She followed the path to the old sugarhouse that was home to Walter and Alice, grateful for her new boots and jacket. Both were warm and fitted perfectly. As she rounded a bend in the trail she smelled wood smoke and heard the steady thump of an ax connecting with a log. There, in a covered area next to the house, was Walter with a pile of freshly cut logs stacked next to him.

Nerves fluttered in her belly. Everything she was

hoping to do for Snow Crystal depended on this man's support. "Am I disturbing you?"

That fierce blue gaze reminded her so much of Jackson. "So you haven't gone back to New York then?"

"No." She stamped her feet to keep warm. "I'm here for a week. Élise sent you pancakes and blueberries."

"These aren't real pancakes." But he removed them carefully from the container and ate them with the little fork Élise had packed, one eye on Kayla. "Thought you might have run out."

"I've never run away from a job."

"You've been talking to people." Walter pushed the log with his foot. "Asking a lot of questions. Heard you've been skiing, too."

Kayla thought about the amount of time she'd spent horizontal in the snow. "I'm not sure you'd call it skiing. Other people seemed to be on their feet. I was mostly on my face."

The corners of his mouth twitched. "You were out there. That's what counts."

"I hope so."

"So did you learn anything useful?"

She glanced around her. Saw pretty curtains in the windows of the house and a whisper of smoke rising from the chimney. "I learned I didn't know much about the place when I arrived a few days ago. I talked when I should have listened."

"So now you're an expert?"

"An interested beginner. Jackson took me on a snowmobile."

Walter grunted. "When I was a boy we used cross-country skis and hauled sleds. Back in those days we didn't have ski lifts or fancy machinery to smooth the snow. If you wanted to go up a slope, you attached skins to your skis and you walked there." He pushed the log with the toe of his boot. "It was all backcountry, and when I say backcountry I mean backcountry. We'd be out there in the wilds and the forest and not see another soul all day."

"You skied, too?"

"We all skied. Had Jackson on skis before his second birthday. Same with Sean and Tyler. Tyler was only interested in going fast, but Jackson—" He paused, smiling as he remembered. "Jackson didn't just love going fast, he loved the mountains and he wanted to know everything from what makes a slope likely to avalanche to how to check that the ice on the pond is thick enough for skating. If he found something difficult, he'd try harder. Every time he fell, he was up on his feet again. Didn't matter if he was bleeding, he'd keep going until a job was done."

Kayla heard the pride in his voice and something else that made her stomach knot tight. *Love.* She wondered why he persisted in fighting Jackson when he clearly loved him so much.

"Snow Crystal means a lot to him."

"The place is in his blood. Even when he was young he understood the importance of protecting the habitat. You can't own nature...you're just a guest. He and I used to spend days together in the forest." Walter shifted the ax in his hand. "I was the one who taught him to recognize claw marks on beech trees. A black bear will mark a tree—" He followed Kayla's nervous glance with a shake of his head. "They won't bother you this time of year. Jackson taken you walking in the forest yet?"

"We cut down a Christmas tree yesterday."

Walter sniffed. "I bet you used the snowmobile.

That's no way to see the forest. You need to walk or get Dana to take you on the sled with those dogs of hers. Gives you a real feel for the place. You ever see a sugar maple?" When Kayla shook her head he waved a hand toward the trees. "These maples need a certain amount of cold to produce sap for maple syrup."

"I just had some on my pancakes. It was delicious."

"Come back in March and I'll teach you how it's done."

"Is that an invitation?" Kayla discovered she was holding her breath.

"It sounded like one, didn't it?"

It felt like a huge step forward. She felt light inside and then he hefted the ax and she remembered how worried Elizabeth was about him chopping wood.

"Can I do that?"

His expression was incredulous. "You?"

"Can't really get a feel for Snow Crystal without having chopped some logs. I've burned through plenty in my cabin. The least I can do is replace them." Thinking about the log fire in her cabin made her think about Jackson, and her insides flipped like one of Élise's pancakes.

It didn't matter how long she put it off, eventually she was going to have to face him.

But not yet.

Walter gave her a long look and then gestured to the log under his foot. "We're cutting it to the right length. Secret is to let the weight of the ax do the work. Doesn't need to be razor-sharp. Blunt is good."

"How does it cut if it's blunt?"

"You're not cutting it, you're splitting it." Walter brought the ax down with a *thwack,* and Kayla flinched.

"Should you be doing that?"

He wedged his foot on the log and worked the ax free. "Are you suggesting I'm too old for this?"

"No." She searched for tact and ended up with direct and honest. "Elizabeth mentioned you had chest pain."

"She fusses. It was indigestion. Too much good food." He brought down the ax again, splitting the log. "There's enough work around this place to keep a whole army occupied, and Jackson doesn't have an army so we all need to do our bit."

That fiercely spoken statement brought a lump to her throat. She wished Jackson could have heard it.

"He loves this place."

Walter stood still, his breath clouding the air. "Maybe he does."

"Maybe?" Kayla wondered how he could doubt it. "He came back, didn't he?"

"Didn't have any choice about that."

"There's always a choice, Walter."

"Not to Jackson." He bent to throw the logs on the pile with the others. "He feels a debt. A sense of responsibility. He's bound to this place. It's a failing and a strength."

"How can it be a failing?"

Walter hesitated. "Because a man shouldn't throw away his whole life doing something that doesn't feel right, just to please others."

Kayla thought about her father. About the years he'd been married to her mother before he'd finally got out and gone to the woman he loved.

"Maybe this feels right to Jackson. But you're right—he needs all the help he can get. So let me help."

Walter wiped his forehead on his sleeve. "You seriously want to chop logs?"

"Yes." She pushed up the sleeves of her fleece. "I've

been known to use the gym when I can't think of an excuse not to. I'm sure I can lift an ax."

Walter handed it to her. "Don't chop your foot off or that grandson of mine will take the next ax to my head. According to him, you're valuable."

Kayla felt the weight of it in her hands. "So I just swing it, right?" She laughed as Walter took a rapid step backward. Then she raised the ax and brought it down hard, as she'd seen him do. The log split. "Wow. I did that!" She grinned with delight and Walter grinned back, his weathered face creasing.

"That's a hell of a move you've got there." He nodded at the splintered wood. "If I'd known you could chop like that, I would have been more polite the other night. You mad at someone?"

"No, not mad." She brought the ax down again and then toed the log she'd chopped with a rush of pride. "Maybe a little, with myself."

Walter picked up the pieces and tossed them on the pile. "For falling in love when you didn't want to?"

Kayla froze. "I can absolutely assure you that—"

"Don't blame yourself. First time Elizabeth set eyes on Snow Crystal, she was gone. Same for my mother."

He meant the place, Kayla thought, not the person. Snow Crystal, not Jackson. "It's certainly special."

"Glad you think so—" The deep male voice came from behind her, and when she turned, Jackson was standing there, arms folded, broad shoulders resting against the tree as he watched her with the same blue eyes that had seen her lose control the night before. "I've been looking for you. Didn't realize you had a date with another man."

CHAPTER THIRTEEN

SHE LOOKED GOOD for a woman who'd had less than four hours sleep, but nowhere near as good as she'd looked lying naked on the rug in the firelight. He wished she were back there now. This was the last place he would have picked for a morning-after encounter. He'd come looking for her, but now he had more immediate concerns.

Jackson eyed the ax and the pile of logs. "I thought we agreed you were going to leave the wood chopping to me, Gramps."

Walter glared at him. "You're already running my business. Got to leave a man something to do."

"There's plenty to do." He was treading a delicate path between ensuring his grandfather felt involved and not giving him anything too strenuous.

"Then go and do it and leave me to talk to Kayla about Snow Crystal."

Lack of sleep added weight to the responsibilities already pressing down on his shoulders.

"I need to talk to you about the restaurant, Gramps."

"If you're here to tell me Darren has gone, I already know."

Jackson cursed himself for not speaking to his grandfather immediately. "He came to you?" Anger flared at the thought of Darren bringing an eighty-year-old man in on the problem.

"Two minutes after he walked out. Came straight over here, ranting about that 'French bitch.' Excuse me." Walter sent a look of apology to Kayla, who tightened her grip on the ax as if she was contemplating bringing it down on someone's head.

"Don't worry. But I might just need to chop another log soon."

"Me, too. I'm steaming mad. Some folks don't know when they're well off—that's the problem." He glared at Jackson, who prepared to do something he never did. Explain his decision.

"I know you took him on, Gramps—"

"Yes, I did. And I reminded him of that when I sent him on his way."

"You—" Braced for a different conversation, Jackson stopped in midsentence. "You did what?"

"I sent him on his way, of course." Walter took the ax from Kayla. "I told him to grow a backbone, get himself right back in the kitchen and do the job we employed him to do." He took a swing. The ax landed with a thud, leaving another two logs to add to the growing pile.

Kayla nodded approval. "Nice one, Walter."

Jackson wasn't sure whether she was referring to Darren or the split log. "I'm assuming he refused."

"He did. Said he already had a better job lined up. Need a turn, Kayla?"

"Yes." She took the ax back while Jackson watched the two of them, noticing the way his grandfather gently adjusted Kayla's grip and then positioned the next log for her.

She hit him with her smile and Walter stepped back, dazzled.

Having been on the receiving end of that smile, Jackson felt sympathy for his grandfather.

He watched as she lifted the ax. Watched as that blond hair swung and a look of determination spread across her face.

Apart from that first glance, she hadn't looked at him.

"I'm going to find a way to chop logs in my office. That way every time a client with no story whatsoever tells me he wants to be on the front page of the *New York Times,* I can chop a log instead of banging my head against a wall." She split the log and her eyes sparkled. "You do this whenever you're stressed?"

"Every damn day." Walter glanced at his grandson. "Never any shortage of firewood around here. Isn't that right, Jackson?"

"Gramps—"

Walter grunted. "You did the right thing. People need to pull their weight. Élise cooks like an angel. She was a find, that's for sure."

It was the first word of praise his grandfather had given him. The first time he'd shown any indication that any of the changes Jackson had made were making a difference.

"I didn't expect Darren to leave."

"Things happen. You dealt with it. That's all you can do in life. Things are changing around here. If people can't change along with us, they'd be happier somewhere else. It's important to keep these logs dry." He spoke to Kayla. "We deliver dry logs to the cabins every day. Sure, only a couple of them are occupied right now, but I'm sure that'll change now you're here. Think you can get us on the front page of the *New York Times?*" His eyes twinkled and Kayla grinned back at him.

"Doubtful. You're hot, Walter, but even you're not hot enough for the front page. But I can get you in other places. If I arrange for a journalist to interview you, do you promise not to eat him in one mouthful?"

Walter rested his foot on the log. "I'm not allowed to be myself?"

"I want you to be yourself. I'm relying on it."

He put the ax down. "Just tell me who you want me to talk to."

"I'll make some calls."

Jackson frowned. "This close to Christmas?"

"There are people still working, and some of them are looking for stories that don't include suggestions for cooking turkey or tips on dieting. I'll get right onto it." She zipped up her jacket, still not looking at him.

"I'm taking you skiing this morning. We're meeting up with Tyler and Jess. Your gear is in the back of my car."

"These are two people whose idea of fun is to bomb down a sheer vertical cliff. I'm sure they're just dying to spend time on a flat slope with someone who can't stay upright for more than five seconds." Her voice was falsely bright. "I'm glad they're bonding, but I need to get back to the cabin and work. I'm starting to get a clear picture of how we can sell Snow Crystal to the press and the public."

He was starting to get a clear picture of the reason she blocked people out of her life. "You can tell me about it as we drive." He took her arm. "Car's parked just over there. See you later, Gramps."

"I guess you will." Walter gave them both a long look but Jackson kept walking. Fortunately Kayla did, too, presumably because she didn't want a scene.

"I had a frank discussion with your grandfather."

"Good. A frank discussion is definitely needed. And

not just between you and my grandfather." He heard her sharp intake of breath.

"Jackson—"

"Get in the car, Kayla." They were the same words he'd spoken to her a few nights earlier when she'd fled from the meeting, only this time he understood more about why she'd fled. He hoped she wasn't going to argue, because he was ready to flatten her to the side of his SUV and kiss her until she stopped arguing, which would give Walter something to stare at other than his log pile.

"You employed me to do a job."

"I'm not stopping you doing that job. I'd like an update, and I'd like that update with strong coffee to make up for the amount we didn't sleep last night. Right now we're going to use this private time to have that conversation you've been avoiding."

She climbed into the car. "I had things to do this morning."

"Things that required you to creep out like a burglar?"

"I was trying not to wake you."

"Yeah, I got that part. Question is, why? Am I that scary?"

"I was busy. I spoke to your mother. I had a conversation with Élise and Brenna. I had a lovely chat with Walter." She fastened her seat belt. "That was what we agreed, wasn't it? That I'd talk to people?"

"Seems you've talked to just about everyone except me so far today."

She took a deep breath. "It was one night, Jackson. Just one night."

"In that case you owe me a couple of hours because

you walked out before it was finished." He waited for her to come back with a smart reply.

What she did was turn the conversation back to work.

"I've decided to go for some feature placements and national TV. People like a human story."

He reined in frustration. "Human story?"

"You gave up your own dream to come home and save the family business."

Tension rippled through him. "You make it sound like some sort of damn sacrifice."

"Would you have come home and run this place if your father were still here?"

"He isn't, so it isn't a question that needs answering." The snap in his voice was directed at himself rather than her, but she had no way of knowing that. He was about to apologize when he felt the gentle touch of her fingers on his thigh.

Remembering how those fingers had felt wrapped around a certain part of him, Jackson almost drove off the road.

"I'm sorry." Her voice was soft. "I didn't mean to be insensitive."

"I'm the one who's sorry. I'm tired and cranky and right now I don't want to talk about this place." He tried to focus on the road and not the touch of her hand. "And I'm not sure Walter should be talking to journalists. I don't want the world to know he doesn't want me here."

"He wants you here. I spent an hour with him this morning. You're all he talks about and he talks with love and pride."

"Family loyalty. He's not going to say anything different to—"

"To an outsider. It's fine…you can say it. And he's

proud of you, Jackson. You have no idea how lucky you are to have that." She withdrew her hand and he had to stop himself from grabbing it. Instead he kept both hands on the wheel and steered the vehicle into the parking area at the foot of the chairlift.

"I should have come home sooner." Guilt gnawed at him, aching under his ribs. "Should have asked some questions. My father was a lousy businessman. He considered a day that wasn't spent outdoors trying to break his speed record flying downhill a day wasted."

"He sounds like Tyler."

"There are similarities, but Tyler loves Snow Crystal. To Dad it was a boulder around his neck stopping him doing the things he wanted to do." He wondered why they were talking about this when all he wanted to do was talk about the night before.

He wondered how she could block it out so easily.

And then he saw her fingers. She was clenching them in her lap, her knuckles white, and he knew she wasn't finding it easy, either.

"I've been thinking that we should invite some of the top international ski journalists for a weekend."

He ought to be interested. He should be listening to her words, not looking at her mouth. "We?"

"You." She leaned forward to remove her boots. "I'll be in New York, obviously."

He swore under his breath. "Look at me, Kayla."

"I think it would be an excellent way of getting coverage and—"

"Look at me."

"I'm just—"

"You're just trying to pretend last night never happened, but I'm not going to let you do that."

Color streaked across her cheekbones but she kept her eyes down. "It happened, but now it's done."

"No, it's not."

She stilled and took several breaths. "You are already the longest relationship I've ever had, Jackson."

"Maybe I am, but that doesn't mean you have to run." It was what she'd done after her parents had split up. It broke his heart to think of her shivering and alone on Christmas night.

He thought about what she'd told him about her life. Adding those pieces to the other bits she'd revealed over the time they'd been together had enabled him to build a picture in his head and it didn't make happy viewing.

She adjusted her socks. "I'm not running."

"I woke up alone."

"I took Maple back to your mother."

"At seven in the morning?" He slid his fingers under her chin and forced her to look at him. "Am I that scary?"

"I'm not scared."

"Sweetheart, you're so scared intruder alarms go off in your head when someone comes close. There are better ways to live your life."

"This way works for me."

Exasperation flashed through him. She was more stubborn than Walter. "Don't trust, don't get hurt—is that right?"

"Maybe it is, but what's wrong with that? I'm only here for a few days. This can't be—anything."

"So we can either play it safe and boring, or we can make those few days count." His gaze dropped to her mouth. "I know which I want."

"Jackson—"

"I don't remember you checking your emails, Kayla." He could see a tiny pulse beating in her throat.

"Enough. You need to back off."

"I'm not good at backing off. That's why I'm still at Snow Crystal."

But he understood why she would think that way. Her most important relationships had proved as unstable and unreliable as the snowpack on a steep slope. One moment she'd been standing on what had felt like a solid surface and the next that surface had gone, sweeping her off the mountain in an avalanche of pain that had left her living in a world where nothing felt secure.

He tried to imagine how it must feel to know your parents had chosen a different life. A life that didn't include the child they'd made.

Family life could be messy—he knew that. Tyler's experience with Janet Carpenter had been harsh, and the O'Neils certainly weren't perfect. Much of the time they drove him half-crazy, but they were his family and they were *there*. Yes, there were arguments. Big, door-slamming arguments. Hell, in Tyler's case the arguments had driven him from Snow Crystal for a while. And Sean wasn't exactly rushing home, either, but no one in the O'Neil family had ever doubted they were loved. The arguments, the irritations, the frustrations all added up to a package he couldn't imagine living without.

And one thing he knew for sure—no one in his family would have spent Christmas night at a police station.

He'd left home because he'd craved independence. He'd wanted, *needed,* to prove himself. But he'd always known he could return at any point. He'd known they had his back and that if life had buried him in an avalanche, they'd be right there digging him out. And he would have done the same for any one of them, which was why he was here now.

Kayla had never had that support from anyone.

She'd had only herself to rely on, with no support from the sidelines. For her, security came from not taking risks in her personal life.

He took it as a positive sign that her guard was up. It meant she felt threatened. And feeling threatened meant she cared.

Presumably she'd work that out for herself if she hadn't already.

Jackson decided to let that kick around in her brain for a while.

"I'm glad we had this talk because now we both know where we stand. Let's go and break the news to Tyler you want him to be a media star."

CHAPTER FOURTEEN

Now we both know where we stand.

Kayla stamped her feet into her skis and zipped up her jacket. She had no idea where she stood. She'd made it clear she wanted him to back off, and he'd made it clear he had no intention of doing that. Part of her wanted to argue further, but she didn't want to prolong a conversation she found terrifying.

He'd accused her of running away, but that wasn't what she did. True, she avoided emotional entanglements, but that was a lifestyle choice. It had nothing to do with running and yet somehow he'd made her feel like a coward.

"Remember what I taught you—" Jackson removed his gloves and bent to tighten her boots.

She put her hand on his shoulder to steady herself and was immediately transported back to the night before. She'd explored the dip and curve of those muscles with her fingers and mouth. She knew the feel of his skin and the power of his body.

He straightened, his gaze holding hers.

Around them skiers whizzed past, their jackets a swirling kaleidoscope of bright color against a background of white, but all she saw was the blue of Jackson's eyes.

Her mouth was dry, her fingertips frozen. "I can't do this."

"Yes, you can. It's an easy run and I'll be right next to you."

"I wasn't talking about the skiing."

"I know." His voice was gentle. "But you need to stop panicking and have some fun. Live a little, Kayla."

"I like the way I live. Is it so wrong to enjoy work?"

"No. But when work becomes something you use to prevent you facing the things that scare you—that's not good."

"You don't understand."

"I'm trying. And I know that when you're scared, the best thing to do is throw yourself into whatever it is that scares you. Just do it. Don't think about what could go wrong. That's a surefire way of never doing anything in life."

"It's a surefire way of getting hurt."

"I'm still not talking about skiing." He covered her lips with his fingers. "Stop assuming something bad will happen."

She tried to ignore the feel of his fingers on her lips. "Maybe I'll fall."

"Maybe you won't." He stared deep into her eyes, and there was humor there and something much, much more serious.

She was definitely falling. Tumbling headlong into something she'd avoided all her life. "Maybe I'll break a leg." *Or something more important, like a heart.*

"Maybe you'll have the most fun you've ever had." His voice soft, he dragged his thumb slowly over her mouth. "And maybe you'll want to do it again and again."

Her heart raced away faster than a downhill skier going for gold.

She tried to ignore it. Tried to ignore *him*. "I'm too old to learn to ski."

"How old are you?"

"Twenty-eight."

His mouth flickered at the corners. "Your age is not getting in the way." He pulled on his gloves. "The only thing getting in the way is your mind."

"There is nothing wrong with my mind. I like my mind."

"I like your mind, too. Doesn't mean I wouldn't like it to shut up once in a while. Now follow me and turn when I turn. That way you won't gain too much speed."

She watched him with a mixture of frustration and fascination thinking that, with the exception of Walter, she'd never met anyone more stubborn. Or maybe Jackson wasn't stubborn. Maybe he just knew what he wanted.

She shivered. *Was that her?*

He was right about one thing. Her mind did get in the way. It made her pick the safe route. But was that so wrong? Was it wrong to protect yourself…or sensible?

As he moved to one side, sure and confident on his skis, she had her first proper view of the slope.

"Oh, God, that's steep! Now I understand why you were giving me the talk about facing my fear." Terrified, she dug her poles and skis into the slope. "The only way I'm going down that is in an ambulance."

"There is no way to get an ambulance up here." He was laughing. "If you fall and you're injured, you'll be pulled down on a toboggan by the ski patrol. It's not the most comfortable of rides."

"Thank you for the motivational speech." The slope fell away beneath her, the smooth groomed surface of the snow sparkling in the bright winter sunshine. The contrast of snowy mountains against blue sky would have taken her breath away if she hadn't already been holding it in sheer terror.

Far below, through the veil of trees, she could see the village nestling in the valley and to the right the lake and the Snow Crystal cabins. "It's comforting to know that if I fall I might just land straight in my bed."

Maddeningly relaxed, he slid away from her. "Ski, Kayla."

"Ski, Kayla," she muttered under her breath. "Can I climb back up to the top? I'll sacrifice my nails if that's what it takes to get me back up to the lift."

He glanced over his shoulder and smiled. "Trust your skis. And me."

He had no idea what he was asking.

"I'm not big on trust."

But he was.

He was a man who trusted family bonds to hold. She'd only ever seen them snap. "We're incompatible."

"Ski, Kayla, or I'll carry you down, and that will make you dizzy."

She was already dizzy, but she let the skis glide, tentatively at first, heard a soft rushing sound and felt the cold air on her cheeks. Her stomach knotted in terror and then she saw him turn, still watching her over his shoulder. She faltered, postponing the moment when she'd have to commit to going straight down the fall line. And then she saw a little girl no more than four years old careering down the mountain with her daddy and remembered what Jackson had said about her mind being the only thing getting in her way.

Holding her breath, she turned, ignoring the instinct that told her she was committing suicide. For a split second her speed increased, and she forced herself to concentrate, forced herself to remember what he'd told her about her weight and the edges of her skis and then she was turning and traversing the slope behind him.

Turn, glide, turn, glide—they went down the mountain, gradually increasing speed, and fear turned to enjoyment and then exhilaration. All worries left her mind as she focused.

There was a sense of peace that came from being out in the mountains, surrounded by people having fun. Her own smile stayed on her face right up until the moment she realized Jackson had stopped and she was going to crash into him.

He caught her easily, stopped her from plowing into the snow heaped at the side of the mountain restaurant, but her ski flew off and they both ended up in a tangled heap.

"And here I am, on my back again." She was laughing so hard she couldn't breathe, and he was laughing, too, and cursing at the same time, as he took good-natured ribbing from two members of the ski patrol who happened to be passing.

"You just ruined my reputation. Thirty-two years I've skied here and I just fell on a baby slope. Do you know what this is going to cost me? I may have to move to Colorado." He showed no sign of releasing her. His arm was around her and she was pressed hard against him. "Are you all right?"

"I'm fine, but I think my skis might have landed in Canada." Her mouth was inches from his, and she was shocked by how badly she wanted to kiss him.

His eyes were intense blue, shadowed by lack of sleep and she knew hers were the same.

It had been the most incredible night of her life.

She rolled away from him and tried to get up. "Why did my skis come off?"

"I adjusted the bindings so that they'd come off if you fell. I didn't want you to break an ankle."

"Did I hear talk of broken ankles?" A man skied to a stop right next to them, showering them both with snow. "That's my specialty."

Jackson swore softly and brushed the snow off his jacket. "You pick your moments to show up." He stood up and rescued both pairs of skis while Kayla stared at the man in disbelief. Apart from the fact he was clean-shaven, she was looking at another version of Jackson.

Jackson dug the skis into the deep snow next to the restaurant. "Kayla, meet my brother Sean."

"Twins," she murmured. "Identical twins. You said you were the eldest."

"I'm the eldest by five minutes."

"We are most certainly not identical." Sean snapped his feet out of his skis. "My taste in wine is much better than his, and he might help you break your ankle but there's no way he'd be able to fix it. Our taste in women, however, occasionally coincides." His smile was as sexy as his brother's. "You must be Kayla. Good to meet you."

"YOU WANT TO offer up a piece of me as part of your PR campaign?" Tyler sprawled in his chair on the terrace of the mountain restaurant, nursing a beer while Jess sat close to him, soaking up each word he spoke.

Kayla poked the creamy froth on her cappuccino with a spoon. "Your skills and reputation add something to Snow Crystal. It's something other resorts can't match."

Tyler winked at his brother. "Are you listening?"

Jackson rolled his eyes. This wasn't the way he'd planned it. It was supposed to be a low-key friendly lunch with Jess and Tyler. He hadn't banked on Sean arriving.

Fortunately Kayla didn't seem overwhelmed.

Instead she seemed fascinated as she listened to Tyler and Sean talking about the performance of a U.S. skier.

"He got sucked low on the top section. The snow was soft."

"DNF'd twice at Val-d'Isère. Hooked a tip halfway down."

Tyler stretched out his legs. "We all have a bad run sometimes. The important thing is to get back out there and race again."

Jess looked as if she was memorizing every word, while Kayla just looked confused.

"DNF?"

"Did not finish." Jackson reached across and knocked a lump of snow off her hat. "Unlike you, who finished in style."

"Flat on my face you mean. I have a feeling DNF could be my specialty. So I know there are two types of ski racing—the one that goes straight down and the one that's curvy."

"Slalom." Tyler looked pained. "It's called slalom."

"Slalom. The one when you turn all the time—" she drew the pattern in the air "—a bit like I was doing just now when I came down the slope."

Tyler lifted an eyebrow in incredulous disbelief. "Honey, you were about as close to slalom as I am to Mars."

"I was just illustrating a point."

"Slalom is one of two technical disciplines, the other

being giant slalom. Do you know *anything* about World Cup alpine ski racing?"

"Not a thing," Kayla said happily, "except that you all wear supertight spandex like Superman. Fortunately skiers seem to have muscles in all the right places, which is a relief because if you put that outfit on the average London commuter it would *not* be a good look."

"The outfit is designed to minimize drag." Tyler scowled at Sean, who wasn't bothering to hide his laughter. "You got something to say?" Without waiting for him to respond, he turned back to Kayla, determined to educate her. "As well as technical, you have speed disciplines. Downhill is the Formula 1 of ski racing. I presume you've heard of Formula 1?"

"Formula? Isn't that what they feed babies?" Kayla grinned. "Just kidding. So it's fast."

"You ski a course like the Lauberhorn in Switzerland, one of the longest and toughest on the World Cup circuit, and you're hitting speeds of around 90 miles an hour, and you're not wearing a seat belt. And when you're up there waiting to start there's nothing but you and the slope. Think about it."

Jess was on the edge of her seat with excitement, but Kayla shuddered.

"I can't think about it without wanting to vomit. I've just skied as fast as I ever intend to."

"Fast?" Tyler choked on his beer. "If you'd skied any slower, the season would have been over and the rest of us would have been sunbathing."

She lived her life like that, Jackson thought. With the brakes on. He wondered what it would take to get her to release those brakes.

"Sunbathing sounds good right now. This place is freezing." Zipping her jacket up to the neck, Kayla sipped her coffee. "So downhill is for adrenaline junkies. I've got that. What else?"

"Then there's the Super-G."

"Super-G?"

"Super Giant Slalom." Tyler glanced at his brother in despair. "Where the hell did you find her?"

"He found me in an office in New York. And I may not be able to stay upright on skis, but I can do my job as well as you do yours. I got my last client on the cover of the *New York Times* and *Time* magazine." She put her cup down and smiled sweetly. "In my business that's the equivalent of two Olympic golds, just in case you're wondering. And under my direction we generated over three hundred million media impressions for that account, which means the number of people who saw that product mentioned was probably higher than the number of people watching your performance on TV."

Tyler narrowed his eyes. "I'd say you crashed and burned your first night here."

Jackson swore under his breath, but Kayla laughed.

"I definitely DNF'd in that meeting. But we all have a bad run sometimes. The important thing is to get back up and race again." Throwing his own words back at him, she leaned forward. "People would pay a great deal to ski with you. To hear you speak about your experiences. You're passionate about what you do. You're an attraction."

"For God's sake, don't tell him that." Sean reached across the table for a bowl of fries. "Who ordered these? Since when do we live on junk food?"

"Since I'm no longer competing." Tyler removed the fries from his brother. "And I'm more of an attraction than you are. I've got medals to prove it."

"All those medals prove is that you ski like someone

on a suicide mission." Sean let Tyler take the bowl but helped himself to a handful. "Not that I'm complaining. It's people like you who keep people like me in a job, so you carry on and snap those bones, bro."

Jackson saw Kayla wince. "Enough medical talk. You're back early, Sean. We weren't expecting you until Christmas Eve."

"I've worked the last four Christmases in a row. Figured I deserved parole." Sean caught the attention of the waitress and ordered a green salad.

"Does Mom know you're home?"

"Of course. Hence the green salad. I'm full of gingerbread Santas and I'm saving myself for dinner. Tonight is family night. Which means Gramps wanting to know why I have to fix bones in Boston when there are plenty of the broken variety around here, Mom stuffing me with food and Grams knitting while Jackson talks profit and loss."

"It's mostly loss, which you'd know if you read your emails."

"I spent ten hours operating yesterday. It was precision work. By the time I'd finished my eyes wouldn't focus enough to read emails."

"I just thought since you own a share of this place you might like to know what's happening."

"I own the wine cellar. That might see a significant loss tonight. I'm thinking we're going to be at least half a crate down." Sean winked at Kayla. "I hope you're joining us for dinner. I need someone to dilute the concentration of O'Neils and add some New York sophistication to the proceedings."

"It's family night. I'm not family."

Jackson knew she was thinking about the last time she'd had dinner with all of them and he waited, knowing she'd refuse. And when she did, he intended to invite her to dinner at his place, which would give them a chance to have a proper conversation, this time without being observed by half the inhabitants of Snow Crystal.

Her gaze met his briefly and then skidded away again.

"Family night." Her smile was fixed. "I'll be there."

She'd be there?

Taken by surprise, it took Jackson a moment to realize what she was doing.

By choosing to eat with the family, she'd managed to avoid an evening with him.

Which meant only one thing.

Kayla Green was running again.

CHAPTER FIFTEEN

SEAN ZIPPED HIS jacket against the shearing winds, stared down the steep pitch of the chute and wondered why he'd agreed to ski with his brother. "So what's going on with Jackson and Miss New York?"

"She's not Miss New York. She's Miss Great Britain. Or Miss—" Tyler paused at the top of the gully, testing the snow. "Frankly I have no idea what she is. She's certainly not Miss Downhill Skier and she's not close to Miss Slalom, either, whatever she may think. But I like her."

Sean thought about the sharp intelligence in those eyes and the way she'd come back at Tyler. He also liked the way she'd laughed at herself when she'd fallen. "I like her, too."

"You're going to have to like her from a distance because your twin has eyes on her. I suspect he's also had hands on her, but you might not want to mention that part just yet. You may have shared a uterus, but last time I looked the two of you didn't share women."

"Didn't say I wanted to share her. Said I liked her. Not the same thing." He digested the news that his brother was involved with a woman.

"You should get to know Élise. You both appreciate good food and wine. The two of you should have a lot in common."

Sean stared straight ahead. Neither of his brothers

had any idea just how well he knew Élise, which was probably a good thing. He was the first to admit his track record with relationships was less than impressive, and he had no doubt Jackson would see him as a potential threat to the well-being of his chef. And what was the point in mentioning it? What they'd shared had been fleeting. One hot summer night where chemistry had gotten the better of both of them. It wasn't going to happen again. This was the first time he'd seen her since that night. They'd had no contact.

Sean studied the narrow chute in front of them.

"Are you seriously expecting me to ski down that? You always were right on the edge of crazy." But he knew it wasn't true. Tyler's judgment when it came to the mountain was close to flawless. He had an almost-preternatural ability to separate the skiable from the unskiable. It was a skill that had put him right up among the elite.

"You skied down it your whole life until you left home. Working in a city has turned you soft."

"I value my limbs. I can't fix other people's broken bones if my own are smashed, and I don't trust anyone else to fix mine." But Sean felt the familiar rush of adrenaline. The pull of temptation that was hard to resist. Normally he forced himself to deny it. It was the reason he'd sold the Ducati even though he'd almost cried doing it. His compromise had been to buy the Porsche. All the speed without the direct exposure to the limb-destroying effects of a motorcycle crash on a hard road surface. "Oh, hell, one run. But you're going first."

"Because you're a coward."

"Because if you trigger an avalanche I'd rather be

above you than below you. But I promise to dig you out."

"If you men could just step to one side—" Brenna shot past them both with Jess close behind her.

"Hey, just wait—" Tyler's words were swallowed by the frozen air as the two girls negotiated the gut-swooping drop that led to the top of Scream gully. Neither hesitated. Neither screamed. But they did whoop. A holler of pure enjoyment as they shot through the air and then turned swiftly on the ridiculously steep slope.

"And there's someone else who borders on the edge of crazy," Sean murmured, watching as Brenna tackled the terrifying slope with effortless ease.

"Are you talking about my daughter?"

"I wasn't, but I think she's probably right there with you. On the other hand she's got your DNA so it's not entirely unexpected. Not that you'd understand. It's science and that's always been beyond you."

"Which is the science that has sex in it?"

Sean sighed. "It's isn't that simple, but I'll make it simple as it's you. Biology."

"I aced that one. You ready? Because I'm damned if I'm going to be outskied by a kid, even if she's my kid."

"You skied Scream at her age. Or maybe you were a year older."

"Your memory sucks. You should talk to a doctor about that. I was seven when I skied Scream, and you know it since you were the one that pushed me off the top."

"It was my duty as big brother to toughen you up."

Tyler grinned. "And you think I'm the one on the edge of crazy?"

FAMILY NIGHT?
Why had she agreed to that?

Because the alternative had meant being alone with Jackson.

Thumping her palm against her forehead, Kayla paced the length of the lodge and back again.

She'd tried to work, but so far her brain refused to cooperate. Halfway through her session, Elizabeth called in to drop off Maple so that she could go and spend time with Élise in the kitchen.

The puppy settled down on the rug and watched Kayla, head on her paws.

Kayla sighed. "You think I was a mess last night? I'm worse today."

Maple wagged her tail and rolled over on the rug.

Kayla put in a call to Brett, knowing he would still be in the office right up until late on Christmas Eve.

While she waited for him to pick up, she drank her coffee. Another fall of snow in the night had added a thick layer to the trees and they glistened in the winter sunshine.

"Kayla? How are things out there in the sticks?" Brett's voice boomed around the cabin, and Maple shot to her feet, barking frantically. "You still there, Green? What the hell's that noise?"

"It's a dog, Brett. Four legs. Tail." She scooped Maple onto her lap. "You have one at home. It's just that you don't often see it because you're always in the office. I'll send you a picture if that would help."

"Didn't know you were a dog person, Green."

She hadn't known, either.

She smiled at Maple, snuggled on her lap. "Turns out I might be a dog person."

"Just don't bring it into the office or go home at lunchtime to feed it. So how are things there?"

Kayla looked at the trees. "Snowy."

"Bet you can't wait to get back to civilization. You're probably so desperate you're willing to leap on the back of Santa's sleigh and grab the first ride out of there." Brett laughed at his own joke while Maple watched her with gentle eyes and Kayla absorbed the fact that she wasn't at all desperate to get back to New York.

She told herself it was because the job still wasn't done. "I've made progress."

"So what do you need to turn progress to profit?"

"I'm going to send the proposal across in the next couple of hours. I'll brief the team, but I want printed and bound copies delivered here ASAP."

"What's wrong with electronic?"

Kayla thought about Alice and her glasses and Walter and his fear of progress. "I want hard copy."

"Think of the trees, Green."

She'd thought of nothing but the trees since she arrived here. "I'm looking at trees, Brett."

"I forgot you were in the dark ages over there. Hard copy. No worries."

"Thanks. And happy Christmas, Brett."

"Why are you wishing me happy Christmas? It's ages until Christmas."

"Two days."

"That's what I mean. Ages. Now get back to work and stop wasting my time. And don't bring the dog with you when you come back to New York." He hung up and left her staring at Maple.

THEY ATE FAMILY dinner in the kitchen. Brenna joined them, but not Élise because she was busy in the restaurant. Instead, she provided a creamy leek-and-potato soup, and Elizabeth cooked lamb shanks.

Jackson barely tasted either.

Kayla had chosen a seat at the far end of the table, as far away from him as possible. She was wearing a soft sweater with black pants tucked into the snow boots she'd bought earlier in the week. Her hair was loose over her shoulders and she was laughing at something Sean had said.

He wondered how long she could carry on pretending this thing between them wasn't happening.

"Are you listening to me?" Brenna poked him in the arm.

"What did you say?" He knew he was lousy company.

"I was telling you a story, but somehow I don't think I have your full attention. In fact I don't think I have any of your attention. I'm not flattered." She picked up her glass. "When you took me out to dinner you didn't look at me like that."

Jackson dragged his gaze from Kayla to Brenna. "Like what?"

"Like the meal was a formality before you got to the interesting part of the evening."

He sighed. "Sorry, Bren—"

"Don't be. You and I never had any chemistry." She sipped her wine. "I like her, Jackson. She can't ski to save her life, but she's genuine."

"I like her, too."

"So do you have a plan?"

"Yes." What he didn't know was whether it was a good plan.

He was going on a hunch. Trusting his instincts.

"I'd give you advice, but I'm no expert."

Jackson eyed Tyler across the table. "How are you finding working with him?"

"About as infuriating as growing up with him."

"That's what I figured. Is it awkward? Should I be worried?"

"No and no. I won't be driven from my home and the place I love by a man with the insight of a boulder. He treats me like a little brother."

"Maybe you should ski naked. Or wear that black dress you wore when we went out to dinner."

"You wouldn't fire me if I taught my class naked?"

Jackson reached for his wine, an excellent sauvignon blanc provided by Sean. "I don't have too many people on my side at the moment. I can't afford to fire you."

They talked for the rest of the evening, mostly about the ski program and how they could expand it. And all the time he was aware of Kayla at the far end of the table, chatting with Sean about the differences between New York and London. It didn't surprise him they were getting on well. What surprised him was how much he minded.

They lingered over the meal and then finally Kayla stood up, thanked his mother and walked across the room to get her coat.

Clearly she thought the evening was over. Right now she was probably congratulating herself on having avoided intimacy.

Then she tilted her head as she heard a noise outside. "What's that?"

Jackson rose to his feet, hoping this was going to play out the way he wanted it to. "That," he said, "is your lift home."

"I can walk."

So far, so predictable.

"I've arranged an alternative mode of transport."

Frowning at him, she wrapped her scarf around her

neck and tugged open the door. Her gasp interrupted conversation. "Dogs?"

"Dogsledding by moonlight. This is one of the oldest forms of winter transportation."

"Jackson—"

"It's a tourist favorite," Elizabeth said happily, walking to the door to wave at Dana. "You can't go home without trying it, dear. I guarantee you won't regret it."

Jackson noticed that this time Kayla didn't recoil from the *dear* or from his mother, who now had her arm around her. She stared at the sled and then finally, *finally* looked at him.

"A sled ride." Her voice was croaky. "You don't give up, do you?"

"I don't know what you mean. This is all part of the Snow Crystal experience."

THEY MOVED THROUGH the magical midnight landscape, weaving and winding along well-groomed snowy trails, the peace broken only by the clink of the harness, the panting of the dogs and the soft crunch of the sled running over packed snow.

Stars sparkled in the velvet black sky and the full moon reflected off the snow, spreading silvery light across the silent forest.

The outside temperature was below freezing but Kayla was warm, snuggled inside a large sleeping bag with Jackson.

She was a coward. She knew she was a coward, because she'd dodged conversation about the night before. In her head she'd tried to dismiss it as a one-night stand, but she knew it was more than that and knowing scared her. She knew what to do after a one-night stand. Walk away. This was different.

She'd avoided it, but there was no avoiding it now as he wrapped his arm around her and hauled her close. Whether that was to add to the warmth, the feeling of security or just because of what they'd shared the night before, she didn't know. And there was no opportunity to explore it, because Dana was behind them, driving the dog team. They surged forward with enthusiasm and excitement. Occasionally she'd call out a command, but otherwise they glided through the moonlight in silence, part of the wilderness, absorbing the unique atmosphere of the forest at night.

It was the most relaxing, magical experience of her life, a million miles away from her job, New York and all the small irritations that punctuated her working day. Here in this snow-covered wonderland there were no complications, no pressures, no decisions to be made. Her whole world was the forest, the silence and the man next to her. It was all about the moment, and she knew it was yet another moment she'd never forget.

The cold stung her cheeks, and she was grateful for the goggles that protected her eyes from snow kicked up by the dogs' paws.

She sat snuggled against Jackson, until Dana brought the dog team to a halt. The lamp on her head showed they were at the junction with another trail leading deep into the forest.

Jackson levered himself out of their cozy cocoon, spoke to Dana and came back moments later holding snowshoes. "I want to show you the forest at night."

Kayla wished she could just stay in the sleeping bag pressed against the warmth of him, but that wasn't an option so she forced herself to wriggle out of the comfort, shivering as the freezing air bit through the warmth of her jacket.

He took a rucksack from Dana. "We'll be half an hour."

Dana walked around to tend to the dogs. "No hurry."

"Half an hour?" Kayla's teeth were chattering. "How long does it take to freeze out here?"

"Not long if you don't have the right equipment. Fortunately we do. These help you walk on deep snow without sinking into the powder." He helped her put on snowshoes and hefted the rucksack onto his back.

"What's in there?"

"Sustenance, just in case we need it." He took her hand and led her along the snowy trail, through heavily laden trees and into the depth of the forest until Dana and the sled were no longer visible and the only sound was the occasional howl of the dogs as they waited impatiently to start running again.

Kayla paused, looking through the trees illuminated by moonlight and his head torch. "I'd spook myself if I were on my own."

"You're not on your own." He curved his arm around her and pulled her against him. "Listen."

It started to snow, big soft flakes drifting down in a steady flow, settling on her hat and her jacket.

"What am I listening for?" She tilted her head. "I don't hear anything."

"Exactly. It's just you, me and the forest. Some of these trees, especially the white pine and the sugar maple, have been standing here for hundreds of years. When I was a kid I used to think that was so cool. I used to wonder who else had walked past and seen these same trees." He stooped and picked up a beautifully shaped pinecone from the surface of the deep snow. "I was fascinated by how the trees could change with the seasons and yet still be here. In the fall, if you stand up on the ridge where we were skiing this morning, it's like looking at a sunset. Reds, golds, oranges—all mixed together."

"It must be spectacular."

"It is, but this has always been my favorite time of year. Not just winter, but Christmas. When I was a kid I used to come up here with Gramps. We'd haul the sled and choose a tree for the lodge. I could never understand why people wanted to cut them down and put them indoors." He studied the pinecone in his hand. "I couldn't understand why folks wanted to spray these silver and put them in a bowl in the center of the dining table with big red bows. A tree belongs in a forest. For me, coming here with Gramps was Christmas. It wasn't the decorations, lights or turkey. It was everything right here."

His words made her eyes sting.

"This is real. The rest is all an illusion."

"It's time you had some new memories of Christmas, Kayla." His voice was as soft and gentle as the snow falling around them. "We're going to make them together so that you have something good to take away with you. That's my gift to you. Merry Christmas."

The sting in her throat became a lump as he slid the pinecone into her palm.

"A souvenir from Vermont. Put it on your desk and it will remind you of the forest when you're back in the craziness of your life."

Kayla stared at it for a long moment and then tucked the pinecone carefully into her pocket, wondering why the prospect of returning to the craziness of her life didn't lift her mood.

It was what she did, and she'd done it for so long

she didn't even question whether there might be another way.

Or maybe she was just too afraid to look.

Maybe he was right about that.

Jackson lifted his hand and brushed snow away from her hat. "We should get back."

The chemistry was a sharp pull in her stomach, a snatch of breath, a pound of her heart—as powerful as ever, drawing them together. She wasn't a romantic person but there was something about the soft fall of snow and the intense blue of Jackson's eyes that made it hard to breathe.

And she knew he was going to kiss her, here in this frozen forest, the trees their only witness.

There was an inevitability to it that made her heart kick at her ribs and when his arms came around her and his mouth finally claimed hers, she gave a soft sigh. His lips were cool, the outside temperature below freezing, but the kiss was perfect—lit by stars and moonbeams, the heat and fire cooled by the soft brush of falling snowflakes on her skin, and she knew that, whatever happened, she would go back with new memories of Christmas.

It had to end, of course. It was too cold to allow such a perfect moment to last, but the warmth stayed with her as they walked back through the silent forest to Dana and the waiting husky team.

They snuggled back down in the sleeping bag, drank hot chocolate to warm themselves and then continued on the trail, along the side of the lake and back to Kayla's cabin.

"Thank you." Kayla shivered as her boots touched the snow. "That was the best experience of my life."

"Top that, Jackson." Dana winked at her cousin. "Want me to run you back to your barn?"

"I do not." A smile touching his mouth, he strolled over to his cousin and hugged her. "Thanks, Dana."

Her eyes twinkled. "You could invite me in for a coffee."

"I could, but I'm not going to." He strolled away from her and took Kayla's arm while Dana gave a dreamy sigh.

"Okay, but just remember I do engagements and weddings. Champagne extra."

Jackson didn't turn his head.

SHE WAS SHIVERING, and he realized with a tug of guilt just how wet she was. "We stayed out too long. You're frozen."

"I loved it." Her teeth were chattering. "That's how I want to commute when I get back to New York. Thank you for arranging it."

Cursing softly, he tugged off her gloves and warmed her freezing hands. "Stay there and don't move. I need one minute, that's all—just one minute."

He'd been planning it all evening, but hadn't expected to use it as a first aid technique.

He did what he needed to do and returned to find her standing where he'd left her, the melting snow sliding off her jacket.

"We need to get you out of your clothes—"

"You have to be kidding." Her hands covered his as he tried to unzip her jacket. "I am not removing a s-single layer. You may be hot, O'Neil, but even you're not hot enough to make me part with layers."

"You need to be naked for what I have in mind."

Her teeth were chattering. "Jackson—"

"Hot tub." He ignored the grip of her chilled fingers and pulled down the zip. "We need to get you out of this wet clothing and into the warmth."

"I c-cannot take my c-clothes off."

"I'll do that part."

"You're all heart, O'Neil."

"Not true. I have other parts." He pulled off her fleece top, steadily undressing her. "Parts you're about to discover."

"Are those parts frozen?"

"Definitely not. Want me to prove it? I'll leave you your underwear, Green."

"Why bother?" She was still shivering but her eyes were dark as she looked at him. "Don't tell Alice, but my underwear isn't thermal."

"In that case it's serving no purpose and has to come off." Resisting the temptation to start the warming process right there and then on the hardwood floor, Jackson relieved her of her underwear and wrapped a warm bathrobe around her. "Come with me."

"I am going to die of hypothermia. Or frostbite—" Her muttered complaints lasted until she slid into the steaming hot tub. "Or maybe I'll just die of bliss—" She closed her eyes and sank down to her neck. "Oh, this is perfect."

Jackson slid in next to her, the heat of the water a luxurious contrast to the freezing air.

She leaned her head back against the side of the hot tub. "I want to stay here and never move. I'm going to make Brett install one in the office for lunchtime relaxation sessions."

"You don't take lunch and you don't relax."

But she was relaxing now, her eyes closed, her long lashes creating a dark shadow against her pale skin.

"Now I understand why you installed a hot tub on the deck of each cabin. It's genius."

"You've never used a hot tub before?"

"Never." Her eyes opened and she looked at the forest and the frozen surface of the lake that glistened in the moonlight. "I bet there aren't many hot tubs with a view like this one."

"I've tried to persuade my grandfather to try it."

She smiled. "I can imagine his response."

"It wasn't polite, but the gist of it was that he thinks it's an unnecessary extravagance."

"Which probably defines my perfect holiday."

"You never take holidays."

"Maybe it's time I did."

"Are you telling me you've fallen in love with Snow Crystal?"

Her smile faltered. A tiny frown appeared on her forehead.

"Maybe. Does that count as being involved with a client?"

"No. But this does." He tried to take it slowly, to savor each moment, because the last time had been a desperate blur of hunger and need and he wanted this to be different. He fought the surge of raw primal lust, tensed muscle to prevent himself from hauling her close, tried to ignore the madness, until holding back became the biggest challenge of his life. She was naked, her skin gleaming wet from the snow and the water. He'd never seen a woman more beautiful. *Never wanted a woman more.*

Her hair was pinned haphazardly on top of her head. Wisps of blond, damp from the steam, clung to the smooth curve of her jaw and neck.

This was a different Kayla Green and this was the woman he wanted.

He might have kept it slow if she hadn't slid a hand over his thigh and eased herself closer to him in the bubbling water. Might even have held back a little if her mouth hadn't brushed against his jaw, the lick of her tongue a tease and a temptation. He turned his head, caught her mouth with his and was lost. Her lips were soft, her kisses hot, her body lithe as she moved gracefully through the steaming water and wound her legs around his.

Her hand cupped him, and Jackson closed his eyes, jaw clenched, brain wiped, reduced to the most basic version of himself. "Kayla—"

"This is your fault—" She nibbled his lip, licked at him, driving him crazy. "I don't do this, so it has to be your fault."

But she was doing it now, and he told himself that was all that mattered. They'd work the rest out later. Or maybe they'd let the rest take care of itself. Right now, he didn't care. All he cared about was not tipping over the edge. Not yet.

Her hands were on his shoulders, on his chest, and she drove him wild with the drag of her nails, the touch of her mouth until he knew he couldn't trust himself to control the pace unless he was the one in charge.

Fighting for control, he locked his hands on her hips and shifted her so that she straddled him. Eyes wide, she tried to sheathe herself with him, but he held her hard, restricting the movement of her hips, his legs pressing hers apart, exposing her to his touch. And touch he did, with slow gentle strokes, his fingers sliding over her feminine softness until she gasped softly against his mouth.

Around them the forest was silent, sounds muffled by the thick blanket of winter and the steady fall of new snow. Her lips were pressed against his, and he felt each sound she made, tasted and swallowed every moan as he stroked and explored with knowing fingers until he tipped her over the edge.

He felt it happen, felt each ripple and pulse of her body with his fingers and he was so hard, so ready, it took all his willpower not to give in to the writhing of her hips and take what they both wanted right there.

But he wanted more—so much more than a steamy encounter in a hot tub followed by a serving of hypothermia.

"Inside." He managed one word and she raised her head and looked at him, eyes unfocused, mouth soft and swollen from his kisses.

"Inside?"

"Now." He'd never been this desperate. Never felt this out of control, not even when he'd hit adolescence and chased everything female. Exercising willpower he didn't know he had, he eased away from her, reached for her robe and braved the freezing air. "Move."

CHAPTER SIXTEEN

HE SECURED THE door behind them, shutting out the cold. Then he grabbed warm towels from the bathroom and tried to dry her hair, but she couldn't keep herself from touching and neither could he so the towel landed on the bedroom floor, abandoned and forgotten.

His robe went next, the moon sending silver light over perfect male physique.

"I've had an idea—" Her mouth was dry as she slid her hand over his chest. "We could just make a poster of you half-naked and slap it on the subway. Snow Crystal would be booked out within minutes."

He gave a slow smile. "I'm already booked. Exclusively."

The word shook her. She'd never felt like this before. Never allowed her feelings to be engaged. But she no longer had a choice in it. She wanted all of him. Wanted to know all there was to know.

"How did you get this?" Her palm traced the scar over his ribs and lingered there.

"I was injured rescuing a litter of vulnerable puppies from a river."

"Really?" She glanced up and the dangerous glitter in his eyes gave her clues as to exactly how he was feeling.

"No, not really—" he spoke through his teeth "—but

this isn't a good time to confess all my misadventures. Kayla—"

"Mmm?" She teased him, took her time, explored him with her fingers and her tongue until finally, when his breathing was shallow and uneven, she dropped to her knees and took him in her mouth, sliding her lips over his silken hardness, taking him deep.

She heard him groan her name, felt the shudder pass through his body as she used her tongue and her mouth, touching and tasting until finally he muttered something unintelligible and lifted her to her feet.

They hit the bed together, rolled, her on top then him on top, his fingers hard on her flesh as he spread her thighs.

She was ready, so ready, but still he postponed that moment, drawing his tongue over her, driving her higher, closer, until her hips shifted against the sheets and her hands clutched at his shoulders. His muscles were pumped up and hard, everything about him completely, aggressively masculine as he used his wickedly expert hands and mouth to seduce her until she was weak with wanting.

"Jackson—" his name left her lips like a plea "—I want— I need— You have to—" The words were as messed up as her thoughts but he knew what she wanted and gave it to her, his mouth on her, his tongue on her as he explored her with erotic precision and a skill that had her sobbing with desperation.

Swamped by exquisite sensation, she felt herself rush toward orgasm, but this time instead of letting her reach that peak alone, he eased away from her briefly, reached for the protection he'd almost forgotten the first time and then drove into her with a smooth thrust that took him deep.

She gasped his name, felt the hardness of him, the thickness of him pulse inside her and felt control slipping. She opened her eyes and stared into the fierce blue of his, and what they shared in that single look was as intimate as the physical connection that throbbed through both of them. He lowered his head and kissed her deeply and then they were moving together in a perfect rhythm, his hand locked in her hair, eyes on hers, inseparable as they took the same wild ride through the storm. It was intense and primitive, her need for him so fierce she thought she'd burn alive with the heat of it. Orgasm ripped through her, and she cried out, consumed by it, the spasms of her body rippling down his shaft and taking him with her. They kissed right through it, mouths fused, bodies slick with sweat, her gaze locked with his the whole time so they didn't just feel what they were doing to each other, they watched it happen.

And afterward they lay, bodies entwined, not moving.

When she'd recovered sufficiently, Kayla tried to pull away only to find herself locked against him.

"You're not going anywhere." His eyes were closed and her hand was on his chest. She felt the steady thump of his heart beating under her palm.

"I need to—"

"I know what you need to do, but you're staying here."

"I was going to say I need the bathroom."

"You were going to say that, but then you were going to run." His eyes were still closed. "And I'm not letting you do that. Not this time. You're going to stay right here and then perhaps you'll discover the world doesn't end if you wake up in my bed in the morning. Go to sleep, sweetheart."

Frustration mingled with panic. "You manipulated this evening. You did it on purpose."

"I planned the part in the forest. The rest just happened."

She sat up, spooked by feelings she had no idea how to handle. "No, it didn't just happen." She turned to him, accusing. "You did this. Magical sled rides through the forest, a hot tub on the deck, skiing, snowmobiling—you were trying to make me fall in love with Snow Crystal."

"Of course. You were supposed to fall in love."

With the place, yes, but not with the man, she thought desperately. Never with the man.

He was someone who believed in bonds, ties, families—all the things she would never allow herself to believe in ever again.

And yet, even knowing that, she was lying here next to him. Again. She'd never been this intimate with a man. Never shared so much.

"Are you going to lie down or am I going to do my caveman thing and haul you back down here?" His tone was mild but the hand on her shoulder was strong. Reassuring. She tried to ignore the lazy stroke of his palm over her bare flesh.

"I can't do this—"

"All I'm asking you to do is lie down. Is that so hard?"

"That's not what I mean—"

"I know, but it's enough for now." He drew her into the circle of his arms and held her there. "You never just live in the moment. You're always ten steps ahead, panicking." His fingers stroked her hair gently, and she closed her eyes because it felt good and that terrified her, too.

"I never imagined it could be like this. And I don't mean the sex, although that was good—"

"Good? Sweetheart, *good* is the first cup of coffee in the morning or a perfect powder day on the mountain. This was off the scale—"

"Good sex is a matter of physical compatibility. It doesn't have to be close—"

"You've had sex like that before?"

"I— No—" He tied her in knots. She couldn't get her balance. *Couldn't breathe.* "Jackson—"

"This doesn't feel close?" He lifted his eyebrows, and she couldn't blame him for that because her limbs were tangled with his, her naked body pressed against his. There wasn't a part of her that wasn't touching him.

"It feels close. And I don't do close."

"Because it's safer to keep yourself distant so you don't get hurt. Yeah, I get that. But just because your parents had a screwed-up relationship doesn't mean all relationships are screwed up."

"Their relationship wasn't screwed up. They never argued."

"And that didn't strike you as strange?"

"Why would it? I assumed it meant they were happy."

"Really? Because that isn't what it would have said to me."

"What would it have said to you?"

"Sweetheart, you can't live with someone, be married to them for years and never disagree on a single thing. How is that healthy?" His hand was warm on her bare back. "There are only two reasons a couple are never going to argue—the first is because they're afraid, maybe because the balance of power is wrong or other complex reasons mostly driven by fear, the second is because they don't care enough. There is a third, which is when they're thinking and feeling the same thing at the same time, but that would make them robots."

She hadn't thought about it before. "There's a fourth—" her hand slid around his waist "—and that's that you don't see each other enough to argue. That's how it was with my parents most of the time. My father stayed away."

"With his other family. And that sucks, and if you want my utterly biased opinion, I confess to wanting to shake the pair of them for not living their relationship in an honest fashion."

"I suppose they thought they did their best."

"Then their best wasn't good enough." His voice was hard. "Either one of them could have said at any point that it wasn't working for them. That they wanted more. Instead they colluded to live a lie and they forced you to be part of that lie. And when that lie fell apart, as it inevitably would in those circumstances, you were left holding the fragments of something that never even existed. You avoid relationships because you're terrified of having that and losing it again—" He curved his hand behind her head and forced her to look at him. "But what you saw wasn't a relationship. It was a tangled mess. And instead of untangling the mess, they just stepped over it and left you there in the rubble. They didn't even try to rebuild something you could be part of."

"Neither of them wanted me living with them." She paused, aware of an emptiness in her chest. "I suppose I'm just not that lovable." It was the first time she'd voiced that feeling, and he swore softly and rolled, pinning her to the bed.

"They told you that?"

"They didn't need to. It was obvious in the lengths they went to not to spend time with me. Those first few holidays when I started at boarding school were hideously awkward. The correct term for it is a blended family, but we were never that." She stared up at him, distracted by the blue of his eyes and the sensual curve of his mouth, feeling more vulnerable than she ever had in her life before. "There was no blending. I used to hear my father's new wife on the phone—'we have his other daughter staying with us'—and then there'd be a pause while whoever it was on the other end of the phone sympathized with her. I stayed in my room as much as I could and then the next year I told them I'd been invited to stay with a friend. Deep down, I hoped they'd talk me out of it. That they'd tell me it was Christmas and they wanted me home."

"But they didn't."

"They were relieved. They gave me money and told me to go and enjoy myself. After that they sent me money every year. Why are we talking about this?"

He stroked her cheek with his fingers. His touch was casual, but the look in his eyes was anything but casual. "I like to know what I'm fighting. You can't remove obstacles until you know what they are. Now I know more about you."

"You don't know me, Jackson."

But he knew more about her than any other person.

"I know that what you believe about relationships is based on one appalling example. I know you're scared." His voice was rough. "I know I'm going to change that."

"You can't. I'm stuck this way now."

"That sounds like a challenge." His mouth was on hers, warm and skilled, and this time when they made love it was slow, deep and rocked the heart of her. And she knew that each time they did this she was making it harder for herself to walk away unscathed.

"Jackson—"

"Close your eyes and go to sleep." He rolled onto his back, but didn't release her. "We still have to catch up on the sleep we didn't get last night, and tonight is half-over."

She lay still in the strong protective circle of his arms, not wanting to move. In the past, staying had been the problem, not leaving. Now that situation was reversed.

But what difference would it make to stay until dawn? What did one whole night really matter?

She'd wake early and do what she always did.

She'd get up and walk away.

SHE WOKE TO bright sunshine and delicious smells from the kitchen. She lay there for a moment, warm and lethargic, hovering between wake and sleep. Sometime during the night it had stopped snowing, and through the window she could see a perfect blue sky, the sun reflecting off snow that had the smooth perfection of a wedding cake.

Still groggy, Kayla groped for her phone and did what she always did first thing in the morning. She checked the time.

Normally it said 5:00 a.m.

Today it said 9:00 a.m.

Nine?

It had to be a mistake. She hadn't slept until nine

since—since—she couldn't remember a time when she'd slept until nine. *She never slept until nine.*

She sprang out of bed, then realized she was naked and grabbed the nearest item of clothing from the pile on the floor, which turned out to be Jackson's T-shirt. It smelled of him and she briefly pressed her face in it before dragging it on and dragging her fingers through her hair.

Flustered, she looked at the bed and then at the open door leading to the living area. So much for her plan to sneak out early.

She ventured into the kitchen and saw him, standing with his back to her, frying bacon. He'd pulled on jeans, but his feet were bare. His chest was bare. Her gaze lingered on the masculine contours of his body. She stared at the swell of his biceps, at the hard strength of his shoulders, at the power in those forearms. He was the hottest, sexiest guy she'd ever met, and he shouldn't be allowed to remove his shirt without issuing a warning.

She thought the moan was in her head, but something must have come out of her mouth because he turned and of course the front view was even better than the back.

"Good morning." His voice was husky, and he turned the heat off under the pan and strolled over to her. His jaw was dark, his hair slightly rumpled, and she knew she was the one responsible for that because she'd had her fingers locked in it for almost half the night.

She had no idea what she was supposed to say but he didn't give her a chance to speak. Instead he cupped her face in his hands and lowered his head. His kiss was long, slow and deep, and she felt fire lick through her veins. Her eyes drifted shut. He could take her from zero to the edge of orgasm at supersonic speed with nothing more than a single kiss. By the time he finally lifted his head she was ready to go straight back to bed. It shouldn't have been possible to feel this desperate, should it? Not after the way they'd spent the night.

Unsettled, she pulled away from him, but that didn't help because now she had a full-on view of his chest. "You should have woken me."

His smile was slow, his eyes an intense blue in the light of the morning. "Why?"

"Because I always wake at five. I don't sleep late."

"But you slept late today." He brushed her lips with his thumb and turned back to deal with the breakfast. "That's good."

"It's not good, Jackson!" She ran her tongue over her lips where he'd kissed her. Everything about him unsettled her, not least the fact he didn't seem unsettled at all. He was so relaxed. So sure of himself. "I have to finish off my proposal, make some calls, wash my hair— Why are you smiling?"

He flipped the bacon. "Because we both know the reason you're panicking about waking late has nothing to do with work."

"I thought you were eager to get this project started, too."

"I am. But I have room in my life for things other than work, and I know you'll get the job done. And your hair looks great, by the way. Can you pass me the eggs from the fridge?"

How could her hair look great?

She hadn't dared look in the mirror but she had to look a tousled mess.

Dazed, Kayla dragged open the door of the fridge and found the eggs. "I wanted to write up the proposal, send it across to the office and then be ready to make some calls this morning."

"You can still do all that." He handed her a bowl. "Break four eggs into that."

She smashed an egg and it landed in the bowl with a broken yolk and pieces of shell.

Jackson sighed and fished out the shell with a spoon. "What did that egg ever do to you? Calm down."

"I'm calm."

"Sweetheart, you're shaking." He covered her hand with his and rapped the egg on the side of the bowl so that it broke neatly. "There. Easy." His hand was warm and strong and suddenly she couldn't breathe.

"I don't know what any of this means."

"It means we're eating breakfast." He squeezed her hand and then released it, removed bacon and added mushrooms to the pan. "Once a week I allow myself a heart attack breakfast. Today is that day. You can join me. Last night didn't kill us—this might but at least we'll die together."

"I don't eat breakfast."

"You don't sleep late, either, but you managed that." His arm brushed against hers, and she realized how strange it felt to be standing side by side in the kitchen with a man, cooking.

"Jackson—"

He sighed. "Relax, honey. You feel out of control, but we can't control everything that happens in life. Sometimes we just have to go where the tide takes us and know we'll cope with whatever comes along."

"I can't live like that."

"We all live like that. Control is an illusion. You think you're in charge and then—whoosh—life happens when you're not looking and you realize the best thing you can do is just roll with it."

She wondered if he was talking about losing his father so suddenly. "I know there are some things we can't control, but there are things we *can* control and I like to control those things. It's what I do."

"That's because to you *everything* is work, but even that can't be completely controlled. If it could, this place wouldn't be the mess it is."

She marveled at the way he handled the pressure. "I know you can turn this place around."

"So do I. Unfortunately, Gramps doesn't, which gives me a dilemma. Do I do what the business needs and upset him, or do I keep him happy and risk losing this place? It doesn't give me pleasure to cause him this much stress."

Kayla thought about the conversation she'd had with Walter the day before. "He worships you."

"I don't doubt that he loves me—" his tone was gruff "—but trust me to run this place? Make decisions and changes? No. And that's the part that counts."

She handed him a plate. "Have you tried talking to him?"

"I've talked to him a million times." He slid the eggs onto the plate and added bacon. "It doesn't seem to help."

"He's scared, Jackson. And you take him ideas that scare him even more, so he fights. Instead of talking about how you're going to change Snow Crystal, maybe you should talk about all the things you love about it. Listen to his vision, and if it seems unrealistic, out of date, maybe you should find a way of helping him see that." She shook her head, embarrassed. "Sorry. I know nothing about working with family. Ignore me."

"No." Frowning, he put the plate down. "You're right. Our conversations are always about the changes I'm making. From the day I arrived back, eighteen months ago, it's been about survival, firefighting, crisis management."

"I suppose that's inevitable."

Jackson cursed under his breath and rubbed his fingers over his forehead. "I stormed back in here like some corporate warrior, sure I knew what I was doing, and sure I could fix things. I was so shaken by losing my father and the discovery that he'd left a mess, I didn't tread sensitively. It's no wonder Gramps doesn't want me here." He stood for a moment and then drew in a deep breath. "I'll go and talk to him when we've finished breakfast. While I'm gone, take a shower and get dressed in something warm. I'm taking you skating on the lake. I promise not to let you fall."

Kayla opened her mouth and closed it again. She was allowed some secrets, wasn't she?

"Sounds like fun." As he turned to her, her breath caught. "Jackson, do me a favor—"

He lifted an eyebrow and a wicked smile tugged at the corners of his mouth. "Again?"

"Very funny—"

His head lowered to hers. "What is this favor?"

"Put some clothes on. Right now."

"That's the favor?" Laughing, he backed her against the countertop, all pumped-up muscle and male virility. "Is there some reason you want me to put clothes on, Miss Green?"

"Yes." She tried to push him away but it didn't work out that way. "I can't concentrate when you're half-naked."

"Is that right?" His mouth was on her neck. Lower.

Her eyes closed. "Jackson—breakfast—"

"You don't eat breakfast." He scooped her into his arms and carried her back to the bedroom.

By the time they eventually ate their breakfast, the eggs were cold.

HE LEFT HER naked and working in bed while he went in search of his grandfather.

He found him sitting on a log, staring at the mountains.

Something about his expression made Jackson's heart tighten. "Need any help?"

"Why?" Turning his head, his grandfather scowled at him. "Are you taking a break from pouring good money after bad?"

Fear, Jackson thought. What he was seeing was fear.

"Nothing I've done has been bad, Gramps." He spoke quietly. "What is it you want for Snow Crystal? I assumed you wanted to keep this place going, and that's what I'm trying to do."

There was a long silence.

"What I want," his grandfather said, "is for you to go back to Switzerland or wherever it is your fancy company is based and leave this place to those of us who know how to run it."

The words lit the fire under the neat stack of frustration that had been slowly building over the past eighteen months.

"There's more than one way to get something done. I've seen you come down a mountain sixteen different ways, and running a business is no different. I may not be taking the route you took, I may not be doing things the way you did them, but it doesn't mean I'm wrong. I can run this place. I can keep it going and build it. Why can't you trust me to do that?"

"Because I don't want you to." Walter stood up and picked up the ax, his knuckles white on the handle. "I don't want you to run this place."

The words drove into his belly like a physical punch.

The silence was broken only by the sound of his grandfather's uneven breathing.

Jackson knew better than to let the first thing in his head come out of his mouth, so he waited a moment. He tried never to let emotions enter into his business decisions, but when those decisions involved family he'd discovered it was all about emotion. He'd trained himself not to take anything personally, but how could this not be personal? "You don't think I can do it."

"I know you can do it." His grandfather thumped the ax into the log and left it there, vibrating with the force of the blow. "You can do anything you put your mind to. I saw it when you were four years old. If something stood in your way and you couldn't get over it, you went around it. You're clever. And you've got a way with people. Those things together—well, it's a real gift."

The shift from insult to compliment was so swift Jackson was left reeling. *Your grandfather is so proud of you.*

"But—" he had to push the words through the roughness of his throat "—if you know I can do it, then why don't you want me here?"

"Because this place swallows you up. It takes all you have and still demands more. And it's never enough." His grandfather sank back down onto the log, his movements unsteady. At that moment he looked every one of his eighty years.

Jackson stared at him, seeing a stranger. "I thought you loved Snow Crystal."

"Love?" His grandfather tilted his head and breathed the air and stared at the mountains. "I've stared at these same peaks since the day I first opened my eyes. You'd think I'd be bored of the view by now, wouldn't you? Truth is, the only thing that lifts my mood more than looking at those mountains is looking at your grandmother, and she's part of this place. Of course I love it. I was born loving it and I'll die loving it, but loving it comes at a price and I didn't want any of you to pay that price. I wanted all of you to be free to live your lives the way you want to live them. If you'd stayed to run this place would you have gone to Switzerland and built your company? Would Tyler have won medals? Would Sean have become a doctor?"

"Nothing would have stopped Tyler skiing or Sean becoming a doctor." Jackson's throat felt raw. His chest ached. "You sent us away. Hell, Gramps, you virtually kicked the three of us out."

"I did it for your own good."

Jackson dragged his hand over the back of his neck, wondering why that possibility hadn't occurred to him. "I thought you didn't want us here."

"I didn't. But it was never because I thought you couldn't do it." His grandfather's eyes were fierce. "I wanted you to choose your own path, not have this one thrust on you. I didn't want loyalty to your family holding you back from doing what you needed to do. This place has been my life. I didn't want it to be yours."

Jackson thought about the burden his grandfather had carried. And he would have carried it alone, because his father hadn't been interested.

"You should have told me how bad things were here. You should have let me come home sooner."

"And tie you up with debts and worries?" Walter reached forward and picked up one of the logs he'd chopped. He rubbed his hand down the rough bark and then threw the log on the pile with the others. "That's not what I want for you. Birds should fly the nest, not be tethered to it. It was our problem, not yours."

"And you didn't think I could make that decision for myself?"

"This place was my father's dream and then it was my dream. It was never yours. A man shouldn't have to carry the weight of another man's dream." There was a sadness in his voice. "I gave that dream to your father to carry and it weighed him down. I have to live with the guilt of that. I wasn't going to put that same weight on you. I may be old, but I can still learn."

Jackson felt pressure in his chest and a thickness in his throat. He'd never had trouble forming words before. "What if it's my dream, too?"

Silence stretched, long and deep.

Walter's throat worked as he stared at the mountains.

Jackson put his hand on his grandfather's shoulder. "What then, Gramps?" He saw the sheen in his grandfather's eyes and the tension in his jaw that came from expending effort to hang on to control.

"I guess that would be different."

The atmosphere shifted.

"Gramps—"

"Is it your dream?"

Jackson was surprised by how easy it was to answer that question. This time there was no pause and no silence. "It always has been. Maybe I had to go away to see it."

Walter's shoulders relaxed. The tension left him. "You'll save this place. You can do anything you want if you put your mind to it."

There was no crash of cymbals to highlight the dramatic shift in their relationship. No fireworks to welcome in a new phase. Just words. But words so deeply felt they changed everything.

"*We'll* save it." Jackson wrapped his arms around his grandfather and felt strength and fire pumping beneath thin bones and fragile flesh. "We'll carry that dream together. We'll save this place together. That's a promise."

CHAPTER SEVENTEEN

"THE LAKE IS usually frozen solid between December and March. Providing the weather is right, we maintain the section of ice closest to the lodge as a rink for pond skating and we maintain a skate trail around the lake. So far, it's been a good year."

"Hey, Kayla—" Tyler was already on the ice "—if you can stay upright we'll make you an honorary member of the O'Neil pond hockey team."

"Ignore him." Jackson gave her elbow and knee pads. "These will help if you fall. We're going to take it slowly to give you a chance to get used to being on the ice."

Kayla secured the knee pads.

Maybe it was wrong of her not to say something, but she didn't see why they should have all the fun.

Sean fastened his skates. "And if you do fall and break something, I'll fix it for a discounted rate."

"You're so generous." Kayla stood still while Jackson fastened her skates.

"Bend your knees slightly and lean forward. Whatever you do, don't lean back." He straightened and held out his hand. "Don't be nervous. The ice is thick here so you're in no danger of falling through."

She ignored his hand and skated onto the ice.

"Kayla—"

"Back in a minute." Enjoying herself hugely, she glided across the ice, getting the feel for the unfamiliar skates. Then she increased speed, flowed into a jump, spun and landed perfectly, executed another couple of spins and glided back to where Jackson and Sean were standing, mouths agape. "You're right. It's fun."

Sean folded his arms, grinning. "Is there something you'd like to tell us?"

Jackson stared at her. "Where did you learn to skate?"

"At school, a long time ago."

"You went to school in London."

"So? They have indoor ice rinks. Not as picturesque as this, but ice is ice." She doubted anywhere in the world could be more picturesque than this.

"You didn't think to mention it?"

"I wasn't sure if I could remember how to do it, or if it would feel different being outdoors. It doesn't. It feels wonderful—" She glided away from them and spun again. When she stopped, Jackson was on the ice next to her.

"You're good."

"Not that good. I won a couple of junior competitions, but I wasn't prepared to practice for hours at a time. I wasn't dedicated enough."

"You skated in competitions? Did you ever wear one of those incredibly short and revealing dresses?"

"Yes."

With a groan, he lowered his head toward hers, ignoring the wolf whistling from his brothers. "Can I tempt you to wear one of those again?"

"You're warped." But her heart picked up pace and she saw his eyes darken.

"Remind me why we got up this morning instead of staying in bed?"

"Because I'm experiencing Snow Crystal, and you wanted to talk to your grandfather. How did that go by the way?"

"It went well. You were right about a lot of things." He seemed about to add something to that comment but then looked over her shoulder and stopped. "Later. Jess is on her way over here."

"Wow, Kayla!" Jess skated over to them, her face alight. "That was *so* cool. Will you teach me?"

"Sure. I'll swap skating lessons for ski lessons."

"Done. I want to learn how to spin."

"You need to glide on your edge, turn your shoulders—" She demonstrated it several times and then they all skated together until Jackson was called away to deal with a problem at the lodge.

Kayla returned to the cabin, determined to work while she could.

She'd just removed her boots and jacket when Elizabeth arrived with Maple.

"Do you mind taking her for a couple of hours? I have to take Alice into the village to do some last-minute Christmas shopping and then Élise is giving me a cookery lesson."

Maple leaped ecstatically at the sight of Kayla, who discovered she didn't mind at all.

"I'm glad of the company."

Which should have surprised her, because normally she resented interruptions when she was working.

She lifted the puppy and was rewarded by canine kisses. "I'll bring her back over later." Was it her imagination or did Elizabeth seem different? There was a glow to her smile and an energy in her step that hadn't been there a few days earlier. "How's it going in the restaurant?"

"Incredibly busy. It's a crazy environment, but you're part of a team and—it's hard to explain, but I feel as if I have a purpose. I feel needed."

"That's because you are needed," Kayla said drily. "Without you, Élise would be slitting her throat with one of her own kitchen knives."

"She's giving me a sauté lesson later."

"Good luck with that." But she was pleased to see Elizabeth looking so happy and pleased that she'd played a part in that.

Left alone, Kayla stripped off the clothes she'd worn for skating, took a hot shower and washed her hair.

She stepped onto the towel, her mind on work, and almost jumped out of her skin as something licked her toes.

Maple wagged her tail and Kayla pressed her hand to her chest and waited for her heart to slow down.

"You frightened the life out of me. I'd forgotten you like to do that." She picked the puppy up and carried her through to the bedroom. "Good job you weren't here last night because you are far too young to witness what went on in this room."

With Maple watching, she pulled on a pair of jeans and a chunky cream sweater and left her hair to dry naturally.

Walking through to the living room, she spread out all her notes while the puppy settled down on the rug.

She worked harder than she'd worked in her life. Every account was important to her, but this was the first time an account had mattered to her on a personal level and she was determined to do all she could to get results.

She lost track of the time and nearly jumped out of her skin when she heard Maple bark and looked up to see Jackson standing there.

"You scared me."

"Yeah, we need to work on that. You're far too jumpy for your own good." He reached down and tugged her to her feet. "I love your hair like that."

"Messy?"

"That's not the word I'd use. You look relaxed. Less uptight. I like it. When did you last eat?"

"Er—breakfast?" She ran her fingers through her hair, self-conscious. "You cooked it. It was cold."

"You've been working all this time?"

"I didn't realize it was so late. I've been finishing up this proposal, making a few calls—" She was excited enough to want to share the details, but decided it would be better to talk to them all at the same time. "When do you want me to present to your family?"

"You're prepared to do that again after what happened last time?"

"Of course. This is a family business."

"How about Christmas Eve? Élise is cooking." He picked up Maple, and Kayla followed him to the door, work forgotten.

"Where are we going?"

"My place. I'm cooking you dinner."

She ran her palms over her jeans and glanced toward the bedroom. "I should change—"

"Don't. I like you like that. I think I might prefer chilled, sexy Kayla to corporate Kayla." He pulled her toward him and delivered a lingering kiss to her mouth. "You look exactly the way you looked when you woke up this morning."

IT WAS THE first time she'd been to his home. It had the same soaring ceilings and large windows as the cabins. The same charm. The same incredible view of the lake. "I love it."

"This barn was built in 1902 to house a couple of hundred cattle." He dug his thumbs in his pockets. "My brothers and I played here as kids. Used to hide up in the hayloft."

"It was your idea to convert it?"

"Didn't seem any sense in keeping it empty, and I needed somewhere that was mine. I added the deck because I liked the idea of drinking beer while watching the sun go down over the lake, but so far that's been wishful thinking. When I've drunk beer it's mostly been while standing up doing ten jobs simultaneously."

She strolled to the large kitchen window. Ice crystals glistened on the surface of the lake, and the bright winter sun sent shafts of light through the trees. "The view is incredible."

"It was this place that gave me the idea of building the log cabins. I loved the position. I figured others would, too."

"That explains why it has the same feel."

"I used to spend hours in these woods when I was young. Some nights the three of us camped out up in the mountains. If we were lost, we followed the river home. We knew how to survive in the wilderness. We have Gramps to thank for that."

She tried to imagine what it must have been like growing up here, surrounded by laughter and family. "So you talked to him?"

"Yes." As he relayed the conversation, her heart ached for Walter.

"He didn't want you to be burdened." She thought

about the love that must have been behind such an unselfish action. "He's a special man."

"It's generous of you to say that after the way he spoke to you on the first night."

"He thought you were wasting precious money and didn't see how PR could help. I didn't do a good job of showing him. He was protecting this place. Protecting you. Everything Walter does is driven by his love for Snow Crystal. And love for his family. You're lucky." She felt his arms come around her and leaned against him. "So you've cleared the air. That's a good Christmas present."

"Yes. What about you, Kayla Green?" His arms tightened around her. "What do you want for Christmas?"

It wasn't something she ever asked herself and certainly no one ever asked her. "A million bookings for Snow Crystal."

"That's work." He turned her to face him. "What about the personal?" Dark lashes shielded sinful blue eyes and she felt her knees weaken. He had to be the hottest guy on the planet.

"I might buy myself something when Christmas is over."

"Do you always buy your own gifts?"

"Why not? I don't need people to buy me things, Jackson. I can buy them for myself."

"People don't buy and give gifts just because the other person can't buy it for themselves. A gift is a symbol. It's a way of showing someone that you care and want to make them happy."

"Yes. I bought my earrings because I cared about me and wanted to make myself happy."

He laughed. "When was the last time you received a gift you hadn't chosen yourself?"

"Brett was pretty generous with the Christmas bonus this year."

"I'm not talking about money."

"Money suits me fine. I know what I want."

"Maybe you don't." He lowered his forehead to hers, and she felt her heart kick against her ribs. He was right there in her personal space, and she was shocked to discover that was exactly where she wanted him.

"So if you were choosing me a gift, what would you give me?"

"I'd give you something you would never buy for yourself," he said softly. "Something you possibly don't even know you want."

Standing this close to him, she could feel the warmth and power of his body. The chemistry was intoxicating, and this time she didn't even bother fighting it. Instead she slid her arms around his neck.

"I know exactly what I want, Jackson."

Fortunately, so did he.

CHRISTMAS EVE DINNER was a special occasion. "In France, Christmas Eve is a big celebration." Élise put food on the table with a flourish, roast duck cooked in a delicious sauce, the ingredients of which she refused to discuss. "It is a secret. I am trying something new."

"So if we're dead on Christmas morning, you know not to feed it to the guests," Tyler grumbled. "I'm not sure how I feel about being one of your experiments."

Kayla was finding it almost impossible not to look at Jackson and wondered how Élise could be so relaxed around Sean. Despite her confession that morning at breakfast, the French girl hadn't glanced once in his direction, nor he in hers.

There was no banter. No exchange of small talk. No comfortable laughter.

They'd been intimate, and yet not once did they look at each other.

And Kayla realized suddenly that they weren't relaxed at all.

She could have sliced through the tension with one of Élise's kitchen knives.

She glanced around the table.

Brenna was arguing with Tyler, and Jess was telling Alice about a run they'd done that morning.

Maybe she was the only one who had noticed. Maybe she was imagining it. She was no expert on relationships, was she?

And there was no time to dwell on it because all too soon the meal was over and she was the focus of attention.

Had it really only been a week since she'd stood here and tried to give the presentation? It felt like a lifetime ago.

Looking at the photographs on the wall she saw Jackson, aged about four, building a snowman with Sean. She could clearly see they were twins and wondered how she'd missed that the first time.

"Kayla?" Jackson was watching her, and the concern in his eyes touched her.

Walter scowled. "Well? Where's your laptop? We're all waiting to hear your miracle ideas."

"I left my laptop in the cabin."

"How are you going to impress us if you don't have all those fancy graphs?"

Jackson sighed, and Kayla quickly smoothed down the spike of tension.

"I'm going to impress you in other ways—for example, by reminding you of my log-chopping abilities."

"What abilities are those?" But Walter's eyes gleamed with humor as she flexed her biceps.

For this presentation she'd chosen to wear a cardigan in a pretty shade of green with her black trousers tucked into boots. She felt so much more relaxed and comfortable than she had that first night in her stilettos and pencil skirt.

"I got through the whole pile of logs this morning."

"You call that a pile? We'll heat the cabins for half an hour on what you chopped, and we almost had your foot along with it. Hardly surprising. All you've ever lifted is a pen. Now what are we going to do about this place?"

We.

She never heard *we*. She'd never been part of a *we* before, and the word threw her more than hostility would have done. Kayla tightened her fingers on the edge of the table.

"When I first arrived here you asked me what makes Snow Crystal special and I couldn't answer you. Now I can."

"Get on with it then." Walter caught his wife's eye. "What? I just want her to hurry up, that's all. I've seen what's for dessert. It's enough to make a grown man beg."

Alice peered at him over her glasses. "The girl is trying to speak. It would serve you right if she walks out."

"She's not going to walk out. She's got grit." He pushed his plate away. "Doesn't change the fact the seasons will have moved on by the time she's finished.

We'll be in summer and what's the point of having taught the girl to ski if we're in summer?"

"Maybe it's bad news." Elizabeth sat down, her face pale. "We're going to need a miracle, aren't we?"

"You heard Jackson. She is the miracle," Walter said gruffly. "Now will you stop panicking or she *will* walk out and I'll get the blame. And then I won't get my just desserts." He winked at Alice, and Tyler groaned and covered Jess's eyes with his hand.

"You're too young to see this. Start talking, Kayla."

"It's not bad news," Kayla said to Elizabeth. "First, the cabins…" She spoke fluently, not once glancing at the notes she'd made as she painted a visual picture of how she saw the cabins being used.

When she finally stopped talking, the only noise in the kitchen was the bubble of food on the stove and the gentle *click clack* of Alice's knitting needles.

Walter put his beer down on the table. "I think—"

"Gramps—" Jackson gave him a warning stare and his grandfather glared back.

"What? If I can speak without being interrupted, I was just going to say I think it all sounds great."

Jackson stared at him in disbelief. "I've been telling you some of this for months. You told me I was an idiot."

"If you'd explained it the way Kayla did, maybe I wouldn't have thought you were an idiot. She needs to give you a few lessons in communication."

Kayla tried not to smile. "Moving on, I want to—"

"Wait a minute—" Jackson held up his hand, his eyes on his grandfather. "So are you finally going to quit telling me to knock the cabins down?"

Walter O'Neil looked innocent. "You heard the woman—they're part of the magic of Snow Crystal.

What would be the point of knocking them down? They're up now. They might as well stay up."

Kayla cleared her throat. "I'd like to—"

"So you admit they were a good idea?" Jackson's gaze was locked on Walter, and Elizabeth sighed.

"Why does there always have to be a winner? Just ignore them, Kayla, and carry on talking. If you wait for silence in this house you'll be waiting forever."

"I've finished. Here's my Christmas gift." She handed out the proposals, neatly bound by Stacy and tied with a red bow to add a festive touch. "Read them, and then I'll answer any questions."

Jackson immediately turned to the back page and scanned the cost breakdown.

"I like the ribbon." Alice twisted it around her fingers. "People think there is only one shade of red, but they're wrong."

Kayla handed the last proposal to Tyler. "You should knit a jumper that color, Alice."

"Just don't knit it for me." Tyler winked at Jess and then everyone started talking, and Kayla fielded their questions until finally Elizabeth stood up and pulled her into a warm hug.

"Thank you for working so hard. Between you and Jackson, I know things will be all right—"

Kayla felt her throat close as she returned the hug. *You and Jackson.*

"Just doing my job."

"You've done much more than that. You could have sat in your cabin, but you've been out there every day, joining in."

"I'm a terrible skier—"

"You truly are," Tyler said, and then caught Jackson's eye, "but we can work on that."

"She is also a terrible cook," Élise said, "and we will *not* be working on that because I do not have the patience. I would kill you and that would lead to bad feeling, but fortunately you have your own job and you're good at it so you don't need to work in my kitchen."

Kayla eased herself out of Elizabeth's embrace.

"That's it." She stared down at her copy of the proposal, realizing with a lurch that this part of her job was done. "If you have any questions, Jackson can always call me."

"Call you?" Alice sounded confused. "Why would he have to call you?"

"Because Kayla is going back to New York the day after Christmas." Elizabeth focused on the document in her hands.

"She could stay. You did. She can share your English Breakfast tea and HP Sauce."

"Kayla has a job, and a life, somewhere else. Now let's all clear the table and make some coffee." Elizabeth was brisk and Kayla watched as she stood up and bustled around the kitchen.

They'd be building the business without her. Every day they'd be working together to build Snow Crystal, and she'd be sitting in her office in New York, managing her team and growing the business for Innovation. Finding new clients, winning new accounts, achieving successes that would be good for her reputation, but which didn't touch her personally.

While they were grooming the trails, chopping logs and baking cinnamon stars, she'd be flying across the country to meet clients.

Alone.

There was a pressure behind her chest.

Usually at the end of a presentation she felt satisfaction. This time she felt numb.

Perhaps the lack of sleep was catching up with her.

She was so desperate to leave the room it was a relief when her phone rang. "It's Brett. Will you excuse me?"

Jackson frowned. "It's Christmas Eve."

"I doubt he knows what day it is." She walked through to the living room. "Brett?" She tried to sound cheerful. "You should be trimming the tree."

"Delegated that job to my kids."

"You're not supposed to delegate Christmas. You're supposed to be part of it." She thought of the O'Neil family gathered around the table next door, enjoying time together.

"So are you finished there, Green? Because I want you back in the office day after tomorrow. The partners are flying in."

He wanted her back in the office.

Which meant Christmas was almost over for another year. She waited for the rush of relief that always came.

"Aren't you taking time off?"

"I'm off now. Got a Christmas gift for you, Green."

"Gift?" She immediately thought of Jackson.

What do you want for Christmas, Kayla?

"I'm moving you up. That vice president role is vacant now that Cecily has moved to L.A. You'll need to jump through a few hoops, but that's just a formality. There isn't a person in this company who doesn't know your name. Sure, you'll be working double the number of hours you work now, which basically means you can forget about sleep for the rest of your working life, but that's the price you pay for achieving your goal, right?"

Vice president.

Stunned, Kayla sank down onto the sofa and Maple

sprang onto her lap. She hadn't even heard the puppy come into the room. Resting her hand on the dog's springy fur, she looked at the Christmas tree, remembering how hard it had been for her to decorate it. Had that really only been a few days before?

"I don't know what to say." She hadn't expected it to happen this quickly.

"You're overwhelmed. You can thank me later. Go and buy yourself something to celebrate. My wife is always telling me a woman can't have too many diamond earrings."

She should be feeling excited.

So why did the thought of standing in front of the window of another jewelers, picking out a pair of earrings for herself, depress her?

She looked down at herself, thinking that diamond earrings would look ridiculous with what she was wearing now.

"Everywhere is closed for Christmas."

"Oh, right, I forgot you were out there in the boonies. Take a few hours off to eat maple syrup with your client or whatever they do up there on Christmas Day, and then get yourself back to the real world."

"I— Thanks, Brett."

"No worries. And congratulations."

As Brett ended the call, Kayla stared at the lights twinkling on the tree and then looked out of the window into the darkness of the forest. Stars studded the night sky like tiny diamonds, sending light sparkling over snow and she knew what she was looking at was more beautiful than anything she'd see in a jeweler's window.

She cuddled Maple close.

Tomorrow was Christmas Day. The day after, she'd be flying back to New York.

Her stay at Snow Crystal was over.

CHAPTER EIGHTEEN

JACKSON WOKE IN the dark to find the bed empty.

He went in search of her and found her curled up on the sofa watching snow fall on the trees.

They'd chosen to spend the night in his barn for the first time. His home. The significance didn't escape him.

"What are you doing out here?"

"I like looking at the trees. Helps me think. And your sofas are so comfortable." She snuggled deeper. "I love what you've done to this room."

She hadn't switched on lamps, but moonlight shimmered on the hardwood floors and the last flickers of the dying fire gave enough light for him to see her expression.

He sat down next to her. "What do you need to think about?"

"That phone call from Brett—I'm being promoted. Vice president. I still have to have an interview with the partners, but it sounds as if it's virtually a done deal."

Jackson felt a rush of mixed emotions. "Congratulations."

"It's my dream. I just didn't expect it to happen yet."

He decided not to say that she didn't sound very pleased for someone who had just achieved her dream.

"Perhaps it hasn't sunk in yet."

"That's probably it." She shifted position and leaned

her head against his shoulder. Her hair was soft and silky and brushed against his jaw.

"You need to come back to bed. If you don't close your eyes, Santa won't come."

"I don't believe in Santa."

There were a lot of things she didn't believe in, but he decided this wasn't the time to talk about any of those, either, so he simply pulled her to her feet, scooped her into his arms and carried her back to his bed.

They had this. They had now.

It was enough.

SHE AWOKE IN his arms and felt weight in her heart. Then she realized she also felt weight on her feet.

"What's that?"

"What?" He levered himself up on his elbows, his eyes sleepy under lowered lids. "Looks like you were wrong about at least one thing, Kayla Green. Santa does exist."

And she saw the cause of the weight. A stocking, lying across the bottom of the bed, the shape distorted by mysterious packages stuffed inside. "That's for me?"

"How would I know? Better take a look."

She sat up, thinking that there could be no better place to wake up than Jackson's handcrafted log canopy bed with its uninterrupted view of the lake and forest. A cobweb of early-morning mist hovered over the trees, but the first rays of sunshine were already peeping through, sending shafts of light bouncing across the frozen surface.

"This place must be stunning in the summer." Reaching down, she dragged the stocking onto her lap, feeling lumps and bumps and interesting shapes. As a child, the lumps had excited her. She'd been intrigued by the anticipation and the endless possibilities that came with not knowing. She'd loved that part so much she'd often prolonged the moment when she'd actually opened the packages. "There's a note— *To Kayla, because you've been a good girl this year—*" Eyebrows raised, she turned to him and slid her hand over his chest. "That's funny, because I thought I'd been quite a bad girl the last few days."

"Yeah, you certainly have." His voice was husky. "I guess Santa didn't see that side of you. Don't worry, I won't tell."

"I can't believe you made me a stocking."

"Honey, I've never seen that stocking before in my life."

She was incredibly touched. And choked. Telling herself she was just tired, Kayla put her hand in the stocking and pulled out the first package, ripped off the paper and laughed.

"Underwear?"

"Thermal. To keep Alice happy, obviously."

She fingered soft fabric and lace. "It's sexy."

"Okay, maybe it's not just Alice who will be happy. I wanted to buy you a black basque for skating but I decided one Christmas night spent at a police station is enough for anyone."

Smiling, she ripped off paper, touched by the thoughtful gifts. There was a pretty bottle of maple syrup, warm ski mittens, sachets of hot chocolate and a couple of hand warmers. As she opened the last packet, she laughed. "A toy moose?"

"For your desk."

"I should have gone shopping. I didn't buy any gifts—"

"You came here. You put up with my family. You

worked until you dropped. And you were the one who made me see how Walter felt." He leaned back against the pillows. "Eighteen months I've been charging around here, burying grief in activity, behaving like a steamroller and not even noticing who I was crushing."

"You didn't crush anyone."

"He was grieving, too. And he was protecting my father's memory. He saw the changes I was making as a criticism of my father, and he couldn't handle that. Couldn't cope with the enormity of losing Snow Crystal."

"He won't. You won't." She leaned across and kissed him, feeling the roughness of his jaw against her lips. "Our campaign is going to rock. We are going to do what it takes to make sure this place is full."

"But you won't be doing the day-to-day work, will you? As vice president you'll be out winning new business and directing strategy on all the accounts. You won't be picking up the phones."

"I can pick up a phone whenever I want to." But he was right, of course. She wouldn't be involved in the detail.

Someone else would be doing that part while she moved on to other things.

He eased away from her, sprang from the bed and walked into the shower without looking back at her. "We'd better get moving."

"Jackson—"

"We're expected over at the house for Christmas lunch. Or are you going to say you have to work?"

Christmas lunch.

She hadn't shared Christmas lunch with anyone in years.

Last year she'd heated up a microwave meal. She hadn't even bothered sitting down to eat it.

"I don't have to work."

He stopped in the doorway. He was naked, every inch of his masculine physique on display. And then he turned and trapped her with that deep blue gaze, holding her there with nothing but a hot look until she was ready to combust.

Her stomach curled, and she could barely string a sentence together. "I just meant there's nothing more I can do here. I've done what I came to do."

"That's what I figured."

Why was he looking at her like that? *What did he want from her?*

Apparently she wasn't going to find out, because he turned and walked into the bathroom without saying a word.

THE MOMENT SHE stepped into the house she was assailed by delicious smells of Christmas and the sound of laughter from the kitchen.

"I shouldn't be here." She turned to escape but Jackson blocked her path, legs spread, arms folded.

"Where are you going?"

"No one wants me here, Jackson."

"We *all* want you here." His gaze dropped to her mouth. "And, more to the point, *I* want you here."

Did he?

He'd been acting strangely since they'd woken up.

"I shouldn't be at your family Christmas celebration." It had the potential to be a supremely awkward moment, but a loud chorus of welcome from the hallway soon dispelled that.

Alice and Elizabeth stood there, their hands full of plates and kitchen implements.

"Kayla! Thank goodness you're here. Can you help lay the table, sweetheart?"

Before she could utter a word, napkins were thrust in her hand along with a box of matches and instructions to light candles.

And that was it. There were no awkward moments, just the usual O'Neil kitchen chaos. And the warmth, of course. Always the warmth.

"Spare candles in the drawer, Kayla." Elizabeth bustled around the kitchen, removing pans from the heat and draining vegetables. "Alice used branches from the white pine by the door to make the table centerpiece. Doesn't it look pretty?"

Kayla lit candles, duly admired the artful twist of pine and the addition of scarlet berries, placed napkins by all the plates and then went to sit at the farthest end of the table, telling herself it would be fine.

She was an expert in the social etiquette of being the awkward extra at holiday celebrations. She'd learned all the rules at an early age. Sit at the end of the table, not in the middle. At least then you didn't get in the way of other people's conversation. Make yourself as inconspicuous as possible.

"You're sitting here, Kayla—" Elizabeth caught her arm and pulled her gently back to the middle of the long table "—in between Jackson and Tyler. Sean across from you—" She organized everyone. "We're three extra. I invited Brenna, of course, and Josh, although he can't stay long because he's on duty. Pete's going to pop in and take a few slices of turkey for Lynn. She can't be cooking with a two-day-old baby." Elizabeth thrust a cloth in Kayla's hands. "Could you rescue the roast potatoes from the oven? Try not to drop them on the floor, dear. Maple doesn't mind flour on her head, but roast potatoes would feel like bullets to a puppy of her size."

"When did Maple have flour on her head?" Tyler was intrigued, and soon Kayla was being teased along with everyone and she was surprised by how good it felt. She'd spent so many holidays hovering awkwardly on the edge of everyone else's celebration. This was the first time she'd felt part of it.

Finally, when everyone was sitting down, Elizabeth placed the turkey in the center of the table.

Everyone oohed and aahed, except Jess, who recoiled.

"I can't eat meat, Grandma. I told you on Monday I'm vegetarian."

Walter shuddered. "Vegetarian? Since when?"

"If she wants to be vegetarian, that's fine by me." Tyler winked at Jess. "Most parents have to nag their kids to eat vegetables. Good to know that's one job off my list."

"Will you carve please, Walter?" Elizabeth gave Jess a quick hug. "I made you a delicious nutty parsnip bake. Élise gave me the recipe. I'm just so glad you're here. It wouldn't feel like Christmas without you."

Walter sharpened the knife. "All I'm saying is a growing girl needs to—"

"Make her own decisions," Alice said firmly, and Walter subsided.

"That's what I was going to say, honey."

"Of course you were, but you were taking your time getting the words out so I thought I'd help." Alice helped herself to potatoes, and Kayla noticed there was a new energy about her. She wondered whether it was because all the O'Neil men were home or because the people around her were happier. Jess was spending all her time skiing with Tyler, and Elizabeth was absorbed in her new role in the restaurant.

"Sean should be doing this." Walter handed him the knife. "He's the surgeon."

Sean raised an eyebrow. "If you want my professional opinion, I'd say this turkey is never going to walk again."

Kayla watched as he carved, sensing tension between him and his grandfather. Or maybe it was just that she didn't know Sean. He was harder to read than Jackson. Physically they were alike—same dark good looks, same killer blue eyes—but Sean seemed more emotionally detached. She wondered if that was a necessary quality for a surgeon.

"Did you operate on Tyler's knee?"

Tyler shuddered. "Are you kidding? I wouldn't let him near me with a scalpel after what he did to me when we were kids."

"I'm the reason you're still walking." Sean served perfectly carved slices of turkey onto plates. "If it had been left to that team in Switzerland, you wouldn't be."

"We were all in Switzerland when Tyler had his accident," Jackson explained, "so Sean was able to take charge. He's an expert on skiing injuries."

Walter grunted. "So why is he working in Boston? If he worked here, he could help out at Snow Crystal when he isn't fixing bones."

Sean didn't respond, but Kayla saw a muscle flicker in his cheek.

Elizabeth sighed. "Do we have to talk about bones at the lunch table?"

"You've raised three boys. No way can you be squeamish. And anyway, you should be proud of him." Walter tried to sneak a slice of turkey onto Jess's plate. "Just try one small slice. It will make you big and strong."

"I didn't say we weren't proud of him," Elizabeth murmured, "just that I didn't want to talk about surgery over lunch."

"I don't want her any stronger than she already is or she'll be beating me down that slope." Tyler forked the turkey from Jess's plate onto his own. "She's faster than I was at her age. And faster than you, Gramps." He pushed the vegetables toward Jess, and Walter brandished the carving knife.

"In my day we didn't have all the fancy equipment you have now."

"She's more stylish than you, Tyler." Brenna helped herself to potatoes. "Your aim was to get down the mountain as fast as possible. You didn't care how you looked."

"The point is to get down as fast as possible." Tyler's eyes glittered. "And I looked awesome."

"You crashed all the time. Jess is amazing."

Basking in the attention and love, Jess glowed like the flame of a candle.

Family could be like a cushion, Kayla thought. Something soft to protect you from the blows of life. You couldn't stop the blows happening, but if you had people who cared around you then the blows hurt less.

She'd learned to live without that cushion. She'd learned to protect herself from the blows of life, but she'd done it by avoiding anything that might hurt. She'd avoided relationships so she didn't have to nurture herself through the pain of an ending.

And she'd avoided Christmas.

She rubbed her hand over her stomach, realizing that

she hadn't reached for indigestion tablets since that first night with Jackson.

"Are you hungry, honey?" Alice patted her hand. "Sean, put some turkey on this poor girl's plate before she starves."

They noticed everything. They looked out for each other. They even looked out for *her*.

Kayla's throat thickened. She'd come here to escape Christmas, and ended up being immersed in it. She'd been cushioned from the usual bruises by the O'Neil family.

By Jackson.

She turned her head and saw him laughing at something Tyler had said.

He'd dropped everything to come home and support his family. He was there for them, all the time, even when they drove him crazy, because Jackson O'Neil wasn't a man who walked away.

She thought about that first night when she'd messed up her presentation and he'd insisted she stay. She thought about the night she'd been on her own and miserable and he'd refused to leave her. She thought about the sled ride through the forest and the times they'd laughed. And she thought about making love with him.

It had felt perfect, and the things that made it perfect were the same things that made him absolutely, totally the wrong man for her.

She sat still, frozen by the realization that she'd allowed herself to care.

How had that happened? *How?*

"Time for presents!" Jess leaped up from her chair, and Maple barked furiously, fired up by the excitement in the room.

Kayla stood, too, like a robot executing a preprogrammed movement. "I ought to be getting back to my cabin."

She shouldn't have come. She should have worked, instead of allowing herself to spend time with them.

"You can't leave now!" Elizabeth took her hand and squeezed. "We're opening presents. You're part of that. Let's go into the living room. We can clear up later."

Before she could even draw breath, Kayla was seated by the Christmas tree she'd helped decorate days earlier.

Maple jumped onto her lap, and Kayla hugged the dog, trying to work out how she'd got in so deep so fast.

Jess was on her knees in front of the tree, sorting through presents.

"This pile is for Grandma—" She read labels and handed out presents while Kayla sat, awkward and self-conscious, grateful for Maple.

"This pile is for Kayla—" Jess dropped them onto her lap next to the puppy, and Kayla stared at the prettily wrapped gifts.

"What are these?"

"Your presents." Jess passed two to Elizabeth and one to Jackson, while Kayla sat there, clutching parcels, her feelings raw and exposed.

They'd given her presents.

"You shouldn't have bought me anything—"

"You gave up your Christmas to be here with us." Elizabeth handed around coffee. "That makes you one of the family."

She wasn't one of the family. She couldn't be. *Didn't want to be.*

"Kayla?" Jackson's voice was soft, and she realized she had to get this over with fast, before she made a fool of herself.

It was just a few presents. She'd open them, make

enthusiastic noises and then go back to her cabin and pack. She'd bury herself in work, and all these feelings would go.

"This is exciting!" Smiling, she opened the heavy one first and pulled out an ax. Her smile wobbled as she glanced at Walter.

"I guess you can't take it on the plane, so you'll have to leave it here," he said gruffly, "and use it when you come and visit."

There was no way she was ever going to be able to come back here.

No way.

"Thanks, Walter. I—" She found it difficult to speak, so instead she went through the presents one by one and managed to smile and say the right things, even though it was the hardest thing she'd ever done. Alice had given her a pretty red scarf, Jess a box of chocolates, Tyler a warm pair of ski socks and Élise a cookery book for beginners.

And then Elizabeth pushed a small box into her hand.

"This is from all of us." She reached down to hug Kayla. "You've worked so hard and we want you to remember us. Merry Christmas, sweetheart. Come back soon."

Choking back her wayward emotions, Kayla undid the bow and unwrapped the tiny silver box. There inside, nestling against dark velvet was a silver snowflake on a chain. "That's so beautiful." It winked and shone like the surface of the snow in sunlight.

"Wear it sometimes so you don't forget us when you're back in New York."

Forget them?

How could she forget them? This was the first time

in her life she'd felt like part of something. The first time in her life she hadn't felt as if she were on the outside looking in.

The first time she'd allowed herself to care.

She lifted the necklace out of its box and fastened it around her neck.

"It looks pretty." Alice put her knitting down. "When will you be back, Kayla?"

Elizabeth started picking up crumpled, torn wrapping paper. "Not for a while, I expect. But I'm sure she'll stay in touch, and Jackson will tell us how she's getting on."

"How can she help us from New York? She's put all those lovely, exciting ideas together, and now she's leaving?"

Kayla saw Jackson looking at her and knew he was waiting for her to tell them about her promotion. But she couldn't. The words stuck in her throat. It wasn't relevant to them. It was a million miles away from life here.

Kayla heard Jackson swear under his breath, but it was Walter who spoke, his voice rough.

"She came here to give us advice and she's done that. Now leave the girl alone."

"But she fell in love with Snow Crystal," Alice said in a stubborn voice. "She told us that."

"Alice, her job is in New York."

"Jackson could give her a job. He's in charge now. He could fix this."

Walter took her hand. "She's going to help us."

"For once in your life will you think about something other than this place." Alice glared at him fiercely, the look giving clues as to why she hadn't been crushed by Walter in the sixty years they'd been together. "People matter more than places."

"I know that. But Kayla has a life in New York."

Kayla fingered her necklace. She had an apartment and a job. That was her life in New York.

"That's enough." Taking charge, Jackson stood up. "You've given her your gifts. Now it's my turn. Put your coat on, Kayla."

Reeling from emotions she couldn't begin to decipher, Kayla stood up. "You already gave me presents—"

"Those were from Santa. I still have to give you mine—" Jackson picked up the scarf Alice had given her and wrapped it around her neck. "Where's your coat?"

"In the kitchen."

"I brought it through for you—" Elizabeth handed it over, eyes shining, a hopeful smile on her face as she looked at her son. "Oh, Jackson—"

Kayla wondered why Elizabeth was suddenly so cheerful. Then she heard the sound of bells, looked out of the window and saw the horse-drawn sleigh. Jess made a happy sound and ran to the window.

"It's Bessie! Oh, wow. Can I go for a ride through the forest?"

"No." Tyler tugged her away from the window, his gaze fixed on his brother. "You can have a turn later."

Jess looked disappointed. "Who is it for then?"

"Kayla." Jackson took her hand. "This is my gift to you. Your last Snow Crystal experience. Merry Christmas."

HE COULD SEE them watching, noses pressed to the window as he and Kayla climbed into the sleigh. He was torn between frustration, amusement and sympathy.

Could his family be any less subtle?

Even Tyler was still standing by the window, beer in hand as he watched.

Jackson hoped Kayla didn't notice them or she'd probably go straight to the airport and sleep in the departure lounge overnight rather than hang around a moment longer.

"Merry Christmas." Pete grinned at them both as he used the reins and his voice to persuade Bessie to move.

"We've had her since she was a foal. Gramps used to do the sleigh rides at one time but now it makes his arthritis worse." Jackson pulled the blanket over Kayla. "You'll need this. It can get cold."

"Thanks. This is fun." But she didn't look like someone who was having fun. She looked wan. Pale. Incredibly tired.

He felt a stab of concern. "Did Alice upset you?"

"No, of course not. She's lovely. Your whole family is lovely." There was a choke in her voice that caught his attention and gave him hope.

"Why didn't you tell them about your promotion? You have a right to celebrate."

But she didn't look as if she was celebrating.

She stared ahead through the trees. "It didn't seem like the right time."

He wasn't sure this was the right time for what he had planned, either, but it was the only time he had so he intended to use it.

He sat, restless and impatient as the sleigh wound along the groomed forest trail, the jangle of bells and the soft thud of hooves disturbing the silence.

"Thank you." She turned to him, her smile strained. "It's been a happy Christmas Day. I was dreading it, but it's been the best ever."

He thought about what he carried in his pocket.

He was either about to ruin that day or make it perfect.

"It hasn't finished yet." They'd reached the part of the trail that led to the frozen waterfall and Pete pulled in and winked at Jackson.

There were times when he wished he lived in a place where a man could have a few secrets, and this was one of those times.

Jackson sprang down from the sleigh and held out his hand to her. "Come with me."

"Where are we going?"

"To the same place we came on the first day." They took a different path, staying on a groomed track until they reached the waterfall.

"I can't believe I've been here a week. I can't believe I'll be back in New York tomorrow."

He took her hand and noticed that she didn't try to pull it away. "How do you feel about that?"

"Excited, of course." Her smile was a little too bright. "Why?"

"Because I want you to stay." He hadn't meant to say it so abruptly. He should have said something fluent and romantic, something that would make her head spin and her heart melt. Instead of which, he'd shocked her. "I really want you to stay."

Instead of looking starry-eyed, she looked stunned. "Stay?"

"Yes. Damn it, Kayla——" he grabbed her jacket and hauled her against him "——I love you."

She stared at him, her breathing shallow. "You're crazy."

"Maybe I am. Or maybe I'm just good at knowing what I want. I think I fell in love with you the moment you landed on your back in the snow and laughed. Or maybe it was when you didn't walk out on that first night, even though my family had been rude to you and you were desperate to get away from us. I know I loved you when I kissed you next to this waterfall. I definitely loved you when we spent the night together, and I think—" he paused, knowing he was taking a risk "—I think you love me, too."

Silence stretched from seconds to almost a full minute.

Then she shook her head.

"No." She planted her palm in the center of his chest, warding him off. "Damn it, no, Jackson. Don't do this—"

"Don't do what? Tell the truth about how I feel?"

"You can't possibly feel that way. We've only known each other for a week. You can't know that."

"I know."

"No—" Panic flickered in her eyes. "You're a risk taker. That's what you do. You leap off cliffs without knowing if you can land safely—"

"I'm still standing here, so that has to prove something about my judgment. I've never been afraid to leap, Kayla, but that's probably because there's always been a bunch of people cheering me on. I know you haven't had that. And I know I'm asking a lot, but I want you to stay, Kayla. Stay and be with me. Don't go."

She gave a choked laugh. "Let me get this straight—you're asking me to give up my job, a job I've worked almost a decade to get, a job most people would kill for, to come and live with a man I met a week ago?"

"I'm asking you to think about what you truly want. What truly makes you happy."

"My job makes me happy."

"Your job makes you feel safe. You feel in control

and it's important for you to feel in control." He kept his voice gentle because he wasn't sure she was ready to hear what he was saying. "You shut people out, because if they're not in your life then they can't hurt you. But that isn't what happiness is, Kayla. Happiness isn't simply avoiding unhappiness. You can spend your life dodging boulders or you can jump on top of one and take a look at the view. See what you're missing."

"Jackson—"

"You came to Snow Crystal because you were miserable. You were lonely. Is that really what you're choosing to go back to?"

"You're asking me to give up work—"

"No, I'm asking you to do a different job and do it here, with me. And maybe that doesn't seem like much of an offer compared to being vice president—" he wondered who thought up those ridiculous damn titles that city marketing companies always used to seduce their staff "—but maybe, there is more to work than a title, a salary and a fancy corner office in a big city. You care about this place—I know you do. I don't believe this is just another account to you."

"I think—"

"I don't want to know what you think because you have the ability to think yourself out of anything." He pulled her against him, his mouth close to hers, "I want to know what you *feel*. Tell me what you feel."

"Right now?" Her voice rose. "Sick." She was shutting him down. Blocking him out.

"What has the last week meant to you, Kayla?"

"Damn it, Jackson, I warned you I don't do relationships. You knew—"

"Yeah, you warned me—I broke the rules—" He knew he was pushing her, but he didn't have the luxury of time and he figured he didn't have anything to lose that wasn't already lost. "But are you really telling me it meant nothing? You didn't check your emails, Kayla. You've been laughing and sleeping late. When did you last look in the mirror? Your hair is curling and you have color in your cheeks. You look healthy! Maybe it's time to take another look at those rules of yours. Maybe it's time to take a look at a different sort of life."

"You can't— I don't—" she breathed. "It isn't possible."

"I know my own mind, Kayla. And you know yours. The question is, will you believe what it's telling you?"

"I've worked hard for what I have."

"And what do you have, Kayla? A corner office? A stomach ulcer? A salary, but no one to spend it on except yourself? Is that really what matters to you?"

"I love my job."

"Yes, but you've let your job fill your whole life because you're afraid of what will happen if you don't. You do that job out of fear. You work those hours out of fear, because you're afraid that if you don't keep moving you might just build connections with people, and the next step to that is becoming involved and that terrifies you. You ran away at thirteen and you're still running away."

Her face was so white it almost merged with the snow around her. "That isn't true—"

"I'm offering you a job *and* a life. And that life includes me."

"I can't believe you're serious."

"Then maybe this will prove it." He put his hand in his pocket and pulled out the box he'd zipped in there the night before.

"No! Jackson—" She moaned his name and gasped

as he flipped opened the box. The diamond sparkled in the winter sunshine. "Oh, *God,* that's beautiful."

He allowed himself a brief moment of satisfaction that he'd got that part right.

"Marry me, Kayla. Stop running, marry me and we'll build a life together."

The healthy glow left her cheeks. Her lips were the only stain of colour in her face. She pulled off her glove and her hand hovered over the ring.

His heart lifted and hope, ruthlessly suppressed, broke free.

Then she curled her fingers into her palm and shook her head. "I can't." The words were a whisper, and she pressed her hand to her mouth. "I'm sorry, but I just can't."

For the first time in his life he knew how it felt to be desperate. "I know you're scared, I know on the surface it seems like a risky decision, but I love you, and that isn't going to change. I'm know I'm asking you to walk away from the safe option, but always choosing the safe option stops you reaching for something more. Is that really the way you want to live?"

She was silent and then finally she looked up at him, her eyes blank. "It's exactly the way I want to live. It's the only way I know how to live. I'm sorry, Jackson. I—I really *am* sorry, but I can't. I have to go back to New York."

CHAPTER NINETEEN

THE CAB ARRIVED at 8:00 a.m.

The snow was already falling heavily, and Kayla lifted her face to it, knowing now that snow was good for the business. Snow meant skiers, and skiers meant money for Snow Crystal.

"Better hurry, lady." The driver threw her bags into the trunk, and Kayla tucked Maple inside her coat.

She'd spent the night alone on the shelf with just the puppy for company. She'd waited for Jackson, her emotions fluctuating between relief and disappointment when he hadn't come.

She didn't blame him. He'd put everything out there, and she hadn't even met him halfway.

How could she?

What he was suggesting wasn't just ridiculous, it was terrifying.

She wondered if Elizabeth had known what had happened. Had Jackson told her?

The cab stopped at the main house and she slid out, still holding Maple. For a crazy moment she wondered if she could have a dog in her apartment in New York, and then she realized she didn't want any dog—she wanted *this* dog and there was no way the O'Neils would part with the puppy. She was as much a member of the family as Jess or Alice, and the O'Neils didn't consider family members disposable. Even when life was tough, they stuck together.

She walked down the path, steady this time in her beautiful new boots, and paused for a moment to stare at the mistletoe bunched above the door before ringing the bell. There was nothing romantic about mistletoe, she reminded herself.

Mistletoe was poisonous.

The door opened. Walter stood there along with Elizabeth, Tyler and Jess.

Kayla forced herself to hand Maple over to Elizabeth. "Thank you. For being so welcoming, for listening to me, for the necklace—" She reached forward and embraced the other woman, and Elizabeth hugged her back.

"You have such an exciting future. We're proud of you, dear, so proud."

Oh, God—

No one had ever said that to her. No one.

"Keep those knives away from Élise in the kitchen." She pulled away before she made a fool of herself, but then Walter stepped forward and hugged her.

And she hugged him back, surprised by the strength in his bony frame, thinking that this man was as much a part of Snow Crystal as the mountains and the snow. "I've set up some interviews. You're going to be a star, Walter." Her voice was croaky. "Just don't scare them too much."

"You'd better come back and keep me in line. And do it soon." Patting her back, he released her and cleared his throat. "Alice isn't good with goodbyes. She's inside. You could give her a wave."

Alice was standing in the window holding her knitting, the lights from the Christmas tree glowing behind her.

Deciding she wasn't good at goodbyes, either, Kayla waved and Elizabeth pressed a small package into her hand.

"A few gingerbread Santas. In case you're hungry on the journey."

"You're not going to cry, are you?" Tyler drawled. "Because if there's one thing I can't stand it's a sobbing woman."

"Dad!" Rolling her eyes, Jess gave Kayla an awkward smile. "Come back soon so you can teach me to skate."

Tyler winked and stepped forward to give her a warm hug. "Take care of yourself. Place isn't going to be the same without seeing you lying flat on your back in the snow every time I turn a corner." He lowered his voice. "Jackson's taken the groomer up one of the trails. He said he'll catch up with you soon."

In other words he hadn't wanted to see her.

And she couldn't blame him for that.

He'd offered her everything, and she'd given him nothing in return. Nothing except her skills at her job, and they both knew that was something she gave freely to anyone with the money to pay Innovation the going rate.

The cabdriver leaned on his horn.

"I'd better be going—" Kayla turned and walked back down the path. As she slid into the cab she felt as if someone had taken one of the boulders from the top of the mountain and pushed it onto her chest.

She sat, flattened by misery and something heavier that she didn't recognize.

The car moved silently along the snowy track toward

the road, and Kayla stared at the lake, her vision blurring. She blinked a few times, remembering the first day she'd arrived here.

"Home for the holidays?" The taxi driver glanced in his mirror and she shook her head.

"I was working. Home is New York."

Her life was in New York.

She'd come here to escape Christmas, and Christmas was over, so why didn't she feel more excited about going back?

Trying to pull herself together, she reached for her phone and tried to check her emails, but the signal was so patchy it was impossible to work. Or maybe it was her concentration that was patchy. All she knew was that her head throbbed and she still had preparation to do for her meeting. The meeting with the partners to discuss her promotion.

She should have been buzzing with excitement.

Instead she kept thinking of Alice's face in the window. Of Walter hugging her. Of Maple licking her toes as she'd stepped out of the shower.

Of Jackson.

Feeling tears burn her throat, she reached into her bag for tissues, and her fingers closed over the envelope she'd forgotten. Her Christmas gift. Numb, she ripped it open and read the card. The message inside was printed, a generic festive greeting that would have been sent to all her father's clients.

She waited for the thud of disappointment, but it didn't come.

Somewhere along the way she'd given up expecting anything different from her family. Given up wanting something they couldn't deliver.

They weren't close, and nothing she did was going to change that.

Stuffing the envelope back into her bag, her fingers scraped against something rough, and she found the pinecone Jackson had given her the night he'd taken her on the sled ride through the moonlit forest.

And suddenly she realized why she wasn't more excited about going back to New York.

She didn't feel as if she was going home.

She felt as if she was leaving home.

Somehow, over the past week, she'd fallen in love with Snow Crystal. And not just Snow Crystal, but with the whole O'Neil family.

And Jackson.

Oh, God, she was in love with Jackson.

Crazily, madly in love with Jackson.

She leaned her head back against the seat.

No, no, no. How had she let it happen?

This was what she'd avoided.

"Stop the car!"

"What?"

"Stop the car—just for a minute—"

She gripped the pinecone, her brain spinning.

What the hell was she doing?

Her life was in front of her, and she only ever looked ahead, didn't she?

She should do the sensible thing and return to New York and her promotion. She should go back to living behind the walls she'd built and keeping herself safe. She'd direct the account, but someone else would do the real work. Someone else would be the one spending time at Snow Crystal with Walter, Alice and Elizabeth.

Someone else would work with Jackson.

And eventually he'd meet someone.

"Lady—"

"Just a minute…" She pressed her fingers to her forehead, feeling as if she were being torn in two directions, like the rope in a tug-of-war.

Jackson was right, she thought. *She was scared.*

Most of her life, decisions had been driven by fear. She didn't form close relationships because she was scared of losing. She was good at building walls, but hopeless at opening doors. Jackson had smashed down those walls, pushed his way through the door she'd never opened and found the person she'd hidden away all those years before.

He knew her better than she knew herself.

She thought about their walk through the forest, about skiing together, about the nights lying in his arms on the shelf while they talked about things she'd never talked about before.

The pinecone lay in her palm and she looked down at it, remembering the night he'd given it to her. The kiss she knew she'd never forget.

And then she thought about the life waiting for her in New York. Promotion. Security. She'd have to be crazy to throw that away, wouldn't she?

The taxi driver glanced in his mirror. "Lady, you need to make up your mind."

Why was she hesitating?

There was only one decision she could possibly make.

JACKSON STOPPED THE snowmobile and examined the damage to the trail.

Trudging back to the snowmobile, he removed the sticks he'd brought up with him and marked the area.

The phone in his pocket rang for the eighth time,

but he ignored it. He didn't want to talk to anyone right now, especially not his well-meaning family.

He knew they were worried about him, but this was one situation he had to handle by himself. Not that he'd done well so far.

What the hell had he been thinking? Had he really expected her to give up her well-paid, secure job to come and work at a place that was teetering on the brink of disaster?

He never should have asked that of her.

No wonder she'd panicked and run.

Right now, he didn't want to talk about it, nor did he want to be fed gingerbread Santas or think about the work facing him.

He was so desperate to be left alone that when he heard the sound of a snowmobile coming up the trail behind him, he swore. The last thing he wanted was company, not even tourists who were essential for the future of this place.

But it wasn't tourists, it was Tyler. And seated behind him was Kayla, wearing Alice's red knitted scarf around her neck.

Jackson stood still. She should have been on her way back to New York.

She shouldn't be here.

Tyler steered the snowmobile to the edge of the trail. "You need to learn to drive one of these things yourself," he grumbled. "I've got better things to do than drive you around."

"I will. I promise." Kayla slid off the back and leaned in to kiss him on the cheek. "Thanks, Tyler."

Tyler threw a wary glance at his brother. "Not my fault. Women just can't help themselves around me."

Winking at Kayla, he drove off without giving Jackson an opportunity to respond.

Which left the two of them alone.

Jackson took a deep breath. "You're supposed to be at the airport."

It wasn't the welcome she'd hoped for, but she couldn't blame him for that. "You didn't answer your phone. I left about a million messages."

"I assumed it was my family. What the hell are you doing here, Kayla?"

What if she'd messed it up by walking away?

"I couldn't leave." She stared through the trees, thinking she'd never been anywhere more beautiful. "You said I needed to experience all that Snow Crystal had to offer and I haven't even touched on it, have I? I haven't built a snowman. Walter says I need to see you tap the sugar maple trees. I want to see the lake when it isn't covered in ice and ride a mountain bike over these trails in the summer. I want to see the fall foliage. But most of all I want—" She broke off and took a slow breath. It felt like stepping off a cliff, especially with him watching her with those blue, blue eyes. "I want you. I want to be with you."

There was a long pause. Just long enough to make her courage falter.

"You said no."

"I panicked. It was all so sudden, so unexpected and—and I'm a coward. You were right about that."

"I never said you were a coward."

"You said I was scared, and I *am* scared. But I don't want to be this way anymore. I can't go back to being the old me. I can't go back to making choices just because they're safe."

He didn't respond, and she felt a lurch of terror that he might have changed his mind.

"I threw myself into work because it was the one thing I could control." She tried to explain. "I could depend on it. And I was successful and that gave me a buzz. I worked hard because success made me feel good about myself and because—" she found it hard to admit, even to herself "—and because when I was working I was never alone. Thinking about work meant I didn't have to think about all the things that were missing from my life. And it became normal for me. I didn't even question it. I never slowed down. Except at Christmas. That's the time of year when it's impossible to miss the fact you have no one in your life."

His gaze was fixed on her face. "So you're back here because you don't want to be lonely anymore?"

"No. I'm back here because I don't want to live without you in my life. We have so much fun together. You make me laugh. You help me be the person I'm too scared to be by myself. You made me feel like one of the family." She was not going to cry. She was *not* going to cry. "And you're indecently hot, of course, and the sex is amazing, and— God, this is the worst speech I've ever made." Hand shaking, she pushed her hair away from her face. "Yesterday, Christmas Day…that is the first family Christmas I've had since I was thirteen and when you all gave me gifts…" Tears clogged her throat.

Shit. So much for not crying.

Jackson frowned and stepped toward her. "Kayla—"

"No, let me finish." She dug her hands into her pockets, knowing this wasn't the time to hold back. "Work is important to me. I'm not pretending it isn't. But I used work to avoid life. I used it to avoid relationships. And you're right that when I get back to New York the work on Snow Crystal is going to be done by someone else. And I realized in the car that I don't want that to happen, because it isn't just an account to me anymore. And you're not a client. I want to be here with my sleeves rolled up doing the work. I want to be with you."

There was a long silence. "So does this mean I should cancel my flight to New York?"

She stared at him. "You booked a flight?"

"You wouldn't stay with me here, so I decided to come to you. I shouldn't have asked you to give up your job." His voice was hoarse. "You love it, and you're so damn good at it. I thought maybe we could find another way. Long-distance can work."

"You'd do that for me?"

"I'll do whatever it takes to have you in my life."

She felt a burst of happiness. "I'm glad you feel that way because I called Brett and told him I don't want the promotion. It was a long conversation, but basically I'm going to stay in my current job. That way I can be more involved with Snow Crystal. And I can work from here a few days a week and commute backward and forward. It might be complicated at first, but I'm willing to do whatever it takes."

"Hell, Kayla—" there was a look of disbelief and uncertainty on his face "—you worked hard for that promotion. And there's no corner office here."

"But there are other things. There are trees, mountains, snow, moose—don't forget the moose—and there's your family—" Tears slid down her cheeks and she wiped them away with her palm. "And there's you. *You're* here. That makes it the only place I want to be."

"Are you sure? I can't believe you did that for me." He closed the distance between them and pulled her into his arms. She clung to him, relief flooding through her.

"I did it for me. For us. I can't believe you booked a flight to New York."

"Good job I had to mend the trail first, otherwise we would have passed each other on the road."

"When you didn't answer the phone I was terrified you might have changed your mind."

"I'm never going to change my mind." He cupped her face in his hands. "You think it's that easy to switch love on and off?"

"I don't know anything about love, Jackson, except that it makes me do crazy things. And you. You're doing crazy things, too. You've known me a week. That's not long enough."

"Do you really believe that?"

She gave a choked laugh. "No. The truth is you know me better after a week than anyone else has after years. I came here to avoid Christmas. I didn't expect to enjoy it. I didn't expect to be welcomed the way your family welcomed me. I didn't expect to feel included. I've been the outsider for so long I had no idea how good it would feel to be on the inside. But it felt good. It *feels* good."

"Kayla—"

"I love you, Jackson. I've never said that to anyone before, but I'm saying it now. I love you, and I want to live my life with you. I want you to be there to pick me up when I fall down and I want to be there to do the same for you."

He hauled her against him and hugged her tightly. "I love you, too. All I want is for us to be together. The rest of it, we can work out."

"I was thinking that in the long-term I might think about starting my own business. You talked about it the other night, and I think it might be something I'd love." She was stammering. "To be honest I have no idea how we're going to do any of this, but I know we'll work it out somehow."

"Are you sure this is what you want? I can spend time in New York, too. If you want that promotion, you should take it."

"Everything I want is right here. You're right here."

"Are you sure? You're a city girl."

"Turns out I'm not as much of a city girl as I thought. And if I stay, I can wear these gorgeous warm boots I bought and the gloves you gave me. I can drink hot chocolate and learn to ski without landing on my face. I can see what summer looks like from your bed." She hugged him tightly. "I love you, Jackson O'Neil, and if you're still carrying that diamond ring in your pocket, now would be a good time to give it to me and ask the question you asked yesterday."

He pulled out the box and slid the ring onto her finger.

It sparkled in the winter sunshine, the diamond catching the light like a snow crystal.

Her throat felt thick. "It's the best gift anyone has ever given me."

He lowered his head and kissed her gently. "Marry me, Kayla."

"And those are the best words anyone has ever said to me," she whispered against his mouth. "Yes."

The sound of bells interrupted them, and they pulled apart, ready to move out of the way of the horse-drawn sleigh.

"Merry Christmas." Walter sat in the driver's seat, his hands on the reins while Alice and Elizabeth sat snuggled together under a rug in the backseat. "This is supposed to be a moment she remembers forever and you pick a hole in the trail and a gas-guzzling snowmobile? Get in the back and do it again so you can tell your kids you proposed in a horse-drawn sleigh."

Jackson closed his eyes. "Gramps—"

"There are still some things I know more about than you. Now get in."

Laughing, drowning in happiness, Kayla jumped into the back of the sleigh and was immediately hugged by Elizabeth and Alice. Maple popped her head out from the protection of Elizabeth's warm coat and barked.

"This is the best Christmas present." Alice took Kayla's hand and studied the ring. "And you're wearing the scarf I knitted you."

"Of course she's wearing it," Elizabeth said. "Why wouldn't she? It's a beautiful scarf."

Shaking his head in disbelief, Jackson sprang up next to her. "Are you sure you want to do this?"

"Of course she's sure," Walter said over his shoulder. "She's here, isn't she? Now get on with it. Just pretend we're not here."

"I've already done it, Gramps. She said yes, although she might be about to change her mind now you've reminded her what marrying me entails."

"I'm not going to change my mind." Kayla couldn't ever remember a moment more perfect. She took Maple from Elizabeth and tucked the puppy inside her coat. "I'm really not."

"Are you sure?" Jackson put his arm around her and snuggled her against him. "I can't pretend it's not going to be a challenge."

"Haven't you heard? Challenge is my favorite breakfast dish, along with a side of difficult marinated in the impossible. Only these days I'm adding in a taste of maple syrup. I find it adds that extra special something."

"I can't believe you're staying."

"I fell in love—" tears shone in her eyes "—and not just with the man. With the place. That's what happens at Snow Crystal. It's magic."

And it felt like magic with his arms around her, his mouth on hers and the soft flutter of snow falling like confetti.

* * * * *

ACKNOWLEDGMENTS

First, a huge thank-you to my readers who continue to buy my books thereby giving me the opportunity to write more.

Special thanks to my brilliant and talented editor, Flo Nicoll, for her enthusiasm and insight. Working together on this book has been more fun than anyone has a right to expect from a job.

I'm grateful to my agent, Susan Ginsburg of Writers House, for her wise advice, and to the fantastic team at HQN and Harlequin UK for their support and hard work.

Without Kimberly Young and Lucy Gilmour I doubt my career would have reached this point. I owe them both a great deal.

Particular thanks to Dianne Moggy for her encouragement and for allowing me to use real-life Maple as fictional Maple in this story. All errors my own.

Love and thanks to Laura Reeth for her friendship, support and astute observations on life.

All writers need writer friends. I am fortunate to have more than I can mention here—you know who you are!—but I am particularly indebted to Carol Marinelli and Nicola Cornick.

Writers also need nonwriter friends. Love and thanks to Sue, who has been there through thick and thin and occasionally forces me to talk about real people as well as fictional ones.

I am fortunate to have a wonderful family. Love to my parents and also to my fantastic children for the hugs and laughs and for never complaining when I'm on a deadline and make them eat pizza.

Finally, love and thanks to my husband for proving that romance can happen outside the pages of a book. I am grateful to him for teaching me to ski and for patiently picking me up when I landed on my face, thus providing me with plenty of material for this story!

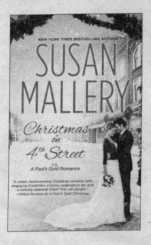

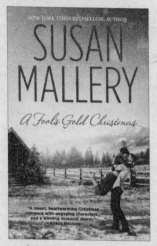

A fun, unexpected and totally addictive story from
New York Times **bestselling author**

KRISTAN HIGGINS

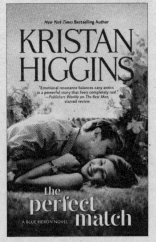

New York Times Bestselling Author

KRISTAN HIGGINS

"Emotional resonance balances zany antics
in a powerful story that feels completely real."
—*Publishers Weekly* on *The Best Man*,
starred review

the
**perfect
match**

A BLUE HERON NOVEL

After being unceremoniously rejected by her lifelong crush, Honor Holland is going to pick herself up, dust herself off and get back out there…. Or she would if dating in Manningsport, New York, population 715, wasn't easier said than done. And charming, handsome British professor Tom Barlow comes with complications. He just wants to do right by his unofficial stepson, Charlie, but his visa is about to expire. Now Tom must either get a green card or leave the States—and leave Charlie behind.

In a moment of impulsiveness, Honor agrees to help Tom with a marriage of convenience—and make her ex jealous in the process. As sparks start to fly between Honor and Tom, they might discover that their pretend relationship is far too perfect to be anything but true love….

"Kristan Higgins not only knows how to write the woo, she
knows how to show her reader a good time."
—*USA TODAY*

Be sure to connect with us at:
Harlequin.com/Newsletters
Facebook.com/HarlequinBooks
Twitter.com/HarlequinBooks

HARLEQUIN® HQN™

™ www.Harlequin.com

PHKH819

REQUEST YOUR FREE BOOKS!

2 FREE NOVELS
FROM THE ROMANCE COLLECTION
PLUS 2 FREE GIFTS!

YES! Please send me 2 FREE novels from the Romance Collection and my 2 FREE gifts (gifts are worth about $10). After receiving them, if I don't wish to receive any more books, I can return the shipping statement marked "cancel." If I don't cancel, I will receive 4 brand-new novels every month and be billed just $6.24 per book in the U.S. or $6.74 per book in Canada. That's a savings of at least 22% off the cover price. It's quite a bargain! Shipping and handling is just 50¢ per book in the U.S. and 75¢ per book in Canada.* I understand that accepting the 2 free books and gifts places me under no obligation to buy anything. I can always return a shipment and cancel at any time. Even if I never buy another book, the two free books and gifts are mine to keep forever.

194/394 MDN F4XY

Name _____ (PLEASE PRINT) _____

Address _____ Apt. #

City _____ State/Prov. _____ Zip/Postal Code

Signature (if under 18, a parent or guardian must sign)

Mail to the Harlequin® Reader Service:
IN U.S.A.: P.O. Box 1867, Buffalo, NY 14240-1867
IN CANADA: P.O. Box 609, Fort Erie, Ontario L2A 5X3

Want to try two free books from another line?
Call 1-800-873-8635 or visit www.ReaderService.com.

* Terms and prices subject to change without notice. Prices do not include applicable taxes. Sales tax applicable in N.Y. Canadian residents will be charged applicable taxes. Offer not valid in Quebec. This offer is limited to one order per household. Not valid for current subscribers to the Romance Collection or the Romance/Suspense Collection. All orders subject to credit approval. Credit or debit balances in a customer's account(s) may be offset by any other outstanding balance owed by or to the customer. Please allow 4 to 6 weeks for delivery. Offer available while quantities last.

Your Privacy—The Harlequin® Reader Service is committed to protecting your privacy. Our Privacy Policy is available online at www.ReaderService.com or upon request from the Harlequin Reader Service.

We make a portion of our mailing list available to reputable third parties that offer products we believe may interest you. If you prefer that we not exchange your name with third parties, or if you wish to clarify or modify your communication preferences, please visit us at www.ReaderService.com/consumerschoice or write to us at Harlequin Reader Service Preference Service, P.O. Box 9062, Buffalo, NY 14269. Include your complete name and address.

ROM13R

Celebrate the holidays with this remarkable McKettrick tale by beloved #1 *New York Times* bestselling author

LINDA LAEL MILLER

With his wild heart, Sawyer McKettrick isn't ready to settle down on the Triple M family ranch in Arizona. So he heads to Blue River, Texas, to seek a job as marshal. But in a blinding snowstorm he's injured—and collapses into the arms of a prim and proper lady in calico.

The shirtless, bandaged stranger recuperating in teacher Piper St. James's room behind the schoolhouse says he's a McKettrick, but he looks like an outlaw to her. As they wait out the storm, the handsome loner has Piper remembering long-ago dreams of marriage and motherhood. But for how long is Sawyer willing to call Blue River home?

**Available now,
wherever books are sold!**

Be sure to connect with us at:
Harlequin.com/Newsletters
Facebook.com/HarlequinBooks
Twitter.com/HarlequinBooks

TM www.Harlequin.com

PHLLM785R